A Handbook

of

Analyses, Questions, and a Discussion of Technique

for use with

MODERN SHORT STORIES: THE USES OF IMAGINATION

Fourth Edition

by

Arthur Mizener
Cornell University

W. W. Norton & Company
New York

ISBN 0 393 95032 8

Printed in the United States of America.

1 2 3 4 5 6 7 8 9 0

CONTENTS

Contents

Part Four

FOREWORD

The material in this handbook is intended to help teachers in the actual classroom use of the stories in this edition of *Modern Short Stories*. There are analyses of every story in the book here—fairly detailed ones of two or three stories from each of the book's four parts, briefer ones of all the rest. Each of these analyses is accompanied by a set of carefully correlated questions that constitutes a structured analysis of the story, based on the discussion of it in the handbook; these sets of questions are, for convenience, also printed at the end of *Modern Short Stories*. These questions mediate between the story and the handbook's analysis of it. (Numbers in parentheses in the analyses refer to pages in the text.) If students think about these questions as they study the story they will come to class prepared for a discussion of it that is based on the analysis in this handbook.

At least with normal luck that will happen. But sometimes, as every teacher knows, we have bad luck. Students carry the discussion off in some unexpected but interesting direction, or they simply fail to see the answer to some question. In the first instance, we need to let them work out their own ideas and then, with questions invented on the spur of the moment, bring them gradually back to the main line of our analysis. In the second instance, we have to invent subsidiary and more leading questions to make them see the point—or, in the last desperate resort, answer the question ourselves. In short, we all know from experience that preconceived classroom plans often go awry, most often with an especially lively class or an unusually torpid one. Under the best or the worst conditions, however, I hope these analyses and the questions in the text that lead to them will give the teacher something to work with.

For teachers who like to begin a study of the short story by examining the major resources of the short story and for those who are primarily interested in the techniques of the short story for their own sake, I have added to this manual a brief discussion of technique and a table of contents of *Modern Short Stories* that is arranged according to the various technical devices the stories illustrate.

A.M.

Cornell University
March 1979

PART ONE

JOSEPH CONRAD
HEART OF DARKNESS

HEART OF DARKNESS is perhaps the greatest of all the stories written by the greatest of twentieth-century romantics. As such it is the nearly perfect example of this kind of story, one that uses all the modern romantic's major resources to create a unified image of his vision of experience. This vision is complex, and it is impossible to consider every important aspect of it in a brief essay. At the same time, Conrad's story is so consistent, its every detail so expressive of its meaning, that once we grasp the essential nature of that vision and the characteristic way the story relates event to meaning, the minor details that refine and enrich its central conception of human experience almost explain themselves.

That conception, very crudely put, is that there is an organic relation between the outward, objective experience of men and their inner subjective life; the salvation of society, of the organized outward activities of men, and the salvation of individual inner lives are similar processes, and the achievement of each depends on the achievement of the other. If enough men are truly civilized, they will make the world civilized; but no man is strong enough to save himself alone; he needs the protection and support of the civilization that surrounds him. Thus the two are interdependent. That is why the heart of darkness that men must —if they are men enough to do so—confront and conquer is at once a darkness at the heart of every man's soul and a darkness at the geographical heart of the world.

To the realization of an image of the world seen in this light Conrad brings all the resources of his remarkable talent, especially his gifts for subtlety of construction and the almost baroque splendors of his eloquence and his irony. The story's structure is fascinating. To begin with, it has a first-person narrator who is also its central intelligence, a man whose gradual realization of the truth of his own experience is a slow revelation of the truth Conrad wishes his story to convey. At the same time that we are watching Marlow's self-discovery, Marlow, as narrator, is describing his discovery of the nature of a man, Kurtz, who had also looked squarely into the heart of darkness, though with a different—indeed, a directly contrasting—result. In addition to the subtle perception of what it is to look into that heart of darkness that this complication of the story makes it possible for Conrad to present, Conrad introduces a further perception by beginning the story, not with the individual looking into his own heart, but with Marlow

contemplating organized society, what constitutes the darkness and the light of communities of men. It is the sight
of London from the Thames, that great, luminous presence in
the surrounding darkness, that sets Marlow to brooding over
his personal experience with Kurtz in the dark heart of dis-
tant Africa.

What London and the Thames make him think of first is
that "this also has been one of the dark places of the
earth. . . . darkness was here yesterday" (7-8). As a result he thinks first of the history of the emergence of
London and England and—ultimately—the British Empire from
tha darkness of savagery, and the meaning of *Heart of Darkness* is thus made in a kind of prologue about England that
is almost complete in itself. Even more, Marlow's accounts
of how he was hired to go to the Belgian Congo and of his
trip down the African coast to take up his job allow him to
describe in the light of his as yet unrevealed judgment of
colonial enterprises both the headquarters of another empire
and some selected examples of colonization at work.

This England was then, as the Congo is now, "the very
end of the world," a place where "the savagery, the utter
savagery, had closed round him [the civilized Roman conquer-
or], —all that mysterious life of the wilderness that stirs
in the forest, in the jungles, in the hearts of wild men"
(9). It is to be observed how precise for Conrad's purposes
that statement—like all his statements—is: this savagery
of the primeval English <u>forest</u> was the same savagery that
now exists in the African <u>jungle</u>; and it exists in the
hearts of the wild men who inhabit the African jungle exactly as it existed nineteen hundred years ago in the hearts
of men who inhabited the English forest the Romans had to
face. Moreover, it had then as it has now "a fascination,
too, that goes to work upon" all men: "the fascination of
the abomination." For just beneath the conscious self of
every man, however civilized, is the savage self that instinctively responds to the appeal of savagery. As Marlow
says when he himself encounters this appeal as he goes up
the Congo, "No, they [the savages] were not inhuman. Well,
you know, that was the worst of it—the suspicion of their
not being inhuman. . . . Ugly. Yes, it was ugly enough; but
if you were man enough you would admit to yourself that
there was in you just the faintest trace of a response to
the terrible frankness of that noise. . ." (43).

The Romans, Marlow says, "were men enough to face that
darkness" in the primitive Britain that they conquered and
and that awoke an echo of its savagery in them. To be sure,
the Romans were conquerors only. Conquest is, at its best,
brutal—"just robbery with violence, aggravated murder on a
great scale" (9). Marlow is not an unrealistic or inexperienced man. "You know I am not particularly tender," he observes, ". . . I've seen the devil of violence, and the
devil of greed, and the devil of hot desire; but, by all the
stars! these were strong, lusty, red-eyed devils, that
swayed and drove men—men, I tell you," such as the Romans

(20). However bad the mere conqueror may be, then, he is
not so bad as the people Marlow finds in the Belgian Congo,
who are less than men, easily driven by "a flabby, pretending, weak-eyed devil of a rapacious and pitiless folly."

     Moreover, the ugly brutality of conquest is sometimes,
like the hearts of the men that carry it out, redeemed by
the unselfish building of a superior civilization in place
of the savage world that has been destroyed by conquest.
"What redeems it [conquest] is the idea only. An idea at
the back of it; not a sentimental pretense but an idea; and
an unselfish belief in the idea—something you can set up
and bow down before, and offer sacrifice to. . ." (9) —and
(the addition is very important for Conrad) work for in a
practical, efficient, effective way; "what saves us," as
Marlow puts it briefly here and at much greater length elsewhere in the story, "is efficiency—the devotion to efficiency." So deeply does Conrad hate fine words and the mere
pretense of high purpose that constitute the tribute paid by
the hypocrisy of mere commercial greed to virtue, that he
infinitely prefers to it the honest savagery of primitive
men, such as—to take the most extreme example among many
mentioned in the story—that of the cannibals who man the
river steamer and show, in their innocent way, an alert and
natural interest in the possibility of obtaining human meat,
an attitude that rises to "a dignified and profoundly pen-
sive attitude" in their headman (49). It is this hatred of
inefficient greed that gives its eloquence to Marlow's description of the horrors of the "inhabited devastation" of
the Company station (19-22). Efficiency, in this world of
meaningless madness—even if the efficiency is being main-
tained in the service of nothing, in a vacuum—is like a
breath of fresh air to Marlow, and he cannot restrain his
admiration for the meticulous bookkeeper he meets there,
dressed in a "high starched collar, white cuffs, a light
alpaca jacket, snowy trousers, a clean necktie, and var-
nished boots. . . . He was amazing, and he had a penholder
behind his ear" (22). With infinite pains this man makes
his "correct entries of perfectly correct transactions; and
fifty feet below the doorstep I could see the still tree-
tops of the grove of death," where the natives conquered by
these pettily greedy agents of civilization were sent to die
—not even out of some deliberate impulse of brutality effectively executed, but just out of the careless inefficiency
of men who could not even be effectively greedy.

     But if pure savagery has its own innocent and sometimes
even its awesome dignity and is thus infinitely preferable
to the so-called civilized men and organizations that have
nothing but greed for motive and are not even efficient
enough to be purposeful in their brutality, that does not
mean that Conrad is in favor of a return to the jungle and a
regression of man to his original savage self. He has not
the least doubt that genuine civilization is infinitely
superior to the jungle and civilized man to savage man.
England was once too one of the dark places of the earth.
But for ages now, men who, to be sure, were "hunters for

gold or pursuers of fame,. . . had gone out on that stream
[the Thames], bearing the sword, and often the torch"; but
these men were also "messengers of the might within the
land, bearers of a spark from the sacred fire" (7). "The
old river in its broad reach [now] rested unruffled at the
decline of day, after ages of good service done to the race
that people its banks, spread out in the tranquil dignity
of a waterway leading to the uttermost ends of the earth"
(6). Here is the heart of a great civilization, the British
Empire. No doubt there had been mixed motives in its emis-
saries; no doubt its conquests had often been as brutal as
those of the Romans. But it had carried with it its idea and
had served that idea efficiently; it had made light where
there had been darkness, and if that process had been costly,
it was nonetheless worth it, so that when Marlow looks at the
map of Africa, he is glad to see "a vast amount of red" (the
traditional map color for the British Empire) "because one
knows that some real work is done in there" (13).

Conrad was no easy optimist; the whole of *Heart of Darkness*
goes to show how difficult he believed the achievement of true
civilization to be, how thin the armor of civilization that
protects the hearts of men from the latent savagery at their
center. Like his contemporary, Kipling, he wanted to warn
his times that complacency was desperately dangerous, to
show them what lay in store for them, if they relaxed their
purpose, by describing to them the civilized brutality of
Leopold II's coldly greedy conquest of the Belgian Congo.
He too wanted to say:

> God of our fathers, known of old,
>   Lord of our far-flung battle lines
> Beneath whose awful Hand we hold
>   Dominion over palm and pine -
> Lord God of Hosts, be with us yet,
> Lest we forget — lest we forget!

This is the source of his fierce condemnation of the Company
with its Dickensian mausoleum of an office in the "city that
always makes me think of a whited sepulcher," from which
they "were going to run an over-sea empire, and make no end
of coin" (12); and of the Company organization in Africa
with its subhuman Manager, its fiddling "pilgrims," its fantastic inefficiency, and its senseless slaughter.

With wonderful delicacy, he suggests the extent to
which the evils of complacent greed are spreading out in the
world by describing Marlow's slow trip down the coast of
Africa. This is a journey into the primitive world that
awakens its echoes in Marlow's own heart, and a glimpse of
what the forces of civilization are doing to "improve" this
vast primitive world. Marlow's description of it is both
visually brilliant and morally significant.

> We pounded along, stopped, landed soldiers; went on,
> landed custom-house clerks to levy toll in what
> looked like a God-forsaken wilderness, with a tin

shed and a flag-pole lost in it; landed more
soldiers—to take care of the custom-house clerks,
presumably.

Here is "civilization" at work: tax-collecting and killing.

Now and then a boat from the shore gave one a momentary contact with reality. . . . They shouted,
sang; their bodies streamed with perspiration; they
had faces like grotesque masks—these chaps; but
they had bone, muscle, a wild vitality, an intense
energy of movement, that was as natural and true as
the surf along their coast.

They may be savages, "these chaps"; but they are not a ludicrously irrelevant fantasy of brute force in the service of
greed.

Once, I remember, we came upon a man-of-war anchored
off the coast. There wasn't even a shed there, and
she was shelling the bush. . . . There was a touch
of insanity in the proceeding . . . and it was not
dissipated by somebody on board assuring me earnestly that there was a camp of natives—he called
them enemies!—hidden out of sight somewhere (17-18).

When Marlow finally reaches the Congo, then, his capacity to sustain a belief in civilization is put to a double
test. He must endure the daily sight of "civilization" at
its worst, and he must face the powerful pull at his heart
of the savage jungle with "its mystery, its greatness, the
amazing reality of its concealed life" (31). Can he survive
those pressures? Can any man? Marlow's own experience of
the terrible appeal of the jungle's savagery to the savagery
in his own heart has given him a special interest in the
career of the mysterious Kurtz, of whom he hears so much.
Kurtz is evidently a man of great talents, "a prodigy . . .
an emissary of pity, and science, and progress" (31), a "man
who had come out equipped with moral ideas of some sort,"
not one of your "sordid buccaneers" concerned "to tear treasure out of the bowels of the land . . . with no more moral
purpose . . . than there is in burglars breaking into a
safe" (37). How, Marlow wonders, has such a man fared?

The first thing he hears about Kurtz is puzzling.
Kurtz has come three hundred miles down river toward the
Company station and then, at the last minute, turned back to
his station in the interior. It is a mystery, and Marlow
starts on his journey up the Congo to Kurtz's station anxious to explain it. "Going up that river was like traveling
back to the earliest beginnings of the world" for him, an
astonishing revelation both of geographical fact and
spiritual reality (40). As they "penetrated deeper and
deeper into the heart of darkness" (42), they became like
"wanderers on a prehistoric earth" that was like "an unknown
planet." "We were accustomed to look upon the shackled form
of a conquered monster"; but here was "a thing monstrous and

free" (43). From the pressure of knowledge like this, "only
a fool, what with sheer fright and fine sentiments, is always safe"; men "must meet [the terrible frankness of
savagery] with [their] own true stuff. . . . You want a
deliberate belief" (44).

Finally they arrive at Kurtz's station. They are
greeted first by "a cry, a very loud cry, as of infinite
desolation" as the river fog lifts for a moment (47). "The
glimpse of the steamboat had for some reason filled those
savages with unrestrained grief" (52). For Kurtz has become to them a god before whom they willingly crawl. Then
the steamboat is attacked as they move up toward Kurtz's
station—by Kurtz's command, as it later turns out.
Conrad gives us one of his marvelous impressionistic accounts of this attack, not telling us "what happened" but
what Marlow, taken wholly by surprise and only gradually
comprehending what is going on, was aware of (53-56).

During this attack the native who has been steering the
steamboat for Marlow is killed. The whole episode constitutes one of those perfect, small images with which Conrad
refines the central meaning of his story. This steersman
was what Marlow calls "an improved specimen," a savage who
had not been civilized but merely trained, just enough to
serve the white man's purposes. "He sported a pair of brass
earrings, wore a blue cloth wrapper from the waist to the
ankles, and thought all the world of himself" (53). When
the fight started, training at first told; the steersman
stayed at his post, though he could not stop "lifting his
knees high, stamping his feet, champing his mouth, like a
reined-in horse" (54). But the temptation was too much for
him; he let go the wheel, snatched up a rifle, and fired
through the window of the pilot house, and then hung out it
"shaking the empty rifle and yelling at the shore" (55). He
is, of course, killed. Marlow misses him because, however
badly, "he had done something, he had steered. . . . It was
a kind of partnership" (61), the bond of actual, practical
accomplishment.

Finally, we meet that remarkable man, Mr. Kurtz—not
directly: Conrad is always happiest when he is working
through a narrator who is commenting and meditating on what
happens. He is even happier if he can put events at the
double remove of two narrators, as he does here by intro-
ducing the young Russian. The young Russian is naive and
humble, the perfect subject for Kurtz's superb powers of per-
suasion. He it is who tells Marlow what he needs to know
about Kurtz's past, coloring it with his devotion to Kurtz
and his puzzlement; and Marlow tells it to us, colored by
his understanding of its meaning. What emerges from all
this is that Kurtz is a remarkable man, a man of splendid if
rather vague ideas of civilizing the savages and of great
eloquence in expressing them. "He had faith . . . he had
the faith. He could get himself to believe anything" (86).
That is to say, he believed in nothing except his own desires, himself; "he was hollow at the core" (69), nothing

except a voice (57). "There was something wanting in him—
some small matter which, when the pressing need arose, could
not be found under that magnificent eloquence" (69). As a
result he had, in the jungle, gradually yielded to the appeal of savagery—"the whisper had proved irresistibly fascinating" (69)—and had made himself into a savage god,
collecting ivory by force and spending more and more time
"getting himself adored" (68). The desire for wealth and
fame had not, of course, died in Kurtz; on the contrary,
even on his deathbed he had grandiose, uncontrolled visions
"of wealth and fame revolving obsequiously round his unex-
tinguishable gift of noble and lofty expression. . . . He
desired to have kings meet him at railway stations on his
return from some ghastly Nowhere" (81-82). The struggle
within him between his ego's self-centered craving for
savage pleasures and for wealth and fame thus made a hell, a
"lightless region of subtle horrors, where pure, uncompli-
cated savagery was a positive relief, being something that
had a right to exist—obviously—in the sunshine" (70).

So strong is the pull of the savage world that Kurtz
crawls on hands and knees—he is too sick to walk—back
toward it the night before the boat starts on its return
trip and Marlow gets him back to the boat only by, as he
puts it, invoking him, because there was nothing Kurtz believed in but himself; "his soul was mad" (79). On the trip
down the river Kurtz discourses. That voice! "It survived
his strength to hide in the magnificent folds of eloquence
the barren darkness of his heart" (81), and "no eloquence,"
as Marlow says, "could have been so withering to one's belief in mankind as his final burst of sincerity" (79)—"The
horror! The horror!" (83)

It is left for Marlow to return a packet of letters to
Kurtz's fiancée, a girl, innocent like all civilized women
as Conrad sees them, who has believed in Kurtz with her
whole heart. Marlow lies to her to save her faith; "I could
not tell her [the truth]. It would have been too dark—too
dark altogether. . ." (92). This is his final commitment to
a belief in the possibility of civilization, for it is the
girl's "stretching out her arms . . . across the fading and
narrow sheen of the window" (91) that persuades Marlow to
tell this lie. That gesture persuades him by reminding him
of another Shade, "tragic also, bedecked with powerless
charms, stretching bare brown arms over the glitter of the
infernal stream, the stream of darkness" (91)—that is, the
dignified and heroic savage girl who had stood on the banks
as the steamboat left Kurtz's post and stretched her arms
toward him while he looked back at her "with fiery, longing
eyes, with a mingled expression of wistfulness and hate"
(80).

Between that dedicated and innocent savage girl and any
of the lesser products of the civilized world, Marlow would
not have hesitated. That is why, for all the sense of its
horror that he and Kurtz share, he can nonetheless understand that girl's appeal to Kurtz and see that Kurtz's

desire for her was, if inescapably corrupt in a civilized
man, nonetheless the corrupt impulse of a remarkable man,
not a weak one. But between that pure savage girl and
Kurtz's Intended, the equally pure civilized girl with her
all too innocent faith in the civilized ideas that Kurtz
as well as she mistakenly supposed Kurtz the almost divine
agent for, Marlow does not hesitate either. Savagery, like
any other evil when it is pure and courageous, has something
admirable about it that makes it far superior to any
cowardly, self-serving pretense of civilization. But
savagery, however admirable, is unquestionably inferior to
genuine civilization.

QUESTIONS (pages 849-850 of *Modern Short Stories*)

1. Marlow begins by saying that "this [London and the Thames] also has been one of the dark places of the earth." What was dark about it? Who penetrated that darkness? What did it take in the way of strength for him to do so? What did he have to fight?

2. What is Marlow's opinion of conquest such as the Romans carried out?

3. What does Marlow think justifies conquest?

4. What does Marlow think of savages, of the cannibals and others he meets during his trip up the Congo?

5. Why does he think contact with such savages and with the jungle is such a test of civilized man? How does it test him?

6. What does Marlow think of the Company? Of its office in Brussels? Of its organization in Africa? Of the manifestations of the spirit of commercial exploitation he sees on his trip down the coast of Africa?

7. What is Marlow's first impression of Kurtz?

8. What impression of Kurtz comes to us from Marlow's report of what the young Russian tells him about Kurtz?

9. What does Marlow learn directly from Kurtz that first night when he has to follow Kurtz and bring him back to the boat?

10. What does he learn from Kurtz on the trip down the river before Kurtz dies?

11. Why does Kurtz write at the end of his pamphlet, "Exterminate the brutes"? Why does he say, "The horror! The horror!"

12. Why does the native say "Mistah Kurtz—he dead" "in a tone of scathing contempt"?

13. Why does Marlow lie to Kurtz's intended when they finally meet?

F. SCOTT FITZGERALD

BABYLON REVISITED

BABYLON REVISITED was originally published in *The
Saturday Evening Post*, though Fitzgerald revised it slightly
before reprinting this version of it in his collection of
short stories called *Taps at Reveille*. But it remains an
interesting illustration of how a story can satisfy the general reader and at the same time achieve greatness. *Babylon
Revisited* does not depend for its effect on unlikely characters and events or on sensational ideas and attitudes.
There is nothing "experimental" about the way it is told;
though Fitzgerald uses the familiar method he has chosen
with a good deal of unshowy skill.

We notice how unobtrusively he omits any explanation of
how Lorraine and Dunc got hold of the Peters' address. We
know Charlie left the address of his hotel at the Ritz Bar
(92-93); we can work out the rest if it becomes a problem
for us, but Fitzgerald clearly prefers the question not to
arise since it is irrelevant to the central interest of the
story, merely a matter of the machinery of the plot. He
therefore does his best—short of omitting to make the plot
feasible—to keep the question from arising at all. We
notice, too, the economy with which the characters and their
attitudes are established for us—Lincoln Peters resting his
hand for a moment on Charlie's shoulder (95), Marion sitting
behind the coffee service in her black dinner dress "that
just faintly suggested mourning" and playing nervously with
the black stars of her necklace (101-102). Lorraine
Quarrles still not feeling old a bit, still longing to steal
butchers' tricycles and to build the important human rela-
tionships of her life on such foundations ("I have thought
about you too much for the last year, and it's always been
in the back of my mind that I might see you if I came over
here." [108]) We notice how unostentatiously the story is
made to begin and end with Charlie Wales sitting in the Ritz
Bar—the once fabulous center of American dissipation in
Paris—contemplating the irredeemable past with its terrible,
meaningless, irresponsible "fun." We notice how naturally
the story manages to place the rigidly neurotic Marion
Peters, with her false stability, on one side of Charlie and
Honoria, and Lorraine Quarrles, with her slightly shabby
frivolousness, on the other.

Above all we notice how skillfully the story reveals,
bit by bit as the need for it arises, the necessary information about Charlie and his wife Helen and about Charlie's
conquest of his drunkenness. At first we know only that
Charlie has had a wild two years in Paris ("I spoiled this
city for myself," [94]) and that his sister-in-law dislikes

him (95). Next we discover that, even during the wildest
escapades of those two years, he was aware that he was ignoring what he really cared for, the wife and child he has
now lost (97). Then, during the second scene at the Peters'
(102-105), we learn from Marion's bitter, jealous references
to the past nearly everything we need to know about the life
Charlie and Helen lived together in Paris. It only remains
for Charlie to remember as he leaves the Peters' exactly how
it had really been that night he locked Helen out in the
snow (106).

Every one of these bits of information comes into the
story where the development of the plot—Charlie's effort to
regain legal authority over his own daughter and Marion's
irrational opposition·to it—requires it. As the story
approaches its climax, Fitzgerald sums up this history of
the past for us once more, now not as facts but as feelings,
as the qualities of experience, in one of those wonderful
images that are the heart of all his best stories: "Again
the memory of those days swept over him like a nightmare
. . .—The men who locked their wives out in the snow, because the snow of twenty-nine wasn't real snow. If you
didn't want it to be snow, you just paid some money" (112).

The distinction of *Babylon Revisited* is in the quality
of its feeling, in its subtle evocation of what it feels
like to live in a certain way in a certain time and place,
and in what a man becomes by doing so. The plotting of the
story, the establishment of its characters, the selection of
scenes for full development are managed with quiet skill;
the story is solidly constructed. But what it exists for,
what makes it more than skillful, is this. That is why it
begins, easily and naturally, with the muted echoes of the
past at the Ritz Bar—the familiar names from the list of a
year and a half ago (92), the details about Claude Fessenden,
that "dandy fellow" who has become what Charlie just missed
becoming (93), the homosexuals whom "nothing affects" (94).
That is why it dwells—irrelevantly so far as the plot is
concerned—on Charlie's taxi ride through the Paris of "fire-
red, gas-blue, ghost-green signs," on the "pink majesty" of
the Place de la Concorde, on the cab horns repeating the
first few bars of *La Plus que Lente* (94). This is the magnificent Paris that the Charlie of nineteen twenty-nine had
never seen. That is why we are taken on Charlie's sober and
disenchanted tour of the Paris he had seen, the Montmartre
where "the catering to vice and waste is on an utterly childish scale" (97).

Against this background of Paris as it really is, so
beautifully evoked by a handful of exactly observed, evoca-
tive details, the story's central feelings develop. The
story begins with Charlie's sense of the past and its deliberate irresponsibility, when he threw away thousand-franc
notes in an unsuccessful effort to forget everything he
really cared for, trying to believe that not only snow but
every other reality of life could be made to disappear simply

by paying some money. "In retrospect it was a nightmare"
(108). Nonetheless, "ghost-green," it returns to haunt him
in the person of Lorraine Quarrles. In the past she had
seemed attractive to him, and if she now seems "trite,
blurred, worn away," he can nevertheless not escape his past
involvement with her and with the life she still lives.
Marion's condemnation of Charlie, when Lorraine and Dunc in-
vade the Peters' house (109), may be unjust, a case of guilt
by association. But they are what Charlie had once been,
his past self; he may now find that past self inexplicable,
may feel "awe that he had actually, in his mature years,"
been like that (108). But he had been, and he has to pay
the full price for it. It is one of the story's nicest
touches that Dunc and Lorraine—careless, irresponsible, uncalculating—should nonetheless have ferreted out with
drunken cunning the Peters' address and tracked Charlie
there.

Charlie is just as anxious to avoid, for himself and
Honoria, the life of the Peters' household. It appears
"warm and comfortably American," quiet, stable, responsible;
but at its heart is an uncontrollably, irrational,
bitterly neurotic woman, a contrasting character to the
Lorraine Quarrles, who embodies the frivolous life. Charlie
now sees the defects in the ways of life represented by both
women; but he is entangled with them both, with Lorraine by
his past friendship with her, with Marion Peters by her
legal guardianship of Honoria—both consequences of the life
he had lived in twenty-nine. Like the apparently joyous
life of Lorraine Quarrles ("we did have such good times that
crazy spring," [108]) that is in fact a nightmare, the
apparently stable life of Marion Peters is like a wall
erected against life, a neurotic woman's self-destructive
shutting-out of experience.

At the center of *Babylon Revisited* is the feeling for
life that Charlie has developed—or renewed—during his
years of recovery in Prague: a belief in the value of hard
work, of disciplined responsibility, of character "as the
eternally valuable element" (96). At the center of that
feeling is his overwhelming love for his daughter who is so
intensely alive—very much a person in her own right—yet
uniquely close to him, his own flesh and blood. She is an
extension of himself back to the time when he was young
"with a lot of nice thoughts and dreams to have by himself"
(113), and he wants to be a part of her life (100). We
catch a glimpse of all that would mean to him during their
luncheon at Le Grand Vatel. This brief escape from the
prison of the Peters' home, behind whose walls Honoria
quickly disappears again, is interrupted by the "unwelcome
encounter" with Lorraine.

The new Charlie Wales has come back to the city he had
been a part of in the past with the serious purpose of re-
gaining his daughter and renewing the life he and Helen had
lived before he had made a fortune in the boom market of the
late twenties and they had lost themselves in the Babylon

Americans had then made of Paris. Almost in idle curiosity
he looks over his old haunts in Paris, wondering how he
could possibly have been taken in by them ("You had to be
damned drunk," [97]), conscious now of the magnificence of
another Paris his old self had never seen at all. The last
thing he is thinking is that the past is inescapable, that
he is not just revisiting Babylon as a sightseer. But he is
not a sightseer; he is an old citizen of Babylon, and bit by
bit the past comes to him demanding that he accept his responsibility for it. In the end he is sitting again in the
Ritz Bar, again refusing Alix's offer of a second drink,
telling himself that "they couldn't make him pay forever"
(113). But we are not at all sure, after what we have seen,
that they cannot.

It is probably unnecessary to add that *Babylon Revisited*
is close to Fitzgerald's personal experience. It was written
in December, 1930, shortly after his wife, Zelda, had broken
down mentally in such a serious way as to make Fitzgerald
fear she would never be well again; at a time when Fitzgerald
was being forced to look squarely at his own uncontrollable
drunkenness; and at a time when he was beginning to worry
seriously over the future of the daughter he loved very much.
A story is not necessarily better for having this kind of
connection with its author's personal life, but here the
connection helps to explain why the voice that is telling the
story is so charged with feeling. That voice is, ostensibly,
the voice of the anonymous, third-person narrator; but almost
from the beginning it carries much of the burden of the
story's feelings. Even when feelings are ascribed to Charlie
Wales, the narrator shares them; they are not merely the
feelings of a character but have the authority of the story's
total experience behind them: they are what the narrator's
voice, by participating in them, suggests life itself is.
It is not easy to write a story that retains a reasonable
objectivity—never becomes an exercise in self-pity and
self-justification—when the narrator's feelings are so close
to those of the central character; Fitzgerald succeeds by
never allowing either the narrator nor Charlie Wales to
justify Charlie's past life or to feel that he is helpless.
As a result the final paragraph, in which the narrator and
Charlie Wales are difficult to separate, is a triumph of
tact. It is a summary of the facts of Charlie's experience
and of its meaning such as only a third-person narrator,
looking at the situation from outside, could give. At the
same time it expresses, almost in the voice of the sufferer,
Charlie's feelings about what has happened to him: though
the words are given us in the narrator's voice, they are in
fact the ones Charlie is using to himself in phrases like
"They couldn't make him pay forever" and "He was absolutely
sure Helen wouldn't have wanted him to be so alone" (113).
The effectiveness of *Babylon Revisited* depends very largely
on the success with which Fitzgerald combines in this way
in the voice of the narrator the authoritative objectivity
of the third-person with the immediate feelings of the
protagonist.

QUESTIONS   (page 850 of *Modern Short Stories*)

1. What kind of person is Lorraine Quarrles? What can we discover about the kind of life she lives from Charlie's recollections of her during his previous time in Paris and from the note she writes him? From the way she behaves when Charlie runs into her and Dunc at the restaurant? When she and Dunc come to the Peters' house?

2. What kind of a person is Marion Peters? What do we learn about her life from Charlie's visits to the Peters' house? From what Lincoln Peters says about her?

3. What sort of life had Charlie and Helen lived in Paris before Helen's death and Charlie's collapse? How, specifically, had Charlie come to lock Helen out in the snow that night? What had that episode done to their personal relations? What had Helen died of? How had Charlie collapsed?

4. What parallel is there between Charlie's present relation to Lorraine Quarrles and his present relation to Marion Peters?

5. Why does the story begin with Charlie talking to the bartender in the Ritz Bar and then taking a taxi ride through Paris? Why does Charlie pay a visit to Montmartre?

6. What is Charlie's life like now? Why is Honoria so necessary to its fulfillment?

7. Why does Charlie, at the end of the story, think Helen would certainly not have wanted him to be alone?

RALPH ELLISON
BATTLE ROYAL

BATTLE ROYAL is not Mr. Ellison's title; this is the first chapter of a novel, *Invisible Man*, and the opening paragraph's description of how it took "a long time and much painful boomeranging of my expectations to achieve a realization everyone else appears to have been born with" (113)— namely, that he is himself and only he can truly know what that is—applies to the whole book; but it also applies with special precision to this particular chapter of the book, because this chapter is a thematic introduction to the novel.

Like *Invisible Man* as a whole, *Battle Royal* combines social realism and moral symbolism in an unusual way to make its point about the black man's life. Mr. Ellison is particularly interested in two aspects of his subject. He wants to trace the psychological process by which the young black boy accepts the white man's theory of the black's place in the scheme of things and to emphasize the absurdity of this theory, its glaring inconsistency with the plain facts of the boy's experience. And he wants to give concrete examples of white society's general methods of enslaving the black man, examples in which the white man's motives are so transparent that the incidents become almost allegorical. The view of the black man's situation in American society on which the story rests is set forth by the narrator's grandfather, a man who seems to the narrator a very "odd old guy" and to the narrator's parents a dangerously mysterious one. On his deathbed, the narrator's grandfather has said that "ever since I give up my gun back in the Reconstruction"—that is, ever since the black man ceased openly to fight against the white man's world—his performance of the grinning, "Yassuh boss" darky's role has been a cover for a traitor and a spy in the enemy's—that is, the white man's—country. At the end of the story, the narrator dreams he finds in his briefcase a directive from the white world about the treatment for blacks like him, "a short message in letters of gold." It says: "To Whom It May Concern. Keep This Nigger-Boy Running." What was literally in that briefcase was a scholarship to a Negro college given him by white men. But it took the narrator years to learn that his grandfather was right, that white man's country was enemy country and the scholarship just a trick to keep him running.

He is incapable of understanding his grandfather's deathbed statement or his own dream, though the events of the evening described in the story shout their meaning at him, because he is deeply committed, psychologically, to the

-15-

view of himself that has been imposed on him by white
society. No matter what happens to him, he remains sure
that subservience to the white man is the only means to success and happiness for him and that the only source of
approval—the only standard of rightness—is the white man's.
The battle royal and the accompanying "entertainments" constitute a systematic demonstration of the falseness of his
view.   The effect of this demonstration is greatly increased
by the way the narrator—like some very young, very black
Gulliver—clings to his ridiculous but psychologically
plausible self-deception as he describes, step by step, the
complacent brutality of the white men who are running the
smoker.

     The narrator wants nothing to do with the other black
boys, who are tougher and more cynical than he and "seemed
to have no grandfather's curse worrying their minds" (115).
Their one concern is to win their five or ten dollars, by
whatever means.   They too are victims, of course, limited to
the small freedom the white man permits them by their own
cynicism, their willingness to accept what they are given.
The narrator is shocked at the smoker "to see some of the
most important men of the town quite tipsy" (116), but he
fails to draw any conclusion from it.   At the worst moment
of the evening, in the almost unconscious despair of
suffering and humiliation, he surprises himself by striking
back, "by trying to topple [a white man] upon the rug" that
was electrified.   Otherwise he does not consciously recognize the white men's responsibility for what is happening to
him, open and obvious though it is.

     It is the school superintendent himself, who has
arranged to bring the narrator to this smoker in the first
place because he has been so impressed by the narrator's
oration on the wisdom of black subservience, who calls out
when the stripper is naked, "Bring up the shines, gentlemen!
Bring up the shines!" (116) Gentlemen.   Then these young
black boys are forced to endure the torturing complex of
feelings aroused in them by this deliberately seductive
white woman, while the white men in effect dare them to respond, half in amusement, half in the hatred that is always
trying·to create occasions for hating.   At the climax, as
the city fathers lose all control and toss the naked woman
in the air, the narrator sees "the terror and disgust in her
eyes, almost like my own terror . . ." (118).   In this way
the smoker begins with an almost allegorical vision of the
way the white man tortures the black man sexually.

     The battle royal is a similar vision of the second
way the white man regularly tortures the black.   Here black
boys, blindfolded and helpless, deprived of all dignity,
stumbling about like drunks or babies, are set to savaging
each other for the amusement of the white men—if amusement
is the right word: at least one of the man present so
enjoys seeing black youngsters hurt that he has to be held
back by main force from joining in the beating.   The black
boys themselves are so cynically, so anarchically committed

to collecting their pittance for hurting one another that
not even the final pair of them can unite against the white
man's scheme. When the narrator whispers to Tatlock, "Fake
like I knocked you out, you can have the prize," Tatlock
says, "I'll break your behind." "For them?" "For me,
sonofabitch!" (121).

In the midst of this naked display of savagery by these
white men—"Kill him! Kill that big boy!" (120)—the
narrator is worrying steadily about when he will get a
chance to impress these wise and important men with his
speech: "How would it go? Would they recognize my ability?
What would they give me?" (120). "I wanted to deliver my
speech more than anything in the world, because I felt that
only these men could judge truly my ability" (121)—these
drunken, goatish, sadistic men; and when one of them yells,
"I got my money on the big boy [Tatlock]," the narrator almost drops his guard, feeling that if the white man is
against him, it would be wrong for him to try to win the
fight (122).

After this demonstration of how white men set black men
to fighting one another, we are shown how white men exploit
black men's greed, trap blacks with promises of quick
riches, which turn out to be both tortures and frauds (the
"gold coins" are brass advertising tokens). For this exploitation too, in spite of all he has already been put through,
"Sambo" is ready and eager: the narrator "trembled with
excitement, forgetting my pain. . . . I would use both hands.
I would throw my body against the boys nearest me to block
them from the gold" (122). As the boys writhe in agony on
the electrified rug, the white men stand over them, roaring
with delight.

Finally the narrator is given a chance to deliver his
almost forgotten speech. The MC introduces him with brutal
playfulness by suggesting that he—like some savage in a
silk hat—"knows more big words than a pocket-sized dic-
tionary" (125). This gives the audience its clue; nobody
listens to the speech except to make jokes about the big
words he uses ("What's that word you say, boy?"). Still,
aching all over from his beating and swallowing blood from
the cut in his mouth until he is nauseated, the narrator
delivers his oration about how necessary it is for people of
his race "not to underestimate the importance of culti-
vating friendly relations with the Southern white man" (125),
that oration which has convinced the school principal that
"some day he'll lead his people in the proper paths" and has
earned him a briefcase and a scholarship to a Negro college,
where the good work of training him for that task will be
continued. When the audience's baiting makes him slip and
say "social equality" (126), the kindest man present says to
him, "We mean to do right by you, but you've got to know
your place at all times" (127).

The briefcase and the scholarship "so moved [the narrator] that I could hardly express my thanks" (127). Everyone shares this feeling: at home everyone is excited; the neighbors all congratulate him.

> I even felt safe from my grandfather, whose death-
> bed curse usually spoiled my triumphs. I stood
> beneath his photograph with my briefcase in hand
> and smiled triumphantly into his solid black
> peasant's face. It was a face that fascinated me.
> The eyes seemed to follow me everywhere I went
> (127-128).

QUESTIONS (pages 850-851 of *Modern Short Stories*)

1. What is the point of the grandfather's deathbed state-ment?

2. What connection do you see between this attitude and the dream the narrator has at the end of the story about the message he finds in his briefcase saying, "Keep this Nigger-Boy Running"?

3. What is the point of the narrator's oration that has so delighted the school principal? What does the principal think it suggests about the narrator's future career?

4. Why is the narrator determined to attend the smoker and to survive throughout the evening?

5. Why do the men at the smoker insist on the black boys' watching the naked woman at close range?

6. What does the conduct of Jackson suggest about the white men's motives for staging the battle royal?

7. Why did the narrator want "to deliver my speech more than anything else in the world"?

8. Under what conditions does he finally succeed in delivering it?

9. What causes him to make his slip about "social equality"?

10. What is his reward for his speech?

MARY McCARTHY

ARTISTS IN UNIFORM

Mary McCarthy's *ARTISTS IN UNIFORM* was first published
in *Harper's Magazine*. A year later Miss McCarthy, roused by
the letters she had received about the story, wrote an article for *Harper's* entitled *Settling the Colonel's Hash*. In
this article she was primarily concerned with what seemed to
her the serious defects of the fashionable way of analyzing
stories as revealed by the letters she had received. What
follows is the analysis of her own story as made in her
article.[1]

Seven years ago, when I taught in a progressive
college, I had a pretty girl student in one of my
classes who wanted to be a short-story writer. She
was not studying writing with me, but she knew that
I sometimes wrote short stories, and one day,
breathless and glowing, she came up to me in the
hall, to tell me that she had just written a story
that her writing teacher, a Mr. Converse, was terribly excited about.

"He thinks it's wonderful," she said, "and he's
going to help me fix it up for publication. . . .
Mr. Converse is going over it with me and we're
going to put in the symbols." . . .

At the time, I thought these notions were peculiar to progressive education: it was old-fashioned
or regressive to read a novel to find out what happens to the hero or to have a mere experience empty
of symbolic pointers. But I now consider that this
attitude is quite general, and that readers and students all over the country are in a state of appre-
hension, lest they read a book or story literally
and miss the presence of a symbol. And like everything in America, this search for meanings has become a socially competitive enterprise; the best
reader is the one who detects the most symbols in a
given stretch of prose. And the benighted reader
who fails to find any symbols humbly assents when
they are pointed out to him; he accepts his mortification. . . .

---

[1]From Mary McCarthy, *On the Contrary*. Copyright 1954
by Mary McCarthy. Reprinted by permission of Farrar, Straus
& Giroux, Inc.

The whole point of this "story" ["Artists in Uniform"] was that it really happened; it is written in the first person; I speak of myself in my own name, McCarthy; at the end, I mention my husband's name, Broadwater. When I was thinking about writing the story, I decided not to treat it fictionally; the chief interest, I felt, lay in the fact that it happened, in real life, last summer, to the writer herself, who was a good deal at fault in the incident. I wanted to embarrass myself and, if possible, the reader too.

Yet, strangely enough, many of my readers preferred to think of this account as fiction. . . . Shortly after the story was published, I got a kindly letter from a man in Mexico, in which he criticized the menu from an artistic point of view: he thought salads would be better for hot weather and it would be more in character for the narrator-heroine to have a martini. I did not answer the letter, though I was moved to, because I had the sense that he would not understand the distinction between what *ought* to have happened and what *did* happen.

Then in April I got another letter, from an English teacher in a small college in the Middle West, that reduced me to despair. I am going to cite it at length. "My students in freshmen English chose to analyze your story, 'Artists in Uniform,' from the March issue of *Harper's*. For a week I heard oral discussions on it and then the students wrote critical analyses. In so far as it is possible, I stayed out of their discussions, encouraging them to read the story closely with your intentions as a guide to their understanding. Although some of them insisted that the story has no other level than the realistic one, most of them decided it has symbolic overtones.

"The question is: how closely do you want the symbols labeled? They wrestled with the nuns, the author's two shades of green with pink accents, with the 'materialistic godlessness' of the Colonel. . . . A surprising number wanted exact symbols; for example, they searched for the significance of the Colonel's eating hash and the author eating a sandwich. . . . From my standpoint, the story was an entirely satisfactory springboard for understanding the various shades of prejudice, for seeing how much of the artist goes into his painting. If it is any satisfaction to you, our campus was alive with discussion about 'Artists in Uniform.' We liked the story and we thought it amazing that an author could succeed in making readers dislike the author—for a purpose, of course!"

I probably should have answered this letter, but
I did not. The gulf seemed to me too wide. I
could not applaud the backward students who insisted
that the story has no other level than the realistic
one without giving offense to their teacher, who was
evidently a well-meaning person. But I shall try
now to address a reply, not to this teacher and her
unfortunate class, but to a whole school of misunderstanding. There were no symbols in this story;
there was no deeper level. The nuns were in the
story because they were on the train; the contrasting
greens were the dress I happened to be wearing; the
Colonel had hash because he had hash; materialistic
godlessness meant just what it means when a priest
thunders it from the pulpit—the phrase, for the
first time, had meaning for me as I watched and listened to the Colonel.

But to clarify the misunderstanding, one must go
a little further and try to see what a literary
symbol is. Now in one sense, the Colonel's hash and
my sandwich can be regarded as symbols; that is,
they typify the Colonel's food tastes and mine.
(The man in Mexico had different food tastes which he
wished to interpose into our reality.) The hash and
the sandwich might even be said to show something
very obvious about our characters and bringing-up,
or about our sexes; I was a woman, he was a man.
And though on another day I might have ordered hash
myself, that day I did not, because the Colonel and
I, in our disagreement, were polarizing each other.

The hash and the sandwich, then, could be regarded as symbols of our disagreement, almost conscious symbols. And underneath our discussion of
the Jews, there was a then sexual current running,
as there always is in such random encounters or
pick-ups (for they have the strong suggestion of the
illicit). The fact that I ordered something con-
ventionally feminine and he ordered something con-
ventionally masculine represented, no doubt, our
awareness of a sexual possibility; even though I was
not attracted to the Colonel, nor he to me, the circumstances of our meeting made us define ourselves
as a woman and a man.

The sandwich and the hash were our provisional,
ad hoc symbols of ourselves. But in this sense all
human actions are symbolic because they represent
the person who does them. If the Colonel had
ordered a fruit salad with whipped cream, this too
would have represented him in some way; given his
other traits, it would have pointed to a complexity
in his character that the hash did not suggest.

In the same way, the contrasting greens of my

dress were a symbol of my taste in clothes and hence
representative of me—all too representative, I suddenly saw, in the club car, when I got an "artistic"
image of myself flashed back at me from the men's
eyes. I had no wish to stylize myself as an artist,
that is, to parade about as a symbol of flamboyant
unconventionality, but apparently I had done so unwittingly when I picked those colors off a rack,
under the impression that they suited me or "expressed my personality" as salesladies say.

My dress, then, was a symbol of the perplexity I
found myself in with the Colonel; I did not want to
be categorized as a member of a peculiar minority—
an artist or a Jew; but brute fate and the Colonel
kept resolutely cramming me into both those uncomfortable pigeonholes. I wished to be regarded as
ordinary or rather as universal, to be anybody and
therefore everybody (that is, in one sense, I wanted
to be on the Colonel's side, majestically above
minorities); but every time the Colonel looked at my
dress and me in it with my pink earrings I shrank
into minority status, and I felt the dress in the
heat shriveling me, like the shirt of Nessus, the
centaur, that consumed Hercules.

But this is not what the students meant when they
wanted the symbols "labeled." They were searching
for a more recondite significance than that afforded
by the trite symbolism of ordinary life, in which a
dress is a social badge. They supposed that I was
engaging in literary or artificial symbolism, which
would lead the reader out of the confines of reality
into the vast fairy tale of myth, in which the color
green would have an emblematic meaning (or did the
two greens signify for them what the teacher calls
"shades" of prejudice), and the Colonel's hash, I
imagine, would be some sort of Eucharistic mince-
meat.

Apparently, the presence of the nuns assured them
there were overtones of theology; it did not occur
to them (a) that the nuns were there because pairs
of nuns are a standardized feature of summer Pullman
travel, like crying babies, and perspiring business
men in the club car, and (b) that if I thought the
nuns worth mentioning, it was also because of something very simple and directly relevant: the nuns
and the Colonel and I all had something in common—
we had all at one time been Catholics—and I was
seeking common ground with the Colonel, from which
to turn and attack his position.

In any account of reality, even a televised one,
which comes closest to being a literal transcript or
replay, some details are left out as irrelevant
(though nothing is really irrelevant). The details

that are not eliminated have to stand as symbols of
the whole, like stenographic signs, and of course
there is an art of selection, even in a newspaper
account: the writer, if he has any ability, is
looking for the revealing detail that will sum up
the picture for the reader in a flash of recognition.

But the art of abridgment and condensation, which
is familiar to anybody who tries to relate an anecdote or give a direction—the art of natural symbolism, which is at the basis of speech and all representation—has at bottom a centripetal intention.
It hovers over an object, an event, or series of
events and tries to declare what it is. Analogy
(that is, comparison to other objects) is inevitably
one of its methods. "The weather was soupy," *i.e.*,
like soup. "He wedged his way in," *i.e.*, he had to
enter, thin edge first, as a wedge enters, and so on.
All this is obvious. But these metaphorical aids to
communication are a far cry from literary symbolism,
as taught in the schools and practiced by certain
fashionable writers. Literary symbolism is centrif-
ugal and flees from the object, the event, into the
incorporeal distance, where concepts are taken for
substance and floating ideas and archetypes assume a
hieratic authority.

In this dream-forest, symbols become arbitrary;
all counters are interchangeable; anything can stand
for anything else. The Colonel's hash can be a
Eucharist or a cannibal feast or the banquet of
Atreus, or all three, so long as the actual dish set
before the actual man is disparaged. What is de-
pressing about this insistent symbolization is the
fact that while it claims to lead to the infinite,
it quickly reaches very finite limits—there are only
so many myths on record, and once you have got
through Bulfinch, the Scandinavian, and the Indian,
there is not much left. And if all stories reduce
themselves to myth and symbol, qualitative differences vanish, and there is only a single, monotonous
story.

American fiction of the symbolist school demon-
strates this mournful truth, without precisely in-
tending to. A few years ago, when the mode was at
its height, chic novels and stories fell into three
classes: those which had a Greek myth for their
framework, which the reader was supposed to detect,
like finding the faces in the clouds in old newspaper
puzzle contests; those which had symbolic modern
figures, dwarfs, hermaphrodites, and cripples, illustrating maiming and loneliness; and those which contained symbolic animals, cougars, wild cats, and
monkeys. One young novelist, a product of the
Princeton school of symbolism, had all three elements
going at once, like the ringmaster of a three-ring

circus, with the freaks, the animals, and the
statues. . . .

It is now considered very old-fashioned and
tasteless to speak of an author's "philosophy of
life" as something that can be harvested from his
work. Actually, most of the great authors did have
a "philosophy of life" which they were eager to communicate to the public; this was one of their
motives for writing. And to disentangle a moral
philosophy from a work that evidently contains one
is far less damaging to the author's purpose and the
integrity of his art than to violate his imagery by
symbol-hunting, as though reading a novel were a
sort of paper chase.

The images of a novel or a story belong, as it
were, to a family, very closely knit and inseparable
from each other; the parent "idea" of a story or a
novel generates events and images all bearing a
strong family resemblance. And to understand a
story or a novel, you must look for the parent
"idea," which is usually in plain view, if you read
quite carefully and literally what the author says.

I will go back, for a moment, to my own story, to
show how this can be done. Clearly, it is about the
Jewish question, for that is what the people are
talking about. It also seems to be about artists,
since the title is "Artists in Uniform." Then there
must be some relation between artists and Jews.
What is it? They are both minorities that other
people claim to be able to recognize by their appearance. But artists and Jews do not care for this
categorization; they want to be universal, that is,
like everybody else. But this aim is really hopeless, for life has formed them as Jews or artists,
in a way that immediately betrays them to the
majority they are trying to melt into. In my conversation with the Colonel, I was endeavoring to play a
double game. I was trying to force him into a
minority by treating anti-Semitism as an aberration,
which, in fact, I believe it is. On his side, the
Colonel resisted this attempt and tried to show that
anti-Semitism was normal, and he was normal, while I
was the queer one. He declined to be categorized as
an anti-Semite; he regarded himself as an independent
thinker, who by a happy chance thought the same as
everybody else.

I imagined I had a card up my sleeve; I had
guessed that the Colonel was Irish (*i.e.*, that he
belonged to a minority) and presumed that he was a
Catholic. I did not see how he could possibly guess
that I, with my Irish name and Irish appearance, had
a Jewish grandmother in the background. Therefore
when I found I had not convinced him by reasoning, I

played my last card; I told him that the Church, his Church, forbade anti-Semitism. I went even further; I implied that God forbade it, though I had no right to do this, since I did not believe in God, but was only using Him as a whip to crack over the Colonel, to make him feel humble and inferior, a raw Irish Catholic lad under discipline. But the Colonel, it turned out, did not believe in God, either, and I lost. And since, in a sense, I had been cheating all along in this game we were playing, I had to concede the Colonel a sort of moral victory in the end; I let him think that my husband was Jewish and that that "explained" everything satisfactorily.

Now there are a number of morals or meanings in this little tale, starting with the simple one: don't talk to strangers on a train. The chief moral or meaning (what I learned, in other words, from this experience) was this: you cannot be a universal unless you accept the fact that you are a singular, that is, a Jew or an artist or what-have-you. What the Colonel and I were discussing, and at the same time illustrating and enacting, was the definition of a human being. I was trying to be something better than a human being; I was trying to be the voice of pure reason; and pride went before a fall. The Colonel, without trying, was being something worse than a human being, and somehow we found ourselves on the same plane—facing each other, like mutually repellent twins. Or, put it another way: it is dangerous to be drawn into discussions of the Jews with anti-Semites: you delude yourself that you are spreading light, but you are really sinking into muck; if you endeavor to be dispassionate, you are really claiming for yourself a privileged position, a little mountain top, from which you look down, impartially, on both the Jews and the Colonel.

Anti-Semitism is a horrible disease from which nobody is immune, and it has a kind of evil fascination that makes an enlightened person draw near the source of infection, supposedly in a scientific spirit, but really to sniff the vapors and dally with the possibility. The enlightened person who lunches with the Colonel in order, as she tells herself, to improve him, is cheating herself, having her cake and eating it. This attempted cheat, on my part, was related to the question of the artist and and the green dress; I wanted to be an artist but not to pay the price of looking like one, just as I was willing to have Jewish blood but not willing to show it, where it would cost me something—the loss of superiority in an argument.

These meanings are all there, quite patent, to anyone who consents to look *into* the story. They were *in* the experience itself, waiting to be found and

considered. I did not perceive them all at the time
the experience was happening; otherwise, it would
not have taken place, in all probability—I should
have given the Colonel a wide berth. But when I
went back over the experience, in order to write it,
I came upon these meanings, protruding at me, as it
were, from the details of the occasion. I put in
the green dress and my mortification over it because
they were part of the truth, just as it had occurred,
but I did not see how they were related to the general question of anti-Semitism and my grandmother
until they *showed* me their relation in the course of
writing.

Every short story, at least for me, is a little
act of discovery. A cluster of details presents itself to my scrutiny, like a mystery that I will
understand in the course of writing or sometimes not
fully until afterward, when, if I have been honest
and listened to these details carefully, I will find
that they are connected and that there is a coherent
pattern. This pattern is *in* experience itself; you
do not impose it from the outside and if you try to,
you will find that the story is taking the wrong tack,
dribbling away from you into artificiality or in-
consequence. A story that you do not learn something from while you are writing it, that does not
illuminate something for you, is dead, finished before you started it. The "idea" of a story is implicit in it, on the one hand; on the other hand, it
is always ahead of the writer, like a form dimly
discerned in the distance; he is working *toward* the
"idea." . . .

The tree of life, said Hegel, is greener than the
tree of thought; I have quoted this before but I
cannot forbear from citing it again in this context.
This is not an incitement to mindlessness or an en-
dorsement of realism in the short story (there are
several kinds of reality, including interior
reality); it means only that the writer must be,
first of all, a listener and observer, who can pay
attention to reality, like an obedient pupil, and who
is willing, always, to be surprised by the messages
reality is sending through him. And if he gets the
messages correctly he will not have to go back and
put in the symbols; he will find that the symbols
are there, staring at him significantly from the
commonplace.

QUESTIONS (page 851 of *Modern Short Stories*)

1.   When Miss McCarthy gets into the discussion in the
club car, where the anti-Semitic Colonel is holding forth,
she discovers that the occupants of the car have quickly
identified her as an artist. How have they done so? Why is
she dismayed that they have?

2.   In what sense are both she and the Colonel "artists
in uniform"?

3.   By what process of reasoning does the Colonel persuade himself that, as an anti-Semite, he is a perfectly
reasonable and normal man?

4.   How does Miss McCarthy set about proving to the
Colonel that he is wrong to think so? Why does she fail?
What weakness in her own attitude contributes to this
failure?

5.   How does the Colonel set about explaining to himself
why Miss McCarthy opposes his views? How has Miss McCarthy
laid herself open to this kind of explanation?

6.   When the Colonel discovers that Miss McCarthy is
married to a man named Broadwater and concludes that Mr.
Broadwater must be a Jew and that that explains Miss
McCarthy's objections to anti-Semitism, how much is he
justified in reasoning this way, even though he has the
facts wrong? Why does Miss McCarthy not tell him he is
wrong in thinking Mr. Broadwater a Jew?

7.   What is the story's final implication about how Miss
McCarthy ought to have dealt with the Colonel? What mistake
does it suggest she made? What does it suggest were the
causes for her making that mistake?

DIANE OLIVER

Neighbors

NEIGHBORS focuses with quiet dramatic force on the essential evil of social injustice: the personal suffering—always homely, domestic, unspectacular—that is the only real reason for hating such injustice. The story's power is the reward for Miss Oliver's perfect control over feelings that must, in some form, have been her own, and the result is not just a literary achievement but a comment on social injustice that has an immediacy, a poignancy, and an effectiveness greater than that of a thousand uncontrolled shouts in the street. It is hard to believe this beautifully conceived story was written by a twenty-three-year-old girl.

Miss Oliver has three main ends to serve with her narrator, Ellie Mitchell. She must make us see Ellie's ordinary, everyday self and her habits of life, so that we can properly interpret her reactions to the special events of the story and appreciate fully their effect on a young girl. She must then show us clearly Ellie's special reactions to this situation as a measure of the psychological cost of a social conflict of this kind. Finally, she must make clear to us the social situation to which Ellie is reacting, the objective, external conditions that constitute her problem. In order to maintain the sharp dramatic focus that gives the story its power, all these things must be done within the terms of Ellie's consciousness, within its natural range of perception, within the limits of its accumulated experience. The precision of Miss Oliver's imagination is nowhere better demonstrated than in the way she finds the exact form each of these things will take for Ellie's understanding: so natural are Ellie's observations, so perfectly suited are her feelings to her character that it is with a kind of delayed explosion that we realize the larger moral implications of what she observes and what she feels.

What we make out first is that Ellie is fresh out of high school, with a young girl's usual expectations of life as yet undamaged by experience: "Saraline had finished high school three years ahead of her and it was time for her to be getting married" (146); neither Ellie nor Sara can figure out why Sara's grandfather does not like Sara's boyfriend, Charlie. Ellie is on her way home from her work as a maid in the white part of town, "clutching in her hand the paper bag that contained her uniform" (145). A job is still enough of a novelty that she is actively enjoying having money of her own to spend on the clothes that, girl-like, she is enchanted by; one of the most painful of the story's many small, precise psycological notations is Ellie's sudden realization that she is not enjoying clothes-hunting anymore: "She stopped to look at a reversible raincoat in Ivey's window, but although she had a full time job now, she couldn't keep her mind on clothes" (146). We are constantly being shown how the innocent and happy young girl in Ellie is being smothered by the anxiety of her special situation, the details of which are still unknown to us. "Everything in the shop was painted orange and green and Ellie couldn't help thinking that poor Saraline looked out of place" (146); "Reverend Davis' car was big and black and shiny just like, but no, . . . her mother didn't like for them to say things about other people's color," which had no doubt been something she and Saraline giggled over in innocent amusement in the past, but which she was beginning to know was not funny (148). The old woman everyone her age used to call "Doughnut Puncher" will not smile for her now, won't remain the inhuman victim of childish fun she has always seemed; Mr. Paul's bitter joke about people's spitting on Tommy angers the child in Ellie, who does not want to grow up to the knowledge that it is true (148).

In this way Ellie's reluctant, painful, psychologically shaking emergence from girlhood into womanhood under the pressure of the situation her family is in is carefully traced for us. Her feelings about this situation begin with the ordinary kind of resentment anyone might feel—too many newspaper photographers being crudely inconsiderate of little Tommy, she thinks (145). But even as she thinks it, she is aware that somehow it is not just that, that her familiar world has become phantasmagoric. She struggles to maintain her sense of ordinary reality, fixing her attention by a deliberate act of the will on the small details of life around her—" . . . at least [it] kept her from thinking of tomorrow" (145). She looks desperately for some way to separate "what was real and what she had been imagining for the past couple of days" (146).

As we are slowly brought in this way to recognize the shaken state of Ellie's mind, we begin to measure for ourselves the effect on her of what she observes when she gets home—of her quiet recognition that her father "hadn't had much sleep _either_" (149); of her watching helpless as her mother's hands begin to tremble more and more uncontrollably, until she whispers, "He's so little" (151); of her listening to Tommy say, "Are they gonna get me tomorrow?" (152) We understand the meaning of her sudden uncontrollable shaking after the bombing and the effect on her of the broken geranium pot and the "red blossoms turned face down" in the blasted yard—that geranium that only hours before, when she had still been a young girl, she had contemplated moving from the porch to catch the rain (148). We recognize the final, mature acceptance of the existence of evil that makes it possible for her, as dawn breaks, "to look at the kitchen matter-of-factly" and "to start clearing up and cook[ing] breakfast." "The hurt feeling was disappearing" (158); hurt feelings are for people who still trust the world. Ellie has been forced into the maturity of full understanding by the particular impact of her and her family of a general social injustice.

This injustice is, moreover, not just a social problem; it is also a destructively frustrating moral dilemma. Her father's friend leans out of his car and says to Ellie, "if anything happens to that boy of his tomorrow we're going to set things straight" (146). Ellie remembers this promise after the bombing: "It would serve them right if some of her father's friends got one of them. . . . What Mr. Paul said was right, white people couldn't be trusted" (157). But if white people can't be trusted, they can't simply be fought, as her father's friend suggests, either: too many children you can't bear to see hurt will suffer; the worst casualties of this war will be your own. Had Mr. Mitchell been aware that the school board, in its terrible unconsciousness of the individual evil it was doing, would make Tommy the lone black child in "Jefferson Davis" school, he would not have had Tommy put up for transfer.

This is the evil Mrs. Mitchell is thinking of when she says, "A hundred policemen can't be a little boy's only friends" (158). ("I told him he wasn't going to school with Jakie and Bob any more but I said he was going to meet some other children just as nice.") This is why she finally says, "Jim, I cannot let my baby go" (159). Mr. Mitchell at first answers in terms of the abstract battle for black rights, consoling himself that, as for Tommy, "He's going to fight them the rest of his life. He's got to start sometime." With a bitterness beyond complaint, Mrs. Mitchell accepts that point without argument; all she argues is that "Tommy's too little to go around hating people. One of the others, they're bigger, they understand about things" (159); and Ellie is present in the story to show us that they are, at however great a cost, old enough.

Because the Mitchells cannot bring themselves to sacrifice a small child to the cause, even though they recognize that sooner or later that child will certainly be wounded, this particular battle for Negro rights is lost. "God knows we tried," Mr. Mitchell says in acknowledging their defeat, "but I guess there's just no use. Maybe when things come back to normal, we'll try again" (160)—as if this were not the normal situation. Mrs. Mitchell accepts the cost of their decision with the stoicism of complete silence. "He's probably kicked the spread off by now," she says of what is clearly a nightly problem with Tommy, and, "without saying anything," Mr. Mitchell gets up and walks toward the bedroom to put the covers back over Tommy.

QUESTIONS (pages 851-852 of *Modern Short Stories*)

1. Why does Ellie observe the people on the bus at the beginning of the story with such microscopic attention?

2. What does Ellie mean, that she wants help to "figure out what was real and what she had been imagining for the past couple of days"?

3. Why "couldn't [Ellie] help thinking that poor Saraline looked out of place" in Tanner's?

4. Why is Ellie angry and impatient with Mr. Paul when he makes his bitter joke about people spitting on Tommy?

5. Why did Ellie laugh aloud at Reverend Davis' car and then stop herself guiltily?

6. What is it that destroys Ellie's mother's composure so that she bursts out crying?

7. What are Tommy's feelings about tomorrow?

8. What is the attitude of Ellie's white employers to the situation in which she and her family find themselves?

9. How had Ellie's father got them into this situation?

10. Why has her father insisted on going through with their commitment even after discovering Tommy is the only black child admitted to Jefferson Davis?

11. Ellie's mother finally refuses to let Tommy go to school because she keeps thinking, "he'll be there all by himself." What is it, then, that is decisive for her?

12. Ellie's father keeps thinking "that the policeman will be with him all day" and that the decision about Tommy's going to school is "not in our hands"; what is it, then, that has made him stick so long to his original decision?

FRANK O'CONNOR

MY OEDIPUS COMPLEX

MY OEDIPUS COMPLEX has a familiar kind of plot; it sets
a problem—the relations of the small boy, Larry, with his
mother and father—and in due course resolves it. Its
special quality depends on the skill with which it manages
to make the objective reality of the situation that confronts Larry—the characters of the mother and father and
the relations between them—quite clear to us and at the
same time does not violate the limits of the small boy's
understanding to which it is confined by its first-person
narrator. This first-person narrator has been chosen, of
course, because the primary interest of the story is in his
character, in the mixture of ignorance and insight, naiveté
and cunning, egotism and need for affection that make it up.

This focus of interest is quickly established for us;
the boy tells us that, while the war lasted, his father
"came and went mysteriously" like Santa Claus and that the
only disadvantage he noticed about these visits was that "it
was an uncomfortable squeeze between Mother and him when I
got into the big bed in the early morning" (161). Here is
the boy's childlike egotism, which makes him assume without
question that everyone exists for his pleasure and has no
reality of his own, so that Father is another Santa Claus.
Nothing is more natural than that the boy should have fallen
into the habit of rushing into his Mother's bedroom to discuss his day's plans every morning or that he should have
been annoyed by his Father's interruption of this customary
practice, but his innocent reference to Father's presence in
the big bed promptly alerts the reader to the kind of shock
the boy is in for when his Father comes home permanently.
It will be a special injury to his ego that, though his
Mother has put him off with the explanation that sleeping
all night in the same bed is unhealthy, she does not use
this argument with Father; he can see no explanation for
that discrimination except that she must like Father better
than she likes him. The extent of Larry's happy self-
assurance that prevents his anticipating any serious competition from Father is indicated by his scornful assertion of
how simple Mother is to think they cannot afford a baby
until Father comes home because a baby costs seventeen and
six (162). Here again we are reminded of the handicap of
unsuspected ignorance Larry labors under.

Before going on to trace the boy's battle with his
Father for his Mother's affection and the pathos of his continued and, to him, inexplicable defeats, O'Connor shows us
where his strength lay, the appeal to his Mother of his

innocence and energy and of his assurance of her illimitable
interest in his schemes. We watch Larry waking at dawn,
"feeling myself rather like the sun, ready to illumine and
rejoice," and rushing into his Mother's bedroom to tell her
all about it (162). We do not need to be told how she felt
about that because we are made to feel something of it ourselves. After Father has come home, Larry looks back on
these mornings of happy confidences with Mother with disgust
at his own simple-mindedness in taking them for granted.
Just imagine him having been fool enough to allow himself to
be persuaded to pray that his Father would return safely
from the war! "Little, indeed, did I know what I was
praying for!" "The irony of it!" (163) Here once more is
the pathos of his essential ignorance, for he does not suspect what the real irony of it is even then, the mysterious
"hold" Father has over Mother.

The first thing O'Connor shows us when Father does return is how thoroughly unsatisfactory Larry finds him as a
companion. Mother sends the two of them straight out for a
walk together so that they can make friends, but no happy
confidence, such as exists between Larry and his Mother, is
established; Father turns out to be hopelessly incapable of
appreciating everything Larry knows to be important because
he is interested in it, and he gives his Father up in disgust (163-164). This conviction that Father is worth little
or nothing makes him even more outraged than he otherwise
would be when he discovers that Father is offering him
serious competition for Mother's attention.

The first signs of the trouble Father is going to cause
that Larry observes are "those ominous words 'talking to
Daddy'" (163). Then come the readings from the newspaper
(164), a shamefully cheap maneuver on Father's part, Larry
thinks, that suggests the man will sink to almost anything:
"Man for man, I was prepared to compete with him any time
for Mother's attention, but when he had it all made up for
him by other people it left me no chance" (164). Finally,
there is the trouble about mornings in the big bed, his
Mother's inexplicable "Don't wake Daddy" (165) and—most
outrageous of all—Father's smacking him when he continues
to do so (169).

Throughout this war, O'Connor never lets us forget
Larry's touching need for his Mother and his courageous if
scornful determination, at once pitiful and selfish, to win
her attention from Father. With admirable directness, he
considers praying God to start another war and send Father
back to it, and when he learns that "it's not God who makes
wars, but bad people," he "began to think that God wasn't
quite what he was cracked up to be" (164-165). The justice
of his position seems to him unassailable. All he is asking
God for is fair treatment. "I wanted to be treated as an
equal in my own home" (166). Yet here was God taking the
most outrageous advantage of his having innocently prayed
for the return of his Father, "a total stranger who had
cajoled his way back from the war into our big bed as a

result of my innocent intercession. . ." (169).   Being who
he was, Larry had of course been successful in this intercession; since that went without saying, his having been
talked into praying for his Father's return becomes for him
all the more ironic: to think that he himself is primarily
responsible for the presence of this bonily uncomfortable,
selfish late-sleeper in "our" bed!

     But he does not fall into despair and self-pity.
Sturdily he sets about analyzing Father's horridly unattrac-
tive but nonetheless apparently winning ways—his common
accent, the noises he makes at tea, the readings from the
newspaper, the pipe-smoking—and devises countermoves,
making up "bits of news of my own to read" to Mother, going
"round the house dribbling into" Father's pipes, making
"noises at my tea" (170).   But none of these moves works;
"Mother only told me I was disgusting" (170), and he was
forced to conclude that "it all seemed to hinge round that
unhealthy habit of sleeping together," though, closely as he
checked up on this habit, "they were never up to anything
that I could see" (170).

     Then the situation changes with dramatic suddenness
when Sonny is born.   "I was no end pleased about that because it showed that in spite of the way she gave in to
Father [Mother] still considered my wishes" (170).   Nevertheless, from the very start, the advent of Sonny caused a new
and unexpected trouble.   Mother "was very preoccupied—I
suppose about where she would get the seventeen and six ..."
(171).   Things rapidly get worse after Sonny is born.   Like
Father earlier, Sonny is a menace in himself; "the child
wouldn't sleep at the proper time" in spite of Larry's
efforts to keep him awake in the daytime by pinching him
well (171).   Moreover, Mother was worse about Sonny than she
had been about Father when he first returned from the war.
In fact, she seemed now to be ignoring Father quite as much
as she ignored Larry.   That suggests to Larry the possibility
of a consolation, poor enough in all conscience, but still,
perhaps, better than nothing; this is an alliance with the
old enemy, Father.   He approaches this possibility with
every caution, planting himself in the front garden with a
pretense of playing trains when his Father comes home from
working and pretending to talk to himself.   He puts out a
delicate feeler to determine Father's attitude toward Sonny;
"if another bloody baby comes into this house," he murmurs,
"I'm going out" (171).   The result is startling.   The next
night that Sonny worked himself into convulsions of howling
and Mother brought him into the big bed, Father arrived in
Larry's.   To be sure, it was no more than he deserved;
"after turning me out of the big bed, he had been turned out
himself" by Sonny.   Still, Larry was no man to be small-
minded about it.   "I couldn't help feeling sorry for Father.
I had been through it all myself, and even at that age I was
magnanimous" (172).   And, though he does not say so, he too
is lonely.   "'Ah, come on and put your arm around us, can't
you?' I said, and he did, in a sort of way. . . . He was very
bony but better than nothing" (172).

<u>QUESTIONS</u> (pages 852-853 of *Modern Short Stories*)

1. What do we learn about Larry from his comments on his father's wartime visits at home? From his comparison of his father to Santa Claus? From his offhand remark that it was uncomfortable having his father in the big bed?

2. Why does Larry think his mother is not getting a baby because of the cost? Why is he impatient with her arguing this way?

3. Why does Larry rush in to join his Mother in the big bed every morning as soon as he wakes up? What does this habit of theirs show about Larry's mother?

4. Why is Larry so disappointed by his father when they go on a walk together?

5. What tactics does Larry devise for winning his mother's attention away from his father? How does he decide on these particular maneuvers? Why do they not work?

6. What does Larry feel when he first hears that there is going to be a baby?

7. What means does Larry use to keep Sonny in what Larry thinks is Sonny's place? What does his doing so make us feel about Larry?

8. What leads Larry to think there is a possibility of an alliance between him and his father? How does he set about suggesting such an alliance to his father? How does the establishment of the alliance finally come about? How satisfactory is it to Larry?

KATHERINE ANNE PORTER
The Grave

Miss Porter's story is one of the most delicately balanced and yet solid stories in this book. It is a straightforward narration of a typical childhood experience — so convincing that the reader feels this happened just as Miss Porter says it did. Indeed, it is hard not to think it happened to Miss Porter herself, and in fact it may have: the Miranda of Miss Porter's stories is often close to Miss Porter's own experience. But what makes the story convincing is its unobtrusive but precise accuracy of fact and feeling. Everything is seen in a wholly natural way, nothing is ever forced, and the balance between what happens and what Miranda feels is just right.

At the same time, despite this supreme naturalness of the represented life, the story is more than a narrative of childhood experience. The clearest indication of that is the episode of the dead rabbit and its unborn young: ". . . there they were, dark gray, their sleek wet down lying in minute even ripples, like a baby's head just washed, their unbelievably small delicate ears folded close, their little blind faces almost featureless" (177). It is a beautifully accurate description; at the same time it is an image of the miracle of conception that — because the rabbit and her young are dead — is also an image of death. The sentence's single simile shows us the relevance of this image. It is unobtrusively introduced as a visual description of the rabbits' "sleek wet down" that is "like a baby's <u>head just washed</u>." But it unavoidably associates these un<u>born</u> rabbits with human young, with a baby; and that is the unexpressed source of Miranda's vivid response to the sight of them.

We are carefully told that Miranda was not at all frightened by what she saw; she was used to animals, including dead ones, and found them "altogether natural and not very interesting" (178). Nonetheless the sight of these unborn rabbits fills her "with pity and astonishment and a kind of shocked delight" (177). "She wanted most deeply to see and to know" and she "began to tremble without knowing why" (177). This is her first conscious knowledge of the miracle of conception, though she is conscious of it only as the explanation of a puzzle, of an ignorance of fact that has bothered her. "I know," she says, "like kittens. I know, like babies" (178). But it is the answer to something far deeper than that, a resolution of the "secret, formless intuitions of her own mind and body" (178). No wonder that, at her first sight of these unborn rabbits, she instinctively

associates them with a baby and trembles to see them and
their mother dead.

We then learn that Miranda "thought about the whole
worrisome affair with confused unhappiness for a few days"—
confused because she did not fully grasp with her conscious
mind what her "formless intuitions" had responded to (178).
Then, in what almost constitutes a metaphysical joke,
Miranda buries her unhappiness deep in her mind, where it
will lie undisturbed for twenty years. That burial is
enough, however, to show the reader the connection between
the episode of the rabbits and the apparently unconnected
cemetery episode that opens the story—that cemetery from
which grandfather, "dead for more than thirty years," had
just been dug up, the second time his long repose has been
disturbed (173). In the now empty graves of the family
cemetery Miranda and Paul find a silver dove and a ring.
The dove, Paul says, "is a screw head for a <u>coffin</u>!" (174).
It is, of course; a fancy Victorian decorative screw head.
It is also an image of the Holy Ghost; and the ring is a
wedding ring. Here is the same combination we have had in
the episode of the rabbits, this time in the forms of the
symbol of marriage and children and the continuity of mortal
life and of the figure in which the Holy Spirit descended at
Pentecost. Miranda's response to these treasures is really
a step in the same direction that the episode of the rabbits
will take her in later. She trades the dove, which she has
found, for the ring Paul has found and wears the ring
"shining with the serene purity of fine gold on her rather
grubby thumb" (176)—both the suggestion of purity and the
suggestion of luxury here are relevant. Thinking of the
ring makes her turn against her overalls and long for her
"thinnest, most becoming dress" (176). She would have liked
to long for more than that, for "luxury and a grand way of
living," but her experience is inadequate for such longings:
these things "could not take precise form in her imagination." But a vision of herself in her best dress, covered
with her sister's talcum, at ladylike ease under the trees
in a wicker chair—that she could and did imagine. Miss
Porter thus precisely records Miranda's first step from the
epicene condition of childhood toward womanhood.

Yet she is still child enough to go hunting with Paul,
though she has never really liked hunting ("What I like
about shooting," she says with what seems exasperating in-
consequence to Paul, "is pulling the trigger and hearing the
noise" [175]); she really goes along for the companionship
and the walk. Then Paul shoots the pregnant rabbit, and the
woman in Miranda, without being quite fully enough developed
to understand what she has felt, confronts the terror of
life.

The conclusion of *The Grave* is as casually natural as
the rest of it. Twenty years later Miranda's memory of this
occasion is released, incongruously but characteristically,
by the sight of sugar candy in shapes of "birds, baby
chicks, baby rabbits, lambs, baby pigs" in a foreign market

(179). It is not just the candy baby rabbits that does it.
There is also the market itself "with its piles of raw flesh
and wilting flowers" that fit Miranda's buried knowledge so
perfectly. There suddenly, before her mind's eye, is that
scene of twenty years past in all the horror of its full
meaning: "She had remembered [it] always until now vaguely
as the time she and her brother had found treasure in the
open graves." Now, for the first time, she remembers it
precisely, and for what it was. Then her "dreadful vision"
fades, because she remembers another vision that is also
true, the "childhood face she had forgotten," the face of
her brother Paul smiling soberly at her, "turning the silver
dove over and over in his hands."

Miss Porter is not ostensibly—as she never is ostenta-
tiously—a religious writer. But powerful religious feelings
are implicit in *The Grave*—that "fine and private place"
where none embrace.

QUESTIONS (page 853 of *Modern Short Stories*)

1. Why is Miranda excited by the sight of the dead rabbit and her young? Why does she tremble at the sight of them?

2. Why does Miss Porter introduce the simile about the baby into her description of the young rabbits?

3. In what way does the sight of the dead rabbit and her young connect with the "secret, formless intuitions" of Miranda's mind and body?

4. How likely is it that Paul and Miranda might have found a gold ring and a silver dove in the empty graves? With what are these two objects associated? What kind of ring is the gold ring? What religious significance has the dove?

5. Why does Miranda prefer the ring to the dove, swap with Paul, and wear the ring on her thumb?

6. Why does the ring suggest to Miranda a dislike of her overalls and a longing to dress up in her best dress?

7. Why does the scene in the foreign market awaken her memory of this scene? What have the "piles of raw flesh and wilting flowers" to do with evoking the memory?

8. What is the "dreadful vision" that comes into Miranda's mind when she first remembers her childhood experience?

9. Why is it driven out by the vision of Paul smiling and turning the dove over in his hand? What has the dove to do with this? What has Paul's age and liking for the dove to do with it?

FLANNERY O'CONNOR

THE ARTIFICIAL NIGGER

Flannery O'Connor's THE ARTIFICIAL NIGGER is a fable of human pride that, in its vanity and self-sufficiency, ventures boldly into the world, sure that—whether as guide and mentor or youthful adventurer—it is adequate to all the world's dangers, like Virgil and Dante setting forth on their journey of exploration (180). The world destroys Mr. Head's confidence in himself as a guide and Nelson's confidence in himself as adventurer, and in their common agony Mr. Head denies Nelson publicly (195) and Nelson, losing faith in himself, finds he needs Mr. Head.

The author makes all this almost too overt when she says at the end of the story that Mr. Head now "understood that [mercy] grew out of agony, which is not denied to any man and which is given in strange ways to children. . . . He stood appalled, judging himself with the thoroughness of God, while the action of mercy covered his pride like a flame and consumed it. . . . he saw now that his true depravity had been hidden from him lest it cause him despair" (199). This very specific and theologically unexceptionable formulation of the story's meaning may be too rigid; it is certainly unnecessary, since the story's meaning is most beautifully embodied in its action.

Nonetheless this flat statement of the story's meaning offers an ideal place to begin an analysis of the story by making very clear the underlying idea the author intends the story to have. The flat statement of this idea alerts us to watch for the less obtrusive evidences of it that occur everywhere in the story. In using it, however, we ought to be careful not to become so preoccupied with this meaning that we ignore all the natural human interest of the story.

As simply country people, Mr. Head and Nelson are touching in their earnest anxiety to carry off the trip to the city properly; they have every man's need to give a good account of themselves and to look well in their own eyes. Both are secretly frightened of the unknown dangers that await them, but their pride—made appealingly human by its naiveté—will not allow them to admit they are. Mr. Head's experience had convinced him that he was "a suitable guide for the young" (180); Nelson is fiercely independent, "never satisfied until he had given an impudent answer" (181). Each is so anxious to score off the other that he fails to notice how much he loves and needs the other, though "they looked enough alike to be brothers" (181)—and were inwardly enough alike to be, too, Mr. Head almost childlike in his inexperienced assurance, Nelson almost an old man in his fierce

independence. They carry the personal conflict of their
prides onto the train with comic self-absorption. Only the
large, flamboyant Negro shakes Nelson's confidence and suggests "that he might be inadequate to the day's exactions."
Mr. Head, too, hates and fears these mysterious creatures
(186).

All this is conveyed to us with a wealth of comic detail that is exactly right—the efforts of each to be up
before the other in the morning, their proud and anxious
efforts to be at home on the train and to carry on, in good
country fashion, easy conversations with everyone but not to
miss any of the train's wonders, such as the plumbing and
the dining car. Behind the author's wonderful comic narration of these events there runs like an obbligato her
special, almost apocalyptic sense of nature, lurid and awesome like some symbol of the truly cataclysmic nature of
man's experience, and usually ignored by people in their
self-centered pride as much as in the true character of
their lives.

The experiences of Mr. Head and Nelson in the city have
the same qualities as their train ride. The city stands
over its sewers like the world over hell (189), Mr. Head
scorns Nelson for "standing there grinning like a chim-pan-
zee while a nigger woman gives [him] direction" (193) when
they are wholly lost, though Nelson, making human contact
with the Negro woman, has felt curiously drawn to her (192).
Finally Nelson is forced to recognize his need for Mr. Head
when he wakes up alone, terrified (194), and Mr. Head his
humiliating, sinful weakness when he denies knowing Nelson
(195). He tries pitifully to persuade Nelson to forget his
betrayal, but Nelson courageously and perversely nurses his
resentment—without being able to separate himself wholly
from his grandfather.

Finally, Mr. Head's pride is broken by his agony, "Oh
Gawd I'm lost!" he cries out, "Oh hep me Gawd I'm lost!"
(197); it is at this point that the author begins to make
the story's meaning overt. "He felt he knew now what time
would be like without seasons and what heat would be like
without light and what man would be like without salvation"
(198). He and Nelson are then both saved from this damnation by the artificial nigger, the figure of a human being
"meant to look happy" with "a wild look of misery instead"
who was neither young nor old (198). "Mr. Head looked like
an ancient child and Nelson like a miniature old man . . .
they stood gazing at the artificial Negro as if they were
faced with some great mystery, some monument to another's
victory that brought them together in common defeat" (199).
They are looking at an image — an artificial Negro — that
reveals the truth about Negroes, the victory they have won
over their pride in the agony of their defeat; recognizing
that mystery, Mr. Head and Nelson see that it is an image of
them too, that those alien and terrifying creatures, the
Negroes, are just like them. That understanding dissolves

"their differences like an action of mercy" (199). So Mr.
Head, when it can no longer be a matter of pride to him,
earns his right to guide Nelson, and even Nelson — "as the
[tempter] train glided past them and disappeared like a
frightened serpent into the woods"—decides he never wants
to be led into temptation again.

QUESTIONS (page 854 of *Modern Short Stories*)

1. Start with the end of the story and the author's
statement of its lesson. What did Mr. Head learn from his
experience?

2. Go back to the start and ask questions about the ad-
venture. Why does Mr. Head want to take Nelson on this trip
to the city? What does he think it will do for Nelson? Why
is Nelson so belligerent about it?

3. What are the feelings of the two on the train. Why
does Mr. Head talk to everyone? Why does he take Nelson on
a tour of the train? What is his attitude to the large
Negro they see?

4. Why does the author constantly bring in descriptions
of the scene outside the train and of the sunrise, that
neither Mr. Head nor Nelson notices?

5. What is the point of the episode when Nelson questions the Negro woman about where they are?

6. What is Nelson frightened of when he wakes up and
finds himself alone?

7. Why does Mr. Head say Nelson is no boy of his after
the accident?

8. What happens to Mr. Head that he admits he is lost?
Lost in what sense?

9. What is the effect of the artificial Negro on them?

JOHN UPDIKE
A SENSE OF SHELTER

There is a brief comment on *A SENSE OF SHELTER* in the
Introduction to Part Three of *Modern Short Stories* (525). A
good place to start with the story is the title, since the
phrase is used almost immediately in the story, at the end
of the first paragraph. This paragraph in turn establishes
the point of the title: there is the great world outside
the high school—damply snowy, cold, unfriendly; and there
is the sheltered world within the high school where William
Young is joyous, even in the dimly lighted gloom, because
"he felt they were all sealed in, safe" (201).

This scene of being sheltered, of being safely sealed
away from the unknown, unpredictable forces of the world
outside allows William to rest comfortably in his knowledge
that he is a success within the protected high school world,
to feel that he is, in his way, in control there. As a
senior and as teacher's pet he feels "like a king" here;
when he notices the snowflakes melting outside he thinks of
them as "drowning on the gravel roof of his castle." The
confidence generated in him by his feeling of security inside that castle permits him to nerve himself to "tell Mary
Landis he loved her" (201). The paragraph that follows and
that describes Mary Landis hovers skillfully between what
William sees and what the narrator wants us to see about
her. Without saying so, he makes us see that Mary Landis is
experienced beyond her years, her face already slightly
hardened by knowledge of the world outside high school, the
"boxiness in her bones" beginning to show, as in a mature
woman. She shows a slightly weary indifference to the high-
school-boy sexual challenge of the leg in the aisle; she
merely "stared down until it withdrew" (203).

The scene in Luke's luncheonette shows William in a
place that is simply an extension of the high school world.
The conversation in the booth shows us teen-agers living in
a half-imaginary world constructed of cheap fiction and
Sunday supplements, a world they do not so much believe in
as feel sheltered enough to play with. It is this almost
conscious exploitation of the knowledge that they are protected from reality and its defeats that makes Mary Landis,
when she comes in for her cigarettes, seem so alien a figure
in their world.

In the study-hall scene we see again the way William
has acquired assurance in this world. He meets all its demands with triumphant success—the thirty lines of Virgil,
the ten trigonometry problems, the Poe story. This easy

conquest of scholarly foes leads him into a pleasant daydream of a future life of academic success rounded off by a
graceful, literary death, the slightly dated model for
which he has found, not of course in life, but in some academic biography of Queen Victoria's poet laureate. After
school he stays to cut a sports cartoon, and when that is
finished he wanders to a washroom on the second floor that
only he seems to know about. There he enjoys "the lavish
amount of powdered soap provided for him in this castle."
"Though he had done everything, he felt reluctant to leave"
(207). If he is thinking he "has done everything," William
has forgotten his resolve to tell Mary Landis he loves her.
The Mary Landis he loves is a part of the high school world
in which William feels secure; but this is not the girl the
reader already suspects is the real Mary Landis. Perhaps
William's impulse to tell his Mary Landis he loves her is
also merely a part of his daydream of a happy future in
which he imagines himself living in the sheltered high
school world indefinitely. If so, the actual expression of
his impulse to the real Mary Landis would scarcely survive
that contact with reality, and perhaps William half-
consciously knows it will not.

     In any event, William's encounter with Mary in the hall
is an accident, and his expression of his love for her is
surprised from him by her flat scorn of the high school
world that is his castle but that she finds so drab. "Don't
quit," he blurts out when she threatens to drop out of high
school. "It'd be n-n-nuh—it'd be nothing without you"
(208). What follows is an unconsciously cruel exposure of
William's misconception of Mary Landis as still a high
school girl and a wounding criticism of the high school
world he finds so satisfactory. Mary is simply expressing
her boredom with school and the despair to which her life
outside it has driven her. "Oh, Billy, if you were me for
just one day you'd hate it" (210). It is as if "in his
world of closed surfaces a panel, carelessly pushed, had
opened, and he hung in this openness paralyzed, unable to
think what to say" (210).

     Then, as if to move out into the world in which she now
lives, Mary decides to go outside to wait "for the person
who thinks [her] legs are too skinny" (210), a "man she met
while working as a waitress in the city of Alton" (205).
This is not William's country, and he tries to get her to
come back in, but she walks silently away into the cold,
"toeing out in the childish way common to the women of the
country" (211). It is a wonderful touch; for all her
maturity, her inescapable awareness of the bitterly cold
world beyond high school, she is still touchingly young and
defenseless.

     Almost from the start of this real encounter with Mary
Landis, William has been disturbed by the way it was devel-
oping. His masculine pride tells him that, once started, he
must go through with it boldly; just the same he is frightened by Mary's "awful seriousness." He makes a bold effort

to lighten the atmosphere by saying that one thing he knows about Mary Landis is that she is "not a virgin." The move is a failure; Mary is long past the time when this question of who is and who is not a virgin titillates the imagination and constitutes a daring subject for dalliance. She has already discovered that the true problem is not a simple sexual one but the total relationship between a man and a woman, a relationship which, in her case, has left her helplessly in love with a man who views her as merely a sexual object, and not a very satisfactory one at that, as he has plainly let her know.

William can see that his gambit about virginity has "been a mistake"; but, caught as he is between his need to see this venture through and his fear that, if he does so successfully, he will be forced out of the shelter of his protected high school life and into the adult world, ". . . in part, he felt grateful for his mistakes. They were like loyal friends, who are nevertheless embarrassing" (211). Eventually they lead Mary to tell him, in effect, that someday he is going to grow up into a good man, something she knows far better how to value than does William, who still wants only to be a hero. When Mary says to him that he is "basically very nice," he feels only humiliation. Nice is not what he wants to be, certainly not basically nice, the possessor of the materials for a quality he is not yet mature enough to have developed. Half resenting this quite justified assertion of his immaturity, half grateful for the opportunity Mary has given him to escape his commitment to love the woman she is now, William says: "Listen, I did love you. Let's . . . let's at least get that straight." It is true; before he had spoken to her and been forced to recognize who the real Mary Landis is, he had loved what he thought she was, what at one time she had perhaps even been. But that love had been the love of a high school boy for a high school boy's idea of what a woman is, and Mary Landis all too sadly knows that women are not that-nor are men William Youngs. "You never loved anybody," she says hopelessly. "You don't know what it is." Then she walks away.

William retreats to the warmth and shelter of the high school building. Part of him had been working to make this retreat possible, but the defeat that had been necessary to make it so was a humiliation that another part of him found hard to bear, the part that could not live with his daydream without believing that he could conquer the real world by an exercise of the same talents that had made him "king of the castle" in his sheltered children's playground. Back in the high school he feels at first smothered and imprisoned; "he had the irrational fear that they were going to lock him in" (211). Gradually, however, he recovers his assurance and retreats once more into the high school boy's dream of omnipotence as he shuts his locker door. "In answer to a flick of his great hand the steel door weightlessly slammed shut." He is king of his castle once more, free of the enslaving realities of the world outside the high school, untouched by its humiliating grubbiness; "he felt so clean and

free he smiled." "The happy future predicted for him"
as a bright high school boy once more seems to him so
assured that "he had nothing, almost literally nothing,
to do."

QUESTIONS (pages 854-855 of *Modern Short Stories*)

1. What does the first paragraph show us is the difference for William Young between life inside the high school
and life outside it?

2. How does Mr. Updike lead us to think of William's
feelings about life in the high school as like a child
playing king of the castle?

3. What are we supposed to think of Mary Landis? What
does William think of her.

4. What is the function of the scene in Luke's
Luncheonette?

5. Why is William reluctant to leave the school at the
end of the day?

6. How is William surprised into telling Mary Landis he
loves her?

7. What state of mind does Mary Landis reveal in her
conversation with William? What has led her to feel this
way?

8. What is Mary Landis's opinion of William? What does
she think of his belief that he loves her?

9. Why is William discontented when he first goes back
into the school after Mary Landis has left him?

10. What relieves this feeling and makes him once more
happy in the sheltered world of the high school?

GRAHAM GREENE

THE INNOCENT

Graham Greene's *THE INNOCENT* complements John Updike's *A Sense of Shelter*. Updike's story shows a boy beginning to recognize the complexity—the loss of innocence—that constitutes maturity, and shows it from the point of view of the innocent boy himself. Greene's story shows us the same experience from the point of view of a mature man. William Young has a terrifying first glimpse of what adult life is like. Graham Greene's narrator discovers what the age of innocence had been like, a thing that, in the years since his childhood, he had forgotten, just as he had forgotten his feelings about Bishop's Hendon, the town in which he had grown up. Both stories show us the sadness—and the inevitability—of growing up, of the loss of innocence, a kind of repetition in the life of every man of the original fall of man.

The Innocent is a very quiet story. With the simplest details it brings home to us what the loss of innocence means. What it means in Graham Greene's story is not so much our becoming evil in any melodramatic sense, though evil of course it is, but our sinking into what might be called a meaningless and unmoving crumminess—which is perhaps what damnation is really like. There is nothing special about Bishop's Hendon to affect the narrator; the town is quite commonplace. "The old grain warehouses across the canal," "the little humpbacked bridge," "the ugly alms-houses, little grey stone boxes" are all insignificantly "grim," as Lola's conventional perception of them shows. What moves the narrator is an unexpected recovery of the feeling of life in childhood, a quality experience had for him then that it no longer has. He had known life then as only the innocent can know it; it had been a time "when, however miserable we are, we have expectations." Remembering it now, he realizes that he knew the place of his childhood "as I knew nothing else. It was like listening to music." "Those years hadn't been particularly happy or particularly miserable; they had been ordinary years, but . . . I thought I knew what it was [about Bishop's Hendon] that held me. It was the smell of innocence." Life had been there with all its troubles; he could remember having watched a middle-aged man run into one of the ugly old alms-houses to commit suicide; he had thought—though he has not been reminded of it yet—of the girl in his dancing class in a perfectly normal physical way. None of these things had then frightened him or made him feel, as he now suddenly does, despair at the meaninglessness of life.

His love of the little girl in his dancing class had
been frustrated in a way that, however painful it was, he
then took almost for granted. Though he had loved her "with
an intensity I have never felt since," he had not even been
able to walk home with her from dancing class and, except in
dancing class, had never touched her. "Now when I am unhappy about a girl, I can simply go and buy another one"—
pick her up in a bar, give her five pounds and pay for their
week-end together, as he does with Lola. Like all the rest
of these girls in his life, "Lola meant just nothing at
all." How general is this sense of adult experience is made
clear for us by the man at the bar at the inn, "a local man,
perhaps a schoolmaster" who was "simply longing to stand
[Lola] a drink."

Lola is a perfect counterpart to the little girl of the
dancing class. "I suppose you used to think of nights like
this when you were a boy," she says. "'Yes,' I said, because it wasn't her fault." He doesn't know it yet, but in
the literal sense, she is quite right; he did think of the
little girl at dancing school, so far as his immature
imagination would allow him to, with physical desire. But
what he thought was purified by their innocence, while what
he thinks about Lola is made meaningless by their lack of
innocence. When he had made the drawing of himself and the
little girl, he had felt that "I was drawing something with
a meaning and beautiful; it was only now after thirty years
of life that the picture seemed obscene." "It seemed a long
journey to have taken to find only Lola at the end of it."

QUESTIONS (page 855 of *Modern Short Stories*)

1. Is there something unusual about Bishop's Hendon that makes it a mistake for the narrator to have brought Lola there?

2. Why does Greene include among the narrator's childhood memories the sight of the middle-aged man who was about to commit suicide?

3. What is it about the narrator's memory of Bishop's Hendon that makes his sense of the first twelve years of his life so strong?

4. "It wasn't," the narrator says, "Lola's fault." Why not? If not, why does he wish she were not there?

5. Why does Greene bring into the story the man at the bar who longs to stand Lola a drink?

6. Why does Greene stress the narrator's memory of his childhood desire to touch the little girl?

7. What makes the drawing the boy left in the hole in the gate obscene? What makes it innocent?

SAUL BELLOW
LOOKING FOR MR. GREEN

LOOKING FOR MR. GREEN is the quiet realization of a complex view of man's experience. The story's purpose is to suggest that the human dilemma is the same for everyone— for the Blacks and the Poles who live in the slums, for Grebe, the son of Chicago's last English butler, for Raynor, his boss, for Yerkes, the financier who built the El, for Field, who has invented a scheme for creating Black millionaires.

This idea perhaps seems more plausible to us than it might otherwise because it is set in the depression of the 1930's, when the common dilemma of the unemployed of all classes seemed more obvious than it does today. Unobtrusively Bellow makes the date of the story clear to us. The checks Grebe carries are not punched for a computer, as they would be today, but for a desk spindle, with holes that remind Grebe of the kind of holes one saw, in the 1930's, in player-piano rolls. It is a world of trench coats, of "huge red Indiana Avenue [street] cars," of cellars full of "canvas-jacketed [steam] pipes," of stair-carpets held down by brass strips. This is the 1930's.

But there is something unusual about the characters of the story. Grebe, though his parents wanted him to be practical and become a chemical engineer, changed schools in order to study Latin and become a scholar. Raynor had worked his heart out to get a law degree and is still struggling with Berlitz-School French and thinking of the civilized life of the diplomatic corps. Getting his law degree, he says with wry amusement (knowing nonetheless that in an important sense it is true), is a way of seeking to see "life straight and true." He longs for "civilization," which, he admits, is also longed for by "office boys in China and braves in Tanganyika." "It's overrated," he says with grim amusement at his own passion for it, "but what do you want?" Then, making a joke of his Berlitz-School French, *"Que voulez-vous?"* Even Yerkes, the financier who apparently lived only for money and success, spent millions to build the Yerkes Observatory out of some need "to find out where being and seeming were identical," "to know what abides." Raynor supposes that Grebe's parents sent him to the university to "find out what were the last things in the fallen world of appearances." This ultimate reality behind the appearance of things, the reality that abides forever and explains everything, haunts mankind. It is the final object of all learning, the essential meaning of civilization, the thing people dream of finding the time and means to know.

But Raynor knows too that we live our lives in a world where we must eat, in the world of what are, ironically, called appearances—ironically because the world of appearances is overwhelmingly actual for us, what determines the way we live. "Don't you think that was clear to your Greeks," Raynor says to Grebe, the classics teacher. "They were thoughtful people, but they didn't part with their slaves."

In an important sense, to be sure, the story recognizes that the remote and final reality behind appearances is fundamental. But the world of appearances is where humanity has always lived. When Grebe sees "Whoody-Doody Go to Jesus" scribbled on the slum tenement wall, he thinks, "so the sealed rooms of the pyramids were also decorated, and the caves of human dawn." As Raynor puts it in his blunt way, "I'll tell you, as a man of culture, that even though nothing looks to be real, and everything stands for something else, and that thing for another thing, and that thing for a still further one—there ain't no comparison between twenty-five and thirty-seven dollars a week, regardless of the last reality."

The human animal has a superabundance of an energy that desperately needs to be "organized" to some purpose. "To be compelled to feel this energy and yet have no task to do— that was horrible; that was suffering; he knew what that was." Cities, states, societies depend on such organization as much as individuals. There is nothing fundamentally real about the organizations that give people's daily lives purpose. They are the result of a kind of unconscious conspiracy, an "agreement" to pretend that the way things are organized is reality. "How absurd [the El] looked; how little reality to start with. And yet Yerkes, the great financier who built it, had known that he could get people to agree to do it." Mr. Field, with his fantastic scheme for making Black millionaires in order to improve the lives of the poor, seems to Grebe another social inventor like Yerkes. His idea is a myth; but it is the kind of myth that just might create actual appearances in which millions of people will live. To Grebe Mr. Field is "like one of the underground kings of mythology, old judge Minos himself." It is terrible when the appearances that organize people's lives and provide a meaningful outlet for their energies collapse and the fact that they are only myths people have agreed to believe in becomes visible.

Desperately Grebe commits himself to finding Mr. Green, to the conviction that his job is important and must be carried out at all costs. To think of going home and having a drink and lying on his bed reading the paper—to think, that is, of having no driving purpose in life—"made [Grebe] feel sick." He knows that "nobody expects you to push too hard at a city job," but his feeling that his life is organized to some purpose depends on his taking his job seriously. So he refuses to give up in his search for Dr. Green. He is

like some deadly serious big game hunter—only "instead of
shells in his deep trench coat pockets he had," he realizes
with grim humor, "the cardboard of checks." He is determined to penetrate beyond the suspicions of these people who
think he is an installment collector or summons-server, or
just untrustworthy because he is white. At bottom, Grebe
can see, these Black people are simply human. "They didn't
carry bundles on their backs or look picturesque. You only
saw a man, a Negro, walking in the street or riding in the
car, like everyone else. . . ." Like everyone else they live
in their own world of appearances, "the men padded out in
heavy work clothes and with winter coats, and the women
huge, too, in their sweaters, hats, and old furs." To them
Grebe looks like a schoolboy, "with his cold-heightened
fresh color and his smaller stature," a stranger from
another world, not to be trusted.

   Grebe's realization that they are all living in their
separate worlds of appearances allows him some perspective
on the situation but does not for a minute change his
feeling of the particular world he lives in or his need to
succeed in it. He can see and even share the amusement of
the Black people at his persistence. But "he was his own
man, he retracted nothing about himself, and he looked back
at them, gray-eyed, with amusement and also with a sort of
courage." In his quiet way he is asserting himself, defining his own reality within his world of appearances, as
much as Mrs. Staikas with her six children, "flaming with
anger and with pleasure at herself," is when she raises
hell in the relief office. This assertion of oneself has
its important kind of truth, even though it is achieved
only in the world of appearances. Like the graffiti in the
pyramids and caves, it is a need as old and persistent as
humanity itself, and the grievances against life—the
suffering—it expresses are too. The Mrs. Staikases, Raynor
observes, will ultimately triumph in the world; "she'll sub-
merge everybody in time, and that includes nations and
governments." Maybe there really is some place in the
universe where "being and seeming [are] identical." People
like Grebe and Raynor—and maybe in their muter ways the
rest of mankind—cannot help searching for it. Meanwhile,
they live and have their being in a world of appearances in
which the ordering of their lives depends on a structure of
the world that exists because humanity consents to an
elaborate set of myths, like the El.

QUESTIONS (pages 855-856 of *Modern Short Stories*)

1. This story takes place in Chicago during the Depression of the 1930's. How does Bellow tell us so?

2. The story's main character, Grebe, had given up chemical engineering to study Latin, and Raynor has struggled to get a law degree and to learn French. Why?

3. Does some motive like Grebe's and Raynor's also affect the financier Yerkes who built the Chicago El? What is it?

4. Why is Raynor consistently ironic about what he calls the world of appearances?

5. Why is the world of appearances important?

6. Why is Mr. Fields, with his scheme for creating Black millionaires, "like one of the underground kings of mythology"?

7. What have Mr. Fields and Yerkes in common?

8. Why is Grebe so determined to find Mr. Green?

9. Why does Grebe compare himself, in his hunt for Mr. Green, to a big game hunter?

10. Why does Grebe sympthize with the Blacks who refuse to help him find Mr. Green?

11. Why does Bellow put the episode of Mrs. Staikes in the story?

PART TWO

HENRY JAMES
THE TONE OF TIME

THE TONE OF TIME shows clearly the method of Henry
James, the great master of the short story as comedy of manners. The story's subject is characteristic—a drama that
occurs almost entirely in the realm of feelings, its most
material manifestation being a painting—but it is not so
complicated as the subjects of the other two James stories
in *Modern Short Stories*. It therefore allows us to watch
closely the characteristic way James concentrates on the
drama of understanding, especially as it occurs in conversations during which the characters infer—sometimes with astonishing insight—one another's thoughts and feelings. As
in many comedies of manners, the basic situation in *The Tone
of Time* is an artificial one, dependent on an extreme coin-
cidence. But that is unimportant, because what matters in
James is the intelligence and subtlety of the attitudes
evoked by the situation and the excitement of the way,
little by little, they emerge for us. The best way to deal
with the story is to watch this process.

It begins with the narrator trying, out of consideration for Mary Tredick's poverty, to throw a commission to
her. He knows that his gift as a painter is for the "given,
the present case," whereas Mary Tredick's is realizing the
imagined past, painting pictures that have "the tone of
time" (246). This gift the narrator casually—and as it
turns out very mistakenly—imagines to be merely "an extra-
ordinary bag of tricks" (249). These points are important.
The narrator's own talent for painting only what he can see
is a measure of his inability to see beneath the surface of
things; his misjudgment of the source of Mary Tredick's
talent is a forewarning of the way the well-meant practical-
ity of his later activities will go wrong.

This commission this narrator has brought Mary Tredick
is from a somewhat dubious woman who has an odd desire for
an imaginery portrait "to symbolise, as it were, her husband, who's not alive and who perhaps never was" (246).
This assessment of the situation by the narrator is true
enough as far as it goes; but, being the kind of man he is,
the narrator easily assumes that the only reason Mrs.
Bridgenorth can want such a portrait is a desire to give
herself social respectability by suggesting that she has
once had a husband when in fact she never has had. She has
not; but she does not want a portrait of one she might have
had simply for respectability. The narrator canvasses his
view of Mrs. Bridgenorth's motive with Mary Tredick and ends
by confidently dismissing the question of Mrs. Bridgenorth's

possibly adventurous past by observing that her past is
"none of one's business," a conclusion that turns out to be
anything but correct.

     With a subtlety that would do credit to one of Poe's
crime-solvers, the narrator then detects something odd about
Mary Tredick's interest in this commission. He is right to
be suspicious, for as we later learn, it has already occurred to her that she can fill this commission, not with a
fanciful portrait, but with a portrait of a lover who had deserted her years before whom she had never forgotten or forgiven. She will have to imagine him, for he has long since
died, but she will be imagining something that was once very
real and that her love and her hatred have kept alive in her
memory. Her portrait will have the true tone of time. But
we know none of this yet. All we know is the narrator's
feeling that there was "something more than, as the phrase
is, met the eye in such response as I felt my friend had
made. I had touched, without intention, more than one
spring" (249). Then Mary Tredick says of the portrait, "I
shall make him supremely beautiful—and supremely base," and
the narrator thinks, "In fact, I had touched the spring"
(249).

     We then turn to Mrs. Bridgenorth. Firmly convinced
that Mrs. Bridgenorth is merely seeking respectability, the
narrator complacently congratulates himself on what he believes the tact of both of them in keeping their conversation superficial and raising no embarrassing questions. "We
remained on the surface with the tenacity of shipwrecked
persons clinging to a plank," talking only of Mrs.
Bridgenorth's present, never of her past (250). But Mrs.
Bridgenorth, as we later learn, is not seeking merely to
hide a disreputable past; like Mary Tredick, she has an un-
fulfilled and unforgotten passion in that past—and for the
same man.

     Mary Tredick then paints the picture into which she has
sought to get both the beauty and the infamy of her lost
lover, but to the narrator the figure in the painting appears rather ambiguous than infamous, as if Mary Tredick
does not hate the original as much as she thinks she does.
Still thinking of providing Mrs. Bridgenorth with the portrait of a man who could plausibly be alleged to be a husband
dead some years, the narrator is most concerned that the
portrait should have what he considers the tone of time, the
obvious, superficial signs of a portrait painted a good many
years before. Not that he and Mary Tredick are pretending
very hard any more that her painting is not a portrait of
her memory of an actual man. That as well as a clear view
of how that man had treated Mary Tredick emerges when Mary
says of the original of her portrait, "I once had everything"; then she says the portrait is all hate; and then she
bursts into tears (253). As if to emphasize the implication
of this action, the narrator observes of her painting that
"the beauty, heaven knows, I see. But I don't see what you
call the infamy" (254). Thus James establishes for the

reader the distinction between what Mary Tredick <u>thinks</u> are
her feelings about the man she has painted and her actual
feelings, and we begin to see her real, if unconscious
motive for having been so interested by this commission.

We now turn back to Mrs. Bridgenorth and James shows us
with beautiful precision the complicated series of her
responses when she sees the portrait and tries to conceal
her feelings about it (255). But the narrator, playing his
role of spiritual detective to the hilt, cross-examines her
and soon discovers that this "is the very head [she] would
have liked if [she] had dared [ask for it]" (256). Mrs.
Bridgenorth's real reason for seeking the portrait is thus
exposed, and we can now see the reason for her former conduct, which the narrator had mistakenly ascribed to a desire
for mere respectability. To Mrs. Bridgenorth the narrator
continues to pretend that the original of the portrait was
only a "friend" of Mary Tredick, and that the vividness of
the portrait is a product of artistic cunning rather than
passion, a view Mrs. Bridgenorth accedes to rather because
she wants to than because she is convinced by the narrator.
In the end she ceases to believe it.

Mrs. Bridgenorth had not, then, wanted this portrait
for respectability but as a reminder—however inaccurate—of
the lover who had never married her; now she has discovered
that it is a portrait of the actual lover, she wants it very
badly indeed. She "bravely" tells the narrator—perhaps
still pretending to herself it is true—that the man represented by the portrait would "certainly" have married her
had he lived (257), but we learn later from Mary Tredick
that there had been plenty of time for him to do so and that
he had not (262). Mrs. Bridgenorth's assertion is false,
and she needs the portrait, not to persuade others that she
had had a husband and is a respectable woman, but to make
the man she had loved and never succeeded in marrying her
husband, at least in retrospect. Mrs. Bridgenorth's reason
for wanting this portrait is very like Mary Tredick's real
reason for having painted it, the reason that will presently
make her determined to keep it.

Then between them—the narrator wishing to relieve Mary
Tredick's poverty, Mrs. Bridgenorth wanting desperately to
have the portrait—they botch its sale to Mrs. Bridgenorth
by offering Mary Tredick too much money for it, with the result that Mary Tredick guesses the truth about Mrs.
Bridgenorth and snatches the portrait back. The final
scene, another scene of James's marvelous dialogue, is devoted to showing us just how much Mary Tredick has guessed.
She is sure Mrs. Bridgenorth is "one of them"—one of the
all too many women the man had known—and almost certainly
the one who almost persuaded him to marry her, the one who
"was the reason [Mary Tredick had lost him]" (262). She
even understands the kind of blundering efforts of the
narrator to give her a chance to earn some money ("It's very
nice—what you're doing for me '. . ." [262]). She has also
now seen her own real motives in painting the portrait. If

"it was painted in bitterness" she will, she now knows, "keep it in joy." By having taught her to recognize her true feelings about her lost lover, the woman who had taken him from her those many years ago, and has kept him for her —in her own thoughts—all the years between has "by a prodigy . . . unwittingly [given] him back" (264).

Mary Tredick's gift for giving her paintings "the tone of time," which the narrator began by thinking a technical trick, a talent for giving paintings the quaint antique look of old portraits (246), has turned out to be the result of a deep commitment to that past, a habit of living in it, in her imagination, because she still loves passionately a man who had deserted her and then died in that past. "If our wonderful client [Mrs. Bridgenorth] hadn't been his wife in fact, she was not to be helped to become his wife in fiction" by Mary Tredick (263), who, thanks to Mrs. Bridgenorth herself, has come to recognize that she still loves this man with a passion as undiminished as Mrs. Bridgenorth's.

QUESTIONS (page 856 of *Modern Short Stories*)

1. Why does the narrator think Mary Tredick a better person to paint the picture for Mrs. Bridgenorth than he is? What does what he tells us about their differences as painters tell us about him?

2. What does the narrator think Mrs. Bridgenorth's reasons for wanting the painting?

3. Why does Mary Tredick take such an interest in this commission?

4. What feelings does Mary Tredick think her portrait reveals about its subject? What feelings does it really reveal?

5. What does the narrator discover about Mrs. Bridgenorth when she sees the portrait?

6. What leads Mary Tredick to guess Mrs. Bridgenorth's connection with the subject of her portrait?

7. How precisely does she guess what that connection has been?

8. What does Mary Tredick's discovery about Mrs. Bridgenorth reveal to her about herself?

9. What does Mary Tredick's discovery about herself show us about Mary Tredick's gift for giving the tone of time to her portraits?

HENRY JAMES
THE JOLLY CORNER

THE JOLLY CORNER is a late James story (published in
1909), written when he had mastered completely the resources
of his particular kind of story. These include most strikingly the marvelous tact with which James handles ghosts and
dreams; he makes these just evidently enough the projections
of the characters' own psyches—of their inner anxieties and
interests and passions—to be plausible to an age that does
not literally believe in ghosts and prognostic dreams. At
the same time, he presents his ghost in an objective—that
is, in a third-person—narration but in an objective narration that, for all its vividness of detail, is in fact an
objective narration not of events but of the thoughts and
feelings of his central character—what James himself called
his "central intelligence." What we are really being told
is what Spencer Brydon <u>thought</u> he saw and felt in the house
on the jolly corner.

This tactic has another great advantage for James. As
The Tone of Time shows, his greatest talent was for the
representation of the drama of understanding, the exciting,
inward process by which a character comes gradually to "see"
and feel his experience. By focusing our attention on what
Spencer Brydon thinks is happening during those long nights
in the house on the jolly corner, James can thus bring to
bear on the task of making the ghost convincing the kind of
narration he did best, the representation of the way Spencer
Brydon's mind moved gradually toward that state in which he
fully believed he saw the ghost of the man he might have
been standing before him in the "watery under-world" of his
house's vestibule. We remain free to suppose, if that will
help us to accept the story, that the ghost was not "really"
there, that Spencer Brydon only imagined it.

We have already been given good reason to believe
Brydon might well imagine it, that is, a full understanding
of the psychological and moral problem Spencer Brydon has
faced with his return to America. This is the problem of
what he might have become had he remained in America and become a successful American businessman—a career for which
he shows, on his return to America, a considerable though
heretofore concealed aptitude that is at first amusing to
him, then disturbing, and finally frightening, since it suggests that somwhere <u>in</u> him is an undeveloped self that might
have been what, to h<u>is</u> developed self, is a horror.

Once that possibility has presented itself to Spencer
Brydon, the need to understand exactly what his undeveloped

self might have been—and actually is in an undeveloped form,
now—the need to confront and know his whole self, becomes
imperative; "He found all these things came back to the
question of what he personally might have been" (273).   This
psychological and moral necessity is completely persuasive,
and if, for Spencer Brydon, the confrontation with himself
takes the form of stalking a ghost in the house on the jolly
corner (a haunting presence in the place that represents all
he can admire in his own American past), that is easy enough
to accept, once we have seen the reality of the psychological
problem.   Psychological problems are perhaps no more "real"
than ghosts; they are certainly no more tangible.   But our
age finds them easier to believe in and take seriously than
it does ghosts, and James uses that fact to make us accept
the ghost.

There is another source of strength for the ghost.
Spencer Brydon's problem, the psychological and moral problem of an American who has deliberately chosen to
Europeanize himself and is anxiously facing the possibility
that no man can wholly extirpate his past—that, do what he
will, there will always be an ineradicable American element
in himself—is not a problem for Spencer Brydon alone.   It
is in some sense a problem for every educated American,
since the cultural past of America is so largely European.
Every educated American must, in one way or another, face
the problem of reconciling his "Europeanized" self and his
"American" self.   The meaning of James's story applies far
beyond the immediate circumstances of Spencer Brydon.

To the task of imagining the dilemma of Spencer
Brydon—and the dilemma of so many other Americans—James
brings a remarkably subtle understanding of the depths of
the problem; to this he added the immensely powerful verbal
resources that the mature James had at his command, especially his gift for witty comparisons that deprecate their
own extravagance at the same time that they use that extravagance to suggest just how violent the psychological
shocks they are describing really are. The first of these
amused, ironic insights the story puts before us is Spencer
Brydon's comic surprise at discovering that the New York he
had, as a young man, thought provincial and stuffy has, with
the passage of time, taken on a charm he had not foreseen.
All these years in Europe he has been living with the complacent conviction that he hated the America of his youth.
Now he has been sharply brought up to date; now "the ugly
things he had expected, the ugly things of his far-away
youth . . . placed him rather, as it happened, under the
charm" (266) as he discovered just how truly ugly the "considerable array of rather unattenuated surprises' that
constitute contemporary New York is (265).   The thirty-three
years of his absence "have organized their performance quite
on the scale of licence" (265).   These new horrors "set
traps for displeasure . . . of which his restless tread was
constantly pressing the spring" (266).

The first consequence of this discovery about America

is his recognition that there is a quite beautiful American
life that fully embodies the past. It is there in Alice
Staverton and in the life she lives, and Spencer Brydon
finds it has a powerful appeal to his own nature; perhaps
his real home is here after all. The tradition kept alive
in that life is, for him personally, represented by the
beautiful old house with its vivid echoes of his own past
and of his ancestors (272), the house he has not lived in.
The second consequence of his return to America is the dis-
quieting discovery that somewhere within him is a skillful
man of business who finds delight in ruthlessly modernizing
his second property and in living successfully the life of
modern New York, that "gross generalization of wealth and
force and success," a mere "vast ledger-page, overgrown,
fantastic, of ruled and criss-crossed lines and figures"
(268). He finds it difficult to resist the temptation this
second property offers him to cultivate his genius for
starting "some new variety of awful architectural hare and
run[ning] it till it burrowed in a gold-mine" (269).

This hitherto unknown possibility in himself takes for
him the form of "some strange figure, some unexpected occu-
pant, at a turn of one of the dim passages of an empty
house" (269)—the house on the jolly corner, the house of a
possible American past, that he has by his own neglect too
long left empty. In short, "he found all things come back
to the question of what he personally might have been"; not,
as he tells Alice Staverton, that he imagines he would like
what he might have become had he stayed in America and become "one of those types who have been hammered so hard and
made so keen by their conditions" (274); rather he sees that
Spencer Brydon as a monstrous, huge, and hideous flower
(241). James means us to notice the parallel between this
figure and the description of Alice Staverton, the product
of another New York, "as exquisite as some pale pressed
flower (a rarity to begin with)" (268).

Knowing now that the bud of this monstrous flower he
might have blossomed into has always been present in his
nature, is now, Spencer Brydon cannot rest until he sees the
flower it might have become, however hideous. In fact, its
hideousness turns out to be intolerable to him when he does
see it and he is driven to desperate denial: "He's none of
me, even as I might have been," he says (296). But Alice
Staverton, who loves Spencer Brydon enough to love and pity
even the self he might have been, has had the courage and
the insight to imagine and "see" this other, possible
Spencer Brydon long before Spencer Brydon himself does; she
has, as she says, already twice seen him, in a dream, and—
it is a marvelous, precise psychological use of this metaphor—when this ghost turns up a third time in her dreams,
after Spencer Brydon has seen him in the house on the jolly
corner and denied him completely, it is she who, out of her
love for the whole Spencer Brydon, loves him too and pities
him and so is warned by the ghost to come to the house on
the jolly corner and save Spencer Brydon, as she would
hardly have known enough to do had the ghost not trusted her

love and come to warn her of Spencer Brydon's danger (297).
So, if Spencer Brydon cannot himself quite face the reality
of his whole self, he does find some one who can in Alice
Staverton, the embodiment of a New York—and America—that
has known how to treasure and preserve into the present, to
keep alive, a true American tradition that will make it possible for Spencer Brydon, with her help, to live in the old
house on the jolly corner in New York.

The core of the story is made up of James's minute,
marvelous account of how Spencer Brydon stalked the ghost of
the self he might have been through the empty house on the
jolly corner. It is evidently—even taken literally—a
psychological process, a slow refining of Brydon's powers of
perception until he can "see" what was not at first visible
at all. Right at the start of Section II of the story James
puts this point in one of his wonderful extended comparisons.
For Brydon, he says, the old house was like "some great
glass bowl, all precious concave crystal, set delicately
humming by the play of a moist finger round its edge. The
concave crystal held, as it were, this mystical other world,
and the indescribably fine murmur of its rim was the sigh
there, the scarce audible pathetic wail to his strained ear,
of all the old baffled forsworn possibilities" (278).

So Spencer Brydon stalks his "poor hard-pressed alter
ego" (280); for the first thing he feels is that the ghost
of his potential self is fleeing him, as if afraid. The
ghost is in fact, as it turns out, afraid, afraid that
Spencer Brydon will find him so hideous that he will not accept and be kind to the ghost who is the fully formed image
of Spencer Brydon's own potential self. Then, almost comically, the situation changes. Gradually, Spencer Brydon
comes to feel that the ghost is following him (281). Clearly,
though Spencer Brydon is anxious to know the self he might
have been, to see its face clearly, he is also frightened to
do so. Therefore he thinks of the ghost as if it were a
cornered rat, ready to turn and fight (282). This judgment,
we know from the scene in which the ghost actually does appear, is wrong. We know from that scene that the ghost has
always, rather pathetically, feared to face the shock of
Spencer Brydon's horror on seeing him. His courage consists
in his being willing to show himself and accept the pain of
that.

The first tentative approaches of the ghost that make
Spencer Brydon feel the ghost is now following him rather
than he the ghost produce a moment of sheer terror for
Brydon in which he simply closes his eyes, "held them tight,
for a long minute, as with that instinct of dismay and that
terror of vision" (283). Confronted with the possibility
that he really will see the ghost, he finds himself unable
to look. Then he recovers his courage, forces himself to go
to the mysteriously closed door and to prepare to open it.
Then it comes through to him that the ghost has somehow ap-
pealed for his pity, has, as it were, begged him not to open
the door, force a confrontation, and expose the ghost (286).

We are not to suppose Spencer Brydon fully understands why
the ghost cannot bear to be looked on, fully appreciates how
horrible, as the ghost knows, he will appear to Spencer
Brydon. It is all the more to Spencer Brydon's credit that,
not fully understanding the ghost's motive, he nonetheless
yields to its plea for mercy and refuses to open the door
and expose the ghost by force—"not, verily . . . because it
saved his nerves or his skin, but because, much more valuable, it saved the situation" (286), though he is aware now
too that seeing the apparition—or even discovering that in
his absence, the closed door of that remote room has been
opened—would drive him to suicide, "would send him straight
about to the window he had left open, and by that window
. . . he saw himself uncontrollably insanely fatally take
his way to the street" (289).

Ironically enough this demonstration by Brydon of a
capacity for consideration and perhaps for pity and forgive-
ness gives the ghost the courage he needs to appear volun-
tarily to Brydon. Therefore, when Brydon—lacking the
courage to look again at the significant door—instead makes
blindly for the great staircase and goes down it to the
front door, he is suddenly confronted by another open door;
the inner doors of the vestibule, never both left open by
him, are now both thrown back. But though Spencer Brydon
does not appreciate it, the ghost is still desperately
afraid to appear; though Spencer Brydon thinks of the ghost
as waiting "there to measure himself with its power to dismay" the ghost is in fact hesitating in the shadow of the
vestibule "as for dark deprecation" (291). Gradually it
nerves itself to appear and comes forward, with its face
buried in its hands for shame. Spencer Brydon "could but
gape at his other self in this other anguish, gape as a
proof that he [Spencer Brydon], standing there for the
achieved, the enjoyed, the triumphant life, couldn't be
faced [by his shamed other self] in his triumph" (292).
Finally the ghost finds the courage to drop his battered
hands and expose the face that would have been Spencer
Brydon's had he become the New York businessman he might
have. It was "the face of a stranger . . . evil, odious,
blatant, vulgar" (292) and Spencer Brydon "dies" at the
sight of it. (The earlier knowledge that he would have
leapt uncontrollably out of the second-story window if confronted by the ghost means that we must take James's word
"gone" at the end of section II thus seriously.)

When Brydon recovers, the first thing he realizes is
that "what he had come back to seemed really the great thing,
and as if his prodigious journey had been all for the sake
of it" (293), as it had been, for it was the only way he
could learn that he needed Alice Staverton, to forgive him
for being partly the man who could have become the ghost he
has seen, as he cannot forgive himself, and partly to make
it possible for him to be the self that can live in the
house on the jolly corner.

<u>QUESTIONS</u> (pages 856-857 of *Modern Short Stories*)

1. It is probably necessary to deal with the use of
ghosts in the story first; this means making students see
clearly James's use of the central intelligence. Does <u>James</u>
say Spencer Brydon saw a ghost?

2. If what James says is that Spencer Brydon believed he
saw a ghost, what does this ghost represent?

3. What qualities has Spencer Brydon discovered in himself, on his return to New York, that might make him think
he had seen such a ghost?

4. What does his renewed friendship with Alice Staverton
mean to Spencer Brydon?

5. What is Alice Staverton's attitude to the ghost?

6. What is Spencer Brydon's attitude to the ghost (a)
when he first starts going to the house; (b) when he thinks
the ghost is following him; (c) when he actually meets the
ghost?

7. What is James's point in having Alice Staverton
rescue Spencer Brydon and accept him as a husband?

HENRY JAMES

THE LESSON OF THE MASTER

THE LESSON OF THE MASTER belongs to the middle period
of James's work, when he was much preoccupied with the subject of the artist and society. Though lacking the almost
artificial neatness of *The Tone of Time*, it shares that
story's balanced subject, its trick of putting two very different people in the same situation and keeping their responses to that situation more or less parallel. It also
has the relative simplicity of subject—at least as compared
to *The Jolly Corner*—of *The Tone of Time* and that story's
dramatic scenes of confrontation between the main characters
with their striking dialogue.

The subject is quite simple; it is the need to choose
between the necessarily dedicated life, if one is to be a
great artist, and what Henry St. George, without bitterness,
calls "the clumsy conventional expensive materialised vul-
garised brutalised life of London" (343), the normal life of
marriage, children, success and society that he has lived.
About the need for dedication, if one is to do the really
great thing, Henry St. George has no doubt at all. He himself had started out with superb gifts and had written three
quite beautiful books (299). He had then compromised,
marrying an attractive woman, and settling into the expensive life it was her ambition to have. No one knows better
than he does how inadequate to his gifts his present work
is. "I think of that pure spirit [of the dedicated writer]
as a man thinks of a woman he has in some detested hour of
his youth loved and forsaken," he says. "She haunts him
with reproachful eyes, she lives forever before him. As an
artist, you know, I've married for money" (339). He is not
trying to force the young and gifted writer of the story,
Paul Overt, not to follow his course; one of the most wonderful things about the story's magnificent central scene, the
long conversation between St. George and Paul Overt that
makes up Section V (335-348), is the way St. George combines
the eloquence of his statement of the splendor of the
artist's dedicated life with an easy, friendly willingness
to confess what it costs and to admit how little any man has
the right to urge another to undertake it (346-347). The
greatness of the story lies in the conception of the character of St. George, with his full sense of his betrayal of
his talent ("Happy?" he says of his life. "It's a kind of
hell," [340]), his unembittered irony about his wife's utter
incomprehension of his art and her earnest, self-confident
management of his life in order that he may produce a profitable quantity of saleable work ("My wife invented it," he
says humorously of his windowless study, "and she locks me up
here every morning," [337]), his clear conception and honest
admission of what a man like him has sacrificed: "He

may still hear a great chatter [about his books], but what he hears most is the incorruptible silence of Fame" (341). It is because he knows and has come to terms with everything about himself that he is so superbly self-possessed, and it is, in turn, James's conception of him as this kind of man that allows James to give him the marvelously eloquent account of his own life, with all its insight and honesty and even amusement.

It is typical of James's sophisticated kind of comedy that he should make Paul Overt, the young writer trying to decide whether to dedicate himself to being a great novelist or to marry Marian Fancourt, the story's central intelligence. Overt decides, after his long conversation with St. George, that he will give dedication to writing a try but not—he imagines—commit himself to it irretrievably, "He had renounced [Marian Fancourt], yes; but that was another affair—that was a closed but not a locked door" (353). He spends two years in Switzerland writing a big novel and continuing to believe that a choice of lives is still open to him (350-351). But that two year's dedication to writing and neglect of Marian Fancourt convinces St. George—as well it might—that Paul Overt has the strength of character—as St. George had not had—to achieve the necessary dedication to his art. When Mrs. St. George suddenly dies, then, St. George feels morally free to marry Marian Fancourt, though he had carefully kept clear as long as Paul Overt was courting Marian and might still have decided to marry her.

The joke here, James expects us to see, is truly on Paul Overt, for St. George is right about him. Paul himself had said, more truly than he then understood, "No, I am an artist—I can't help it!" (347), and he has now shown St. George that he is capable of dedicating himself to the artist's life. The only person who has not recognized that is Paul himself, so that when he hears of Marian Fancourt's engagement, thinking as he does that he may still decide he wants to marry her, he takes St. George's engagement to her as a betrayal, and even thinks that perhaps St. George had talked as he did in their long conversation about the artist merely to trick Paul into leaving Marian to him (353). But of course that is absurd. As St. George himself reasonably points out in their last conversation, he could not possibly then have foreseen the death of Mrs. St. George and planned to marry Marian Fancourt (356).

Sympathetic as James is to the life of the artist as against the ordinary life of society, disenchanted though he is about the pleasures of upperclass society, he nonetheless does the appeal of these things full justice. Marian Fancourt is very attractive; she displays in her scenes with Paul Overt a real if slightly naive charm (310-323, 329-333). But we are also aware that she is more enthusiastic about great writers than aware of the meaning of literature, that her charm is her beauty and youth rather than real understanding. About this, in the unembittered clarity of his understanding, St. George is never in doubt. "Doesn't she," he says, "shed a rosy glow over life?" (318); and he does life itself the justice of recognizing that it may, after all, 'matter more than art does, even for a man of genius. "Ah, there it is—" he says, "there's nothing like life" (323). But he never pretends to Paul Overt that Marian Fancourt will be any different as a wife from Mrs. St.George, either for Paul or for himself, and we know that is true (345).

We see her true taste in that room of hers, "draped with the quaint cheap florid stuffs that are represented as coming from southern and eastern countries, where they are fabled to serve as the counterpanes of the peasantry" (329). Her true taste shows, too, when, without cost or consideration, she speaks to Paul at the party after her engagement in "her old liberal lavish way." "Perhaps," Paul thinks, "in other days it had meant just as little or as much—a mere mechanical charity. . ." (355). In short, it is all too evident that she is going to make St. George just such another wife as Mrs. St. George had been, and would have made Paul that kind of wife too. But Paul, in his soreness of heart at losing her so unexpectedly to St. George himself, cannot see this as we can, and the story ends with the narrator making a joke of Paul's suspicions of the pair. True to his announcement to Paul at their last meeting, St. George "has published nothing [since his new marriage] but Paul doesn't even yet feel safe" (359). It is only he, sadly enough, who does not.

QUESTIONS (page 857 of *Modern Short Stories*)

1.   What kind of a woman does Mrs. St. George appear to
be when Paul Overt first meets her?

2.   What kind of person does Marian Fancourt appear to be?

3.   What do we deduce from Henry St. George's apparent
interest in Marian Fancourt during the weekend at Lady
Watermouth's?

4.   What does St. George reveal about the way he lives
and the way his wife manages his life in the smoking room
conversation with Paul? What does he reveal about his own
books?

5.   In the long conversation between Henry St. George and
Paul Overt in St. George's study after the dinner party,
what do we learn about (a) St. George's method of work;
(b) the kind of books he produces by this method; (c) the
reasons he writes such books by this method; (d) his judgment of the general life he lives; (e) his judgment of what
marriage to Marian Fancourt will do to Paul Overt as a
novelist; (f) his hopes for Overt as a novelist?

6.   What does Paul Overt do as a result of this conversation?

7.   Why is Paul upset to discover, when he returns to
London after two years, that St. George and Marian Fancourt
are engaged?

8.   What is Paul's impression of Marian at their last
meeting?

9.   Was Paul right or wrong to think St. George had not
played quite fair with him?

EDITH WHARTON
ROMAN FEVER

ROMAN FEVER is an almost ideal illustration of the
short story as comedy of manners. It manages in almost neo-
classical fashion to give us the essential elements of a
story of violent passion sustained for twenty-five years by
showing us a single scene, and that one a quiet conversation
between two middle-aged women sitting on a hotel terrace.
Almost deliberately, Mrs. Wharton begins the story with the
departure of the daughters, Barbara and Jenny, the only characters we feel are likely to do anything. We hear just
enough of what these daughters say about their mothers as
they depart to understand that, for them, in the provincial
confidence of their youthfulness, the life of knitting they
visualize for "the young things" suits their characters exactly (359). Their point is emphasized by the first ex-
change between the ladies themselves, when they comment rue-
fully on the passive roles assigned to them as mothers by
modern custom. They protest mildly against these roles:
"The new system has certainly given us a good deal of time
to kill; and sometimes I get tired of just looking—even at
this," says Mrs. Ansley (360). But we do not take this complaint very seriously; probably, we think, they are not
fundamentally different from what their daughters think them.

"This"—the scene the ladies are looking at—is the
panorama of Rome, one of the great sights of the world, and
we can take Mrs. Ansley's remark that even this tires her as
simply a reference to the splendor of that view. In fact it
is anything but that; as we eventually will learn, Mrs.
Ansley is looking at the place—the Forum—where she lived
the one evening of her life that determined its whole
meaning, and did so because of something Mrs. Slade had done.
Mrs. Wharton keeps everything, like this, that the ladies
say strictly in character, and yet at the same time she
manages to make everything they say express their unrevealed
selves and their concealed experiences. Their revealed
characters—what each, looking "through the wrong end of her
little telescope" (363) can see of the other—are neatly set
forth almost at once as "the two ladies, who had been intimate since childhood, reflected how little they knew each
other" (361). This again sounds like a commonplace—the
sort of thing that occasionally occurs to everyone as he contemplates his friend; but it is going to turn out to be
shockingly true for both ladies. Meanwhile, the reflections
of each give us a clear picture of the public self of the
other, and—unintentionally—a revelation of herself.

To Mrs. Slade Mrs. Ansley has always been hopelessly

conventional, and she and her husband—that "estimable pair"
—have led a drab, passionless life. "Funny," she thinks,
"where she [Barbara, the Ansley's daughter] got it [her
"edge"] with those two nullities as parents" (362). Twenty-
five years ago Mrs. Ansley "had been exquisitely lovely"
("You wouldn't believe it, would you?" [361]). Mrs. Slade's
bland suggestions that Mrs. Ansley has never been anything
but wishy-washy reveal a good deal about Mrs. Slade's own
character, and these qualities of her character are emphasized by her recollection of her own life with Delphin
Slade, which had been for her a life of decisive self-
expression: "She had always regarded herself . . . as con-
tributing her full share to the making of the exceptional
couple they were" (362). She has evidently been an effective but self-assertive companion for the successful and
worldly Delphin Slade—striking looking and efficient, and
no doubt as positive when she was wrong as when she was
right: "brilliant; but not as brilliant as she thinks," as
Mrs. Ansley sums it up (363).

There is a hint of overassertion in all Mrs. Slade's
recollections, as if she were not so sure of her triumphant
success as she would like to be; and indeed, she is not, for
deep in her heart she still hates Mrs. Ansley, as she would
not if she were quite sure she had completely defeated Mrs.
Ansley when they fought over Delphin Slade twenty-five years
ago. So far as she consciously understands, however, she
had won a complete victory; she believes she is sure she had
her triumph back then and, in addition, had revenged herself on Mrs. Ansley for the impertinence of having challenged her, by tricking Mrs. Ansley into the humiliating defeat of her night's visit to the Forum. Since she believes
she is assured of all this, she cannot understand why she
continues to hate Mrs. Ansley. She admits to herself that
she had been afraid of Mrs. Ansley's appeal to Delphin
Slade in the old days, "afraid of you, of your quiet ways,
your sweetness . . . your . . ." (369), and the truth she
does not face is that she is still afraid, as if she somehow
felt, beneath her conscious confidence, that Mrs. Ansley's
quiet sweetness had been too powerful a force to have
allowed Mrs. Slade's energetic, unscrupulous nature the un-
alloyed triumph she has always assured herself she won.

There is even something just a little pathetic about
the self-doubt of this self-assured woman, something
touching about her faint suspicion that, however masterful
she has always been in dealing with headwaiters and other
inferiors, however energetic she was in meeting the "existing
and unexpected obligation[s]" of life with Delphin Slade,
there may always have been some inadequacy in her, something
she never could give Delphin Slade that perhaps the much
scorned Mrs. Ansley could have—though she is much too sure
of herself to suspect that Mrs. Ansley ever actually did so.
"One might almost imagine," she thinks to herself, "(if one
had known her [Mrs. Ansley] less well . . .) that for her,
also, too many memories rose from the lengthening shadows of
those august ruins [of the Forum]" (366). Mrs. Ansley is a

quiet woman, "less articulate than her friend" (363) even
when she is thinking to herself. She too has her blindness,
her tendency to see Mrs. Slade's boldness as less brutal
than it really is. Knowing what she does about that night
twenty-five years ago (and perhaps giving Mrs. Slade more
credit than she deserves for having guessed it)—she sees
Mrs. Slade's life as "full of failures and mistakes" (363).
Underestimating both Mrs. Slade's insensitivity and her
boldness, Mrs. Ansley never suspects the audacity of what
Mrs. Slade did that night.

All this secret knowledge and the miscalculations the
two women base on it is working just beneath the surface of
their conventional conversation. It is there in the stress
Mrs. Ansley puts on "me" when she says that the view of the
Palatine and the Forum "always will be, to me [the most
beautiful view in the world]." It is there in the "indefin-
able stress" of her "Oh, yes, I remember" what things were
like when she and Mrs. Slade were here as girls (360). It
is equally there in Mrs. Slade's confident references to
moonlight and sentimentality (361); she means, of course,
that in the old days she had, in her firm, unsentimental
way, played on Mrs. Ansley's soft, sentimental nature to win
Delphin Slade away from her.

Thus what each of these women does and does not understand about their common past is an outgrowth of her character, and their conceptions of the past are—just as are
their characters—complementary. Moreover, it is typical of
Mrs. Slade's commanding nature to precipitate a crisis between them when her hatred of Mrs. Ansley—kept alive by her
unconscious doubts about the past—nags her into trying once
more to hurt Mrs. Ansley. It is equally in character that
Mrs. Ansley, having been fulfilled as far as her quiet
nature requires fulfillment—as Mrs. Slade, despite having
been married to Delphin Slade for twenty-five years, has not
been—feels no need to hurt Mrs. Slade; she even tries to
hold back out of pity for Mrs. Slade, though her pity is
based on a partial miscalculation of Mrs. Slade. When Mrs.
Slade wonders if Mrs. Ansley knows what it means to be
frightened because one is too happy, Mrs. Ansley says, "I—
yes . . ." (367) so quietly that we hardly suspect the
truth, that she has felt such fear far more deeply than Mrs.
Slade ever has, because she was made overwhelmingly happy by
the letter she thought Delphin Slade had written her, had
always believed that she had, in truth, been his "one
darling" and that he was truly "only your D.S." (368). On
the strength of her belief in all his letter had said, she
had—for all the quietness of her nature—gone boldly out to
meet him in the Forum that night twenty-five years ago, had
conceived his child, and had hastily married Horace Ansley
in a successful effort to conceal the real cause of her
pregnancy. In her quiet way she has lived out her life content with the knowledge that she had had Delphin Slade's
real love and had borne his brilliant child, Barbara. She
has felt no need, such as has driven Alida Slade, to shine
herself or to punish her rivals or to possess Delphin Slade

legally. So she pretends to Mrs. Slade that she does not
remember how lovers met in the Forum or how people said that
her innocent desire to see the moon rise there had caused
the illness that eliminated her from the battle to win
Delphin Slade (367).

Mrs. Ansley's gentleness, her content, only irritate
Mrs. Slade. She begins by trying to control her hatred of
Mrs. Ansley and fails; and, failing, she tries once more to
injure Mrs. Ansley. And she succeeds, for what she tells
Mrs. Ansley destroys one of the two convictions by which Mrs.
Ansley has lived all these years. She has now to give up
her belief that Delphin Slade had unequivocally expressed
his love for her and face the fact that—all unwittingly—in
answering the letter she thought was from Slade, she had in
fact taken the initiative, had invited him to meet her in
the Forum. Such boldness would doubtless have come easily
enough to Alida Slade, but to a woman of Mrs. Ansley's
nature it would be a humiliation to recognize that, to
Delphin Slade, she must have seemed, not the proudly quiet
woman responding bravely to the true passion of the man she
loved, but a desperate woman who took the course of propos-
ing to him that he give her the meager consolation of a
hasty assignation in the notorious Forum. The meaning that
meeting had always had for her—her belief that, however
secret the fact had to be, she was Delphin Slade's only real
love—has now been destroyed. The letter and all it had
made her believe, that memory on which she has lived for
twenty-five years (370), is gone. No wonder she says, yes,
when Mrs. Slade says, "You tried your best to get him away
from me, didn't you? But you failed; and I kept him.
That's all" (370). Up to now Mrs. Ansley has believed that,
in the way that matters most to her—the possession of
Slade's real love—she had not failed but had got him away
from Alida Slade; she has thought of Alida Slade as having
achieved only a hollow victory, only the outward appearance
of possession, and of therefore having lived a life of
"failures and mistakes" (363). Now all she can think of is
that she never did possess Slade's love—or at least that
the evidence of that love she had always counted on never
existed. For a moment, overwhelmed by this revelation, she
thinks of herself as having failed entirely and answers Mrs.
Slade, "Yes. That's all." She is admitting that, with re-
spect to the only thing that counts for her, sentiment, she
failed.

But Mrs. Slade cares nothing for sentiment ("I never
should have supposed," Mrs. Ansley quite truly says, "you
were sentimental, Alida" [361]). What matters to her is
physical fact and appearance. She therefore assumes Mrs.
Ansley means by her answer that the letter's effect had been
just what Mrs. Slade planned to have it, that Mrs. Ansley
had spent that long-ago night "waiting round there [the
Forum] in the dark, dodging out of sight, listening for
every sound, trying to get in—" (371). The sheer brutality
of Mrs. Slade's plan had been such that Mrs. Ansley had
never suspected her of forging the letter from Slade. In

the same way, the heroism of Mrs. Ansley's love for Delphin
Slade that made her—despite her apparent meekness and
conventionality—boldly accept the letter's proposal and
answer it at once has been beyond Mrs. Slade's imagination:
she has never suspected what Mrs. Ansley in fact did. When
she is shaken by the discovery that Mrs. Ansley had really
met Delphin Slade in the Forum that night and been possessed
by him, Mrs. Ansley begins to recover from her shock, seeing
that she still has something of the kind that counts for
her. What hurts Mrs. Slade is the physical fact that Slade
was Mrs. Ansley's lover; but that physical fact is insignificant to Mrs. Ansley; what matters to her is its result,
that she has had Slade's child, the brilliant Barbara who is
so much like Slade. From the wreckage of this moment, she
thus recovers something that to her makes life worth living,
even though she must now reconcile herself to the knowledge
that Slade never loved her as she had supposed he did.

But the thought of Barbara renews her pity for Mrs.
Slade, whose son—so like his father—is dead, whose
daughter, Jenny, is not the least brilliant. So she again
holds back, trying not to tell Mrs. Slade that Barbara is
Slade's daughter: when Mrs. Slade presses her to explain
why she is sorry for Mrs. Slade (a thing intolerable to Mrs.
Slade), Mrs. Ansley only says, "because I didn't have to wait
that night" (371). But when Mrs. Slade, not willing to
leave well enough alone, insists with her "unquiet laugh" on
rubbing salt in the wound and says, "After all, I had everything; I had him for twenty-five years. And you had nothing
but that one letter he didn't write," Mrs. Ansley strikes
back. "I," she says, "had Barbara," the true heir of
Delphin Slade, the possession of whom Mrs. Slade cannot take
away from Mrs. Ansley as she had taken away the letter from
Delphin Slade. Just once in her life, Mrs. Ansley had displayed the boldness Mrs. Slade—not without reason—thinks
characteristic of herself and inconceivable in Mrs. Ansley.
She had done so, not because she was habitually bold as was
Mrs. Slade in her self-confidence and her desire for visible
triumphs, but because her quiet nature was capable of depths
of love that were quite beyond Mrs. Slade's nature and that,
when stirred, made her do without hesitation whatever that
love required. Without hesitation, Mrs. Ansley had, for the
sake of her love, given everything without hope of compensa-
tion; as a result she now has all that, by her standards,
still matters, Slade's daughter Barbara—who is also, by
Mrs. Slade's radically different standards, all that also
matters to her. So, as the two women leave the hotel
terrace, Mrs. Ansley "move[s] ahead of Mrs. Slade." Morally
speaking, in spite of her appearance of quietness and con-
tented inferiority, she always has.

Throughout the story Mrs. Ansley's superiority to Mrs.
Slade has been a moral one; the essential quality of her
character is that she cares for the substance of things, not
their appearances, and is content with knowing the truth in
her own mind. This ending in which, like another Mrs.
Slade, she insists on using her special knowledge quite

deliberately to injure Mrs. Slade appears to be a gesture
inconsistent with her character that Mrs. Wharton could not
resist because it rounds off the plot of *Roman Fever* with
wonderful neatness. The brutality of Mrs. Slade's initial
attack on Mrs. Ansley is here repaid with a comparable piece
of brutality that grows directly out of Mrs. Slade's initial
attack, and the story ends with a surprise that makes it a
kind of psychological O. Henry story.

This tendency to make carefully concealed sacrifices
to the unquestionably brilliant neatness of the plot is
evident elsewhere in *Roman Fever*. For its sake we are asked
to believe that Barbara's resemblance to Delphin Slade is
the consequence of her being his daughter; the effectiveness
of the story's ending depends in part on this idea, and it
is in itself not improbable. But it raises a difficulty;
why, if it is true, is Jenny, also Delphin Slade's daughter,
not only not the least like him, but even like Horace
Ansley? Both the women in the story were as busy, during
that tense time twenty-five years ago, as a pair of
Napoleons maneuvering against Delphin Slade. But as
Napoleon himself once said, victory would be easy if the op-
posing force would stand still while you maneuvered. What
was Delphin Slade doing to control events all that time? We
are asked to believe he was a brilliant and decisive man;
but he does nothing except respond (cynically or how?) to
what must have seemed to him Mrs. Ansley's sudden and unlikely proposal, and then to surrender to Mrs. Slade's determined attack.

No doubt it would be possible for an ingenious reader
to invent plausible explanations of these details, but no
explanations are offered or even clearly implied by the
story itself. Difficulties of this kind are the risks of
the tightly plotted story, and it is arguable that Mrs.
Wharton—like Mrs. Slade—was not quite humble enough about
the risks she ran. Yet it remains true that *Roman Fever* is,
because of the neatness and ingenuity of its plot, a remarkable story. The situation it reveals gradually is a solid,
subtle, convincing one, and the moral natures of the two
women who caused it are not only subtly conceived but fully
realized by the development of the plot.

QUESTIONS (pages 857-858 of *Modern Short Stories*)

1. What impression of Mrs. Slade and Mrs. Ansley do we get from the remarks of their daughters and their comments on these remarks? How true is this impression?

2. What impression of each lady do we gain from the thoughts of the other?

3. What is it that Mrs. Slade has always feared in Mrs. Ansley and that makes her hate Mrs. Ansley now?

4. What hints are we given about Mrs. Ansley's real feelings about the view of the Forum?

5. What actually happened that evening twenty-five years ago when Mrs. Ansley received the letter from Delphin Slade that Mrs. Slade had forged?

6. Why does Mrs. Slade now reveal that she had forged this letter?

7. Why does this information upset Mrs. Ansley?

8. Why does Mrs. Ansley's revelation that she had actually met Delphin Slade in the Forum upset Mrs. Slade so much?

9. Why does Mrs. Ansley's revelation that Barbara is Delphin Slade's daughter disturb Mrs. Slade even more?

ERNEST HEMINGWAY

THE GAMBLER, THE NUN, AND THE RADIO

THE GAMBLER, THE NUN, AND THE RADIO has one important characteristic in common with Scott Fitzgerald's *Babylon Revisited* in Part One of this collection. Like Fitzgerald's narrator, Hemingway's is often close in feeling to the central intelligence of the story, Mr. Frazer. Moreover, we feel—no doubt rightly—that the narrator and Mr. Frazer are not unlike Ernest Hemingway himself: Mr. Frazer's life has a good deal in common with Hemingway's and he often sounds like Hemingway.

But in *The Gambler, the Nun, and the Radio* the voice of the narrator is steadily if mildly ironic, as it is not in Fitzgerald's story. It is typical of this irony that the story begins, "They brought them in around midnight and then, all night long, every one along the corridor heard the Russian," and adds almost immediately, when the fight is being described, "the Russian crawled under the table" (372). The real point of this beginning is not the conduct of the Russian at all, but the conduct of Cayetano, the Mexican. We are told the Russian had hidden in order that we may notice—though we are not told—that Cayetano did not; we are told that the Russian, who was not seriously wounded, screamed all night in order that we may notice that Cayetano, who was so badly wounded he was not expected to live, never made a sound. This kind of irony, this making of points by dwelling on their opposites, is pervasive in the story, as when the decent but insensitive detective says, "If I could talk spick it would be different," and the interpreter says, "You don't need to talk Spanish" (375). Mr. Frazer contemplates the possibility that the musicians he hears on the radio "kept their instruments at the place they revelled" (376), thus emphasizing not only the absurdity of the name of this band—The Revellers—that plays at six A.M. but also the sleepless desperation that makes Mr. Frazer listen to them. The lamp's knocking out Mr. Frazer "seemed the antithesis of healing or whatever people were in the hospital for" (376-377), a remark we ought to remember when we come to Mr. Frazer's description of the people in the ward with their largely incurable ills (387).

This irony is directed by the narrative voice against Mr. Frazer himself, even when Mr. Frazer is summing up what appears to be the moral of the story in his meditation about "the opium of the people." "What was the real, the actual, opium of the people? He knew it very well. It was gone just a little way around the corner in that well-lighted part of his mind that was there after two or more drinks in the

evening; that he knew was there (it was not really there of
course)" (388). This meditation of Mr. Frazer's is set off
by a minor character, one thin Mexican, and seems to have no
clear reference to anything we can infer from the main figures of the story—Cayetano, Sister Cecilia, Mr. Frazer—or
to what has happened to them. It does have, of course, but
only by dramatic implication.

Mr. Frazer's meditation is not, directly, a moral for
the story, and if we take it as one, we miss the real point,
which is not merely that the finest and bravest people need
some belief to keep them going, some opium ("Why should
people be operated on without an anesthetic?" [388]), but
also that—in a sense the thin, dogmatic Mexican has never
dreamed of—he may be right. If everything, including the
very impulse to keep alive, is a delusion that is needed to
keep men going, if even "bread is the opium of the people"
(388), then perhaps there is no reason for keeping going.

This ironic qualification of the story's ostensible
moral puts everything in it at a slight distance from the
reader, despite our feeling that what Mr. Frazer thinks is
substantially what Ernest Hemingway thinks, as far as it
goes. Irony, then, adds a dimension to the story. It is
not that we do not take Mr. Frazer's meditation seriously;
that meditation is an impressive explanation of the human
situation, probably the best Hemingway could offer. Nevertheless, the irony with which Mr. Frazer's meditation is
presented deliberately creates in our minds the impression
that this explanation may be a lot of foolishness: ". . .
bread was the opium of the people. Would he remember that
and would it make sense in the daylight?" There remains the
real possibility that life itself does not make sense.

Much the same dramatic distancing is effected by the
story's structure. At first reading the story seems to have
very little plan; we watch Cayetano's unexpected recovery
from his wounds as Sister Cecilia reports it to Mr. Frazer
and talks a little about herself while going about her business as a nurse; we hear about Mr. Frazer's interest in
listening to the radio late at night. These things seem to
have very little connection, at least in the causal sense in
which the connection of events make a plot of some kind; the
most we can say of them at first is that they all show the
way the trivial, routine activities of hospital life take on
for the hospital's inmates an exaggerated importance:
"Everything is much simpler in a hospital, including the
jokes" (377). The story has, in short, a beautifully convincing air of lifelikeness, of the random drift of small incidents that make up—at least for our ordinary contempla-
tion of life—its reality.

Yet when we look more carefully, we see that nothing in
the story is really random or purposeless. What Hemingway
is doing is setting in parallel three people who, however
stunningly different their lives are according to conventional ideas, have one thing in common—the problem of

finding a belief by which they can live in a world that
seems to offer men only continuous bad luck, suffering, and
unendurable pointlessness. It is typical of Hemingway's
irony that the story's three central characters should be a
gambler, a nun, and a man who survives by anesthetizing himself with "a little spot of the giant killer and . . . the
radio" (389).

    Cayetano, the gambler, has great dignity and behaves
always with consideration for others. In spite of his
terrible pain, he is constantly aware of—and deeply embarrassed by—the smell of his gangrened wound and never fails
to apologize for it; and he never makes a disturbance.
There is nothing pretentious about his courage. "If I had a
private room and a radio," he says, "I would be crying and
yelling all night long. . . . It is very healthy. But you
cannot do it with so many people" (385). He is capable of
this dignity and consideration for others because he is, in
his unexpected way, a devout man, a man who loves something
more than himself. He can make fun of what he believes—"I
am a poor idealist. I am the victim of illusions"—but his
jokes, like the jokes of Catholics about their religion, are
more an expression of the strength of his faith than of any
doubts. Cayetano lives by his "illusions"; otherwise he
would not always be broke. He does not deceive himself about
what his life has been, but when Mr. Frazer says to him with
deceptive casualness, "Why continue? . . . what is there to
do?" he says without anxiety, "Continue, slowly, and wait for
luck to change" (386). Cayetano loves gambling the way
Sister Cecilia loves being a saint, and that love gives his
life a purpose that makes integrity (he will not squeal on
the man who shot him), dignity, and consideration possible
for him.

    Sister Cecilia is utterly innocent. It is typical of
her to think she can relieve Cayetano's loneliness by speaking to "that O'Brien boy at Police Headquarters" and getting
a few Mexicans sent to coo him (and it is typical of life
that they turn out to be friends of his assailant). As a
girl Sister Cecilia had thought all she had to do to become
a saint was to renounce the world and go into a convent. It
has not worked out for her, but she is undiscouraged: she
still wakes up some mornings thinking she will be a saint.
Meanwhile, her incurably innocent love of sainthood makes
her incapable of doubting for a moment the point of her
simple good-heartedness. Mr. Frazer cannot talk to her seriously, as he can to Cayetano, who is a sophisticated and
unillusioned believer. When Sister Cecilia asks him to write
about Our Lady he can only put her off gently. But he can
and does admire her essential goodness and her ability to
act on it, however simple-mindedly and—sometimes—even
ludicrously with sustained enthusiasm.

    Sister Cecilia makes a striking contrast with the
story's doctrinaire believer, the thin Mexican. Sister
Cecilia reaches out indiscriminately to life: she prays for
the Notre Dame football team and even the Athletics enthusi-

astically. But the thin Mexican lives by a life-denying
dogmatism. Alcohol, he finds, mounts to his head. Non-
drinkers are seldom admirable in Hemingway's stories; they
suffer from what St. Thomas called, in another context,
"avarice of the emotions." This thin Mexican has got himself hooked on a simplified Marxist doctrine about religion
that has mounted to his head with a vengeance. "This one,"
as the smallest Mexican says, "is very strong against
religion," in a way that we see as not only unsophisticated,
as is Sister Cecilia's faith, but rigid and lifeless, as
Sister Cecilia's faith is not.

There remains Mr. Frazer himself. Mr. Frazer finds it
impossible to believe in anything, but he is wise enough to
envy those like Cayetano and Sister Cecilia who can believe.
He knows from humiliating personal experience how difficult
it is to retain human dignity without the support of some
"illusion," knows how fast the nerves "become tricky." But
if Mr. Frazer is too intelligent for the simple and unattrac-
tive dogmatism of the thin Mexican, he is also too honest to
pretend to the kind of devotion Cayetano and Sister Cecilia,
in their remarkably different ways, have. In place of
Cayetano's love of gambling and Sister Cecilia's love of
sainthood, he has his radio. Cayetano jokes about his
"idealism"; Mr. Frazer cannot even pretend to have any. All
he has is the deliberate anesthesia of his "Revellers" and
his giant killer. "He played [the radio] all night long,
turned so low he could barely hear it, and he was learning
to listen to it without thinking" (383). The best he hopes
for is to live "in Seattle from two o'clock on" (383) or to
arrive each morning at six o'clock at the studio in
Minneapolis with his friends the Revellers. It is all a
quite deliberate effort not to think about life at all;
"usually he avoided thinking all he could, except when he
was writing. . ." (387-388).

What else can he do? If religion, music, patriotism,
sexual intercourse, gambling, ambition are all—whatever be-
lievers may tell themselves—in truth merely anesthetics to
keep people from thinking about what life really is, why
should he not use the opiums that work for him? ". . .
drink was a sovereign opium of the people, oh, an excellent
opium. Although some prefer the radio, another opium of the
people. . ." (388). "They would go now in a little while, he
thought [of the Mexicans], and they would take the Cucaracha
with them. Then he would have a little spot of the giant
killer and play the radio, you could play the radio so that
you could hardly hear it" (389).

Once one sees this pattern of characters and their
common preoccupation with the question of how men can live
with dignity and grace, one sees the economical orderliness
of the story's design beneath the apparent casualness of its
narration. That order consists of alternating scenes that
deal with the story's three kinds of opium and that bring in
very ingeniously several others, like music and education.
Notice that the breaks in the story are used to mark the

divisions between the three. The opening incident (372-375) describes, apparently quite objectively, Cayetano's situation. But all through this incident Cayetano's character is being quietly built up for us: his refusal to squeal, his wry humor even as he suffers ("an accident that he hit me at all, the *cabron*" [373]), his unaffected pity for the cowardly Russian, his soft "I believe him" when the detective says this is not make-believe like the movies, his magnificent manners in inquiring about Mr. Frazer's injury (374).

The second section of the story (375-376) looks at first like a continuation of the description of Cayetano, and it does in fact tell us something more about him by mentioning his fine gambler's hands and the "badness" that Sister Cecilia finds so appealing. But these references to Cayetano are really only a transition; this second section of the story is a sketch of Sister Cecilia. It is followed by a section that describes Mr. Frazer's addiction to the radio (376-377). Thus the first three sections of the story are used to establish the story's three main ways of confronting despair, though they never mention the despair or even the beliefs that underlie the characters' conduct; they simply describe that conduct for us.

From then on each section of the story adds something to our knowledge of all three characters with their different ways of confronting life. The next one, the fourth (377-383), also brings in the three anonymous Mexicans who live by their awful music and—in the case of the thin one—their intellectual pride. The fifth section takes us back to Mr. Frazer's radio (383), the sixth to Sister Cecilia's sainthood (383-384), and the seventh to Cayetano's love of gambling (384-387). In the eighth and final section of the story (387-389), Mr. Frazer, listening to the gaiety in the ward and thinking of how much suffering there is in the lives of those innocently happy inmates of the hospital, is driven in spite of himself to think about the opiums of the people. A little drunk, he tries to explain to the thin Mexican, gives it up, and goes back to his radio and his giant killer.

It is worth noticing the unobtrusive skill with which these sections of the story are linked to one another and conceal their focus on particular characters. We have already noticed the transition between sections one and two, but notice how the neat irony about people with radios who hate the hospital's X-ray machine makes a transition between sections three and four, and how Sister Cecilia's bustling kindliness is used to link sections five and six and make the revealing dialogue between Cayetano and Mr. Frazer possible.

The Gambler, the Nun, and the Radio is a comedy of manners, a story that focuses deliberately on the ironic contrasts of manners and styles among people from radically different backgrounds who are brought by accident into the intimate, simplified contact of hospital life. But the

story is using this representation of manners for the most
serious purpose, the exploration of the reasons why men
sometimes live with dignity and grace and sometimes fail to
—and sometimes fail to go on living at all.

QUESTIONS   (pages 858-859 of *Modern Short Stories*)

1.   Where was the Russian wounded, how dangerous was his
wound? Where was he when he was hit? Why does the story
mention the way he screamed all night when he was brought
into the hospital?

2.   Does the story use this ironic indirectness to make
its points elsewhere?

3.   What moral for the story is contained in Mr. Frazer's
meditation about "the opium of the people"?

4.   What further meaning does Hemingway intend us to see
in the story? How does he communicate his further meaning?

5.   Define the character of Cayetano and point out the
things in the story that reveal it to us.

6.   What makes Cayetano a "poor idealist"?

7.   Why does Cayetano go on living a disciplined and
hopeful life despite his continuous defeats?

8.   What kind of a person is Sister Cecilia? What makes
her go on living with interest and enthusiasm despite her
disappoinment at not becoming a saint?

9.   Why is the thin Mexican who is "very strong against
religion" in the story?

10.   What does Mr. Frazer depend on to keep him going and
save him from despair? How well does it work? If not very
well, why does he not do something else?

11.   If the purpose of *The Gambler, the Nun, and the Radio*
is to compare three apparently unlike characters who have in
common the problem of the belief they live by, show how the
story is constructed to bring these three characters into
parallel.

JAMES THURBER
A COUPLE OF HAMBURGERS

There is a brief analysis of *A COUPLE OF HAMBURGERS* in the Introduction to Part Two of *Modern Short Stories*. The important thing to do with this story, as it is with all comedies of manners, is to infer from the particular incidents and remarks in the story the general attitudes of the characters toward one another and, eventually, toward life itself.

QUESTIONS (page 859 of *Modern Short Stories)*

1. Why does the husband insist on using expressions like "dog-wagon," "stay our stomachs," and "stick to your ribs"?

2. What offends the wife about these expressions?

3. What lies behind the wife's queer ideas that diners with nicknames are all run by Greeks and are therefore bad and that diners set at an angle are always poor? Why do these ideas so annoy her husband?

4. Why is the husband so scornful of his wife's suspicion that she has heard a "funny noise" in the car?

5. Why does the husband enjoy singing old popular songs?

6. The wife finally relaxes, content to wait—for her husband to stop singing, for her supper, for the car to break down. Why?

PHILIP ROTH

DEFENDER OF THE FAITH

The thing that makes *DEFENDER OF THE FAITH* so skillful
a comedy of manners is the unobtrusive authoritativeness of
its details of army life. They never dominate our attention, are never displayed for their own sake. Mr. Roth
always uses them to imply something that is relevant to the
central problem of the story, the conflict between Nathan
Marx and Sheldon Grossbart. That is a conflict between two
different kinds of defenders of the faith. It is obviously
relevant that Sergeant Marx is a real soldier who has fought
all the way across Europe and even succeeded in denying "myself the posture of a conqueror—the swagger that I, as a
Jew, might well have worn as my boots whacked against the
rubble of Wesel, Munster, and Braunschweig" (400), while
Grossbart is an inefficient and goldbricking recruit. But
the conflict is more complicated than that, because it involves—however much Grossbart may simply be trading on the
fact—one's loyalty to one's own immediate kind: Sergeant
Marx has constantly to ask himself whether, in being a good
soldier, he is in fact doing the best for his own people,
defending his faith, in a better way than he might by dis-
playing the simple, immediate family loyalty that Grossbart
is always appealing to. Sergeant Marx's problem is that,
however much Grossbart may merely be using this appeal to
serve his own selfish interests, the appeal may be right.

What the story requires us to grasp at once is the way
the details of the customary life of the army—and of the
New York Jewish community—are being used to give life and
reality to the conflict between Marx and Grossbart, and the
way Grossbart's sincerely false use of their common
Jewishness complicates Marx's problem. The use of army life
to give precise definition to the characters and their con-
flicts is everywhere in the story; the simplest example of
it is the "polished helmet liner pulled down to his little
eyes" worn by the slightly comic Captain Barrett (394), who
represents in his imperceptive but nonetheless admirably
sincere way the thing to which Sergeant Marx has committed
himself. Or there is Grossbart's trick of sitting on
Sergeant Marx's desk, from Grossbart's point of view a gesture of intimacy with which Grossbart tries to persuade
Sergeant Marx that all that matters is that they are both
Jews, from Marx's point of view a piece of military impertinence (395). Or there is Grossbart's typical use of army
ritual, which does not exist for him except as a means of
currying favor, when he continues to call Sergeant Marx
"sir" or creates "the awful suspicion that, behind me,
Grossbart was <u>marching</u>, his rifle on his shoulder, as though

he were a one-man detachment" (406).

Perhaps the most skillfully managed of the story's
small details of manners is the way Mr. Roth makes us see
how successful a soldier—in every way—Sergeant Marx is;
that shows in his being the pitcher on the non-com's base-
ball team, in the character of his relations with the other
non-coms—on the soft-ball team, when talking to them on the
telephone—and in his relations with Captain Barrett. There
is something slightly comic about Captain Barrett's earnest
insistence to Grossbart that Sergeant Marx is a hero. But
we know Marx really is, and that is not an easy thing for a
story to convey about its first-person narrator.

The first episode that reveals the full complexity of
the conflict between Grossbart and Marx occurs when Grossbart
makes it clear that he not only wants to go to shul Friday
nights but wants to do so without creating the impression
that he is ducking the G.I. party (395-397). It is, he
thinks perfectly sincerely, "unfair" for people to complain
about it—as it would be, were he sincere in his desire to
go to shul instead of delighting to "let the goyim clean the
floors" (401). "I just want my rights!" he says, and he
wants to get them, not by insisting on them with open recalcitrance but by using influence, without making "trouble"—
"the first thing they throw up to you" (396). The difficulty
for Marx about the situation Grossbart creates is that he
knows everything Grossbart says has a good deal of truth in
it. Grossbart is not in fact meeting any special discrimination in this story, but no doubt there is some in the
barracks. More important than that, the whole appeal
Grossbart is making to the special character of Jewish life
is very powerful with Marx. That life exists and Marx has
known it in his childhood; it will always be a part of him.
Reminded of it by Grossbart, Marx is moved by it to go to
shul, while Grossbart, despite his pious assertion of it, is
going out of a combination of quite different desires—to
get out of cleaning the floors, to assert his specialness,
to get his "rights" in season and out (400); it also makes
Marx try to explain to Captain Barrett the special character
of Jewish family life (404).

Grossbart clearly has no trouble with the army food;
he eats like a hound (409). But the chaplain at shul puts
it into his head that he <u>ought</u> to find the *trafe* the army
serves him offensive; that makes it one of the things he
feels it his right to complain about. When Marx catches him
out writing the letter for his father to send to his Congressman to complain about the food, Grossbart says he
really faked the letter for his friends Halpern and Fishbein
(409), but that is not true either, for in their different
ways they have accepted the army food (402). Grossbart is
completely sincere. With a cunning almost like that of a
man with systematic delusions, he justifies himself to himself in everything he does and is convinced beyond the
slightest doubt that everything he has done has been morally
impeccable (409). This is what makes him formidable. Marx

imagines for a time that Grossbart has turned back from the
course he has been following, "before he plunged over into
the ugliness of privilege undeserved" (411), but Marx
quickly learns better from the episode over the passes for
the Passover dinner in St. Louis. Grossbart was never, of
course, invited by an aunt to St. Louis for a Seder, and
after he has been there with Halpern and Fishbein and eaten
his Chinese dinner, it never occurs to him in his sublime
righteousness to conceal the fact from another Jew who will,
he assumes, share his feeling that anything goes when one is
outmaneuvering the goyim or ministering to the personal
needs of homesick Jewish boys from the Bronx. He brings
Sergeant Marx a bit of Chinese egg roll and happily explains
the whole affair to him (419). This is his idea of the way
to persuade Marx to cheat in order to keep him from having
to ship out to the Pacific.

Marx has broken his own rule in asking a non-com friend
in C. and A. where his unit is going and—out of his deep
feeling for his own Bronx past and his sense of community
with others who have known that life—he is shocked, "as
though I were the father of Halpern, Fishbein, and Grossbart,"
to hear they are going to the Pacific (417). As he says
quietly when he pleads with Fishbein to be straight with him,
"I'm just like you—I want to serve my time and go home. I
miss the same things you miss" (416). It is this that
weakens his resistance to Grossbart's skillful and dishonest
appeals to their common Jewish background. Then Marx discovers that Grossbart has used his tricks on another Jew,
Corporal Shulman in C. and A., to get himself—but not
Fishbein and Halpern—sent to Monmouth instead of the
Pacific. It is too much for him and he uses his influence
to get Grossbart put back in the orders for the Pacific (420).

The final scene between Marx and Grossbart sums up the
conflict between them beautifully. As he always has,
Grossbart sincerely believes that any interference with his
"rights" is a clear evidence of anti-Semitism ("There's no
limit to your anti-Semitism, is there?" he says to Marx; and
"That's right, twist things around" [421]). When Grossbart
says angrily, "You call this watching out for me—what you
did?" Marx says, "No. For all of us" (422). Marx is defending the Jews by seeing that no Jew is given undeserved
privileges, that each Jew does his share as he himself has
done; that is his commitment, and though he has been seduced
by Grossbart's appeals to their common inheritance into be-
traying that commitment in several small matters like the
weekend pass, when it comes to who must face combat duty he
is not going to allow Grossbart to cheat, especially when
Grossbart is cheating Fishbein and Halpern as well as the
rest of the men. Bitterly Marx thinks to himself that
Grossbart is too cunning not to be able to cheat himself to
safety even in the Pacific. "And, I thought, so would
Fishbein and Halpern be all right, even in the Pacific, if
only Grossbart continued to see—in the obsequiousness of
the one, the soft spirituality of the other—some profit for
himself." "And then, resisting with all my will an impulse

to turn and seek pardon [from Grossbart] for my vindictive-
ness [in getting Grossbart sent to the Pacific] I accepted
my own [fate]" (422) — the fate of always feeling guilty when
acting as he thinks right in situations where he is being
criticized by Jews like Grossbart.

QUESTIONS (pages 859-860 of *Modern Short Stories*)

  1. How good a soldier is Sergeant Marx and what things
in the story provide the answer to this question?

  2. What are Grossbart's reasons for taking the attitude
he does in his relations to Sergeant Marx? How sincere
would you say he is in doing so?

  3. What does Sergeant Marx think of Grossbart's
maneuvers?

  4. How does Sergeant Marx react to Grossbart's appeals
to him?

  5. Is Grossbart ashamed of writing the letter for his
father to send his Congressman about the army food? Why
not?

  6. Why does Sergeant Marx give the three soldiers week-
end passes for St. Louis?

  7. Why does Grossbart reveal to Sergeant Marx how he has
fooled him into giving the passes to them?

  8. Why is Sergeant Marx shocked when he hears that his
unit is being sent to the Pacific?

  9. Why does Sergeant Marx use his influence to get
Grossbart back in the orders for the Pacific?

  10. What is Grossbart's judgment of why Marx did this?

  11. Why does Sergeant Marx have to make an effort not to
beg Grossbart's pardon for having done it?

JAMES ALAN McPHERSON
GOLD COAST

Mr. McPherson has the kind of dramatic imagination that
perceives life not as abstract ideas in a logical order but
as the concrete experience of actual people. At the same
time, the lives of these people have a consistency of implied
meaning that gives his description of them a special force.
Nothing in *GOLD COAST* is mechanically symbolic or comes in
where it does because some argument requires it to; these
people are almost opaquely natural, and what happens dis-
courages the drawing of easy morals by being so remarkably
(and confusingly) like ordinary life. At the same time, the
story has the authority of experience envisioned according to
some consistent feeling about human existence. It is possible
to isolate this feeling in our minds, and it will help us to
see just how purposeful all the apparently casual details of
the story are.

The story is concerned with people's need to store up
treasure, to fulfill their natures in the actual world, or at
least of a man's tendency to "drift off to sleep lulled by
sweet anticipation of the time when my potential would suddenly
be realized . . ." (422-423). Because it is seldom possible
for a man to realize what he supposes his potential, most
people, when they are old and finished as James Sullivan is,
feel themselves—and perhaps are—"a cut above" what they have
turned out to be, victims of "circumstances" (440). The deadly
quiet of their lives, broken only by berserk rages like Meg
Sullivan's or hatreds, usually snobbish, like Miss O'Hara's,
often makes the young want to "knock on a door and expose
[themselves] just to hear someone breathe hard for once" (424).
But in moments of prosperity and happiness, when they have an
"apartment, a sensitive girl, a stereo, two speakers, one
tattered chair, one fork, a job, and the urge to acquire"—when
they have "all this and youth besides"—they pity James
Sullivan (424).

There is something terrifying about people who have
reached the point where they recognize they have all they will
ever get and are in danger of losing even that little, even the
dirty, half-crazy dog that is the last thing left them to possess with love; and know that they will "be dead inside of a
year" (439). Robert, who is fastidious, hates James Sullivan's
dirtiness and the smell of his basement and his flat (though
not so much as he fears "something about [the flat] I cannot
name" [429], the metaphysical smell of old age and despair), as
he hates the obsessive cleanliness of the equally lonely Miss

O'Hara, who keeps herself alive by hating the Sullivans and their dirt.

But even more he pities them. He understands that the old can forget their despair and loneliness only when they are drunk or warmed by old hatreds—whether of the AMA, the Medicare program, hippies, or neighbors—before an audience they know is bored but need so desperately that they try to believe they are not "burdening it unduly." James Sullivan had watched two generations of the Harvard rich "pass the building on their way to the Yard"; "he had watched the cycle from when he had been able to haul the [garbage] cans out for himself, and now he could not, and he was bitter" (426). He had had "a whole lifetime of living in the basement of Harvard" (427). Not that he was not still struggling in his seriocomic way—"If any of these sons of bitches ever ask you to do something extra, be sure to charge them for it" (425).

We may sympathize with the desperate old, we may even (out of a scarcely understood need to do unto others as we know we will one day desperately need to have others do unto us) sacrifice oneself to help them, especially when we have lost some treasure like Jean and momentarily experienced the kind of despair James Sullivan lives with. Jean had been for Robert a rare possession: "I was happy because she belonged to me and not to the race, which made her special. It made me special too because I did not have to wear a beard or hate or be especially hip or ultra-Ivy Leagueish. I did not have to smoke pot or supply her with it, or be for any other cause at all except myself" (432). So, when he and Jean stood in that subway car, the blacks tense and hating on one side, and the whites tense and hating on the other, and endured and aged (437), and did not make it, he got a glimpse of the deprivation James Sullivan was enduring and felt differently about him; ". . . having him there was much better than being alone. After he had gone I could sleep and I was not lonely in sleep" (440).

But Robert recovered, and then "there were girls outside and I knew that I could have one now because that desperate look had finally gone somewhere deep inside. I was young and I did not want to be bothered" by lonely old people like James Sullivan (442). For James Sullivan, however, despair was permanent; he could not, like the young, recover from it, begin again to believe he had escaped. That was all right when Robert too felt despair; but when he recovered it was not: "I disliked him more every time I heard a girl laugh on the street far below my window" (442). To this Robert, James Sullivan was a tirelessly talkative death's-head at the feast.

Walking in the early dawn and seeing the Summer School fellows sneak out of the girls' dormitories in the Yard gave me a good feeling, and I thought that tomorrow night it would be good to make love myself so that I could be busy when he called (435).

What he thinks of to himself when James Sullivan is around is
not making love but old Meg's endless screaming, for whom the
only hope is that she will die before Sullivan does (434); is
not the fellows sneaking out of the girls' dormitories but
those "sad-eyed middle-aged men [watching] them from the
bridge" while "down by the Charles happy students were making
love" (424). The old are constant, painful reminders that,
no matter how good it is to be young and to go to sleep each
night dreaming of the fulfillment of one's potential, there
are always many fierce disappointments along the way and at
the end, simply an end. Man, as Yeats said, is in love and
loves what vanishes. Even if, by some miracle, we get all we
dream of getting, the newness of all the gold seacoasts of
Illyria wears away; the treasure we store up, no matter how
big our pile, rusts.

At the end of the story, Robert avoids James Sullivan,
not simply because Sullivan depresses him with his suggestion
that Robert's life will close in on him too, will make him not
just an apprentice janitor but a man who has to be a janitor.
Far worse, Sullivan makes Robert think that every man is bound
to end up barely able to struggle through Harvard Square with
arms too tired to carry the necessities of life, helplessly
exposed to the young who—gaily brutal in their confidence
that they will never be old—call back over their shoulders at
him and Meg: "Don't break any track records, Mr. and Mrs.
Speedy Molasses" (430). No wonder Robert did not want to be
reminded of the implications of his discovery "that nothing
really matters except not being old and being alive and having
potential to dream about, and not being alone" (440). No
wonder he wanted to avoid James Sullivan, that walking proof
that soon we shall all be old and barely alive, without potential and alone.

This feeling about life underlies every detail of the
story. Take for example the corruscation of jokes about his
janitor's job that Robert starts with. First he notices with
irony the complementary absurdities of the hippies' approval
of him and of the squares' "wondering how the hell I had
managed to crash the party"; then he does a parody of the
trade-unions' fatuous rationalizations for their vicious discrimination ("I haven't got my card yet. Right now I'm just
taking lessons. There's a lot of complicated stuff . . .");
then he makes an almost metaphysical joke about the human
nature that underlies race nature ("I don't keep [Jews and
Negroes who are passing] out [of the apartment house]," he
says. "But if they get in it's my job to make their stay just
as miserable as possible. Things are changing."); finally he
finishes off the liberal he is talking to—"'Don't hate me,' I
would call after him to his considerable embarrassment.
'Somebody has to do it'" (423). But all these jokes are manifestations of a single basic feeling, Robert's deep sense of
freedom, of the infinite possibilities of his life, of the
omnipotence of youth. He is playing at being a janitor ("I
did not really have to be one and that is why I did it" [423]),
though after Jean leaves him, he feels as if "I was really a

janitor for the first time" (437). Like these opening jokes,
all the apparently random comments of the story manifest, in
one way or another, the story's controlling concern with
man's uncontrollable passion for storing up treasure that
will not last and cannot be taken along, youth's sad illusion that it is free and has all the time in the world.

QUESTIONS (page 860 of *Modern Short Stories*)

1. What aspect of trade-union policy is Robert satirizing
when he says of his job as an "apprentice janitor," "I haven't
got my card yet. Right now I'm just taking lessons. There's
a lot of complicated stuff you have to learn before you get
your card and your own building"?

2. Why, after he has said he does not keep out Jews and
Negroes who are passing but only makes their stay as miserable
as possible, does Robert add, "Things are changing"?

3. Why does Miss O'Hara ask Robert five times if the dog's
barking bothers him, force him to take a fudge brownie, and
ply him with offers of root beer, apples, and cupcakes?

4. Why does James Sullivan keep telephoning Robert at
2:00 A.M., begging him to come down to the basement for just
one drink?

5. Why does Robert go when James calls?

6. What change takes place in Robert's attitude toward
James Sullivan after Robert loses Jean?

7. What causes Robert's attitude toward James Sullivan to
change again, so that "I disliked him more every time I heard
a girl laugh on the street far below my window"?

8. Why does McPherson keep coming back to those "sad-eyed
middle aged men watching from the bridge" over the Charles
while "happy students were making love" below?

9. Why, despite his dislike of the terrible smell of the
Sullivans' flat, does Robert go there when James asks him to?

10. "Sullivan," Robert says, "did not really hate the
Jews." How, then, does he feel about them, and why?

11. Why does Robert pretend not to see James Sullivan that
last time he passes Sullivan in Harvard Square?

12. What does Robert mean when he says at the beginning of
the story that he did not really have to be a janitor, "and
that is why I did it"?

SHIRLEY JACKSON

THE FLOWER GARDEN

THE FLOWER GARDEN is a story about race prejudice, but to call it simply that is to falsify its meaning. What the story does is to confront a conception of life with someone who quite innocently fails to share it. The attitude of the local people is deeply ingrained, so habitual to them that they act on its imperatives with the simple assurance of people who are incapable of imagining any other conception of life and are thus incapable of understanding anyone unlike themselves.

The story's central figure, young Mrs. Winning, is momentarily caught between the local people and the "foreigner," at least to the extent that—like Mrs. MacLane —she has dreamed of living free in the little cottage rather than imprisoned in the dark, gloomy Victorian house that is the expression of the sense of life that governs the leading local family she has married into. She has dreamed of having a garden—in her heart, one might say, as well as around her cottage. All she has been able to do so far is plant a few nasturtiums beside the Winning house and, in a rare moment during the summer night, just touch her husband's arm and hope that he and that third Howard Winning, her son, will show her more than "the perfunctory Winning affection."

Mrs. Winning has long since given up her dream of living in the cottage and become accustomed "to the big old house at the top of the hill where her husband's family had lived for generations." All she has left is a hope that some happy young people will come to live in the cottage. Then Mrs. MacLane and her son move into it. On an "irresistible impulse" Mrs. Winning knocks on the cottage door and introduces herself to Mrs. MacLane. It is a last flash of that self that had dreamed of living in the cottage. That self can still see the Winnings and herself with a kind of objectivity, see them as like "some stylized block print from a New England wallpaper; mother, daughter, and granddaughter, with perhaps Plymouth Rock or Concord Bridge in the background." But she now belongs to the Winning family and must adopt their attitude, speaking with Winning sharpness to Tom, the grocer, about the butter, though as a girl she had dreamed of marrying Tom.

She can be friends with Mrs. MacLane and share her feelings about the cottage and the garden so long as Mrs. MacLane does nothing that runs counter to the local values that are second nature to the Winnings. So, though she feels a little awkward at the bold informality of her

approach to Mrs. MacLane and "this little house she had so
longed for," she takes the risk, and even invites Mrs.
MacLane to tea, "all without the permission of her mother-
in-law." "It had been a very long time since young Mrs.
Winning had said the first thing that came into her mind."
Winnings do not do that, but the cottage is such a contrast
to the dark old Winning house with its bolted front door and
its oddly-matched, austere bedrooms that she cannot resist
the impulse. In her innocent way Mrs. MacLane likes the
Winning house. "I love old houses," she says of it; "they
feel so secure and warm, as if lots of people had been perfectly satisfied with them and they *knew* how useful they
were." She is quite right, except that she has no idea of
what that security costs in a lack of what she calls
"warmth," any more than Mrs. Winning knows what the beauty
of the cottage and its garden costs in insecurity.

Then comes the incident with Billy Jones. Mrs. Winning
rebukes her son Howard for calling Billy a nigger, as a
Winning should. "Howard," she says, "leave Billy alone"—
altogether alone. But Mrs. MacLane, hopelessly ignorant of
the proper local way of dealing with the Joneses, treats
Billy as just another little boy. In her choked New England
way Mrs. Winning tries to make Mrs. MacLane, the "foreigner,"
understand. "The church takes care of them, of course, and
people are always giving them things." But she cannot make
Mrs. MacLane understand that she ought not to have "*that*
kind of help" when Mr. Jones comes to work for her and Billy
begins to play with her son. When it becomes clear that
Mrs. MacLane means to keep Mr. Jones, Mrs. Winning, "after
looking at her for an incredulous minute, turned and
started, indignant and embarrassed, up the hill," away from
the cottage, toward the Winning house.

Helen Harris, from a family that had been Winning
servants, can tease Mrs. Winning because they are both local
people and share the feeling that makes Mrs. Harris laugh at
Mrs. MacLane's shoes that are "so inevitably right for Mrs.
MacLane's house, and her garden," and so radically different
from Mrs. Winning's solid white oxfords. Mrs. Winning
faintly resents—a last echo of her love of what the cottage
and Mrs. MacLane stand for—Mrs. Harris's blunt advice that
she "ought to stop all this running around," but she has
begun to realize that, in "running around," she is on the
edge of offending the town's standards and may soon find
that people are telling "someone else to speak to *me*." She
is frightened when Mrs. Burton asks her if it's all right
with her if Mrs. Burton does not ask Mrs. MacLane's son to
a birthday party, so she sides with Mrs. Burton against
Mrs. MacLane, laughing with Mrs. Burton over having asked
Mrs. MacLane where her little boy is just after having said
to Mrs. Burton that "she's like a second mother to Billy,"
a quite strikingly brutal remark when we remember that
Billy's white mother has run off with a white man and
deserted her children.

Thus Mrs. Winning joins the local people in rejecting Mrs. MacLane, and the garden wilts in the summer heat. Now Mrs. Winning even finds that something in herself which she does not quite understand enjoys saying to Mrs. MacLane, "I don't know what you mean," when Mrs. MacLane asks her what has gone wrong, though some residual awareness of Mrs. MacLane's value, if not any longer, of what she represents, makes Mrs. Winning want to "take Mrs. MacLane's hand and ask her to come back and be one of the nice people again." But when Mrs. MacLane asks her if the trouble is that Mr. Jones works for her, Mrs. Winning thinks indignantly, "The nerve of her, trying to blame the colored folks." There speaks all the village's happy assurance that it is good to "the colored folks" because "people are always giving them things" and its comfortable ignorance of its brutality to them. Finally Mrs. Burton's tree falls on the garden and Mr. Jones, in helpless rage against what has gone wrong with the garden and his life in the village, tries with all his strength to lift the branch off the garden; "but the branch only gave slightly and stayed, clinging to the garden." And Mrs. Winning, without speaking, starts with great dignity back up the hill toward the old Winning house.

QUESTIONS (pages 860-861 of *Modern Short Stories*)

1. At the beginning of the story, young Mrs. Winning sees herself, her mother-in-law, and her daughter as figures in an old New England wallpaper. Why? At the same time she wishes the New England cold would not last so long. Why?

2. "Long ago" Mrs. Winning had wanted to move into the cottage. Why?

3. Why is the flower garden an important part of the cottage to both Mrs. Winning and Mrs. MacLane? What kind of flower garden has Mrs. Winning?

4. How do Mrs. Winning and Mrs. MacLane differ when Howard and Davy call Billy a nigger?

5. Why does Mr. Jones say to Mrs. MacLane, "Like to work this garden. Could be a mighty nice place"?

6. Why does Mrs. Winning send Howard straight home after Mrs. MacLane hires Mr. Jones?

7. What does the scene in the grocery store between Mrs. Winning and Mrs. Harris tell us?

8. Why is Mrs. Winning upset when Mrs. Burton asks her about inviting Davy to the birthday party?

9. Explain Mrs. Winning's response when Mrs. MacLane asks her why everyone is treating her so coldly?

10. Why does Mrs. MacLane describe leaving to Mr. Jones as going "back to the city where I'll never have to see another garden"?

J. F. POWERS
A LOSING GAME

Father Fabre in *A LOSING GAME* is a sensible man who has
taken his work at the seminary seriously and has thought, as
he says in another story, that "the chancery had wanted a
man at Trinity to compensate for the pastor" and that he was
that man. (He comes to think differently after a few more
episodes like the one described in *A Losing Game.*) Father
Fabre is, in short, a reasonably intelligent, reasonably ambitious young man who dreams of doing great things as a
priest at Trinity. He thinks of the pastor as a man who is
maneuvering against him, as he is certainly maneuvering
against the pastor whose conduct of the parish seems to him
lamentably old-fashioned and ineffectual. But the pastor
seems to out-maneuver him at every turn. Yet there is a
mystery here that is shown by the final episode of the chair.
It arises from the fact that the pastor is not maneuvering
at all; he is quite unconscious of "their little game" and
its rules. By the end of the story we recognize, despite
all Father Fabre's assumptions to the contrary, that the
pastor is merely being himself, quite uncalculatingly.

That self is certainly unusual. The pastor has no idea
of running his parish along modern lines. He has no elaborate scheme of parish activities and makes no effort to go
about among his parishioners, except as his duty to the sick
and poor requires; he has no building plans for the church;
to say nothing of being tactful and charming, he hardly ever
says anything. In short, his ideas appear old-fashioned and
crotchety, if harmless—thoroughly unenlightened by the
standards of young men fresh from the seminary, as Father
Fabre is.

These are the ideas Father Fabre fixes on as definitive
of the pastor's character. But in fact, as we see by the
end of the story, it is the pastor's character itself we
should be looking at; it is the character of a genuinely
simple man, a man with no interest in material display of
any kind, even without an idea that it is possible to have
such interests. The pastor is direct and uncalculating; and
by being so he appears to Father Fabre to outmaneuver him at
every turn, and does, quite unconsciously, bring to nothing
all Father Fabre's little schemes. The story is made amusing by being told from Father Fabre's point of view, so that
we are made to see the events as he sees them, as a sustained
battle between him and the pastor. In the end it makes the
serious point that, despite his unmodern ideas, his odd but
actually practical ways, and his total lack of public front,
the pastor is not only a supremely good man, but a successful

one, where Father Fabre, for all his up-to-dateness, though
he is not a bad man, is certainly no better than most and,
while not unintelligent, certainly no match for the pastor.

Since much of the amusement as well as the meaning of
A Losing Game depends on the pastor's innocence, it is probably a good idea to start with the ending of the story and to
investigate the pastor's motives in giving Father Fabre the
chair (476). These motives turn out to be simple, earnest
kindliness; "No one knew better than the pastor where soft
living could land a young priest, and yet there it [the
chair] was . . ." (476). The curate has been hurt in the
cellar; in the kindness of his heart, the pastor wishes to
give him what he most wants—or at least has said he most
wants—the old mohair chair. Moreover, the pastor and his
old friend, the janitor John, who has lugged the chair up
from the basement to Father Fabre's room, are waiting
eagerly outside Father Fabre's door to enjoy his delight in
this new luxury. He must pretend for them that he is truly
delighted by it. "He thought of disappointing them, of
holing up as the pastor had earlier. But he just couldn't
contend with the man any more that day" (477); as he sees it
he has been defeated and exhausted by the pastor's unremitting tactical skill.

The reference to the pastor's earlier holing up takes
us back to the opening of the story, where Father Fabre
attacks the pastor on the subject of a table, and—as he
thinks—maneuvers skillfully, though he is temporarily
balked by the pastor's retirement, ostensibly for his collar
but actually, as Father Fabre sees it, as a deliberate move
to frustrate him (469). With wonderfully misplaced cunning,
Father Fabre works it out that "though he had lost, he had
extended the pastor as never before" and this belief gives
him the energy to attempt another maneuver. He "would get
the best of [the pastor] yet" (469). He deliberately lets
John know he is going to break into the church basement,
where all the junk is stored, knowing John will alert the
pastor to the fact (470). Sure enough, this move brings the
pastor to the basement. "The pastor voiced no complaint"—
quite simply because it never occurs to him that he has one;
but Father Fabre of course takes this to mean that he "had
taken a trick honorably, according to the rules [of the
game]" and that the pastor is merely being a good sport about
it (470).

The pastor then goes through the wonderful comic but
sensible business of the light fuses and the combination pad-
lock ("Father Fabre leaned forward like an umpire for the
pitch, but saw at once that it would be impossible to lift
the combination" [471]), puts on the black cap that makes him
look "like a burglar in an insurance ad" but is no doubt in
its odd way very practical in the dusty basement, arms himself—again quite practically—against the rats, arms Father
Fabre too, and they move off into the jungle (472). It all
looks quite mad, yet when Father Fabre questions the pastor

about his way of dealing with the rats, the pastor makes
very good sense.

Father Fabre then begins to maneuver ingeniously to get
the beautiful maple table. The pastor, in his simple way,
has no notion it is beautiful; material possessions mean
nothing to him and he has not the faintest interest in their
possible beauty or value. He is full of the drabbest common-
places about men's lives—"It isn't always what we want
that's best for us" (473) and so on—that are in fact quite
true, not least in this situation: what is Father Fabre
doing yearning for "a noble piece of furniture that would do
wonders for his room"? Not that the longing is not quite
human and normal but that, ideally at least, he ought as a
priest to rise above it, as—in his odd, unostentatious way
—the pastor does.

With elaborate cunning, Father Fabre pretends to want
the maple table only mildly, but to yearn for the old, beat-
up mohair chair, on the theory that the pastor is sure to
give him what he does not want rather than what he does. He
is then hit by the richochetting .22 slug, about which the
pastor—assuming without thinking about it that Father Fabre
is as unself-regarding as he is—says, "Just a flesh wound.
You're lucky" (474). But Father Fabre, full of self-pity
and intent on having everyone treat him with the utmost consideration, is outraged by this casual good sense. "He'd
let the old burglar shoot him down and this was what he got
for it" (475).

But the pastor is not without reasonable consideration
for Father Fabre. It occurs to him that under the circumstances he might spoil Father Fabre a little by giving him a
comfortable easy chair; he knows the dangers of such things
for young priests, but no doubt thinks this a time not to
stand too rigidly on principle. Father Fabre, still playing
his hand, as he thinks, with skill, says the terrible old
easy chair is "<u>too</u> good" (475), thinking to himself that he
is both outmaneuvering the pastor and scoring off with a
sarcasm. The pastor smiles, actually with the innocent
happiness of a simple man taking Father Fabre at his word.
He is, as Father Fabre knows, "of a self-denying nature himself, famous for it in the diocese." Father Fabre concludes
from this that the pastor is pleased to have him refuse the
chair as too good for him, as the pastor no doubt is. What
he fails to see is that, in his simple way, the pastor also
sees the chair as an opportunity to do Father Fabre a kindness to make up for his unfortunate injury and is already
planning to give it to him.

The pastor has offered to remove the bullet from Father
Fabre's leg, but Father Fabre takes his injury very seriously.
He is not going to have the pastor "pinch the bullet out with
his dirty fingers" (474); he will go to the hospital, he assumes under the solicitous care of the pastor. "Better take
the car" (476) the pastor then says sensibly but to Father
Fabre's outrage. Assuming that his assessment of the danger

of his injury is correct, Father Fabre can only assume the
pastor is not driving him to the hospital because "the man
was afraid of public opinion" (476). The truth of course is
that the pastor rightly thinks it is unnecessary—or, to be
exact, is incapable of imagining that Father Fabre so exag-
gerates his danger as to think it is necessary. We know
this because, at the hospital, in spite of all Father
Fabre's efforts to make them take his injury seriously, they
only laugh at him. It is obviously hopeless for him to try
to score off the pastor by having the hospital staff report
the incident to the police. "Only a flesh wound, they said"
(476), exactly as the pastor had, quite rightly, in the
first place. So Father Fabre returns home to find the
mohair chair in his room.

    In his utter disregard for material things and for ap-
pearances, the pastor looks both ridiculous and ineffectual
rather than innocent, perhaps even saintly, as in fact he
is. By being so he completely defeats all Father Fabre's
carefully planned maneuvers—without ever noticing that
Father Fabre is conducting a campaign against him.

QUESTIONS (page 861 of *Modern Short Stories*)

    1. Why in fact does the pastor give Father Fabre the
chair at the end of the story?

    2. What happens at the beginning of the story when
Father Fabre asks for the table?

    3. Why does he think this happens?

    4. What does he do about it?

    5. What does Father Fabre think of the pastor's prepa-
rations for going into the basement?

    6. What are we meant to think of them?

    7. Why does the pastor not respond to the table as Father
Fabre does but accept Father Fabre's praise of the chair?

    8. Compare Father Fabre's reaction to his wound and the
pastor's; which is more reasonable?

    9. What does the scene at the hospital show us?

    10. What final conclusion about the pastor does the story
lead us to draw?

DAN JACOBSON

BEGGAR MY NEIGHBOUR

Mr. Jacobson's story is delicately balanced between realism and symbolism, perhaps because for Mr. Jacobson reality itself is. Mr. Jacobson wants us to think simultaneously about race relations as a personal experience and as a sociological problem. He means his story to represent a convincing individual experience that also clearly implies the generalized attitudes that constitute the social problem. He does so by showing us in convincing detail Michael's schoolboy experience with the two piccanins; and then, by twice resorting to devices that allow him to explore Michael's unconscious, he shows us the powerful, irrational feelings that make Michael representative of all ordinary white people confronted by Africans. The first of these devices is Michael's addiction, as an only child, to daydreaming, when the more or less unconscious feelings come close to the surface (481); the second is the fever dream that constitutes the climax of the story (485-486) and shows us a simplified, exaggerated, and therefore revealing image of the conflict of feelings within Michael.

These devices are not strikingly novel in themselves. What is remarkable about them in this story is the way they are used, the way Mr. Jacobson keeps the events that occur in them just a single, logical step beyond reality. Michael's fantasies are very close to his actual relations with the piccanins, partly for this reason and partly because the actual relations have in their turn a faintly fantastic air, are given delicate touches of strangeness. As a consequence, as we read the story, the life of reality and the life of dreams fade into one another and we feel the continuity between Michael's conscious experience with the two African children and the fantasy life of the powerful, unconscious responses—common to him and all white men—that underlies his conscious experience. Thus the story becomes a fable of race relations without ceasing to be a realistic story of a personal experience.

There is a fine illustration of this effect in the very first paragraph (477). Walking home from school through the curiously empty streets of the white man's orderly middle-class world, Michael sees the two African children suddenly rise before him, as if the alien and blinding glare of African light, which no amount of neat suburbia can wholly exclude, "had suddenly condensed itself into two little piccanins with large eyes set in their round, black faces" (477). Michael is not conscious of anything like this. The phrase the boy uses—"Stukkie brood" is the phrase at

Michael's school for all African children, and hearing it
makes him think of these two children, not as human like
himself, but as the stock, disinfected, mechanical creatures
to which the schoolboy cliché reduces all Africans; these
two are as remote for Michael as robots. In fact, they are
"about Michael's age, about twelve" (477), but their lives
differ unimaginably from Michael's. He is the only child of
comfortable, devoted parents; these creatures are parentless
and homeless. Apart from home, the shaping force in
Michael's life is school; these two do not go to school (478).

But as Michael is moving casually away from this first
encounter with them, he glances back and sees them holding
hands. It is not much, but it does make Michael conscious
that these creatures have in common with human beings the
capacity for affection; to that extent they become something
like him—perhaps as a clever dog might—and he thinks of
"how hungry they must be." Michael is a decent, kindly boy
and so, without thinking about it much one way or the other,
he takes the two home, gives them bread, and, with twelve-
year-old solemnity, repeats with them the ritual his parents
use with him by making them say thank you. It is a natural
image of the white man's paternalistic stance. The two
children stand there holding the bread, the girl's mouth
working a little with anticipation and Michael confronts
them, wanting to "share their pleasure" in eating the bread,
half with a natural fellow feeling for their hunger, half
with an unconscious, corrupting sense of power over them; it
is a wonderfully suggestive moment, and it is reinforced by
Michael's innocently revealing attitude at their second
meeting. "What," Michael calls out jovially when he catches
his second sight of them, "Another piece of bread?" This is
the dangerous joviality of the assured superior. A moment
later we also catch the first faint note of the bullying
attitude that always accompanies that attitude: "And how do
you know that I am going to give you bread?" Michael says to
them (479).

It is therefore a shock to Michael, behavior unsuited
to the role he has unconsciously cast them in, when he finds
them still waiting after dark that night to thank him (480).
It is true he has taught them this trick, but this is to use
the ritual, not as a trick, but as a gesture of human
feeling. It disquiets Michael and his first impulse is to
reject this implicit claim to be recognized as human like
himself. "You mustn't wait," he says to them (480). But
their act has made him unavoidably aware of them; he even
notices, half-consciously, the slightly sexual pathos of
"the nakedness and puniness of [the girl's] black thighs"
(480). As a result, his first impulse of rejection is followed almost immediately by a second impulse of affection;
he wants to give them something, and hands them his torch.
Like the street lights that blaze up a moment later, the
torch is suggestive. Africa is, we remember from the first
scene in the story, flooded with a glare of natural light so
intense that it is like darkness. Like all whites and
blacks, these children really see each other only intermit-

tently, in unexpected flashes of artificial illumination.
Then, as the two African children scamper away with the
torch, "the thought of his own generosity helped to console
[Michael] for the regret he couldn't help feeling when he
saw the torch carried away from him" (481).

This alternation of rejection—of a desire to think of
these black neighbors as unhuman—and of acceptance—of a desire to love and be loved (though always as an unquestioned
superior) dominates Michael's daydreams. In these dreams
there is "ample scope to display his kindness, generosity,
courage and decisiveness"; but strictly *de haut en bas*.
There is never any real relation between him and these two
piccanins, as there never is in actuality; "they were too
dirty, too ragged, too strange, too persistent" (481). In
this state of mind he shows them his pen-and-pencil set.
They are to admire it as something far beyond their humble
ambitions that is, however, something quite proper for
Michael to possess. But they surprise and disturb Michael
by being human here too. They are not content merely to
look; they long to possess as much as Michael. Once more
Michael is shocked to discover that they have needs and desires like his. Again his impulse is to deny their possession of such feelings, not just to refuse to give them the
pen-and-pencil set but to assert indignantly the wrongness
of their even desiring it. Then he tries to put them back
into the roles he has cast them in from the start, to return
the situation to what he has wanted from the start to suppose it. "I'll tell Dora to bring you some bread," he says,
and flees (483). But when Dora takes the bread to them,
they have disappeared, as if they refused to accept bread
alone. Michael understands what has happened well enough to
expect to feel guilty (483). He is surprised that his only
conscious feeling is relief, the relief of a mistaken belief
that he has now escaped these African children with their
implicit demands on his humanity, his affection, that he is
unconsciously reluctant to accept.

When they return, his unconscious guilt fixes on their
dumb, helpless need, what seems to him a lack of proper
dignity, as an excuse for scorning them; he starts to tease
them harshly, in a bullying way, though he cannot somehow
reject them entirely. Now his fantasies are full of
brutality instead of heroic kindness. But instead of being
driven away, the children come oftener and oftener. Finally
Michael orders them never to reappear. "From then on they
came every day" (485). Thus, the more violently Michael
strives to rid himself of this silent demand on his humanity,
the more these two haunt him. "He hated them now; even
more, he began to dread them" (485). His old, comfortable
sense of power, whether as kindness or bullying, is gone;
these two will not stay put in the roles of pets. In some
inescapable, frightening way they demand Michael's full
humanity, his serious love—or hate.

Then he falls into his fever dream. The dream begins
with an echo of his earlier awareness of the girl's thighs;

he dreams of committing "lewd, cruel acts upon the bare-thighed girl" (486); her brother shrieks "to tell the empty street [where Michael had first seen them] of what he was doing." Finally he dreams of smashing in the boy's head; but "the one remaining eyeball still stared unwinkingly at him" (486). Then "Michael thought he was awake," though he has only moved into the other half of his dream, the part where he longs to love and accept these two black children instead of to hate and destroy them. In this half of his dream, he suddenly thinks that they—being human like him—must have been doing to him in their dreams what he has been doing to them and he finds himself weeping, for them all.

Now he feels, "with the same [oversimplified] fixity of decision that had been his in his dreams of violence and torture," that he must love them. Never having touched them before, he now caresses them. Taking them by the hands in imitation of the gesture of affection he had first noticed between them, he leads them into his own private world, and for the first time they smile at him. At the beginning of this half of his dream, he had asked them, as he had the night he had given them the torch, "What are you waiting for?" Now, in his own room, he gives them, not stukkie brood, but what he had thought it impossible to give; kisses them both and then asks, "What do you want now?" But they want nothing, now. Taking hands, they move off, stopping only for "a silent, tentative gesture of farewell" (487-488). Then, suddenly, Michael truly wakes up, filled with grief that this episode has been only a dream. He never sees these two piccanins again.

Beggar My Neighbour thus gives us, with marvelous honesty, the terrifying struggle that all white men go through, the struggle between unconscious rejection—with all its uncontrollable hate and its temptations to exploit the white man's power and the African's helplessness—and the impulse to love our dark neighbors. It also reminds us that probably (as a white man Mr. Jacobson can only infer this and he does not attempt to describe it) they have much the same feelings about us that we have about them. Best of all, perhaps, the story does this in such a way as to make us know it as a convincing individual experience and at the same time to show us that Michael's experience is a paradigm of all men's.

The story's title obviously reminds us of "Love thy neighbor." But it is equally a reminder of the card game for children (of "eight to twelve," Hoyle says) called "Beggar My Neighbour," in which the object is to reduce one's opponent to beggary by the sheer luck of turning up from one's pack the face cards and aces at the right moments.

QUESTIONS (page 862 of *Modern Short Stories*)

1. How does Michael feel about the two African children when he first meets them? Does he think of them as like him?

2. Why is Michael shocked when the two African children wait, long after dark, to thank him the second time he gives them bread?

3. Why is Michael upset when the two African children gently ask him to give them his pen-and-pencil set?

4. Why, after Michael refuses to give them the pen-and-pencil set, do the African children disappear before Dora can bring them bread?

5. Why does Michael begin to hate and even to dread these two children?

6. Why does Michael, when he has a fever, first dream of being lewdly cruel to the girl and brutally violent to the boy and then dream of taking them by the hands and kising them?

7. Why is this story called *Beggar My Neighbour*?

8. Why does the author make Michael an only child who daydreams a great deal?

THOMAS PYNCHON

ENTROPY

ENTROPY is both an odd story, and one that is superbly written, with striking precision of observation and range of perception, and with a dazzling virtuosity of expression. How exactly right is that "15-inch speaker . . . bolted into the top of a wastepaper basket" (489). The quartet has the same authenticity. They know it was Gerry Mulligan's "Love for Sale" that had neither piano, guitar, nor accordion to provide "root chords," not "I'll Remember April." They find irresistible (or perhaps it is Mr. Pynchon who does) the nostalgic, period charm of their songs: "'You want me to sing it? A cigarette that bears a lipstick's traces, an airline ticket to romantic places.' Krinkle scratched his head. 'These Foolish Things, you mean!'" (500-501).

The fullness and precision of details like this makes frequent occasions for the kind of historical irony that gives the story's characters the quaint pathos of distance.

> This was early in February of '57 and back then [all of three years before the story was published] there were a lot of American expatriates around Washington, D.C., who would talk, every time they met you, about how someday they were going over to Europe for real but right now it seemed they were working for the government. Everyone saw a fine irony in this. . . . They would haunt Armenian delicatessens for weeks at a stretch. . . . They would have affairs with sultry girls from Andalucia or the Midi who studied economics at Georgetown (489).

It sounds like F. Scott Fitzgerald—except that Mr. Pynchon is always putting out signals to show that he knows it sounds like F. Scott Fitzgerald, that in some way it is parody, as when Callisto remembers "the sad sick dance in Stravinsky's *L'Histoire du Soldat*" and thinks:

> what had tango music been for them after the war, what meanings had he missed in all the stately coupled automatons in the *cafés-dansants*. . . . And how many musicians were left after Passchendaele, after the Marne? . . . Yet with violin and tympani Stravinsky had managed to communicate in that tango the same exhaustion, the same airlessness one saw in the slicked-down youths who were trying to imitate Vernon Castle and their mistresses, who simply did not care. *Ma maîtresse.* Celeste. Returning to Nice after the second war he

> found that cafe replaced by a perfume shop which
> catered to American tourists. And no secret
> vestige of her in the cobblestones or in the old
> pension next door; no perfume to match her breath
> heavy with the sweet Spanish wine she always
> drank (498-499).

It is wonderfully done—those "automatons in the *cafés-dansants*" that evoke the stiff, doll-like, and romantic figures of the age of Irene and Vernon Castle; that graceful modulation of memory from these people of World War I to *"Ma maîtresse.* Celeste" of World War II; and how wittily romantic to think that no perfume from the shop that replaced Celeste's cafe could match her wine-sweet breath. Callisto is composing, as in a poem, images of exhaustion and airlessness—of the void of some cultural equilibrium—from the history of the twentieth century.

What is troubling about Callisto's poem is its air of self-indulgence, of too easy sentiment. Its images are delicately commonplace, consciously literary. It is like an elegant montage of old newsreel clips from both wars. And every so often a sentence or phrase crosses the line into the obvious clichés of such writing ("And how many musicians were left after Passchendaele, after the Marne?" ". . . their mistresses, who simply did not care"). Those cobblestones and that old pension look more like a scene from an early reel of *Casablanca* than experience. The same air invades the story's account of Callisto's present life. Where is its reality? Are we expected to accept Aubade, that dawn-dream vision of a girl part French, part Annamese, with her exquisitely orderly aesthetic imagination? Or is she a pure image, a figure not in the least probable except as a fancy that satisfies one of man's most persistent longings, real only as a symbol? This is a question that arises about every image in this story, where images appear to have no firm roots in actuality, to exist seriously only as idea—no matter how minutely Mr. Pynchon observes the objects that constitute them.

It is as if Mr. Pynchon truly felt the Fitzgerald kind of nostalgia but recognized that this was an attitude impossible any more to experience directly, without echoing earlier expressions of it—and perhaps, too, an attitude that hovers on the edge of a special kind of sentimentality. The past was never what nostalgia thinks it until it became the past, the "lost and gone"; nostalgia is not a feeling about what has passed: it is a feeling about the pastness of it. But this feeling is nonetheless very important to Mr. Pynchon, for what you might call ontological reasons. It is a way of resisting time's destruction of the meanings and values that accumulate around things people have lived with and through. The "sure obliteration"—the phrase is Wallace Stevens'—of these things is an entropy as frightening as the entropy Gibbs thought must overtake the physical universe. It is not, of course, in any scientifically literal sense, entropy. Mr. Pynchon gets from the entropy accumulating in the physical universe to the "entropy" accumulating in individual lives and the lives of

cultures by metaphor. Why not? If images in the mind are
more reliable, if possibly not more real, than the alleged
objects these images stand for, are not correspondences among
them—metaphors—more reliable than some set of equations that
purport to represent a process linking the alleged objects?
Mr. Pynchon has noticed that even scientists—or at least
mathematicians—have taken to using the idea of entropy meta-
phorically, in information theory, to describe the meaningless
randomness of "noise."

Love and Power, Henry Adams's Virgin and Dynamo, are
alike, then (491), and what makes the nebulae precess and the
boccie ball spin makes the world of human experience go 'round
too. If Power is subject to slow decay, an irreversible
accumulation of entropy, so too must human experience be. If
Clausius is right, "that the entropy of an isolated system
always continually increases" (494), then each human being and
every culture as well as each galaxy and every engine must be
moving inexorably from the Condition of the Less to the Condition of the More Probable, declining into a powerless, love-
less, indiscriminate chaos. This correspondence is, to be
sure, put forward, not by the author, but by Callisto, who is
at the same time described—in a phrase borrowed from the unhealthy sentimentality of Shakespeare's Orsino—as "in the sad
dying fall of middle age" (494).

But, as so often in his work, Mr. Pynchon seems to be
asking himself in this story if the experience of his time does
not force one to some such view as Callisto's. Do we not live
in an America where everyone dreams of going to Europe "for
real," but meanwhile works for the government? Have things,
possibly, always been something like this? It is certainly
true, at least, that the rich proud cost of felt meanings embodied in things—no matter how indestructibly "brass eternal"
they have been—has always been destroyed by time. In an
effort they cannot resist making even while they recognize its
uselessness, writers like Mr. Pynchon struggle to remember, to
resurrect in imagination the past, as if by doing so they can
stop the process by which entropy accumulates until life—for
an age, for an individual—reaches final equilibrium. "Sade,
of course. And Temple Drake, gaunt and hopeless in her little
park in Paris, at the end of *Sanctuary*. Final equilibrium.
Nightwood. And the tango" (498). Again, this is not the
author's meditation; it is Callisto's. But Callisto's limiting
defects—his inclination to a sophisticated, Wallace-Stevens-
like sentimentality, to the cultivated man's clichés—are not
such as to destroy his point, only such as to allow Mr. Pynchon
to have his cake and eat it too.

What thus makes it difficult for the reader to know where
he is in Mr. Pynchon's story is its essential idea, its conviction that the most significant characteristic of life itself—
or at least of the consciousness of life—is our uncertainty of
where we are. The only things Mr. Pynchon is sure of are the
images that fill his imagination. These images are therefore
for him not perceptions of solid, intractible objects that

exist independent of his idea of them. They are final terms;
and for him reality is a theory about these images that orders
them as ideas and, if possible, makes them interesting, surprising, entertaining. The heroine of Mr. Pynchon's second
novel, *The Crying of Lot 49*, tracks down, like some spiritual
private eye, what she believes is a secret postal system that
has, for centuries, kept communications open among the unoffi-
cial undergrounds organized around special perceptions of
meaning and value, undergrounds that refuse to conform to the
values of established society and therefore dare not keep in
touch through its official communications system. But Oedipa
is never sure she is not suffering from hallucinations or even
a put-on by the enormously rich (and highly symbolic) lover
who has died and left her the executor of his will.

> Either way [she thinks], they'll call it paranoia.
> They. Either you have stumbled indeed, without the
> aid of LSD or other idole alkaloids, onto a secret
> richness and concealed density of dream; onto a net-
> work by which X number of Americans are truly com-
> municating whilst reserving their lies, recitations
> of routine, arid betrayals of spiritual poverty, for
> the official government system; maybe onto a real
> alternative to the exitlessness, to the absence of
> surprise to life, that harrows the head of everybody
> American you know, and you too, sweetie (170).

She sees very clearly where thinking in this way leaves
her.

> . . . there either was some Tristero [the under-
> ground she thinks she has found] beyond the appear-
> ance of the legacy America [her rich lover has left
> her], or there was just America and if there was just
> America then it seemed the only way she could con-
> tinue, and manage to be at all relevant to it, was as
> an alien, unfurrowed, assumed full circle into some
> paranoia (182).

The correspondences Oedipa perceives are not among things—at
least she is never sure they exist among things, out there in
actuality. All she is sure of is that they exist among
images in her mind, so that for her the operation of the mind
is not a process of checking hypothesis by objective observation of nature; the only positive exercise of the intelligence
available to her is a search for correspondences among the
images in her mind, a making of metaphors, an attempt to
arrange images in such a way that they make an imagined—and
perhaps also imaginary—world that can be endured, "some
secret richness and concealed density of dream," not "just
America." "The act of metaphor then," Oedipa thinks, "was a
thrust at truth or a lie, depending where you were: inside,
safe, outside, lost" (129). Live in the belief that the world
actually is what the metaphor creates and you are "safe";
otherwise, you are "lost," are in "just America," the present,
the obvious, a place so dull and terrible that any escape—

either Oedipa's "orbiting ecstasy of a true paranoia" (182)
or her husband's LSD—is preferable.

What Mr. Pynchon does in *Entropy* is what Oedipa Maas does
in *The Crying of Lot 49*; that is, he constructs a metaphor "of
God knows how many parts." Since the metaphorical relations
among the images of the mind are the final reality, Mr.
Pynchon's main business as a writer is to remark them; like
Callisto, he seeks correspondences (498), the full implications of which he does not—perhaps cannot—always make
entirely clear.

The basic correspondence for this story is the one
signaled by its epigraph from *Tropic of Cancer* between the
entropy accumulating in the physical universe and the "entropy"
accumulating in the consciousness of men. "The weather will
continue bad" as the physical universe moves toward a powerless and chaotic equilibrium, and "there will be more death,
more despair" as the cultural universe does the same thing.
Both Meatball and Callisto—the wholly inelegant hero and the
wholly elegant one who live in flats one above the other but
have no contact except random noise (and whose stories come to
us in arbitrary alternation), have lived on Callisto's
machiavellian assumption that *virtù* and *fortuna* are roughly
50-50 and that one therefore has a fighting chance to experience meaningfulness, to live Oedipa Maas's life of otherness,
of "the secret richness and concealed density of dream," and
perhaps even give it some sort of aesthetic order that will
focus its meaning. But this assumption has now been badly
skewed, consciously for Callisto by Gibbs's theory, implicitly
for Meatball, who discovers that half of what he says to Saul
is only noise, not information—"It's a bitch, ain't it," as
Saul rightly says—and that the quartet now plays silently.
What Gibbs's "spindly maze of equations" suggested, that not
only galaxy and engine but human being and culture "evolve
spontaneously toward the Condition of the More Probable" (494),
has now to be faced by both Callisto and Meatball.

They have worked in opposite ways to live meaningfully,
ways determined by their ages or by the generations they belong to, but their objects have been the same. Callisto has
built himself an hermetically sealed flat, "a tiny enclave of
regularity in the city's chaos, alien to the vagaries of the
weather, of national politics, of any civil disorder"; he has
"perfected its ecological balance," and "with the help of the
girl its artistic harmony" (491). It is alive, this system,
but the motions of its life are birdlike and as stylized, as
"integral as the rhythms of a perfectly-executed mobile." The
girl can make it so because she lives in an imagined world of
musical order. ". . . she lived on her own curious and lonely
planet, where the clouds and the odor of poincianas, the
bitterness of wine and the accidental fingers at the small of
her back or feathery against her breasts came to her reduced
inevitably to the terms of sound: of music which emerged at
intervals from a howling darkness of discordancy" (491), exactly as information emerges—if at all and perhaps only sub-
jectively—from "noise," the random chaos of meaningless sound.

The architectonic purity of her world was constantly threatened by such hints of anarchy: gaps and excrescences and skew lines, and a shifting or tilting of planes to which she had continually to readjust lest the whole structure shiver into a dis- array of discrete and meaningless signals. Callisto had described the process once as a kind of "feed- back": she crawled into dreams each night [like Oedipa Maas of *The Crying of Lot 49*] with a sense of exhaustion, and a desperate resolve never to relax that vigilance (494).

This musical structure in Aubade's mind rises "in a tangled tracery: arabesques of order competing fugally with the im- provised discords of the party downstairs, which peaked some- times in cusps and ogees of noise," Gothic improvisations by life as against the neoclassic order of Aubade's sleepless imagination, "that precious signal-to-noise ratio whose delicate balance required every calorie [of heat-energy] of her strength" (498).

Meatball meets the common problem by opening his door— and even his windows—wide to all experience of whatever kind until his party reaches a climax of disorder and noncommunica- tion and "the noise . . . a sustained, ungodly crescendo" (501). Anything alive and moving, that has a chance of being meaningful, is welcome to Meatball, who is apparently hopeful of reducing it to some minimal order—"to calm everybody down, one by one," to keep the "party from deteriorating into total chaos," final equilibrium (501)—as Callisto, having estab- lished perfect order in his hermetically sealed room, hopes to keep his sick bird alive. For Meatball, "the day before it had snowed and the day before that there had been winds of gale force and before that the sun had made the city glitter bright as April, though the calendar read early February" (490). But for Callisto, "for three days now, despite the changeful weather, the mercury had stayed at 37 degrees Fahren- heit"; and when his sick bird dies, he is convinced that his efforts to communicate life to it, "or a sense of life," have failed because the transference of heat-energy has ceased (502). (This is a little puzzling: 37 degrees Fahrenheit is a reasonable outside temperature for Washington in February, but 37 degrees Centigrade is bodily heat—98.6 Fahrenheit. Possibly this play on temperatures is meant to suggest that human power depends on the gradient between the temperature of the human body and normal natural winter temperature, and that "the final absence of all motion" will occur when they level off at the normal natural temperature.)

These are the dominant images of *Entropy*, but a host of minor images surround and support them with a complication of implications that appear endless. There is, for example, the story's omnipresent musical image of the aesthetic order imagination imposes. It creeps in everywhere as verbal figure: the February weather is "a *stretto* passage in the year's fugue" (490); Callisto and Aubade are "scraps of melody" from an

"intricate canon," they move into "series of modulations"
(499), and finally resolve into a "tonic of darkness" (444).
But this image also sends out branches and capillaries
throughout the story in the form of further correspondences
(such as the architectural image used to describe the musical
structures in Aubade's mind), or as actual events (such as
the flicked cigarette ashes that "dance around" in the
speaker cone [489], like molecules moving in thermodynamic
order), or as symbolic subplot (such as the actions of the
Duke di Angelis quartet).

The quartet's one recording before they took to playing
in silence, *Songs from Outer Space*, sounds like a slightly
ironic parody of a sophisticated popular song. But there are
no songs of outer space; outer space is soundless ("Just
listen," as Duke says. "You'll catch on" [500]). "Back to
the old drawing board," says Meatball when the quartet gets
mixed up in its silent improvisation. "No, man," Duke says,
"back to the airless void" (501). The outer spaces of consciousness about which the quartet is making its silent music
are where people know Oedipa Maas's "orbiting ecstasy of true
paranoia" (182). With this music a man is never sure he is
with anyone else, and may discover himself hard at work on
"I'll Remember April" when the next man is playing "These
Foolish Things."

> "I have this new conception, man," Duke said.
> "You remember your namesake. You remember Gerry."
> "No," said Meatball. "I'll remember April, if
> that's any help."
> "As a matter of fact," Duke said, "it was Love
> for Sale" (499-500).

Duke's new conception "is to think everything. Roots, line,
everything" ("Well," he says modestly in a characteristic
example of the kind of irony Mr. Pynchon directs at himself,
"there are a few bugs to work out" [500]). Duke is carrying
to its logical limit not only Gerry Mulligan's omission of
piano, guitar, or accordion but the earlier reduced instrumen-
tation of Stravinsky's tango ("Almost as if any tiny troupe of
saltimbanques had set about conveying the same information as
a full pit-orchestra" [498]).

Three days earlier—Meatball did remember—"the city
glitter[ed] bright as April, though the calendar read early
February" (490). But (and here the story makes another of its
leaps into the metaphysical reality of correspondence) since

> the soul (*spiritus, rauch, pneuma*) is nothing, sub-
> stantially, but air; it is only natural that warpings
> in the atmosphere should be recapitulated in those
> who breathe it. So . . . . there are private meander-
> ings, linked to the climate as if this spell were a
> *stretto* passage in the year's fugue . . . months one
> can easily spend in fugue, because oddly enough,
> later on, winds, rains, passions of February and

        March are never remembered in that city, it is as
        if they had never been (490).

—and who knows, perhaps had not. In any event, Meatball will
not remember April, which, "as Sarah Vaughan has put it,
. . . will be a little late this year" (490)—delayed, no
doubt, about as long as the final equilibrium of perfected
entropy can delay it.

        Correspondences like these, each with its hint of a
meaning, are everywhere in the story. For instance, what
Saul's wife Miriam threw at him was a *Handbook of Chemistry
and Physics*; when it missed Saul, it broke a window, and Saul
"reckon[ed] something in her broke too" (495), and in him, as
something broke in Callisto and Aubade and perhaps in the
universe itself at the time Aubade broke the window of their
flat. Saul has entered Meatball's flat through the window
("Sort of wet out," he says [493]). Saul and Miriam had been
quarreling about communication theory, "which of course makes
it very hilarious": somehow, the "precious signal-to-noise
ratio" has gone awry for Miriam. "She'll be back," Meatball
says, and Saul says, "No" (495).

        "Tell a girl: 'I love you.' No trouble with two-
        thirds of that, it's a closed circuit. Just you
        and she. But that nasty four-letter word in the
        middle, that's the one you have to look out for.
        Ambiguity. Redundance. Irrelevance, even.
        Leakage. All this noise. Noise screws up your
        signal, makes for disorganization in the circuit"
        (496).

the disorganization that information theory calls "entropy."
Saul concludes that "successful" marriages are compromises:
"You never run at top efficiency" (497). They are, in short,
closed circuits in which entropy is steadily increasing and
"the secret richness and concealed density of dream" steadily
decreasing.

        "Entropy" is a dance of metaphors, arabesques of ordering
correspondences that have been created, like the architec-
tonically pure world in Aubade's imagination, as a counter-
image to that image of man's culture and consciousness
gradually sinking into an equilibrium of meaninglessness
that is the subject of the story.

QUESTIONS (pages 862-863 of *Modern Short Stories*)

1. What is the effect of the story's nostalgic, historically analytical way of describing the way things were back there in '57?

2. How do you think the story wants us to respond to Callisto's description of how he went back to Nice after World War II looking for his mistress Celeste?

3. What is entropy?

4. How is the idea of entropy involved in Callisto's anxiety about the temperature outside? About the death of the sick bird?

5. The implication in Henry Adams' image of the Virgin and the Dynamo is that inhuman power and human love are alike; if that is so, what kind of entropy must operate in human affairs?

6. In information theory, by a metaphorical extension the tendency for noise to increase and meaningful sound to decrease is called "entropy"; had this fact any bearing on Pynchon's introduction of the conversation between Meatball and Saul?

7. Has it any bearing on the fact that the Duke di Angelis quartet has taken to playing soundless music?

8. Was Callisto right in agreeing with Machiavelli that in life the influences of *virtù* and *fortuna* are roughly equal?

9. What has Aubade in common with the di Angelis quartet? Why?

10. Identify some of the musical figures of speech in the story and explain why Pynchon uses them so frequently.

11. What metaphysical proposition do you think *Entropy* is trying to persuade you to accept?

JAMES AGEE
THE WAITING

THE WAITING is a quietly intense account of how a
person learns to face disaster and suffering. What gives
the story its peculiar power is the ordinariness of the
people and their circumstances. Not only is there nothing
unusual in the conditions that surround these people and no
recourse to rhetoric in Agee's description of them; there is
nothing exceptional about the people themselves: Mary experiences what any ordinary person must experience when confronted by sudden disaster, because she is herself an ordinary person. If we remind ourselves, at the end of the
story when Andrew comes in and Mary knows that Jay is dead,
how, at the beginning of the story, Mary rushed downstairs
to prepare the bedroom for him, just in case Jay's injury is
slight enough to allow him to be brought home instead of
taken to the hospital, we will see how far Mary has come
during the waiting. But each step of that change has been
so slight and so overwhelmingly natural that as we follow
the process, we are hardly aware of any change at all.

The way Agee gives his description of this quite complicated, ordinary experience its special intensity is by
imagining in minute detail every move Mary makes and every
thought that passes through her head. There is a minimum of
explanation of Mary's thoughts and actions; by telling us
what Aunt Hannah, who has lived through a similar experience
herself, sees in Mary's conduct, Agee gives us what little
we need to have in the way of general statement about Mary;
there is no false mystification in the story. But its power
comes from Agee's showing us what happens in such convincing
detail that we know for ourselves exactly what the state of
Mary's mind and feelings at any moment is.

The first thing to notice, then, is the overwhelming
naturalness of the story. The man who calls Mary from
Powell Station is quite ordinary, tactful and considerate
but not particularly subtle; he does not really succeed in
concealing the fact that Jay is dead. When Mary asks about
sending a doctor, the man says, "That's all right, ma'am.
Just some man that's kin." Mary says she will send
her brother right away and thinks, "Walter's auto" (504).
Here is the instinctive, unconscious human impulse to evade
a terrible truth until the consciousness can prepare itself
to face that truth; Mary's mind is busy with planning something she can do; about death she can do nothing, and that
she cannot yet consciously face.

Mary's immediately subsequent conduct follows the same

pattern. From somewhere deep in her subconscious there rises
a terror she can hardly explain; "she found she was scarcely
standing"; "she drew another deep breath; she felt as if her
lungs were not large enough" (504). The possibility of
Jay's death that causes this terror is pushing at her consciousness and, by busying herself getting the downstairs
bedroom ready, she attempts to suppress it. "By the way he
talks he may be—She whipped off the coverlet, folded it,
and smoothed the pad"; "although he did say it's serious, or
it can . . . A light blanket, this weather. Two, case it
turns cool" (506). The details of the bedmaking (smoothing
the pad, taking the pillow between her teeth, etc.) are not
only minute and accurate; they are professional, as one
might say, the things an experienced housekeeper does. They
are not only what Mary is doing but what she is making a
desperate effort to fix her whole attention on so that the
awful possibility that Jay may be dead cannot emerge in her
conscious mind. The strain of trying to do so is so great
that it almost stupifies her: "for a few seconds she was
not sure where she was or why she was doing this" (506).
This process can also be seen during the early part of the
waiting with Aunt Hannah, who has to make an effort to let
Mary busy herself with tea and talk to avoid thinking of
what she knows somewhere must be the truth. Aunt Hannah is
thinking that "it was probably better for her not to face it
if she could help until it had to be faced" (509).

After a time Mary is ready to approach, at least at a
tangent, the possibility of Jay's death. "Why didn't I ask?
. . . I didn't even ask! How serious! Where is he hurt!
Is he living or dead!'" (511). That last sentence is spoken
as if it were an extravagant idea, used merely to illustrate
how she had not asked the simplest question. But, though
Mary may not yet be consciously facing it, it is really what
she means when she says waiting to find out is what is
unbearable. "We both know, Hannah said to herself. But
it's better if you bring yourself to say it" (512). Mary
then backs off from the terrible thought that Jay is dead
and again starts circling futilely over what the man could
have meant by saying the accident was serious. She is
further reprieved by her father's telephone call and by the
discussion it leads to about the family's disapproval of
her marriage to Jay (514-517).

But as such discussions will, this one has an unfortunate accidental consequence. "In these past few months,
Aunt Hannah," Mary is saying, "we've come to a—kind of
harmoniousness that . . ." Then she breaks down at this
sudden vivid thought of her happiness with her husband and
blurts out, "it's just like a post-mortem!" (515-516).
This is Mary's last real evasion; in a moment she is saying;
"quiet and amazed," "If he dies, if he's dead, Aunt Hannah,
I don't know what I'll do. I just don't know what I'll do"
(516). She is, as Aunt Hannah realizes, "absorbed beyond
feeling . . . in what she was beginning to find out and to
face" (516-517). "Her soul," as Aunt Hannah puts it, "is
beginning to come of age." She can now face the truth that

"whatever is, is. . . . all there is now is to be ready for
it, strong enough for it, whatever it may be. . . . It's all
that matters because it's all that's possible" (517). Like
all human disasters, this one had come on Mary when she was
quite unprepared for it; like them all, it could not have
been prepared for, since no one can possibly know what to
prepare for until he has experienced it. "It just has to be
lived through" (518).

        Mary then prays and—marvelous touch—needs to go to
the bathroom; "it was this silly, strenuous, good, humble
cluttering of animal needs that saw us through sane, fully
as much as prayer," Aunt Hannah thinks (520). Mary can now
say, "But I'm all but certain he is [dead], all the same"—
and a moment later, "Oh I do beseech my God that it not be
so" (522). But it is, and it is Mary who has the sanity and
the courage to say so when her brother Andrew comes in, unable to speak (522-523).

QUESTIONS (page 863 of *Modern Short Stories*)

    1. What do we learn from the telephone call to Mary?

    2. What do we learn about Mary's thoughts from the way
she reacts to that call? From her immediate thought of how
Andrew will get to Powell Station? From her rushing to make
the bed in the downstairs bedroom? From the thoughts that
go through her conscious mind as she does so?

    3. Why is it that, during the process, she has a moment
of not being "sure where she was or why she was doing this"?

    4. What is Mary thinking when she says to Aunt Hannah,
"Is he living or dead"?

    5. What happens when Mary starts to think about the im-
proved relations between her and her husband?

    6. What does Aunt Hannah deduce from Mary's saying,
"whatever is, is"?

    7. What is the point of Mary's having to go to the
bathroom?

    8. Where does it tell us that it is Mary who says her
husband is dead when Andrew comes into the house?

PART THREE

D. H. LAWRENCE

ODOR OF CHRYSANTHEMUMS

ODOR OF CHRYSANTHEMUMS is a story characteristic of
Lawrence's strange, powerful, romantic vision of experience.
(For a fuller description of Lawrence's vision, see the
analysis of *The White Stocking*, pp. 128-133 below.) The
story gives us an intimate sense of the everyday life of the
miner's family; one feels he has lived in that house with
the handsome, embittered Elizabeth and the two children.
Lawrence produces this effect the way any good writer does,
by a skillful selection of precise details that will evoke
the experience of that life for us. Ford Madox Ford once
analyzed the first paragraph of *Odor of Chrysanthemums* to
illustrate how a good writer works, pointing out, for
example, the effect of Lawrence's observation about the locomotive that "the colt is startled from among the gorse, . . .
outdistanced it at a canter." "This fellow," Ford says,
". . . doesn't say: 'It was coming slowly,' or—what would
have been a little better—'at seven miles an hour.' Because even 'seven miles an hour' means nothing definite for
the untrained mind. . . . But anyone knows that an engine
that makes a great deal of noise and yet cannot overtake a
colt at a canter must be a ludicrously ineffective machine"
(*Portraits from Life*). It is Lawrence's use of detail in
this way throughout the description of the miner's household that makes us feel we have lived in it.

But though the routine of life, including husbands who
drink and proud, embittered, discontented wives, is very
real for Lawrence and is made very real for us in this
story, it is not the whole of reality or even its most important aspect for Lawrence. Its crucial aspect for him is
the unique and, indeed, sacred, integrity of the individual,
and what he is most interested in in *Odor of Chrysanthemums*
is the revelation that comes to Elizabeth as she contemplates the impenetrable isolation of her husband in death,
the realization that all along he had been a self, an overwhelmingly real, unique self that she had never understood
or known, had never, in her demand that he be what he was
not, be what she required him to be, even tried to know.
They had been man and wife; but they had never been at one
with one another, because Elizabeth had wholly refused to
accept Walter for what he was, had always insisted that he
be something else, something he was helpless to become. It
was only when she saw Walter's nakedness dead and could not,
by physical contact, reach him any more, that she realized
how little contact, for all their physical intimacy, there
had ever been between them when he was alive, how profoundly
she had rejected him.

The first sign of Elizabeth's awakening to the truth
comes as she looks down at Walter's naked dead body. She
"felt countermanded. She saw him, how utterly inviolable he
lay in himself. She had nothing to do with him. She could
not accept it. Stooping, she laid her hand on him, in claim.
. . . Elizabeth embraced the body of her husband, with cheek
and lips" (546). We are meant to see that she has always
heretofore taken her wifely possession of him for granted,
as a thing of course, that only now does she realize that
she does not possess him. "She seemed . . . trying to get
some connection. But she could not. She was driven away.
He was impregnable" (546-547). Alive, he had not been, but
she had not tried then. "Each time he had taken her, they
had been two isolated beings, far apart as now" (548).

The implications of this discovery soon emerge for her.
"Was this what it all meant—utter, intact separateness, ob-
scured by the heat of living?" (548). "I," she thinks,
"have been fighting a husband who did not exist," one she had
as it were invented to suit her purpose. "He existed all the
time . . . apart all the while, living as she never lived,
feeling as she never felt" (548). Now, for the first time,
Elizabeth knows—"She had denied him what he was—she saw it
now. She had refused him as himself. . . . He had been
cruelly injured, this naked man, this other being, and she
could make no reparation" (548). Now, then, for the first
time in her life, "how awful she knew it . . . to have been
a wife" (549). "They had denied each other in life. Now he
had withdrawn. An anguish came over her. It was finished
then: it had become hopeless between them long before he
died. Yet he had been her husband. But how little!" (549).
How little, anyhow, in the tremendous sense in which
Lawrence, in his romantic idealism, thinks it is necessary
for a man and a woman to be husband and wife if they are to
fulfill their unique, individual selves and truly live their
lives. Thus it is that Lawrence realizes for the reader the
aspect of life—so seldom dealt with in fiction—that seems
to him most important, that makes it possible for men and
women to realize their selves in all their "intact separateness."

<u>QUESTIONS</u> (pages **863-864** of *Modern Short Stories*)

1. What means does Lawrence use at the beginning of the story to make the life in the miner's house vivid and familiar to us?

2. Why does Elizabeth touch the dead body of her husband and then kiss it?

3. Is she successful in what she is trying to do?

4. What does this experience reveal to her about their relations when he was alive?

5. What light does this throw on the thoughts she had had when she had been waiting for him to come home, thinking that he was in the local pub drinking?

6. What does she now think of the way she had treated her husband?

D. H. LAWRENCE

THE SHADOW IN THE ROSE GARDEN

In *After Strange Gods*, where he was anxious to maintain
the desirability of men's disciplining their instinctive natures to a set of public moral standards, preferably those
of the Anglican Church, T. S. Eliot criticized *THE SHADOW IN
THE ROSE GARDEN* as both cruel and conscienceless, pointing
to the cruel way in which the woman is forced to recognize
that her former lover is a lunatic and the brutality with
which she reveals her previous affair to her husband, and
observing that she does so without any apparent sense of obligation to consider her husband's feelings. No doubt, had
Eliot not been anxious to prove a point here, he would have
admitted that such a complete absence of what he was looking
for could not have been accidental but must represent
Lawrence's considered sense of the way men and women really
are, the moral reality, as it were, of their natures which
must necessarily determine what their real obligations are.
Mr. Eliot may be right that to accept this aspect of man's
nature as basic and even to admire and praise it when it
fulfills itself, as Lawrence does, is very dangerous — is, as
Eliot's title suggests, whoring after strange gods. Nonetheless, Lawrence has, in *The Shadow in the Rose Garden*,
given us a powerful and convincing account of the way this
aspect of men's natures, working through their sexual and
their class feelings — for "no writer," as Eliot says, "is
more conscious of class distinctions than Lawrence" — may,
rightly or wrongly, control their consciousnesses and thus
their conduct.

This is what Lawrence has his attention on in his description of the husband and wife on their honeymoon. He
begins with the husband. The husband is a small, alert man,
capable of a properly masculine self-confidence and pride
that shows in his "alert interest" at the sight of himself
in the mirror (550) and in his easy laughter when he thinks
of his wife's request that he not give her away as a sign of
submissiveness (553). But "he was only a laboring electri-
cian in the mine, she was superior to him" (559). Moreover,
"she had never loved him" (559). She makes some effort to
make their marriage go, leaning on his arm (551) and trying
to feel her way "delicately" toward understanding him (552).
But her own nature, with its unconscious sense of social
superiority and its profound commitment to a refined, even
upperclass romantic view of relations between the sexes, dictates her conduct most of the time and leads her to hurt and
humiliate her none too confident husband again and again.

She has brought them here on their honeymoon, rather than going to his kind of place, Bridlington (a Yorkshire summer resort), because she is clinging to the memory of the love of her life, which occurred here; living in this memory, she closes out her husband completely, humiliating him and destroying his masculine confidence. "She looked apart from him and his world. . . . It irked her husband that she should continue abstracted and in ignorance of him" (551). Though he attempts to assert himself and the dignity of his class's ways, planting himself masterfully on the hearth rug, he cannot help watching his wife "rather uneasily" all the time to see if she is—as she is not—accepting him as a man (551).

All this Lawrence conveys with the most marvelous delicacy of detail. The husband is up early: he is a working man used to early rising; the wife sleeps later. The husband's way of saying it is a beautiful morning is to say, "You might as well be in a pit as in bed, on a morning like this," and the wife, with unconscious cruelty, says easily, "I shouldn't have thought the pit would occur to you, here" (551); clearly this is her largely unconscious upperclass distaste for her husband's working-class habits, particularly strong at the moment because "here" has brought back for her so overwhelmingly the memory of the gentlemanly lover she had had in this place. The husband—painfully self-educated, one guesses—is careful to disapprove of the Victorian "The Stag at Bay" (550) but does not notice "the glory roses . . . in the morning sunshine like little bowls of fire tipped up" (550) that constitute so powerful a part of the wife's remembrance of her love affair.

The wife's great longing is to renew the past here, and with an attempt at tact that does not deceive her husband at all, she gets rid of him this first morning of their honeymoon, leaving him "suppressedly angry" (553). She then makes her way to what is for her the fairy-story rectory garden that she had shared with her lover. There, for her, the open doorway "shone like a picture of light in the dark wall" and "in the magic beyond the doorway . . . a green lawn glowed" and "a bay tree glittered," though the rectory itself, with symbolic ominousness, "looked black and soulless" (553). Into this garden of almost smothering lusciousness, of "great, dark red gooseberries, over-ripe" (553) and a host of roses, shining and glowing for her, she moves like a somnambulist, "like one who has gone back into the past" (555). This past had been cut short before it could fulfill itself, and she feels, coming back into it, both pain and joy (555); she is like "a white, pathetic butterfly," or "a rose that could not quite come into blossom, but remained tense" (555).

Then, as in a dream, her lover who, she had thought, was dead appears in the garden. For a moment her whole consciousness is fixed on his hands, "her symbols of passionate love." There is the physical "shape she had loved with all her passion." "And it was not he," for her lover is now a lunatic (557), and she stumbles away, "blindly, between the sunny roses, out from the garden, past the house with the blank, dark windows" (557), into the reality she now inhabits, in a state of the soul that "was as if some membrane had been torn in two in her" feeling as if "it might be blood that was loose in her torn entrails" (557).

She goes back to the bedroom like some sick animal wanting to hide to recover, and there her husband, "an air of complacency [as it seems to her] about his alert, sturdy figure" comes to her. Wanting only to be alone to deal with her suffering ("He did not exist for her, except as an irritant"), her self-centered anguish occupying her consciousness completely, she is unable to keep up even the pretense of a relation with him but strikes out at him "in hate and desperation" until he winces "with ignominy" and rage. Remembering her graceful lover and especially his hands, she finds herself disgusted by "his workman's hands" (560)—"His hands seemed gross to her, the back of his head paltry" (561).

Her husband, his natural pride and self-confidence shattered by her bitter, cutting hatred of him, is at first enraged ("His anger rose, filling the veins of his throat,") (558); he tries to master her, "as if," it seems to her, "he would oppose her eternally, till she was extinguished" (560). He tries to get the better of her by wounding her (561); "white with fury" he says with deliberate cruelty and—to her—with lower-class vulgarity, "You mean you had your fling with an army man, and then came to me to marry when you'd had done—. . . Do you mean to say you used to go —the whole hogger?" (562). This way of describing what she has been remembering as her love for a fairy prince in a fairy-story rose garden is an unbearable outrage to her and she strikes back as brutally as she can. Then she tells him that her lover is now a lunatic, and they are both, in their different ways, so shocked at the full knowledge of the barrier that now stands between them that they are incapable of any contact at all, even the relation of hatred: "they were impersonal, and no longer hated each other" (562).

Lawrence says at the conclusion of the story that "The thing must work itself out" (562), but it hardly seems likely that it ever will. The wife had committed her deepest passional self to a lover whose whole nature, particularly his unconscious class characteristics, satisfy all her unconscious, and particularly her class, demands. That commitment of herself has gone too far ever to be redeemed so that she can commit herself in the same way to another man, and her chances of making even a nominal commitment to the man she has married are drastically reduced by her largely unconscious dislike of his class characteristics. For his part, his wife has destroyed, surely beyond recovery, his ability to think of himself in relation to her with a proper sense of masculine pride and assurance. Unlike her, he has no real assurance that his own class habits are unquestionably

superior; he is in fact deeply uncertain about them. But
they are bred into him. At most he can hope to cover them
with a thin veneer of painstakingly acquired, self-conscious,
upperclass manners and tastes, without ceasing to be, at the
center of his nature, a workman. In any serious sense, no
real relationship between the two seems possible; it is hard
to believe even a workable pretense of one is possible. All
this we feel because Lawrence has made the movements of the
deep, instinctive and habitual feelings in both characters
so vivid and real for us.

QUESTIONS (page 864 of *Modern Short Stories*)

1. What impression do we get of the husband as we watch
him moving about before his wife wakes up?

2. What impression of the wife do we have when we first
see her with her husband?

3. What evidence of class differences emerges in these
two similes?

4. What is the wife feeling as she goes back to visit
the garden where she had been courted by her former lover?

5. How does Lawrence use exaggerated descriptions of
flowers and similes drawn from nature to make us understand
her feelings?

6. Why does she focus so hard on the man's hands while
they are in the garden together?

7. Why does the wife not want to see the husband when
she gets back to their room and feel irritated when he
comes in?

8. Why does the husband deliberately give a gross description of the former relationship the wife has just revealed to him?

9. Why is the grossness offensive to the wife in a way
he has not foreseen?

10. What is the result of the wife's revealing the fact
that her former lover is now a lunatic?

D. H. LAWRENCE

THE WHITE STOCKING

The power of *THE WHITE STOCKING* is in its characterization. The essential situation is simple enough; here are two young people, simple and attractive in their youthfulness but unexceptional—neither specially brilliant nor specially beautiful. They are happily married, but there remains between them the shadow of Sam Adams, a florid, crude man of considerable physical magnetism for whom Elsie had worked before her marriage. Among the many girls Sam had been attracted to was Elsie, and he had once—at a dance before Teddy and Elsie were married—deliberately focused the power of his physical magnetism on Elsie. She had escaped him then, but with "the persistence of [his] cynicism" (575), he continued to pursue her after her marriage, waiting for his chance, sending her expensive presents, taking advantage of chance meetings to give her exciting invitations.

Summed up in this way, *The White Stocking* sounds familiar, even commonplace, like a minor story by Arnold Bennett or Frank Swinnerton. So far as the main situation goes—the Edwardian shopgirl caught between her young man and her cynical sexually experienced employer—it is. Nor is there anything startling about the story's basic plan or its execution. The structure is simple and workmanlike. In the first scene (Section I) we see Elsie and Teddy on the morning of Valentine's Day; the scene ends when Teddy goes off to work. In the second (Section II) we see the dance where Sam Adams attracted Elsie. In the third (Section III) we see Elsie and Teddy together when Teddy comes home from work the evening of Valentine's Day. The plot of the story is handled with similar directness. We begin by being as innocently unsurprised as Teddy is when Elsie rushes to the door at the sound of the postman: Elsie rushes everywhere, we think. But as the story develops, Lawrence makes us see that she had a special reason for being up early this morning, for being even more vivacious than usual—and for rushing to answer the door. He does so neatly and unspectacularly, in the way any competent storyteller might.

What no merely competent writer could do, what gives *The White Stocking* its distinction, is Lawrence's realization of the forces within these characters that make them do what they do. In the ordinary sense of the word, there is nothing unrealistic about the way he does even this. Our first impression is that Lawrence has a remarkably sharp eye for vivid characterizing details. Elsie, we see, is a "quick,

pretty, almost witty little thing" (569), "flicking her
small, delightful limbs," glowing with her careless abandon,
"singing in her snatchy way" (563). We do not wonder that,
when she leaves the room, Teddy feels "as if all his light
and warmth were taken away" (563). Teddy, on the other
hand, at once appears heavy and reliable. "The stairs creak
under his weight" when he comes down (563). "His eyes were
very blue, very kind, his manner simple" (565). Sam Adams
is "a bachelor of forty, growing stout, a man well dressed
and florid, with a large brown moustache and thin hair"
(569).

Yet from the very beginning Lawrence is extending these
impressions of his characters to include a perception of
them that is unusual, making us see aspects of their natures,
of their responses to one another and of their own feelings,
that are unexpected and yet convincing. Elsie and Teddy are
unusually—unusually for a story, not for life itself—aware
of the physical presences of one another and of the selves
these physical presences express. Teddy watches "the quickness and softness of [Elsie's] young shoulders, calmly, like
a husband, and appreciatively" (563). Teddy's physical
presence gives Elsie "a feeling of warmth and slowness" (565);
"his neck was white and smooth and goodly" (566); "she loved
the way in which he stood washing himself. He was such a
man" (568). When the action of the story begins with the
arrival of the valentine from Sam Adams and the quarrel between Elsie and Teddy, it involves without difficulty the
powerful, obscure parts of the human consciousness that
Lawrence is reminding us of in these phrases.

Elsie's sense of her triumph over Sam Adams and her delight in its visible rewards is childlike. As she runs into
the sitting-room to try on the ear-rings Sam has sent her,
"she had her lower lip caught earnestly between her teeth"
(565); like a child too, she cannot help laughing at her own
airs and dignities, "could not help winking at herself [in
the mirror] and laughing" (565). Nonetheless, "she was
drawn to the mirror again, to look at her ear-rings" (565).
For behind her innocent delight is something stronger than
she understands, an important part of what determines her
conscious self, her feminine nature. She does not really
recognize how much being "glad because of her pearl ear-
rings" has to do with her whole state of mind (569). She
has never understood the ultimate cost of exercising her
powers as a woman, even when she came close to paying it
that night when she danced with Sam Adams. To her the exercise of that power is quite innocent and harmless, though
she does know it is not strictly according to the rules and
must for some not very important reason be hidden from Teddy
when the ear-rings come.

Thus, when she decides to tell Teddy the truth about
the white stocking, she is aware only of apologizing for
having lied to him. Her very reliance on her confidence in
his affection has encouraged her in what she imagines to be

only an innocent flirtation with Sam Adams, and now it makes
her believe that Teddy will not be seriously angry if she
tells him the truth: "He was so sure, so permanent, he had
her [she thought] so utterly in his power. It gave her a
delightful, mischievous sense of liberty. Within his grasp,
she could dart about excitingly" (568). Yet at the very
moment when she is thinking that what she has done is only
darting about, she is also dissatisfied with Teddy for not
taking her seriously: "She was not satisfied. He ought to
be more moved" (567). But when he is seriously moved, when
his masculine pride is hurt by what she thought merely innocent fun—her going into the Royal with Sam Adams for a
drink—and he says to her, "You'd go off with a nigger for a
packet of chocolate," she is outraged. "Teddy—how beastly!"
(568).

     To Elsie what she has done is harmless—the exercise of
her feminine power to gain an occasional treat. But Teddy—
unconsciously aware of the sheer sexual tension that had
been created between her and Sam Adams long ago at that dance
and thus deeply jealous—sees what she has done in the lowest
possible terms. Both are at once right and wrong. So far
as Elsie consciously understands, she has been as innocent
as she assumes; so far as the real destructive force of the
power she has been toying with is concerned, "Teddy's estimate—though not his conclusion about Elsie's intentions—is
right. It is his jealousy that makes it impossible for him
to see Elsie does not share his estimate of those powers and
to be "hurt . . . so deeply" by what he supposes were her intentions (569). In her innocence Elsie is "aggrieved" by
Teddy's brutal description of her conduct, and being
aggrieved, encourages herself in her belief that what she
has done is nothing more than take "giddy little flights
into nowhere" without a thought of not always returning to
Teddy as a "permanent basis" (569).

     In Section II of the story Lawrence goes back in time
to describe the relation between Elsie and Sam Adams and let
the reader judge for himself how serious Elsie's involvement
with him was. The description of the two dancing together
is one of Lawrence's vivid realizations of the power of the
large sexual responses that operate far beneath the conscious
understandings of men and women. That description is all
the more effective because Sam Adams, an experienced
womanizer, has at least a working sense—if no real understanding—of what is happening between him and Elsie, and is
deliberately exploiting it for the narrowest sexual purposes. All Elsie understood during that dancing was that
"a curious caress in his voice . . . seemed to lap the outside of her body in a warm glow, delicious. She gave herself
to it [without suspicion]. She liked it" (571). Lawrence
makes us understand exactly how she felt in the paragraph
that describes how Elsie "seemed to swim away out of contact
with the room . . . into another, denser element of him, an
essential privacy" (574). All that saves her from complete
surrender to him is her unconscious perception that Sam

Adams is deliberately using the pressure he sees he can put on her. "He did not speak to her. He only looked straight into her eyes with a curious, gleaming look that disturbed her fearfully and deliciously. But also there was in his look some of the automatic irony of the *roué*. It left her partly cold. She was not carried away" (572). It is Adams' cynicism that saves her, however little she may consciously understand that it is. All she understands is in her fumbling plea to Teddy afterwards: "Be good to me. Don't be cruel to me" (579). This is her effort to express her need for what Adams had made her feel—the possibility of a complete fulfillment of her feminine nature—uncorrupted by Adams' cold cynicism. But Ted is much too inexperienced to understand what she is driving at and can only say with equally fumbling love, "No, my pet. Why?"

Sam Adams still has the white stocking he had picked up when Elsie dropped it during that dance long ago. He uses it with all the *roué's* skill, and Elsie, like a child playing with fire, responds. "She knew he had always kept an unsatisfied desire for her. And, sportive, she could not help playing a little with this, though she cared not one jot for the man himself" (580). When Teddy comes home on the evening of the day they have quarreled over Sam Adams' valentine, then, all the conditions necessary for a violent, incomprehensible quarrel between them have been established. Each has been roused to hurt anger by the injury to elements in his own nature that are beyond the reach of his reason. The result is one of those magnificent scenes Lawrence could produce, in which the characters act on feelings that work at a level beneath their conscious, rational minds. They scarcely know from one moment to the next what they are going to do or—when they do it—why they did. Yet there is a profound truth to experience in the nature of these uncomprehended feelings and in the apparently irrational order in which they occur. What these scenes show us is the real conflict of the sexes, the struggle between a man and a woman to preserve the essential integrity of their selves—of the masculine and feminine elements within them that define their natures—in a relationship so close and intimate that it forces each to expose himself to the other completely. For both it is a particularly terrifying struggle because neither can anticipate what he may feel and do next.

We are made to see this at once. Teddy is "in a state of suppressed irritation." Elsie cannot "help goading him" (580). Yet neither knows why he feels this way, or even—very clearly—that he does. When Teddy's irritation reveals itself in the "strong and brutal" tone of his voice, Elsie cannot control her impulse to answer him "flippantly." Elsie then has what Lawrence, with marvelous accuracy, calls "another little inspiration," for without understanding quite why, she knows what she is about to do will enrage Teddy. She put on her white stockings and comes downstairs and, pulling up her skirts to her knees, begins "to dance slowly around the room, kicking up her feet half reckless,

half jeering, in a ballet-dancer's fashion" (581). She is
obscurely frightened: what will Teddy do if she goads him
too far? But she is defiant and resentful of the tyranny he
is trying to exercise over her. "There was a real biting
indifference in her behavior" (581). "He knew somehow that
she would like Sam Adams to see how pretty her legs looked
in the white stockings" (581-582). What he does not know is
that she means no serious consequences to come of that. But
she does mean now to hit Teddy where it will hurt him most,
and without understanding quite why this will or why she
wants it to, she knows the right thing to do. "She was
rousing all his uncontrollable anger. . . . And she was
afraid herself; but she was neither conquered nor convinced"
(582).

Finally she succeeds. Teddy becomes incoherent with
masculine rage at her; "scarcely responsible for what he
might do," he is just able to stifle the impulse to strike
her violently and to get himself out of the house. When he
comes back in Elsie stands looking at him, "a small, stubborn figure with tight-pressed lips and big, sullen,
childish eyes, watching him, white with fear" (583). But in
spite of her fear, she is not able to stop fighting back in
ways that intensify Teddy's rage. She plays her last card,
the secret of the amethyst brooch and the ear-rings. Then,
"transfixed with terror," too frightened even to scream, she
watches Teddy coming slowly, purposefully toward her. He
strikes her, hard, but that is only the beginning: as Elsie
crashes against the wall, she sees Teddy still coming after
her; "his lust to see her bleed, to break her and destroy
her, rose from an old source against her. It carried him.
He wanted satisfaction" (584). Yet, almost simultaneously,
"seeing her standing there, a piteous, horrified thing," he
is filled with "shame and nausea" (584). This is an almost
perfect example of the moment of crisis in sexual conflict.
The forces loosed by the quarrel between Elsie and Teddy are
very powerful—astonishingly so to simple, conventional
people like these two. Yet we recognize that in moments of
intense feeling such as Teddy is experiencing, this illogical
combination of blood lust, pity, and shame is very real.

Unable to help herself, Elsie has deliberately goaded
Teddy into a masculine rage before which she now finds herself helpless and terrified; it is at once the evidence of
her success and of her defeat. All that prevents Teddy from
killing her is his awareness of her pathos, of her fundamental helplessness and her obscure innocence. "They both
trembled in the balance, unconscious" (584). Teddy's complex state of feelings is too intense to last; its very intensity destroys it, leaving him emotionally exhausted for a
moment. "A weariness came over him. . . . He did not care
any more. He was dreary and sick. . . . He could see it, the
blood-mark [on Elsie's handkerchief]. It made him only more
sick and tired of the responsibility of it, the violence,
the shame" (584).

There follow a few moments when they are both in this state of emotional exhaustion, incapable of feeling anything. Then, as Elsie looks at Teddy "with eyes all forlorn and pathetic," "a great flash of anguish [goes] over his body," and suddenly they are in one another's arms. "I never meant—" she says, not knowing any better now than she had when it happened what she had meant, only knowing she now wishes these terrible feelings had never been; and Teddy says, "My love—my little love—" "in anguish of spirit" (585). Neither of them has made a rational decision to change his attitude. Their feelings now, like the ones they had experienced a moment ago, come unbidden, from a source beyond their wills. Yet, like all the feelings that have preceded them in this scene, these have a special rightness, a psychological coherence of their own, however incoherent they may seem to the rational mind. The whole sequence of feelings in the scene is overwhelmingly convincing because it is true, not to what the reason tells us people ought logically to feel, but to what—if we have the power to see into ourselves—we know people actually do feel.

As he does in this story, Lawrence writes a great deal about what we loosely call sex. But for him sex is not the simple, surface mechanisms of desire and satisfaction. These are only the superficial, though necessary, means of expression for something he believes lies at the very center of the natures of men and women and is the source of energy for their whole beings. But even if sex is understood in this sense, Lawrence is not really concerned primarily with sex. He is concerned primarily with the life that goes on— largely below the level of consciousness—in the realm of the irrational and powerful emotions that dictate so much of conduct. Many of these emotions are deeply affected by sex as Lawrence understood it; but they are not exclusively sexual. Nonetheless it is in the realm of these emotions that Lawrence finds the defining characteristics of manhood and womanhood that realize themselves most fully in love. As the beginning of *Lady Chatterley's Lover* perhaps shows most clearly, Lawrence had all the idealizing romantic's intense hatred of sex for the sake of sex alone. What he believed in with evangelical fervor was a love so complete that it expressed the whole natures of the man and the woman. But there was a toughness in Lawrence, an almost peasant realism, that made him see how powerful the energies involved in love are and how easily they can mutate from sympathy to repulsion—how difficult love is. It is these things—the centrality of fully experienced love to human fulfillment, the difficulty of achieving such love—that *The White Stocking* so magnificently shows us.

QUESTIONS (pages 864-865 of *Modern Short Stories*)

1. Why does Lawrence suggest to us at the beginning of the story that Elsie is a lively, energetic, gay young woman? How does this momentarily mislead us as to her reason for rushing to the door when the postman knocks? Why does she rush to the door so eagerly?

2. What is it about Elsie that Teddy is most acutely aware of? What is Elsie most acutely aware of about Teddy?

3. What makes Sam Adams' presents and treats so interesting to Elsie?

4. What does Teddy feel about Adams' giving these presents to Elsie when he learns about them?

5. Why is Elsie so upset by Teddy's attitude?

6. Is Teddy right about the meaning of these presents, or is Elsie?

7. What happens between Elsie and Sam Adams at the dance?

8. How does Elsie feel about what happens at the dance? How does Sam Adams feel?

9. Why does Elsie say to Teddy after the dance, "Be good to me. Don't be cruel to me"?

10. When Elsie and Teddy quarrel the evening of Valentine's Day, what does Elsie do to irritate Teddy? Why does she do it? How does she feel while she is doing it?

11. Why does Teddy strike Elsie? How does he feel as he is doing it? How does he feel afterwards?

12. How are Elsie and Teddy reconciled?

13. Define as clearly as you can the kind of human feelings Lawrence has been dealing with in this story.

VLADIMIR NABOKOV
PNIN

The central purpose of *PNIN* is to make us feel the
heroic struggle of Pnin himself to live without losing his
own soul in a world that will always be alien to him. Without stressing the point, Mr. Nabokov makes us see—partly by
the contrast of the "pseudo-colorful Komarovs" (593), partly
by the "impressive Soviet documentary film" (599)—that
Russia is as surely a part of this alien world as is
Waindellville. Both are grotesque when compared with the
home of Pnin's heart:

> In a haze of sunshine—sunshine projecting in
> vaporous shafts between the white boles of birches,
> drenching the pendulous foliage, trembling in eye-
> lets upon the bark, dripping onto the long grass,
> shining and smoking among the ghosts of racemose
> bird cherries in scumbled bloom—a Russian wildwood
> enveloped the rambler. . . (600).

As Pnin trudges "back to his anachronistic lodgings" in
Waindellville from seeing the Soviet documentary film, he
finds himself walking down the old forest road that tra-
versed that wildwood. It is where he lives.

It is his unconsciousness of his own deprivation that
gives Pnin his pathos. He is not making a deliberate effort
to preserve in this alien world his identity—the tastes,
the inherited feelings, the *antikvarniy liberalizm* created
in that childhood world. In his "old-fashioned, humorless
way," he never conceives of the possibility of changing
these things; he sees his own attitudes as absolutely
natural—including his acute sensitivity to noise, his
absent-minded inaccuracy, his Rube-Goldberg ingenuities for
circumventing the inconveniences of modern life ("Wearing
rubber gloves to avoid being stung [a wildwood verb] by the
amerikanski electricity . . ." [597]). As long as the world
does not remind him inescapably that it does not share these
attitudes, he therefore carries on with easy confidence of
success, "rippling with mute mirth" at his own incomprehensible classroom jokes, speaking out with firm dignity in the
English he does not know is always a little off ("Mrs. Fire
permit me to ask something or other" [537]), never accepting
defeat in his losing battle with the workmen who continually
dig holes in the street ("Brainpan Street, Pningrad") and
with "the monstrous statues on primitive legs of stone" that
tramp grimly about the houses he lives in.

Whenever he moves to a new room, he removes all traces of former occupants and tries to make it his, a home; only he overlooks—and probably never will notice—"the funny face scrawled on the wall just behind the headboard of the bed" (588). He adorns his new office with a wooden desk, an ancient Turkish rug, "a small steel file with an entrancing locking device," and "a highly satisfying, highly philo-sophical [pencil sharpener] that goes ticonderoga, ticon-deroga" (591). These fittings perfectly reflect the soul of Pnin, the old-fashioned liberal; they are promptly pushed into an obscure corner to make room for Dr. Bodo von Falternfels' stainless-steel desk.

When Pnin is forced to recognize the world's surprise at what seems to him quite natural, he feels no self-pity. On the contrary he meets the world's judgment with indigna-tion at its manifest inferiority. He is full of scorn for the Komarovs and their ideal Russia of "the Red Army, an anointed monarch, collective farms, anthroposophy, the Russian Church and the Hydro-Electric Dam" (593); he never notices that everyone thinks the Komarovs "grand people" and Pnin droll. He snubs Komarov over the volume of *Sovetskiy Zolotoy Fond Literaturi* with its pictures of the Russia he loves, only to be driven to undefeated silence by Komarov's "Not interested" (593). When he inquires with frosty formal-ity who has asked to have Volume 18 of *Zol. Fond Lit.* re-turned to the library, that eager scholar proves to be Timofey Pnin, who has incorrectly filled out a slip request-ing a different volume. He does not take this defeat lying down either: "I put the year correctly, that is important! . . . and send to me a more effishant card when 19 avail-able" (595). No doubt the librarian, if not Pnin, notices that, despite his claim that the date is the important thing, Pnin refers to the volume in question by its number. He is quietly proud of his English, and is interested to discover that the 1930 edition of Webster does not stress "interested" on the third syllable, as he does: no doubt it is out of date. He has nothing but scorn for the pingpong fiends of his boarding house: "I don't any more play at games of infants" (586).

He does not play at games of infants. But as he watches the intellectually insulting Soviet propaganda film—

"I must not, I must not, oh it is idiotical," said Pnin to himself as he felt—unaccountably, ridiculously, humiliatingly—his tear glands dis-charge their hot, infantine, uncontrollable fluid (600).

All during the special day in Pnin's life described in this story—as perhaps it does every day of his life—the lost world has been rising unsummoned to disrupt the life of the cultivated and reasonable professor of Russian Pnin bravely imagines himself to be. When the students laugh as he comes perilously close to collapsing his chair at the climax of

his brilliant critical revelation about the date of
Pushkin's death, unbidden there flashes into his memory the
clowns and the piano stool—where was it? "Circus Busch,
Berlin!" (590). As he reads the advertisements in the
Russian-language paper, "for no special reason [he] suddenly
saw, with passionate and ridiculous lucidity, his parents
. . . facing each other in a small, cheerfully lighted
drawing room on Galernaya Street, St. Petersburg, forty
years ago" (596). He runs his hands lovingly over the
"Russian classics in horrible and pathetic cameo bindings,
whose molded profiles of poets reminded dewy-eyed Timofey
of his boyhood" (597). "With a not unhappy sigh" he loses
himself in the ancient, familiar world of "Kostromskoy's
voluminous work (Moscow, 1855)" (597). It distresses him—
for the world's sake; it is merely an annoyance, he
imagines, to him—that "'*Gamlet*' *Vil'yama Shekspira*" is not
in the Waindell Library: "whenever you were reduced to look
up something in the English version, you never found this or
that beautiful, noble, sonorous line that you remembered all
your life from Kroneberg's text in Vengerov's splendid edition. Sad!" (598).

     It takes him off guard, then, when the tears start at
the propaganda film's shot of the Russian family starting
off for a picnic in the Russian countryside. These tears
seem to Pnin unaccountable, ridiculous, humiliating. But
later that night, "as drowsiness overcame Pnin, who was
fairly snug in bed with two alarm clocks alongside, one set
at 7:30, the other at 8, clicking and clucking on his night
table," he fell into a dream that sums up the whole complex
experience of his day. A birthday party is in progress, for
—though Pnin has not consciously noticed it—today is his
birthday. "This was Tuesday, O Careless Reader" the
narrator tells us as Pnin reads the library's latest issue
of the Russian newspaper, that of Saturday, February 12. If
last Saturday was February 12, then today, Tuesday, is
February 15 (595). "By the Julian calendar into which he
had been born in St. Petersburg in 1898," Pnin was born
February 3 (589). But Pnin never celebrates his birthday
nowadays. For one thing, he existed during the academic
year "mainly on a motuweth frisas basis" (a Monday-Tuesday-
Wednesday-Thursday-Friday-Saturday-Sunday basis) (589). For
another, ever since he left Russia, his birthday has "sidled
by in a Gregorian disguise (thirteen—no, twelve days late)."
Thus we are informed that Pnin's birthday, February 3 in the
Julian calendar, is February 15 in the Gregorian and that
the day described in this story is February 15.

     In Pnin's birthday dream, Komarov, dressed in his fake
peasant blouse, tunes his guitar, no doubt preparatory to
playing some of those "more or less phony folk songs" of his
to celebrate, in a way that will thoroughly annoy Pnin,
Pnin's birthday (600-601). A calm Stalin casts with decision
the only vote ever cast in Russian elections, for govern-
mental pallbearers—no doubt those needed for the funeral of
Pushkin-Pnin. Pushkin's lines about his own death—"And

where will fate send me death, / in flight, in travel, or in
waves" (590) — flash in beautiful, ironic variation through
Pnin's dreaming mind: "In flight, in travel . . . waves or
Waindell" — and Dr. von Falternfels, who always smiles happily over his own writing, raises his head for a moment and
chimes in, "Wonderful!" Now the thud of Stalin's ballot
falling into the ballot box becomes louder: the statue of
Waindell's first president, which holds "by its horns the
bronze bicycle he was eternally about to mount" (593), suddenly begins to make an extravagant fuss over his broken
bronze wheel. And Pnin — "in fear and helplessness, toothless, nightshirted" — comes fully awake to the unabashed
amerikanski uproar of Isobel Clements happily returning,
like a school-girl back from summer camp, to her home,
tramping upstairs to her old room — the room Pnin had worked
so hard to make his — and preparing to kick open the door of
the dream Pnin never suspects he has — in defiance of all the
interruptions — always lived in.

Pnin's character can be so subtly and beautifully defined for us because the story's narrator, though profoundly
sympathetic with Pnin, is also a man acutely aware of the
realities of the world around him. However much he may
share Pnin's feelings, he can always see the wonderfully
comic incongruity of Pnin's innocent self-confidence that
only he is in step. The first important effect of this
double perspective on Pnin's life is the addition to the
story of its remarkable observation of American life, with
its affection for the incurable humanity of that life and
its amusement at its absurdity. It is the narrator who introduces all the sharp detail that Pnin himself would never
notice to support Pnin's judgment of American life.

It is this narrator who notices, for example, the uni-
formity of American houses in which Pnin only knows he is
uncomfortable — the almost invariable clapboard, the inescapable presences of Hendrick Willem van Loon, Dr. Cronin, Mrs.
Garnett "impersonating somebody" (like Tolstoy) — and the
Toulouse-Lautrec poster (587). It is he who notices the
"routine smell of potato chips and the sadness of balanced
meals" in the college dining hall (592), the magnificently
awful bronze statue of Alpheus Frieze in sports cap and
knickerbockers mounting his bicycle (593), the incredible
portrait of President Poore "in a mauve double-breasted suit
and mahogany shoes, gazing with radiant magenta eyes at the
scrolls handed him by Richard Wagner, Dostoevski, and
Confucius" in Oleg Komarov's mural (592). It is he, too,
who consciously observes the beauty of the world that unconsciously moves Pnin, as does "the violet-blue air of
dusk, silver-tooled by the reflection of the fluorescent
lights of the ceiling, and, among spidery black twigs, a
mirrored row of bright book spines" of the library window
(597). And it is of course he who notices the inept English
that makes Pnin's most dignified remarks comic, the inefficiency that mars the effect of his firmest protests
("'*Huligani*,' fumed Pnin, shaking his head — and slipped

slightly on a flag. . ." [594]).

Most important of all, it is this narrator who unobtrusively suggests the larger meaning of Pnin's life, the
meaning that Pnin himself—again unconsciously—feels but
never formulates and that dictates his unremitting struggle
against the world. He, for instance, tells us that the
accumulation of rooms in Pnin's memory, from one to another
of which he has fled since his central European days, is
like "those displays of grouped elbow chairs on show, and
beds, and lamps, and inglenooks which, ignoring all space-
time distinctions, commingle in the soft light of a furniture store beyond which it snows, and the dusk deepens, and
nobody really loves anybody" (586). The concluding phrase
of that passage is introduced very casually, almost as if it
were a mere piece of rococo verbal decoration. But it is in
fact the story's first and prompt indication of the way the
imagined life Pnin so bravely strives for makes an image of
eternal home, where the marvelous clown of the Circus Busch
remains, forever playing on, "in a seated, though seatless,
position, with his rhapsody unimpaired" (590), and the
actual life Pnin lives makes an image of human loneliness
and exile, of the brevity and isolation of all life, from the
moment of birth in that cheerful house in Galernaya Street in
St. Petersburg on February 3—no, no, February 15—1898 to
the moment (and "this was 1953—how time flies!") when, like
the victim of that highly philosophical pencil-sharpener that
says ticonderoga, feeding on the yellow finish and sweet
wood, he "ends up in a kind of soundlessly spinning ethereal
world as we all must" (591).

Pnin's anecdote about Pushkin's obsession with death
and dates, particularly the date "that would appear, somewhere, sometime upon his tombstone," and his dramatic assertion that Pushkin in fact "died on a quite, quite different
day!" fails, like most things Pnin attempts, to come off.
Somehow he manages to miss the point he is driving at, triumphantly asserting that Pushkin did not die on December 26,
1829 at 3:03 P.M. in St. Petersburg. But this is the date of
the poem's composition, not the "future anniversary" of
Pushkin's death Pushkin is seeking in the poem. Pnin's
happily unconscious muffing of his point—together with the
ominous cracking of the chair that, in his excitement, he
brings close to dumping him on the floor—effectively di-
verts the attention of Pnin's students—and possibly of Mr.
Nabokov's readers—from the point here, what Pnin feels
about time and death.

But that point is really made quite clear. The narrator
has just noticed (though to be sure he has not quite <u>told</u> us)
that today is the birthday Pnin never quite remembers; Pnin
then dwells on Pushkin's poem about his seeking to discover
his deathday. But, cries Pnin triumphantly, he didn't die
on December 26, 1829, etc., but on a quite different day.
In the touching optimism of his conscious mind Pnin seems almost to think he has now triumphed over death. He has not,

in fact, triumphed at all, since he has badly muddled his
argument; but had he triumphed, it would have been only over
Pushkin's belief that he could identify the correct day of
his death. But whatever Pnin thinks, it ought not to escape
our attention that Pushkin is quite as dead as if he had
correctly identified his deathday, as dead as Pnin will soon
be, "as we all must" be.

It is also the narrator, not Pnin, who consciously
notices for us how the blind President Poore moves, not unlike Pnin and the rest of us, "in his private darkness to an
invisible luncheon" in Frieze Hall. This "figure of antique
dignity" is no less tragic for the absurdly bad taste of his
surroundings, including his own bad portrait on the wall of
Frieze Hall—just as Pnin is no less tragic for his ineffec-
tuality. It is the narrator who arranges—so we can see why
Pnin's mind catches on it—the description of the curious
verbal association that turns out to be the account of
Ophelia's death (598). And it is the narrator who describes
Charlie Chaplin in such a way as to make us see how like him
Pnin is, not least in his confidence that Chaplin is not
funny at all (599).

Ridiculously toothless and absurdly garbed in a night-
shirt he would be indignant to be told was old-fashioned to
the point of absurdity Pnin may be; but the fear and helplessness with which he confronts the dark night that is like
a fever and an infection is nonetheless real and recogniz-
able as the fear and helplessness of everyone who confronts
the truth of his experience. Pnin's uncompromising mainte-
nance of his old-fashioned *intelligentski* ways make him
commonplace in an unusually funny way; the narrator's own
images are also carefully kept commonplace: they are all
drawn from everyday experience—the furniture-store window,
the pencil-sharpener, the college movie. Both work to make
Pnin—like Leopold Bloom—everyman; but Pnin is everyman in
the fullest sense; he is magnificent, absurd, inexplicable—
the glory, jest, and riddle of the world.

QUESTIONS (pages 865-866 of *Modern Short Stories*)

1. What life does Pnin dream he is living as he walks back from the film-showing to his room in Waindellville?

2. How does Pnin conduct himself during his daily life in Waindellville? What conception of himself leads him to conduct himself this way?

3. What failures in the conduct of his daily life make Pnin look absurd? Is he aware of these failures?

4. Why does Pnin scorn the Komarovs? Is his attitude toward them justified?

5. Why does Pnin cry at the film? Why does he think his doing so unaccountable, ridiculous, humiliating?

6. Why is Pnin constantly remembering episodes from the past? Does he understand why he does so?

7. Explain how we know that the day of the story is Pnin's birthday.

8. Explain the reasons for the things Pnin dreams of that night?

9. How does the narrator make us understand things about Pnin's life that Pnin does not understand?

10. Why is Pnin fascinated by the pencil sharpener? Why does the narrator think it significant?

11. What does the narrator wish us to understand from Pnin's discussion of Pushkin's poem?

12. Why does the story end with Pnin's being awakened by the return of Isobel Clements?

SHERWOOD ANDERSON
THE EGG

The interest of *THE EGG* is centered in the naive, passionate, personal consciousness of the narrator's father. We are kept carefully aware of how this man appears to outsiders—mainly by being kept aware of Joe Kane's feelings throughout the climactic scene—but only so that we may measure the extent to which the father is unconscious of how he looks to others, is governed by his own, private conception of what the world is and how he must act in order to conquer it and be popular and successful. Partly because the boy's mother feels a natural maternal ambition for her son, partly because both she and his father have been infected by "the American passion for getting up in the world" (602), they decide to start a restaurant at the local railroad station. They had both been seduced by the advertisements about the wealth to be made from raising chickens and had worked themselves to the bone trying to realize this dream of success; for ten years they struggled with the hard reality of chicken farming, clinging stubbornly to their American dream of making it a profitable success. But it is, like life itself, a hopeless effort; "one hopes for so much from a chicken and is so dreadfully disillusioned. Small chickens. . . are so much like people they mix one up in one's judgments of life" (603). Then they give up and decide on the restaurant.

The father's approach to this enterprise is a demonstration of the special version of American commercial initiative that he has in his slow, naive way worked out in the privacy of his soul. As a chicken farmer he had, in his private version of the enterprising man's keenness for the potentially profitable rarity, specially treasured the rare, grotesque chicks born on his farm. He lived too much with chickens to feel, himself, any sickening disgust at the sight of these objects, and—imprisoned as he is in the world of his private consciousness—it never occurs to him that others may possibly feel differently about them; with each that is born, "he dreamed of taking the wonder about the country fairs and of growing rich by exhibiting it to other farmhands" (605)—a scheme that might, just conceivably, have worked with other farm hands; it never occurs to him that as the *pièce de résistance* of a restaurant these exhibits will have a somewhat different effect.

Once the restaurant was established, "the American spirit took hold" of the father once more (606). He adopted the American idea that it is a man's sacred obligation to be ambitious and started, in the sincere simplicity of his

heart, to work out schemes for making the restaurant popular.
With a characteristic, touchingly naive belief in the omnipotence of public relations and a pathetic disregard of his
incapacity for the kind he settled on, he decided to "adopt
a cheerful outlook on life," to fill the restaurant with
"bright, entertaining conversation" so that all the young
people of Bidwell would love to come to it; "something of
the jolly innkeeper effect was to be sought" (607). It is
usually supposed that the false friendliness and charm laid
on by American businessmen for commercial purposes is a disgusting prostitution of what ought to be genuine human
sentiments. One of the remarkable things about Anderson's
story is that, by making us intimate and therefore sympathetic with the father's feeling, it makes us see how innocent
of fraud the father was, how the naive sincerity of his
dream of succeeding and "getting up in the world" and his
equally naive belief in the American methods of doing so
made this whole public relations scheme quite innocent and—
because it was doomed to ludicrous failure by the father's
ignorance of the world he was trying to interest—pathetic.

   With passionate intensity, the father planned his first
venture in public relations, working out in the privacy of
his imagination exactly what he would do, how brilliantly it
would succeed, and how delighted his audience would be. So
concentrated was he on his performance, when he did get an
audience in young Joe Kane, that he altogether forgot what
little sense he had ever had of the real world outside, as
distinguished from the audience he had imagined. As a result, though he made a convulsively nervous effort to be the
hail-fellow-well-met, leaning over the counter suddenly to
shake Joe Kane's hand, the impression he made on Kane was
that he was an angry man (609). So intense were his private
feelings, which were quite inconceivable by Joe Kane, that
he seemed to Kane "beside himself with the duplicity of
Columbus"; quite unaware of what he was doing, "he muttered
and swore." As he tried to make the egg stand on end, he
"mumbled" to himself the patter that was supposed to impress
his audience; he was really playing to the audience in his
imagination, only occasionally becoming aware of Joe Kane,
the real audience before him, and even then without the
faintest suspicion of the impression he was making on that
audience. Thus he was astonished and disconcerted when,
after repeated failures, he succeeded in making the egg
stand on end for a moment, only to discover that Joe Kane
had long since lost interest and was no longer watching.

   To fill the interval while he decided on his next
dramatic delight for his audience, he took down the bottles
containing the poultry monstrosities from the shelf to show
them to Joe Kane. His assumption that they would delight
Joe Kane because they fascinated him is perfectly sincere;
he was quite incapable of seeing that Joe Kane was made a
little sick by the sight of what he treasured. His efforts
to be, as showman, extroverted and jolly as "he reached over
the counter and tried to slap Joe Kane on the shoulder as he
had seen men do in Ben Head's saloon" (610) were equally

sincere attempts to be the insincere salesman-entertainer.
When Joe Kane, instead of being fascinated and enthusiastic,
as the father's dream called for him to be, started to
leave, the father "grew a little angry and for a moment had
to turn his face away and force himself to smile" (610); it
is impossible to think of this reaction as anything but
pathetic, so earnest, innocent, and anxious was his desire
to dazzle Joe Kane—not in any sense out of vanity, but out
of an almost impersonal desire to make his restaurant a
success.

With renewed confidence he then attempted his most
brilliant trick, stuffing the egg in the bottle. With
assurance, he told Joe Kane how to use the trick to make
himself popular: "Don't tell them. Keep them guessing."
Confidently he "grinned and winked at his visitor," who
"decided that [he] was mildly insane but harmless" (610).
When Joe Kane's interest again failed, the father never suspected the reason; it seemed to him inexplicably unreasonable; nevertheless he went "cheerfully to work." When he
could not get the egg into the bottle, he still kept his
courage, not despairing or losing faith in himself but only
growing angry at the unreasonable recalcitrance of his
materials: "He worked and worked and a spirit of desperate
determination took possession of him" (610). Just as he
imagined he was about to succeed, the train Joe Kane was
waiting for arrived and he started to drift casually out of
the restaurant. The father desperately redoubled his
efforts to complete the trick before his audience went and
the egg broke; and Joe Kane laughed.

At that the father's determination and hope collapsed;
he was reduced to incoherent rage at the refusal of the
objective world around him—the egg, the vinegar, the hot
pan, the audience—to behave in the way his dream of success required them to. In despair he roared with anger,
shouted inarticulately, and frankly displayed his hatred of
the audience that only innocent commercial ambition had made
him try to please by throwing an egg at Joe Kane.

He had given his all in an effort to do what he had
imagined was required for the achievement of that popularity
he supposed necessary to make the restaurant a success and
give him the importance in the community he had been taught
to believe it the duty of every man to achieve. What we
have to see is the innocence and pathos of what is for the
father this inexplicable defeat, and the intensity of his
despair at failing in the scheme of entertainment he had
worked on so hard and had been so sure, in the privacy of
his own imagination, was just the thing to succeed. It is
when we understand this that we feel the sadness of his
dropping by his wife's bed and crying like the boy he
really is.

QUESTIONS (page 866 of *Modern Short Stories*)

1. What had been the motives of the boy's father and mother in starting a chicken farm?

2. Why had they stuck to it so long?

3. How did the boy's father plan to make a big success of the restaurant?

4. Why is this plan so unlikely to succeed?

5. Why do we feel sorry for the father rather than outraged by his commercialism?

6. Why does the father not realize that Joe Kane is not interested in his trick of standing the egg on end?

7. Why does he not realize that Joe Kane will be sickened by his monstrous chicks in alcohol?

8. Why does he burst into a rage when Joe Kane walks out on his final trick?

9. Why does he fall on his knees beside his wife's bed and weep?

JAMES JOYCE

ARABY

ARABY is the story of how the impassioned imagination
of a young boy projects itself onto the world and, when it
is focused by the accident of first love, transforms reality
for him. So accurate in fact and precise in detail is
Joyce's representation of both the world of reality and the
world of the boy's imagination, so little—until the last
sentence—does he allow any comment to intrude on the story,
that it is easy to miss the implications of many of the details of the story.

The street the boy lived on was in fact a self-
consciously respectable, middle-class street where the
houses, "conscious of decent lives within them, gazed at one
another with brown imperturbable faces" (612), where strag-
gling gardens that concealed rusting bicycle pumps were backed by
dark muddy lanes. But the characteristically energetic
boyish imagination of the narrator lends enchantment to all
of it; "the space of the sky above us was the color of ever-
changing violet. . . .. The cold air stung us and we played
till our bodies glowed"; for him, the horses in "the dark
odorous stables . . . shook music from the buckled harness,"
and the "light from the kitchen window . . . filled the
areas" as if by magic (613). All this excess energy of
imagination lends enchantment to the world; then almost by
accident it is focused on Mangan's sister, by "her figure
defined by the light from the half-open door" as she waited,
and by the way "her dress swung as she moved her body and
the soft rope of her hair tossed from side to side" (613).

The boy is overwhelmed, not by Mangan's sister, but by
what his transfiguring imagination has made of her, so that
"when she came out on the doorstep my heart leaped," and
"her name was like a summons to all my foolish blood" (613).
The crude actuality of life was still there; he "walked
through the flaring streets, jostled by drunken men and bar-
gaining women, amid the curses of labourers, the shrill
litanies of shop-boys, . . . the nasal chanting of street-
singer. . ." (613): to him it meant only that he had to
bear "my chalice through a throng of foes," the Galahad
whose eyes were filled with tears of ecstasy, whose "body
was like a harp and her words and gestures . . . like fingers
running upon the wires" (614). All this happens, not because
he has become intimate with Mangan's sister and is affected
in this way by what she really is; in fact he has never
spoken more than a few casual words with her (613). She is
an image that he has filled with the existence his own desires require her to have.

   This image is fixed for him by the one occasion when
she does speak to him to ask him, in the most commonplace
way imaginable, if he is going to *Araby*, the bazaar. But
when she did so, she stood, "bowing her head towards me.
The light from the lamp opposite our door caught the white
curve of her neck, lit up her hair that rested there and,
falling, lit up the hand upon the railing. It fell over one
side of her dress and caught the white border of a petticoat,
just visible as she stood at ease" (614). So intensely does
this sight concentrate his powerful, inchoate feelings that
he blurts out a promise to bring her something from the
bazaar. It must have seemed to Mangan's sister the most
casual of remarks; to him it is a sacred promise. It even
lends to the name Araby, with its suggestions of "Eastern
enchantment" (614), some of the magic of his feelings about
Mangan's sister; it is, after all, now the place to which he,
as fairy prince, will go to get the gift suitable for the
fairy princess of his vision.

   Beside himself with impatience he waits for the days to
pass until Saturday night, when he is to go to the bazaar.
When his uncle is late that night, he alternates between
tense irritation and hour-long brooding on his vision of
Mangan's sister touched discreetly at neck, hand, and petticoat by the lamplight (615). Finally, with his florin
clutched tightly in his hand, he starts off, very late, for
the bazaar. The "street thronged with buyers and glaring
with gas" starts to penetrate his dream with the reality
around him; still, he is dominated by that dream: the train
seems to delay intolerably, to creep out of the station with
inconceivable slowness. But when he arrives at the bazaar
reality presses in on him irresistible. There are the
weary-looking man who takes his shilling at the entrance
(616), the half darkened hall, the men counting money in
front of the "*Café Chantant*"; the place is so unlike what
his vision had required it to be and made him anticipate it
would be that he can remember only with difficulty why he
had come there at all (617). He goes up to one of the
stalls, only to hear a horrible, all too real parody of his
love, the almost incoherent, flirtatious conversation
between the young lady serving the stall and two gentlemen.
Then the upper part of the hall goes completely dark and,
sick with the defeat of his dreams, "gazing up into the
darkness, I saw myself as a creature driven and derided by
vanity; and my eyes burned with anguish and anger" (617).

QUESTIONS (page 866 of *Modern Short Stories*)

1. What impression does the story give us of what the street the boy lived on was really like?

2. What does it look like to the boy?

3. How well does the boy know Mangan's sister? What, then, is it that makes her so fascinating to him?

4. What connects Mangan's sister and the bazaar, Araby, for the boy?

5. What affect does this actual visit to the bazaar have on him? What is it that makes him feel as he does there?

6. Why does his experience at the bazaar make him feel he has been "driven and derided by vanity"?

JOYCE CAROL OATES
Out of Place

This story gets its striking effect by being strictly
objective about Jack Furlong's injury in Vietnam. He has
lost a leg, his face has been grotesquely damaged, and he
has "some trouble with my 'vision.' My eyes." That
touching shift from the technical phrase he has learned
from the doctors and his own simple description of being
barely able to see fixes our attention on the story's main
object, the state of the boy's mind and feelings. That
state is no less complicated because he was, before his injury, an ordinary nineteen-year-old boy and because he must
now wrestle with the half-suppressed memory of his agony
and terror when he was wounded; and, in his more "normal"
moments, try to think out his future. He is a teenager,
everyone's son at that stage of life when a boy knows a good
deal but understands very little of it, forced to come to
terms with disaster and horror.

The technical achievement of this story is hard to
overstate. The author has undertaken to show us, without
comment, the tragedy of this boy's life. She keeps strictly
to what the boy himself sees and understands about himself
and the world around him. What he understands is limited by
his immaturity and by the psychological damage done him by
the land mine that so nearly killed him. Occasionally he
shows flashes of the shrewdness of the young, as when he
recognizes the shock his appearance gives the head waiter
when they arrive for dinner at the Grotto Room and realizes
why the people at the next table change seats. He pretends
not to notice these things, as he pretends not to notice his
parents' clumsy efforts to pretend everything is normal.
"It is better that way."

For all their surface simplicity, his thoughts and
feelings are complicated. By making us see them plainly,
by making us see all the suffering the boy endures without
quite recognizing it as suffering, and by also making us see
all the tragedy there is in the boy's situation, the story
makes us respond directly to what has happened to the boy.
What makes this response so powerful is that it is a direct
response to the facts themselves, not a response to some
rhetoric about them. We see the boy as if we were there
ourselves, watching.

The story achieves this effect with a modified version
of the interior monologue. We are told only what the boy
himself understands about himself; we do not follow the
movement of his interior monologue but only his comments on
it. Still, as in the interior monologue, the narrative

follows the pattern of the boy's meditation rather than the logical order of third-person narration; he tells us things as they come into the mind of some one who knows them, not in the order they would have to be given to explain them to someone else.   (It is, incidentally, worth comparing this use of this method with Virginia Woolf's use of it in *The Mark on the Wall*, pp. 644-651.) Much as we would if we were observing life itself, we have to pull together bits of imperfect information scattered throughout the story in order to understand the boy's situation and to figure out the reason—which he does not always himself understand—for his feeling as he does. The author does not push this interior monologue to the limits of apparent free association that some authors use; the information we need is reasonably available. As early as the first paragraph we learn that the boy is in a hospital and that he is nineteen. Perhaps we also notice some strange things about his meditation that will not in fact be explained till later. He says, "I am nineteen, now, *I think*," as if his memory were damaged and his knowledge of himself uncertain. We do not know, because he does not know himself, why his mind hovers so lovingly over "this memory" of going to the movies with "kids my age" when he was thirteen. We are puzzled that this apparently insignificant memory is more important to him than his mother's delight in his approaching birthday and that he stresses the fact that "there is something pleasant about this memory."

But when we come back to this paragraph after finishing the story, we can see that he has unconsciously shown us why this memory matters so much to him; it is all there, it we read carefully enough. "The movie house, yes, and the kids, *and I am one of them*." "We are all in line waiting and no one is out of line [no one, that is, is out of place]. *I am there, with them*." This is the memory of a past when everything was in place and secure, when he felt safe and happy, untouched by the terror that now lies just below the level of consciousness and can errupt so violently and with so little warning. It is for this reason, too, that getting home from the hospital is so important to him; there "everything is in place" and safe, as it was before he went to Vietnam, not—as the story's title tells us it is now— forever "out of place."

Though he does not make the connection, we soon realize that it is sitting on the hospital terrace watching the children playing across the street that sets off this memory (when the children quarrel and seem to fall apart it frightens him and Ed). But remembering "is unhealthy"; the doctors have told him so. We understand that they want him to live in the present in order to free him from the memory of the horror of the explosion that wounded him and killed his friend, his agonizing weeping over whom he now remembers as some one else weeping over a "buddy," as if his subconscious mind cannot endure to face the full reality of that experience. "But I have already forgotten these things," he

says; and, as a matter of conscious habit, he has. He remembers the bare facts of the explosion of the land mine in
which he was lucky not to be killed. In the simplest sense
it is true he was lucky. Many died; he survived. Moreover,
that is the only truth that will make it possible for him to
go on living; "in the end it is only truth you can stand."
What you can't stand is the other truth that lies just below
his consciousness and emerges at regular intervals, things
like the memory of his actual experience of the explosion
with its unendurable horror and suffering; or the longing he
feels, though he does not fully understand it, for a normal
life. It is this longing that evokes the memory of going to
the movies with a crowd of friends when he was thirteen. It
is so strong that he is caught off guard by the girl who is
not horrified by his terribly damaged face and smiles at him
("It was strange that her face showed nothing, unlike the
other faces that are turned to me all the time"). His unconscious need for her friendship "excites" him so much that
he cannot speak coherently, and the boy with the girl,
looking at him differently, says, "He deserves it."

    This, then, is the way the story slowly reveals to us,
almost the way life itself rather than a story might, the
boy's situation and the way he thinks and feels about it.
Fascinated by the miraculous mechanics of the human body as
the result of the damage to his own and Ed's, he dreams of
becoming a doctor. "I mean if things get better." It makes
his mother cry to hear him say so. Crying, he says,
"embarrasses" him; he cannot stand to cry himself, as he
sometimes does. Only later do we learn why; "Crying makes
me think of someone else crying, a soldier holding another
soldier's hand, sitting in some rubble." We know from his
parents' clumsy efforts to conceal it that things will never
"get better" for him.

    We understand too, though he doesn't, why visitors and
stories about his cousin Betty and Harold Spendor "are like
rays of sunlight" to him. They make him feel nothing has
changed and that presently he will be back in the safe world
that was there when he was a child living at home and going
to the movies with his friends. Only these moments of sunshine do not last, and sometimes, right in the midst of
them, that "terrible" door opens into the blackness. He had
once, when he was young, caught a glimpse of fear, when he
stopped at night to help a man with a flat tire. "What if
something had happened to me?" He does not say so, he does
not know, that he is remembering this experience because now
something has happened to him and he will never be free—
however unconscious the fear may be—of fear.

    So we leave him, delighting his mother by succeeding in
making a choice of his own of how he will have his lobster
done at his twentieth-birthday-party dinner and hearing in
the back of his mind what the irritated boy had said when
his girl smiled at Jack in the hospital ("he deserves it")

and the scream of the wounded in Vietnam, "Don't leave me!"
—out of place.

QUESTIONS (page 867 of *Modern Short Stories*)

1. The school children across from the hospital affect
Jack in two quite different ways. What are they?

2. Why does Jack feel there is "something pleasant
about" the memory of standing in line for the Western movie?

3. Why do the screams of the school children sometimes
upset Jack?

4. What are the facts behind Jack's confused memory of
"a boy somewhere who was holding onto the hand of his
'buddy'"?

5. Why do Jack and Ed want to be doctors? Why do Jack's
parents behave oddly when he talks about it?

6. Why is Jack happy when he says that "if this hadn't
happened . . . I guess I'd be just the way I was"? Why
does his mother cry when he says it?

7. Why does Jack enjoy the family gossip about his
cousin Betty and Mr. Spendor so much?

8. What is the "terrible door" that opens in Jack's mind
sometimes?

9. Why does Jack remember he was frightened when he
stopped to help the man with the flat tire and think, "What
if something had happened to me?"

10. Why is Jack so excited by the girl who says to him,
"I know you, don't I?"

11. Why is coming home such a happy day for Jack?

12. What is the matter with the manager of the Grotto
Room when they arrive for dinner? Why do the people at the
next table change seats?

13. Why are Jack's parents so pleased when he chooses
lobster and decides on "the Skyway Lobster"?

KATHERINE MANSFIELD
HER FIRST BALL

T. S. Eliot once put with a precision that is at once just and rather daunting the characteristic quality of the Katherine Mansfield story. "The story," he said, "is limited to . . . feeling and the moral and social ramifications are outside the terms of reference. As the material is limited in this way—and indeed our satisfaction recognizes the skill with which the author has handled perfectly the minimum material—it is what I believe would be called feminine." It is not necessary to accept the slightly pejorative implications of "minimum" and perhaps also "feminine" to recognize the accuracy of Eliot's definition of Katherine Mansfield's purpose. Her story is wholly concentrated on representing the movement of Leila's feelings at her first ball, to defining and distinguishing each of them, to following their shifts and changes, to making us know them—in the special sense in which to share the exact feelings of an experiencer is to know.

It is possible to argue either that personal feelings —sincerity—constitute reality or, less extravagantly, that unless we concentrate on feeling what it is to have an experience, we know it only imperfectly. To people convinced of one or another of these propositions (as Eliot is plainly convinced of neither), Katherine Mansfield will seem a wholly satisfactory writer, one whose work comprehends all significant reality. But it is quite possible for those who do not take that view to participate in the feelings of the heroine in a story by Katherine Mansfield and to recognize how brilliantly she does what she sets out to do. In any event, it is probably as well not to raise this question with students until late in the discussion; taken up too soon it may divert them from appreciating what is fine in *Her First Ball*. It is time enough to raise this larger question when they have worked carefully through the story and done that.

The exclusiveness with which the story focuses on Leila's feelings is made evident at the start by its resort to the kind of fantasy which frankly—if ostensibly playfully—ignores literal fact in order to convey the reality of intense feeling. Leila is so excited by her anticipation of the ball that she feels as if she were already there when she enters the cab; "the bolster on which her hand rested felt like the sleeve of an unknown young man's dress suit," and the cab seems to her to bowl "past waltzing lamp-posts" (629). Such was the intensity of her delighted anticipation. She struggles to act grown-up and sophisticated about it all,

tries "not to care"; but it all seems so precious to her
that she knows she will "remember [it] forever" and longs to
treasure up, as if keepsakes will keep the feeling of it
alive, even the wisps of paper from Laurie's new gloves. So
heightened are her feelings that for a moment she thinks she
will cry over the beauty of the brother-sister relationship
between Laurie and Laura that she, an only child, will never
know.

Then they arrive, in what seems to Leila's excited
feelings a blaze of light in which "gay couples seemed to
float through the air" and "satin shoes chased each other
like birds"; and she is "lifted past the big golden lantern,
carried along the passage, and pushed into the little room
marked 'Ladies'" (630). In the ladies' room the gas jet
quivers and leaps, as if—she feels—it shared her inability
to wait for the dancing to begin (630) and even "the little
quivering coloured flags strung across the ceiling were,"
(631) it seemed to her, "talking" with excitement. When she
thinks to herself, "How heavenly; how simply heavenly!" she
is not using a mere form of words; she is speaking the simple
truth of her feelings; she can conceive no greater happiness
than she feels at this moment.

When the music begins, she is beside herself with
ecstasy; "if her partner did not come . . . she would die at
least, or faint, or lift her arms and fly out of one of
those dark windows that showed the stars"; and when her
partner does at last come, "she floated away like a flower
that is tossed into a pool." Naively she tries to explain
to her partners her feelings; in their commonplaceness and
their familiarity with balls, they are uncomprehending. But
Leila is much too lost in her own feelings to be affected by
their attitude ("Perhaps it was a little strange that her
partners were not more interested. For it was thrilling.")
until the older, balding man dances with her (633).

He is an image of time denied, of the attempt to go on
being young long after one is not young. "It gave [Leila]
quite a shock again to see how old he was . . . he looked
shabby" (633). But he has the wisdom of his experience and
uses it—tactlessly, even inconceivably, if we are thinking
of character treatment in a realistic way. But Katherine
Mansfield is not; she is thinking only of Leila's feelings.
What this elderly beau is made to say, however implausibly,
sounds "terribly true [to Leila]" (634). It is, of course;
but what counts about it in the story is that it makes the
dance music sound to Leila, for a moment, "sad, sad," and
makes her feel that "forever wasn't a bit too long" for
happiness to last; and "deep inside her a little girl threw
her pinafore over her head and sobbed" (634-635). Not that
Leila is capable of really feeling the possibility of age;
she can conceive it only as a contrast to her happiness,
something that emphasizes by that contrast the joy of the
moment; and "presently a soft, melting, ravishing tune began,
and a young man with curly hair bowed before her. . . . her
feet glided, glided," so that when she bumps into the

elderly fat man, "she smiled at him more radiantly than ever.
She didn't even recognize him again" (635).

QUESTIONS (pages 867-868 of *Modern Short Stories*)

1. How does Leila feel when she gets into the cab to go
to the ball? How does Katherine Mansfield convey that
feeling to us?

2. Why does Katherine Mansfield say that the cab seemed
to go past "waltzing" lamp-posts?

3. Why is Leila moved by the brother-sister relation
between Laurie and Laura?

4. Why does Leila think the lamp jet in the ladies'
room is leaping and quivering?

5. What state of feeling is conveyed by Katherine
Mansfield's saying Leila "floated away like a flower that is
tossed into a pool" when she began to dance?

6. What effect does the conversation of the elderly
dancer have on Leila? How long does it last? What puts an
end to it? Why?

BERNARD MALAMUD
TAKE PITY

TAKE PITY is the story of two people, neither of them young or beautiful or rich, who love one another in the unglamorous, almost comically practical way that is a necessity where there is no money to make refinements possible, but who yet have great delicacy of feeling and pride of heart. Each of them is in his own way a capable person: Rosen is, in a small way, a thoroughly successful coffee salesman, and Eva an attractive and capable woman. Their capability gives them a confidence about their ability to cope with life independently that is—as the story suggests it is for all men—unjustified. That confidence is, in turn, supported by their pride, which makes it impossible for either to accept anything about which there is the faintest suggestion of charity. Each of them can give, with generosity and sympathy. But neither can take anything, least of all pity.

The pride and justified confidence in his own knowledge of the grocery business that makes Rosen so sure a judge of the prospects for the Kalish's store makes him, quite unintentionally, particularly trying to sensitive people. He feels himself to be the shrewd, successful, American businessman talking kindly to the inexperienced immigrant: "Kiddo, this is a mistake. This place is a grave. Here they will bury you if you don't get out quick!" (637). It is perfectly true, but it is surely galling to the Kalishes to be told it with such assured authority. Rosen is a kind man, but he is also a proud man, pleased with his shrewdness and his success; that makes it comparatively easy for him to be kind so long as, in being so, he can indulge his innocent pride by a small display of superior business acumen.

With his immigrant's almost total lack of business judgment and his stubborn, peasant reliance on incredibly hard work, Kalish struggles—hoping against hope—to make a success of the store he knows in his heart is doomed. He has to bear the extra burden of Rosen's confident and—alas, —correct assurances that he has not got a chance. Finally, as Rosen puts it, "Broke in him something"—his ability to believe and hope any longer—and he dies, leaving his wife and two little girls in a perilous situation.

Rosen loves them, more than his pride in his pose of rich uncle will allow him to admit, even to himself. He sets out to deal with their problem with his usual confident —and grossly imperceptive—good sense. Get out of the store while you can, he tells Eva. "You are a nice-looking young

-156-

woman, only thirty-eight years. . . . You're young yet.
Sometime you will meet somebody and get married" (639). For
Eva, who loves Rosen and is proudly anxious that he should
love her so that she can give herself and her two girls to
him as a gift, this is like a slap in the face—"Sometime
you will meet somebody and get married" indeed. In bitter
despair, Eva is now convinced that Rosen does not need or
want her at all, that he just pities her in a way she cannot
endure. "No, Rosen, not me," she says. "With marriage I am
finished. Nobody wants a poor widow with two children."
When Rosen, with common sense all on his side, denies this,
she says "I know," meaning, "I know from what you have just
said that <u>you</u> do not," and "never," Rosen adds, "in my life
I saw so bitter a woman's face." In her hurt pride, in her
detestation of humiliating pity where she had wanted grateful love, Eva is now determined at all cost not to accept
anything from Rosen. It leaves her no alternative but to
try—without hope, with only a desperate and determined
pride—to keep the store going. Rosen, wanting badly in <u>his</u>
pride to think that all he feels for Eva and the girls is
pity, tries everything to save her except the right thing.
One night he brings "a nice piece sirloin" to them (640) but
it is not well received. "So what else could I do?" he says.
"I have a heart and am human." He is still determined to
think what he feels is pity, not needful love. But, remembering that moment now as he tells the story to Davidov, he
weeps. Then, with elaborate, loving, self-deceiving care,
he offers to set Eva and the girls up. Eva, feeling in-
sulted all over again by this new evidence that she is not
needed or wanted by Rosen, "looked on me in such a way, with
such burning eyes, like I was small and ugly . . . I thought
to myself, 'Rosen, this woman don't like you.'" (640) The
truth is, of course, just the opposite; she loves him, and,
loving him, she wants in her pride to give, not to receive—
above all, not to receive from mere pity. When she says to
Rosen with heroic dignity, "Thank you very kindly, my friend
Mr. Rosen [how bitterly she must have thought that "friend"]
. . . but charity we are not needing," Rosen is beside himself with an exasperation that—though he does not know it—
really arises from the anxiety of his love. "Who charity?"
I cried to her. "What charity? Speaks to you your husband's
friend." He could hardly have said worse from Eva's point
of view.

Then the thought that Eva may be suspecting him of
wanting to make her his mistress occurs to him. "This made
me think of something that I didn't think about before," he
says with almost sublime self-deception. He decides to
marry her, but merely as a kindness, not accepting anything
in return: "What did she have to lose? I could take care
of myself without any trouble to them." In these terms he
proposes: "For myself, Eva, I don't want anything. Absolutely not a thing" (641). It is a moment of terrible
temptation to Eva, not only because she needs Rosen badly
but because she wants desperately the chance to love him.
But pride wins out. "She was with her back to me and didn't
speak," Rosen remembers. "When she turned around again her

face was white but the mouth was like iron," and she says,
"No, Mr. Rosen." When he presses her, she lies bravely,
saying precisely the opposite of what she feels—"I had
enough with sick men"; then she breaks down and begins to
cry because Rosen will not allow her what she so desperately
wants, the chance to give herself where she is greatly
wanted.

"I went home," Rosen says, "but hurt me my mind. . . .
Why should somebody that her two children were starving
always say no to a man that he wanted to help her?" Why indeed? Even Rosen, blinded as he is by his deep need not to
be pitied as a sick man, might have guessed. But he did
not; and he is still insisting to himself that "all that I
felt in my heart was pity for her." So he proposed to find
her "a strong, healthy husband" through a marriage broker
and give her a dowry, and she screams with rage at him.
Then he begs her, "on my bended knee," to allow him to re-
stock the store for her and "she cried, it was terrible to
see" (642). Next he tries sending her money anonymously;
she is not deceived and sends it back.

Finally Rosen is forced to recognize the strength of
Eva's refusal to be given anything. "'Here,' I said to myself, 'is a very strange thing—a person that you can never
give her anything.—But I will give.'" For his proud determination to give without receiving is as stubborn as hers.
He makes everything over to her and puts his head in the
kitchen stove and turns on the gas.

He is presumably dead, continuing to exist in some
place "in space" where they regularly send an agent, "the
census-taker," to check up on him. "That was part of the
cure, if you wanted a cure," as Davidov thinks. This place
is not much different from the world Davidov has always
known; certainly none of the defects of either his own
nature or his environment are different there; it is a
grubby, institutionalized, interfering place, and Davidov is
exactly what he was before he died. The problem remains the
same, and perhaps will remain so, if not for eternity, at
least for the long, long time of purgatory, for Davidov has
not yet begun even to want to be cured. The state will "try,"
in its not very efficient way, to help, but Davidov will
here, as in life, have to cure himself if he is to be cured
at all.

Davidov, who has been listening to all this, had asked
at the start why Rosen insisted on sitting without light,
with the shade of his room pulled down. Now he can bear this
gloom no longer and "before Rosen could cry no, [he] idly
raised the window shade." And there stands Eva outside the
window "staring at him with haunted, beseeching eyes. She
raised her arms to him" (643). Now, because Rosen is a
broken man, she is able to express her love freely, as an
offer to give him anything. But to Rosen this love looks
like pity and he will not take it. Infuriated by the very
thought of it, he shakes his fist at her and shouts, "Whore,

bastard, bitch. Go 'way from here. Go home to your
children"—whom he supposes her really to love, where she
only pities him. Davidov makes "no move to hinder him as
Rosen rammed down the window shade"; the situation, he sees,
is hopeless. Loving one another, neither of these two can
accept. Both will die before they will take pity.

Malamud presents this story with great skill. By
having Rosen tell it, under pressure—he is too proud and
bitter to want to tell it—Malamud deliberately puts himself under the necessity of presenting the events as Rosen
understands them. All that we are given directly, therefore, is Rosen's view of himself as a successful, generous,
kindly man and of Eva as an inexplicably stubborn, self-
destructive woman. With great skill, however, without ever
having Eva say or do anything that will force Rosen to
recognize her real motive, Malamud makes us see what Eva's
feelings are. This, in turn, forces us to consider what
Rosen's real motives are, the things that will not allow him
to recognize either why Eva acts as she does or why he fails
to say what is true, that he loves her.

This way of presenting the story to us also allows
Malamud to use Davidov, with the quiet drama of understate-
ment: Davidov is, after all, ostensibly in the story only
to listen, to mark for us the pity of the story. He does so
most notably when Rosen, trying to read Davidov's notebook
in which the writing has degenerated to illegibility under
the stress of Davidov's emotions, says, "It's not English
and it's not Yiddish. Could it be Hebrew?" and Davidov
merely says, "No. It's an old-fashioned language that they
don't use it nowadays"—that is, the language of true pity
that at least Rosen and Eva, if not "they," don't use nowadays. By having Rosen tell the story in his own words,
Malamud also makes it possible for himself to tell it in the
colloquial language that most intimately expresses Rosen's
mind and heart. This gives the expression of his feelings
the wonderful eloquence that any feelings have when they are
expressed in exactly the terms in which they are thought of
by the person who experiences them. They are only more
moving because there is a touch of comedy about the Jewish
colloquialisms of Rosen's speech: they express perfectly
the maddening, stubborn, thorny, blind, and blinding pride
of Rosen's nature.

QUESTIONS (page 868 of *Modern Short Stories*)

1. What conception of himself is revealed by Rosen's manner of advising the Kalishes that their store is doomed?

2. Why does Eva so decisively reject Rosen's first scheme to get her out of the store where she can meet somebody and marry again? Why is she sure she is right that the scheme will not work?

3. Why is Eva even more offended by Rosen's second scheme, to set her and the girls up comfortably at his expense?

4. What offends Eva so greatly in Rosen's reply to her assertion that they do not need charity?

5. What offends her about the way Rosen proposes?

6. Rosen's final scheme for giving money to Eva and the girls looks insane; is it rationally explicable?

7. Why is Eva standing outside the window stretching her arms toward Rosen at the end of the story?

VIRGINIA WOOLF

THE MARK ON THE WALL

THE MARK ON THE WALL is one of the first (it was published in 1921) of the stories writers like John Barth have
written in the 1960's and 1970's. These stories are difficult, or at least puzzling, so perhaps it is best to begin
with a general statement—the kind these writers despise—
about what this story is doing. Its purpose is to represent
its author's notion of what is finally real for all of us.
Virginia Woolf has a specially vivid visual sense of life
that serves her well for this purpose. "How readily," she
says, "our thoughts [meaning what we imagine] swarm upon a
new object"; certainly hers do. "In order to fix a date,"
she adds (or to grasp anything as far as she is concerned),
"it is necessary to remember what one saw"—not, that is,
what ideas one had. So, when she thinks for a moment that
the mark on the wall is a nail put in for one of the
previous tenants' pictures, a miniature, she immediately
imagines the miniature itself, a lady "with white powdered
curls, powder-dusted cheeks, and lips like red carnations."

What Virginia Woolf's story does is to show us a person
seeing life as she believes we all see it when we are most
sharply aware of it. Reality, she is convinced, is life
perceived by the imagination, not something "out there,"
separate from the person who sees it, about which he thinks
out some theory. Reality is life imagined, something immediate and alive in our minds, a "mighty world / Of eye and
ear, both what they half create, / And what perceive." And
if that is so, a story must be, not an illustrated analysis
of life, but the representation of an imagination in the act
of seeing and creating it. What determines the kinds of
things the speaker is conscious of and the order in which
she thinks of them is the way the imagination acts—with
occasional interruptions from ordinary conscious with its
awareness of Whiteaker's Table of Precedency and the dull,
routine thoughts of a relaxed mind. In her honesty about
these interruptions, Virginia Woolf is not unlike her great
contemporary, James Joyce, whom she disliked, perhaps because, despite her disapproval of him, he was a good deal
like her. But she does not, as does John Barth for example,
speculate at length in a rather professorial way (Barth is
a professor) about the special techniques of writing stories
like this one, though she is convinced that "the novelists
in future will realize more and more the importance of these
reflections" of life in the mirrors of our imaginations—as
indeed, novelists have.

Virginia Woolf's kind of story has, then, three main
purposes: first, to conceive reality as life imagined;

second, to describe that reality, not by an illustrated
argument about the imagined life, but by showing the imagination in action; and third, to work out a way of talking
that will show the imagination in action. She realizes that
these purposes are not easy to achieve. The greatest difficulty is that we cannot live continuously at the level of
intensity imagination requires. If the imagination keeps
moving out into life from the mark on the wall, sooner or
later that mark brings the mind back, reminding us that the
tiresome world of newspapers is everywhere around us and
that we cannot escape the world of messy housekeeping that
allows a snail to crawl up the wall. (A snail! How odd;
what the imagination could not do with that!—in another
story.)

     One must also guard against fantasy—the unreal inven-
tions of the mind that betray the imagination. We must not
let childish fancies of crimson flags and castles and
knights take the place in our minds of the imagination's
grasp of actual life. Even more troublesome—perhaps
unconquerable—is the effect of the passage of time. What
have the lives of the previous tenants of her house been?
She can never see them again; she is torn from them as she
speeds through life "as one is torn from the old lady about
to pour out tea and the young man about to hit the tennis
ball in the back garden of the suburban villa as one rushes
by in the train," like some one "blown through the Tube at
fifty miles an hour—landing at the other end without a
single hairpin in one's hair! Shot out at the feet of God
entirely naked! Tumbling head over heels in the asphodel
meadows like a brown paper parcel pitched down a shoot in
the post office! With one's hair flying back like the tail
of a race horse." These vivid images of the way we are
rushed through life by time, never staying anywhere long
enough to imagine it completely and understand it, have a
fine comic lack of dignity, as if, for all our seriousness
about life, it were a sort of joke played on us by time.
For all the intensity of our effort to imagine the reality
of life fully, to grasp it all and understand it, we lose
most of it without even noticing we've done so—as we have
lost the Queen Anne coal-scuttle, the bagatelle board, and
the rest. "Oh, dear me, the mystery of life; the inaccuracy
of thought! . . . What an accidental affair this living is
after all our civilization. . . ." No doubt the after life
will be the same.

     But maybe we could imagine continuously, uninterrupted
by the ordinary perception of things; perhaps we could
charge our lives with imagination without interruption. Let
us try imagining Shakespeare. But no, that is thinking of
history, always more fancy than imagination, not thinking of
the here and the now of actual life. Well, then, let us
imagine ourselves, in a favorable but not grossly flattering
way; is not this?—but no, generalizations are worthless.
They are like the lifeless rules of behavior of our childhood, or like the ridiculous ritual of public life, of

cabinet ministers and archbishops, from which we escape into
the freedom of imagining the actual life around us—if, to
be sure, there is any such thing as freedom.

But perhaps the mark on the wall is not flat but a
protuberance, like a small tumulous, such as antiquaries investigate, making a pleasant existence for them and their
elderly wives until the Colonel dies of a stroke, thinking
not about his wife and child but about the arrow head dug
from the tumulus that now rests in the little local museum
with the foot of a Chinese murderess and other priceless
sources of knowledge about the human situation. "No, no,
nothing is proved, nothing is known. . . ." Scientists are
the descendents of witches and hermits; let us rid ourselves
of such superstitions and try to find "beauty and health of
mind," a world of flowers in open fields, not of professors
or specialists or house-keepers with the profiles of policemen. But no, again; this vision of an underwater world
where one can slice through life with the imagination as a
fish slices through the water is hopelessly idealistic, a
waste of energy, in a world of Whiteaker's Table of
Precedency. So nature, the mark on the wall, calls the mind
back to where we are, to an imaginable reality, not an un-
realizable vision of an ideal world, but a charged vision
of the actual world—in which, for example, a tree, if we
imagine it carefully enough, can be seen living out its
life, and its after-life, too, in bedrooms, in ships, on
pavement, even in living rooms like this one in which the
narrator is still smoking the after-tea cigarette she was
smoking when her imagination first took off from the mark on
the wall to travel over life.

But no, yet again; one cannot live forever in the
imagined world, however real it may be. Suddenly the everyday, unimagined world comes crashing in and the imagined
world falls in ruins. "Where was I? What has it all been
about?" "Ah, the mark on the wall? It was [really?] a
snail."

QUESTIONS (pages 868-869 of *Modern Short Stories*)

1. "How readily our thoughts swarm upon a new object," says Virginia Woolf. What kind of thoughts do so in her story?

2. Why does she dislike "that old fancy of crimson flags, etc."?

3. What is the resemblance between her losing track of the previous tenants and losing sight of things seen from a train?

4. Why is life like being "blown through the Tube at fifty miles an hour"?

5. What makes her dislike her own speculations about what future novelists will do?

6. To what conclusion does thinking about antiquarians lead her?

7. To what conclusion does her speculating about a peaceful underwater world lead her?

8. What bothers her about leading articles, cabinet ministers, and Sunday afternoon walks?

9. What makes her worship the chest of drawers when she wakes up in the night?

10. ". . . but something is getting in the way. . ." What is getting in the way of what?

JOHN BARTH

LOST IN THE FUNHOUSE

LOST IN THE FUNHOUSE is typical of the way writers like
Barth deal with what one critic has called "the mess of our
culture and our daily lives, in this intricate and possibly
devastating century," or—as he also calls it—"the condition of exhaustion and . . . strategies for overcoming and
escaping that distinctively modern trap." The suggestion in
these remarks that there is something specially difficult
about our time is a provincial exaggeration, as if "exhaustion" (acedia) were not as old as man, as if nearly all
centuries have not seemed to those who lived through them
"devastating." But these quotations do describe Barth's
sense of life quite accurately. The only escape from the
funhouse horror of life that Barth can see (this idea turns
up in nearly all his stories) is Love. "For whom is the
funhouse fun?" he begins. "Perhaps for lovers." (651)
Barth's sense of life is complicated, and so, therefore, is
the story in which he tries to communicate it to us. "What
is the story's theme?" (658) he asks at one point, as if
speaking for us, as the story meanders on, through apparently irrelevant interruptions, parodies, and non sequiturs.
But these things are all relevant to its theme, as the final
paragraph makes clear.

Lost in the Funhouse has three main concerns, all of
which it must deal with. The first is the human situation
as a whole; even God is represented by the image of the funhouse at one point: ". . . even the designer and operator
have forgotten this other part [of the funhouse], that winds
around on itself like a whelk shell." (661) The story's
second concern is the painful experience of growing up that
Ambrose goes through, his uncertainties about his own
nature, his attempts to become as secure as adults appear to
be, his comforting daydreams of heroic behavior: "Somewhere
in the world there was a young woman with such splendid
understanding that she'd. . ." (669). The third is the
author's own struggle to write a story that is not conventional and unconvincing but a true image of life—or, to be
precise, of Barth's perception of life. All three of these
experiences are constantly being compared to getting lost in
the funhouse in which Ambrose "actually" does get lost
during the family's holiday (holiday!) visit to Ocean City.

Barth is painfully aware that a story is a trick, an
artifice constructed to deceive the reader, at least for
the moment, into thinking he is seeing life itself. Barth
has the romantic's deep distrust of artifice, and is at the
same time aware of the irony of his using artifice, the art
of narrative, to escape artifice. Words themselves, not to

mention absurd devices like italics, are arbitrary and ludicrously unlike the things they represent. So are devices
like metaphor, plot, narrative pose (first person? second
person?). He keeps interrupting his story to talk to the
reader about these things, to make quite sure they are not
deceived by the unreality of the only devices he has for
showing them his own vision of reality. These interruptions
are frequently written in a deadpan, textbook style that is
comically unpersuasive beside the lively and convincing
style of the devices they are meant to expose. (But if they
were not written in this style, they would become falsely
literary too.)

     These comments take us out of the imaginary world of
the story of Ambrose's trip to Ocean City and into a world
—imaginary too, though less obviously so—where the author
is struggling to write the story. These comments are not
the only means Barth uses to alert us to the artificiality
of art. Quite often, when he is using conventional narrative with all its tricks quite seriously, he will suddenly
slide into a form of it so laboriously artificial as to look
ridiculous ("The occasion of their visit [to Ocean City],"
he will say solemnly, "is Independence Day, the most important secular holiday of the United States of America" [651].)
We begin to doubt whether we should take Ambrose's story
seriously, and that mixed feeling is exactly the one Barth
wishes to create. Barth is himself lost in the funhouse of
creating funhouses, and he wants to make sure we know we are
lost in the funhouse he has created, as we are lost in the
funhouse of life itself.

     Nevertheless, Barth is not really lost in the funhouse
of story writing; on the contrary, he is making a quite
lucid image of being so lost. A large part of *Lost in the
Funhouse* is a representation in a perfectly familiar narrative style, third-person narration, of what Ambrose sees and
feels on the trip to Ocean City; however often Barth slides
away into parody of this method of narration, it works
seriously much of the time. We watch through Ambrose's eyes
the ride to Ocean City, the walk along the boardwalk to the
funhouse, and so forth; and because the narrative is a
representation of Ambrose's consciousness, we also get to
know his painful social self-consciousness, his sufferings
over the slow process of growing up, his childish dreams of
success, above all his sexual responses (often conceived by
him in his own mind in the touchingly formal language of his
age—"Her figure was very well developed for her age," etc.).
We are made to understand just how intense these responses
are by the cunning device of having Ambrose remember, with
almost incredible precision, every detail of the scene with
Magda, down to the number of strings in the lyre that lay on
the marble bench beside the laureled and loose-toga'ed lady
in the picture on the cover of Uncle Karl's old *El Producto*
cigar box that was in the toolshed to hold stone-cutting
tools (656).

One of the great advantages of using third-person narration to present what amounts to the first-person perception of the story's action by one of the characters is that
it allows the author to slide unobtrusively away from the
character's limited perception to his own "omniscient" view
whenever it serves his purpose. Barth often does so in a
familiar enough way by making observations hardly possible
for a thirteen-year-old boy, such as those that tell us this
story is taking place during World War II. There are a lot
of these and they are quite brilliantly precise—like the
reference to the family's "black 1936 La Salle sedan" or to
the white wrapping that Lucky Strike cigarettes so fatuously
announced at the time that it was adopting as a contribution
to the war effort (653). Having done so, Barth carefully
points out to us that such observations would hardly be possible for the thirteen-year-old boy who is supposed to be
making them. Anyhow, he adds, what do such characteristic
features of realistic stories have to do with the story he
is telling?

Interruptions like these are Barth's second, more
radical way of intruding on the narrative, and he frequently
uses such interruptions to talk about the artificial tricks
of writing in general, such as italics (651), blanks (652)
and metaphors (653). Sometimes, too, he uses them to bring
in absurdly pointless examples of such devices, as when we
are suddenly told that excursion trains are mentioned in
Dos Passos' *42nd Parallel* (or rather, "in the novel *The
42nd Parallel* by John Dos Passos"). And sometimes the narrative will shift abruptly into a comically old-fashioned
narrative style ("Nowadays [that is, in 19__ , the year of
our story] . . . [652]"). Sometimes he will let a sentence
of narration simply drift away, as if he cannot endure
it any longer ("The smell of Uncle Karl's cigar smoke reminded one of." [653]) He even plays for a moment with the
idea that he might get behind all this artifice by somehow
giving us a "true" portrait of the author himself, and then
reduces this scheme to absurdity by a laborious genealogy
that suddenly turns into a specific account of the various
sexual encounters in which these earlier generations were
generated. If this reduces the portrait of the artist as
genealogy to a muddle of undignified beddings, and thus
destroys the idea that we can get at reality that way, it
also reminds us of Barth's dislike of artifice, which will
certainly make him dislike the refined circumlocutions of
conventional descriptions of love as much as he dislikes
the artifices of art. He even goes to some trouble to suggest that the physical process of love itself involves the
fierce struggle of the spermatozoa to "grope through hot,
dark windings, past Love's Tunnel's fearsome obstacles"
(659). Barth has written a whole story, *Night-Sea Journey*,
about this journey of the spermatozoa.

On top of this, Barth frequently interrupts Ambrose's
story with criticisms of the kind conventional critics are
likely to make of the story: the ultimate effect of these

interruptions is to remind us of how irrelevant the standards of conventional story-telling are to this story. "A
long time," he will say, "has gone by already without anything happening; it makes a person wonder. We haven't even
reached Ocean City yet; we will never get out of this
funhouse." (656) That last remark makes it clear that the
story is such a muddle because life is. The author is
struggling against the fact that all stories—including
even stories like this one that try to escape—are artifices, funhouses for readers, the creation of which is a
long losing struggle by the artist through a kind of funhouse that is quite as bad as our struggle to get through
the funhouse of life that he struggles to represent for us.

> He wishes he had never entered the funhouse.
> But he has. Then he wishes he were dead. But
> he's not. Therefore he will construct funhouses
> for others and be their secret operator—though
> he would rather be among the lovers for whom
> funhouses are designed. (674)

QUESTIONS (page 869 of *Modern Short Stories*)

1. Why does Barth keep interrupting the story with remarks about how such things as italics work?

2. What does Barth himself use italics for, as in such
phrases as "*psychological coeval*" and "*stimulated by the
briney spume*"?

3. What is the point of the story's references to
writers like John Dos Passos and James Joyce?

4. What makes Ambrose remember in such minute detail
the picture on the cigar box in the toolshed?

5. Why does Barth keep interrupting his story to complain that it is not getting anywhere?

6. Why does the story refer so carefully to the "black
1936 La Salle sedan" and the white Lucky Strike package?

7. "Diving would make a suitable literary symbol," says
Barth as they watch the young people at the pool. In what
way and of what?

8. The funhouse is obviously a symbol too and of more
things than one. What does it symbolize in Ambrose's life?

9. What does the story's last paragraph suggest about
the author?

10. Why does the story begin, "For whom is the funhouse
fun? Perhaps for lovers"?

PART FOUR

WILLIAM FAULKNER
THE FIRE AND THE HEARTH

THE FIRE AND THE HEARTH is a fine illustration of how
traditional and conservative, in the best sense of these
terms, much of Faulkner's work and of a great deal of
Southern fiction in general is. Even the slow, meditative,
steadily accumulative style in which Faulkner writes — though
in some stories like the famous *The Bear*, it can develop to
the point where it looks very strange and experimental indeed — is essentially the ancient style of the fire-side
story-teller.

The technique of *The Fire and the Hearth* is also the
traditional one; the plot is complicated and ingenious, the
characters vivid, often close to extravagance, the conclusion a triumph for a proud but nonetheless cunning and unscrupulous picaro. *The Fire and the Hearth* has one long
flashback in which Lucas recalls how close he came to
killing his cousin and lifelong friend, Zach Edmonds. Like
the insert narratives of much traditional fiction, this one
has no cunning symbolic parallel with the main narrative; it
is relevant to the main narrative quite simply as a further
revelation of the natures of important characters, as a
further explanation of their relations, and as evidence that
those relations have their tragic as well as their comic
aspect.

The values embodied in the story are also conservative.
What is real in it is the slow accumulation of tradition,
especially of family tradition that descends in the blood
line. This reality is the source not only of Lucas's outrageous but genuine pride but of his conviction that it is
anyway his duty to be proud in order to uphold the family
honor ("I knowed what I wanted to do, what I believed I was
going to do, what Carothers McCaslin would have wanted me to
do" [696]).

These family traditions and their precise distribution
among the members of any generation — especially whether they
come down to them through the male or the female line — are
so important to the characters and to our understanding of
their motives that we need to have them very clearly in
mind; the geneological table on page 679 of *Modern Short
Stories* will help to keep them clear. The essential consideration in *The Fire and the Hearth* is, of course, that Lucas
Beauchamp, despite the fact that he bears his mother's
family name, is a direct descendant through the male line of
the founder of the family Lucius Quintus Carothers McCaslin,
and his namesake. (He is also a descendant from Carothers

through the female line since not only was his father, Tomey's Turl, a son of Carothers McCaslin, but his grandmother, Tomasina, was a daughter of Carothers.) The Edmonds who now own the McCaslin plantation—Zachary, Lucas's contemporary and boyhood friend with whom he quarrels over his wife nearly to the death, and his son Roth (Carothers) Edmonds—are, on the other hand, descended from Carothers McCaslin only through the inferior female line, and are more remote from him than Lucas too. The reader will see more of Roth Edmonds—and more of the McCaslin family's inescapably tragic division into black and white branches—in *Delta Autumn*.

But the consequences of these family relations imagined by Faulkner are almost endless. One of the most fascinating is Lucas's fiercely uncompromising scorn of Isaac McCaslin. Lucas has all the violent arrogance of his grandfather, Carothers McCaslin, and as a consequence he thinks of Isaac, who has long since relinquished his inheritance of the McCaslin plantation out of a profound sense of right and justice (as Faulkner shows us in *The Bear*), as having "weakly relinquished the land which was rightfully his to live in town on the charity of his great-nephew" (686), thinking with grim satisfaction that "old Cass Edmonds, this one's [that is, Roth's] grandfather, had beat him [Isaac] out of his patrimony." The thought makes Lucas consider Roth Edmonds almost a worthy opponent for the direct male descendant and rightful spiritual heir of Carothers McCaslin.

This feeling that the most important qualities of character are inheritable gives them stability and permanence. Superficially, families may change, even almost beyond recognition by the vulgar eye: "to the sheriff Lucas was just another nigger and both the sheriff and Lucas knew it, although only one of them knew that to Lucas the sheriff was a redneck without any reason for pride in his forbears nor hope for it in his descendents" (689). Lucas has that reason, and men with any sense do not fail to see that the McCaslin qualities are present in Lucas despite the superficial fact that Lucas is a Negro. It is to this inheritance, for example, that Roth Edmonds appeals when he is most serious with Lucas.

Moreover, the inheritance is not there in Lucas alone; it is a matter of pride to him that it is also there in that beautifully slim, deerlike creature with the "high, sweet, chanting soprano" (711), his daughter Nat, who not only outsmarts even Lucas but is bold enough to blackmail him and blackmail him—at least temporarily, for Lucas wins in the end—successfully. When she confronts Lucas, "her voice was defiant, not hysterical. 'It wasn't me that told Mr. Roth to telefoam them shurfs!' she cried" (707). But she catches on like a flash when Lucas silently decides to make a deal with her: "He looked at her until even the defiance began to fade, to be replaced by something alert and speculative. He saw her glance flick past his shoulder to where George stood and return. . . . Her hand, the long, limber, narrow,

light-palmed hand of her race, rose and touched for an instant the bright cotton which bound her head. Her inflec-
tion, the very tone and pitch of her voice had changed"
(707). While Lucas watches her with silent admiration, she
drives a very hard bargain with him about the price he will
pay for her support against Mr. Roth.

The sense of permanence and stability created by this
continuance from generation to generation of the same human
qualities is reinforced by the stability of physical circum-
stance. Not only has Lucas lived on the McCaslin plantation
all his life, hunting "over every foot of it during his
childhood and youth and manhood too" and working "on it ever
since he got big enough to hold a plow straight" (683), so
that he knows every inch of it and can find his way in the
pitch dark anywhere; he also knows without stopping to think
the whole history of everything on the place, as he knows
the plantation house "—the two log wings which Carothers
McCaslin had built and which had sufficed old Buck and
Buddy, connected by the open hallway which, as his pride's
monument and epitaph, old Cass Edmonds had enclosed and
superposed with a second story of white clapboards and faced
with a portico" (689-690).

By continuing forever, these characteristics of life
provide a stable source of pride and a reliable set of rewards for those who live it. They do so, of course, at the
cost of setting equally permanent and unbreakable limits
within which a man has to assert his pride and win his rewards, and there are, equally of course, always fools about
like George Wilkins who are too stupid to recognize these
limits and are therefore sure not only to fail themselves
but to make things twice as hard for smart people like Lucas.
"George Wilkins was a fool innocent of discretion, who
sooner or later would be caught, whereupon for the next ten
years every bush on the Edmonds place would have a deputy
sheriff squatting behind it from sundown to sunup every
night. And [Lucas] not only didn't want a fool for a son-
in-law, he didn't intend to have a fool living on the same
place he lived on" (682-683).

These, then, are the conditions that confront Lucas,
and Faulkner shows us how Lucas goes about getting rid of
George with all the marvelous insight into the admirable,
outrageous, comic arrogance of "the oldest McCaslin" that is
Faulkner's own inheritance from his forbears and the culture
they created. Lucas's first plan is simple enough. He will
get Roth Edmonds to send George Wilkins to the penitentiary
for running a still and thus remove at one blow George's
competition with his still, the risk of George's ignorant
foolhardiness that can so easily get them both caught, and
the danger that George may marry Nat and burden him with a
fool for a son-in-law. (We should not, in the complicated
twists and turns of the plot, overlook the fact that as
Lucas's true daughter Nat has outmaneuvered Lucas here too
by secretly marrying George "in October of last year," almost a year before Lucas begins to plot George's downfall,

710). In order to do so, he must of course hide his own
still where it cannot possibly be found; in his arrogant
scorn of redneck sheriffs and their deputies, he does not in
fact hide it well enough; the hiding place he chooses is almost the first place they think to look. But by that time
things have, luckily for Lucas, developed to the point where
Lucas wants the sheriff to find his still (704).

It outrages him that he must do the job all by himself,
not being able to trust the discretion of his wife, Molly,
and knowing full well that his daughter Nat is George's ally
and his archenemy; though at first, underestimating how much
McCaslin there is in Nat, he underestimates how formidable
an opponent she is going to turn out to be. It outrages him
that he must do the job by himself, not because of the
physical labor or even the loss of revenue from the neglect
of his crop this involves, but because of the offense to his
dignity as "not only the oldest man but the oldest living
person on the Edmonds plantation, the oldest McCaslin
descendant" (683). Then, while he is burying his still, he
finds the old gold coin and becomes completely convinced
that there is treasure buried in the old Indian mound to be
had merely for the digging. His faith in the existence of
that treasure is absolute. All he even thinks of is the
consequences of possessing it—"In a way he was a little
sorry to give up farming. He had liked it . . ." (688)—and
the outrage that he has had to "wait until I am sixty-seven
years old, almost too old to even want it," to be rich (702).
The only serious question in his mind is how to go about
digging up the treasure. One thing, however, is sure; there
must be no sheriffs poking about; George and his still will
have to be left unharmed for a while. In his eagerness to
find the treasure quickly Lucas is even tempted to enlist
George's help, "on a minor share basis," of course, to do
the digging (686). But he quickly recovers. "He, Lucas
Beauchamp, the oldest living McCaslin descendant still
living on the hereditary land . . . to share one jot, one
penny of the money which old Buck and Buddy had buried almost a hundred years ago, with an interloper without forbears
and sprung from nowhere and whose very name was unknown in
the country twenty-five years ago—a jimber jawed clown who
could not even learn how to make whisky. . . . Never" (686).

Then he discovers that Nat has followed him and been
watching him all the time. That settles it; it is now no
longer a matter of a mere still but of a treasure of gold
that George and Nat must be kept from interfering with.
Therefore George must go. That means sheriffs all over the
place who will surely notice the old Indian mound has been
disturbed. They must not dig in it; they may find the gold.
Therefore they must be allowed to find Lucas's still just
beneath its disturbed surface so that they may believe that
is why the mound has been disturbed, will search it no
further, and will leave him free to dig the treasure out of
it. For these reasons he returns to his original plan of
reporting George's still to Roth Edmonds, thinking rather
complacently as he falls asleep that night that George is

young yet and a couple of years in jail will no doubt do him good—"be a lesson to him about whose daughter to fool with next time" (703). (George is not so much of a fool as not to know Lucas thinks this way. When Lucas later remarks to him that he is in trouble, George replies, "Yes, sir. Hit look like it is. I hope it gonter be a lesson to me" [707]; at the end of the story George admits that he really has learned that lesson [713].) The next evening, then, Lucas goes to Roth Edmonds' house to report George's still, and looking at Roth, he is reminded of Roth's father Zach, with whom Lucas had grown up like a brother, and of the deadly battle Lucas's McCaslin pride had involved him in with Zach over Lucas's wife Molly, because "the same thing made my pappy that made your grandmaw. I'm going to take [Molly] back" (691). And did.

When Lucas tells Roth about George Wilkins' still, it works better than he had dreamed, because Roth thinks Lucas is trying to protect George as his future son-in-law ("All that worry," Lucas thinks. "I never even thought of that," [701]). But once more Lucas is in trouble because he has underrated Nat. She has followed him to Roth Edmonds' house and heard all he has said; as a result, at her suggestion, she and George spend the rest of the night moving George's still and his stock of whisky to Lucas's porch, where in due course the sheriff finds it, catching Nat and George at the work of moving some of it there at the same time. Both George's guilt and Lucas's are thus established, even to the nice detail of George and Nat's giving the sheriff—and Edmonds—the interesting information that Lucas has been running whisky on the Edmonds' place for twenty years (705).

So Lucas has to make his deal with Nat to give George the money to repair his house so that Nat can live there with him in the dignity becoming a McCaslin, and Nat can reveal that she has been married to George for nearly a year so that neither she nor George can legally testify against either George or Lucas; and the judge is left with nothing to do but destroy the two stills and chase them out of his office in a rage.

Meanwhile, Lucas has known all the time that with the money Nat had thought she was forcing him to put up for the repair of George's house George will simply buy a new still. "At first he thought that two or three days at the outside would suffice—or nights, that is, since George would have to be in his crop during the day, let alone getting himself and Nat settled for marriage in their house" (711). But it is in fact nearly a week before Nat arrives in tears to tell them that George has not only not spend a cent on repairing his house but has been away somewhere all the previous night. Lucas then drops quietly down to George's house and says, "Where is it?" and receives George's assurance that "They aint going to catch me this time. I done had my lesson. I'm gonter run this one the way you tells me to" (713).

Not that George is not still George: "That porch and well money liked two dollars of being enough," he says gen- erously, "but I just made them up, without needing to bother you" (713). But George has at least been taught that not even Nat, to say nothing of George himself, can in the long run successfully back Lucas, so that Lucas now has his still and his whisky business in operation again, and has some one else—if not very satisfactory, at least not himself—to do all the night work of running it. George still has his problems. "What I cant keep from studying about is what we gonter tell Nat about that back porch and that well" (713). But that "we" is a mistake; he and Lucas are not partners, least of all in this, where Lucas's admiration for the de- termination and cunning that Nat comes by so naturally, as well as his love for her, put him on her side rather than George's; let George figure out a way to find the money for Nat's porch and well; Lucas is not going to find it or to help George figure out a way to persuade Nat to do without these improvements. "What we is?" he says to George first, showing him there is no hope of his getting more money out of Lucas; and then, showing him there is no other kind of help to be expected from Lucas either, "I don't give no man advice about his wife" (714).

QUESTIONS (pages 869-870 of *Modern Short Stories*)

1. What is Lucas Beauchamp's relation to Carothers McCaslin, the founder of the family?

2. What is Roth Edmonds' relation to Carothers McCaslin?

3. What signs are there in Lucas' character that he is descended from Carothers McCaslin?

4. How strong is Lucas' attachment to the McCaslin place? How well does he know it?

5. Why does Lucas want to get rid of George Wilkins and his still?

6. What is Lucas' plan for getting rid of George?

7. Why is Lucas angry that he must carry out alone the physical labor his scheme against George demands?

8. What is the effect on Lucas of finding the gold coin in the Indian mound?

9. Why does Lucas want his still as well as George's found when he revises his plan after discovering that his daughter Nat has been spying on him?

10. What did Lucas resent about Molly's living in Zack Edmonds' house after Zack's wife died?

11.   Why did Lucas want to kill Zack Edmonds?

12.   How did he fail to kill him?

13.   What unexpected consequences follow from Lucas' reporting George's still to Roth Edmonds?

14.   What bargain does Nat strike with Lucas before she agrees not to give evidence against him?

15.   Why does Lucas let her talk him out of money?

16.   What arrangements do George and Lucas make about the new still?

17.   What advice does Lucas give George about explaining the situation to Nat?

WILLIAM FAULKNER

DELTA AUTUMN

There is a discussion of *DELTA AUTUMN* and a genea-
logical chart to explain the complicated but significant
relations of the characters in the story in the Introduction
to Part IV of *Modern Short Stories*.

<u>QUESTIONS</u> (pages 870-871 of *Modern Short Stories*)

1. Explain by reference to the geneological chart in
Modern Short Stories the relation between Roth Edmonds and
the Negro girl and her son.

2. Why does Roth Edmonds react so harshly when he sees
something by the road, brakes abruptly, and then is teased
by Legate about having a doe in this country?

3. Why is Roth so bitter about patriotism?

4. Why, that night around the campfire, is he so
egregiously rude to Uncle Ike about "the other animals you
lived with"?

5. Why does Roth Edmonds react so violently when Uncle
Ike speaks of that moment "when it dont even matter whether
[a man and woman] marry or not"?

6. Why does the girl who comes to the tent with Roth
Edmonds' child call Isaac McCaslin "Uncle Ike"?

7. If the girl knew all along that Roth Edmonds would
never marry her and went into the affair with her eyes open,
what is she doing in Uncle Ike's tent now?

8. What does Uncle Ike mean he says, "It's a boy, I
reckon. They usually are, except that one that was its own
mother too"?

9. Why does Uncle Ike give the girl the hunting horn?

10. Why is Uncle Ike so sure the deer Roth has killed
that morning is a doe?

WILLIAM FAULKNER
RAID

RAID is the third of seven stories in Faulkner's book
The Unvanquished. *The Unvanquished* is half way to being a
novel: all its seven stories deal with the same group of
characters and the stories are in a chronological order that
begins with the fall of Vicksburg (July 4, 1863) and ends in
1874, when the book's leading character, Bayard Sartoris,
then twenty-four years old, has to accept the responsibility
of dealing with his father's murderer and is forced to
choose between the Christianity of Granny Millard and the
vengeful pride of his cousin Drusilla. The three attitudes
represented by these three characters are the governing concerns of *The Unvanquished*. They are given dramatic intensity by the conditions in the Deep South as the
Confederacy goes down to defeat in the Civil War, but
Faulkner clearly thinks their conflict inherent in all human
experience.

On the one hand, there is Granny Millard with her
Christian faith and her sense of family responsibility.
These qualities are tested to the limit by her efforts to
preserve her family and her people—white and colored—
during the catastrophe of defeat. On the other hand, there
is Bayard's cousin Drusilla and his father, John Sartoris,
at first conventional enough people, but driven by their
suffering and the suffering of their people into an attitude
of arrogant and desperate pride. Between these two influences are Bayard and Ringo, who have to struggle to maturity
amidst the physical and moral disintegration of their
society. At the climax of Bayard's life, than, when he must
decide whether to kill the man who has shot his unarmed
father, the struggle within him is a struggle between the
values of Granny Millard, who brought him up, and the values
of Drusilla, who had ridden through the last desperate years
of the war with John Sartoris's cavalry company and been his
"wife" (it is one of Faulkner's perfect touches that they do
not bother with a conventional service until after the war,
when old Mrs. Habersham makes them), and had come to share
John Sartoris's passionate dream of rebuilding the South and
to sympathize with his quickness to kill, who had had to
kill too many men in the war. It is Bayard's bad luck—as
well as a measure of his distinction—that he loves Drusilla.

Not all these concerns bulk equally large in each story,
but all three are likely to be at least touched on in each,
as they are in *Raid*. *Raid* is primarily concerned with
Granny Millard's effort to recover the family silver, an
effort that accidentally involves her in taking care of more

Negroes than she ever has time to count and the poor whites
in the hills back of Sartoris—and gives her the mules to do
it with. *Raid* also shows us Bayard and Ringo (who is, as
John Sartoris says, a little brighter than Bayard and does
so faster) moving with a rush from boyhood rivalries over
who has seen a railroad to the adult life of outsmarting
Yankees. It even gives us a glimpse of the third concern of
The Unvanquished in Drusilla's bitter emptiness—"So, all
you have to do is show the stick to the dog now and then and
say, 'Thank God for nothing.' You see?" (752)—and its consequence—"and Dru leaned down to Bobolink's ear and said,
'Kill him, Bob,' and the Yankee jumped back just in time"
(744-745).

Like the other stories in *The Unvanquished*, *Raid* is
substantially independent (all but the last of the stories
in *The Unvanquished* were published separately in magazines),
and it is not necessary to know the others in order to
follow its action. Nevertheless, it gains something if the
reader knows certain facts that emerge in these other
stories. For instance, in *Ambuscade*, the opening story,
rumors reach Sartoris after the fall of Vicksburg that the
United States army is approaching. Bayard and Ringo, who
are twelve, decide they must protect Sartoris, and they watch
every day for the enemy. One day they see one of them,
sitting on his horse on the big road and scanning the place
through his field glasses. They rush back to the house,
snatch down the loaded musket over the fire place, carry it
back to their hiding place, and somehow manage to fire it at
the officer. When the smoke clears, they are astonished to
discover that the officer's men—what Ringo calls "the whole
army"—have arrived. They run back to the house and into
the room where Granny is, shouting with innocent and doubting
confidence, "We shot him, Granny! We shot the bastud!"
"Then we heard the boots and spurs on the porch," and Bayard
says, "Granny! Granny!"

Granny sits down in her chair, spreads her skirts, and
hides the boys under them. When the Federal troops come
pouring in, it turns out the boys have killed only a horse,
but the horse was the favorite for Sunday's race and the men
are furious. Then the Colonel of the regiment—who is the
Colonel Dick of *Raid*—comes in. "Do I understand, madam,"
he asks Granny, "that there are no children in or about this
house?" and Granny looks him in the eye and says, "There are
none, sir." He accepts her word, knowing perfectly well
where the boys are, but he cannot resist talking about what
a wonderful place this would be for boys to grow up. He
knows; he has three of his own. When Granny offers him re-
freshment, however, he says, "No, no. I thank you. You are
taxing yourself beyond mere politeness and into sheer
bravado." When he and his men have left, Granny says,
"Bayard, what was that word you used?" But first she kneels
and prays to be forgiven her lie (and the boys kneel with
her); then the boys get their mouths washed out with soap.

In *The Unvanquished's* second story, *Retreat*, when the

boys are nearly fourteen, Federal troops just miss capturing
John Sartoris at the plantation. When he escapes, the
troops burn down the house and carry off the silver, whose
hiding place has been revealed by Loosh, the son of Joby and
Louvinia. When the troops leave, Loosh does too, taking his
reluctant wife Philadelphy with him. "I'm going," he says.
"I done been freed. . . . I don't belong to John Sartoris
now; I belong to me and God." "But the silver belongs to
John Sartoris," Granny says. "Who are you to give it away?"
"You ax me that?" Loosh says with impassioned irrelevance.
". . . Let God ax John Sartoris who the man name that give
me to him."

These are the circumstances out of which the events of
Raid grow. Granny cannot do anything about John Sartoris's
house; it is gone, and they now all live in the slave cabin.
But she can do something about John Sartoris's silver and
his mules and his Negroes. She has made the acquaintance of
Colonel Dick, and however far away he and the silver now
are, she means to find them. But she is going to do it—as
she does everything—right, as a lady and a Christian. She
will not derogate from her own dignity by calling on Colonel
Dick improperly dressed, even if she must borrow hat and
parasol from Mrs. Compson; if she must borrow horses—all
hers having been stolen by the Federal troops—she will
treat them with more care than if they were her own. She
will ask Colonel Dick for precisely what is hers and no more.
"I shall inquire until I find Colonel Dick, and then we will
load the chest in the wagon and Loosh can lead the mules and
we will come back home," she says (737).

Granny is an old lady who has lived all her life in the
provincial world she was born in. But ignorant though she
may be of the world beyond Jefferson, she lives up to the
religious and social obligations of the world she does know
with an integrity that makes her brave enough for anything.
She never wavers in her conviction of the rightness and
sufficiency of her training: even in her moment of greatest
danger, when she is caught in the mindless Negro mob at the
river, with the wagon slipping down toward the water and
"Mrs. Compson's hat knocked to one side of her head," she
shouts firmly to an unknown Yankee officer, "I want my
silver. I am John Sartoris' mother-in-law! Send Colonel
Dick to me!" (754) Her faith makes her indomitable. At the
same time, the minutiae of her code make serious difficulties
for one whose only real weapons are stealth and cunning.
Already, in *Ambush*, she has had to look Colonel Dick in the
eye and lie to him; and worse is to come in *Raid*.

Ringo suffers no such restraints except at second hand,
through Granny. He is freed from the restraints as he is
freed from the opportunities of the white man's life by the
color of his skin. He understands his situation all too
well. If he were as childish as Joby and the Negroes who
seek the river, he would not have to, but, as Bayard later
thinks, Ringo has "some outrageous assurance gained from too
long and too close association with white people" (*An Odor*

of Verbena). Like his grandmother Louvinia who—John
Sartoris says in *Ambuscade*—"would have to be white a little
longer" without being white, Ringo loves and supports
Granny, who has brought him up, and Bayard, with whom he has
grown up. But he loves them in his own outrageously assured,
sardonic way. He is never free—as they are—to decide what
shall be done; but he is, as they never are, free to do what
he can in the most practical and efficient way. Child
though he is in *Raid*, he sees at once the practical inefficiency of Granny's scruples about the horses' being used for
a trip into Jefferson. Considering the strain she herself
is going to have to put on these horses, the trip to
Jefferson is not worth fussing about (736).

   Not that both Ringo and Bayard are not still boys. As
they pass the ruins of the burnt-out house, what Bayard
thinks of is that among those ruins, "Ringo and I found the
insides of the big clock too" (737). (The "too" means, "as
well as the barrel of the musket Joby has just been trying
to put in the wagon.") Ringo's main concern during the
journey is "that railroad you tells about" (738). Each of
them has "a boy's affinity for smoke and fury and thunder
and speed" (747); they are like the ten-year-old Denny, for
whom the railroad is also all that counts (742). They cannot wait to hear Drusilla tell about the locomotive. When
it looks as if they will have to listen to Drusilla's report
about the Negroes at the river first, Ringo says, "I been
having to hear about niggers all my life. I got to hear
about that railroad" (745). Beneath the child's awareness,
that locomotive is for Bayard "the momentary flash and glare
of indomitable spirit" (749) to be fixed forever in the
memories of his people, as it is for Ringo a symbol of his
people's "impulse to move . . . darker than themselves . . .
a delusion, a dream" too (738).

   Ringo's people are very much on the move. With her in-
exhaustible determination to help her people, black and
white, Granny has already tried to talk sense to one Negro
girl they have come across, who will only say, "Hit's Jordan
we coming to. Jesus gonter see me that far." But it is
Granny who sees her that far, willing to help even if it is
only helping the woman satisfy her dream of Jesus and Jordan,
Sherman and the river, the Negroes' fuddled expression of
their scarcely conscious urge to be free. When the woman
gets off Granny's wagon to join the other Negroes hidden in
the bottom, Granny tries once more. "You go back home,
girl," she says; but when the woman just stands there, she
gives up again. "'Hand me the basket,' Granny said. I
handed it to her and she opened it and gave the woman a
piece of bread and meat." Now, at Hawkshurst, close to the
river, they discover that thousands of Negroes have been
heading for Jordan, so many that they have created a problem
the Federal troops are unable to handle. But to Granny—and
to Drusilla—it is neither here nor there that "the Yankees
brought it on themselves," as Aunt Louisa says. "These
Negroes," as Drusilla puts it, "are not Yankees"; and Granny
says, "I reckon I will [go to the river]. I've got to get

the silver anyway." And the wholly adult, sardonic Ringo
emerges for a moment to add, "And the mules; don't forget
them. And don't yawl worry about Granny. She 'cide what
she want and then she kneel down about ten seconds and tell
God what she aim to do, and then she git up and do hit. And
them that don't like hit can git outen the way or git
tromped." Then the child again, "But that railroad—"
(746).

The next day they are at the river. As the mass of
Negroes closes around the wagon, there is Granny "in Mrs.
Compson's hat sitting bolt upright under the parasol which
Ringo held looking sicker and sicker" at the pitiful delusion
and suffering she is helpless to relieve. The catastrophe
that follows, when the Federal troops are across the bridge
and it is blown just as the rearguard and the Negroes reach
it is given one of those brilliant impressionistic descriptions Faulkner always did magnificently—the troops crossing
the bridge; the blood-streaked officer suddenly at the
wagon's side shrieking, "Get back!" and suddenly gone again;
the bridge vanishing in a bright glare; the dead horse and
his rider rising and then sinking again "exactly like a fish
feeding"; and Granny hitting with Mrs. Compson's parasol the
drowning Negroes about to tip the wagon over as it floats
across the river (754-756).

When they finally reach the Federal camp on the other
side, Granny has fainted, but when some one suggests she be
taken to the hospital, she opens her eyes and says, "Just
take me to Colonel Dick" (756). When Colonel Dick sees her,
he can only say, "Damn this war. Damn it. Damn it." Then
he looks at Bayard and Ringo and says, "Ha! I believe we
have met before also"—invisible though they may have been
under Granny's skirts. Then there arises one of those human
tangles of misunderstanding that Faulkner always delighted
in. Despite her shaken condition, Granny makes with pains-
taking accuracy her request for her one chest of silver,
easily identifiable by the new hemp rope around it, her two
runaway Negroes and her two lost mules, carefully distinguished by name. What she says—in her Mississippi accent
blurred by exhaustion—is, "The chest of silver tied with
hemp rope. The rope was new. Two darkies, Loosh and
Philadelphy. The mules, Old Hundred and Tinny." The
Northern orderly who is writing down what she says seems a
little surprised, but says, "I guess the general will be glad
to give them twice the silver and mules just for taking that
many niggers"; for what he has heard is something like, "Ten
chests of silver tied with hemp rope. The rope was new too.
Darkies, loose near Philadelphia [Mississippi] mules, a
hundred and ten"; and that is how—dressed in properly dignified army prose—the general's order to return Granny her
property comes out (759).

When the general's order is being executed and Granny
sees something has gone wrong, she tries to stem the flow of
manna and Negroes: "But that ain't—We didn't—" But they
interrupt her, long enough for her to begin to see what this

mistake can mean for them all. By the time the Lieutenant
gives her a chance to speak—"You want to let some of the
women ride?"—she has fatally weakened. "Yes," she whispers.
Since there are not one hundred and ten Mississippi mules in
the camp, but only sixty-three, the general adds, with his
compliments, a hundred extra Negroes (758). So they set out
for home, with ten chests of silver, sixty-three mules, and
more Negroes than they ever have time to count (758).

When they are clear, Ringo says, "I reckon you gonter
take um back now" (759). It is a desperate moment for
Granny. She has all but stolen the silver and mules, and
she knows it makes no difference that—as Ringo later points
out—"[the Yankees] stole them 'fore we did" (762). On the
other hand, she can see as well as Ringo that the mules are
a godsend, that with them she can feed not only the Negroes
she has on her hands but all the starving people, black and
white, back home in Mississippi. Granny does not deceive
herself. She knows very well what she is doing, and in the
next story in *The Unvanquished*, *Riposte in Tertio*, where we
see her using copies of the general's order, beautifully
forged by Ringo, to steal more mules in order to continue to
feed her people, she begins each Sunday's distribution in
the church by bearing public witness to her sin. "She didn't
look sick," Bayard thinks; "that wasn't it." What she looks
is what she is, a woman living with a conviction of her continuing sinfulness, which the needs of her people have forced
on her. "I have sinned. I have stolen, and I have born
false witness against my neighbor, though that neighbor was
an enemy of my country. And more than that, I have caused
these children to sin. I hereby take their sins upon my
conscience," she says when it is all over and she makes the
boys kneel with her in the church. Then with that characteristic positiveness that Ringo so admires ("Granny . . .
'cide what she want and then she kneel down about ten
seconds and tell God what she aim to do . . ."), she explains
to God that she was "the best judge" of what she had to do.
Best or not, she was the only one; she had no one to help
her. But what she has done with such positiveness and success is no less a sin to her because it was she who decided
it had to be done.

So, when Ringo says to her that first morning, "I
reckon you gonter take um back," and Bayard adds that the
general's order also makes it possible for them to requisition from the Federal army food for the Negroes and fodder
for the mules, she says, "Yes. I tried to tell them better.
You and Ringo heard me. It's the hand of God" (759). But
she can scarcely have anticipated the consequences of this
decision. The first Federal patrol they meet she offers her
paper, merely as a *laisser-passer*, but the officer in command—assuming she intends to requisition some of his mules
—says, "How many do you lack?" "I reckon," says Bayard,
"it was Ringo that knew first what he meant. 'We like
fifty,' Ringo said." The Yankee officer is so busy checking this figure—"Count 'em!" he says; and when he discovers
they have sixty-three, "Get forty-seven mules! . . . Think

you can beat me out of three mules, hey?"—he fails to
notice he has been done out of forty-seven mules. "Hah!"
says Ringo when they are out of hearing, "whose hand was
that?" (760). Some of Granny's authority thus passes to
Ringo; he takes over the driving, and it is he who requisi-
tions a dozen horses from the next patrol they meet. He
does it in Granny's name; "Granny say come here," he shouts,
and when Granny's hand comes away from her chest, it is
holding the general's order (761). But though she is
nominally in charge it is Ringo who makes the decision.
"They ain't hardly worth fooling with," he says thoughtfully.
"Still, they's horses." And it is he who speaks for them
when the horseless soldiers beg to have help sent them:
"They's some of yawl twenty or thirty miles back that claim
to have three extry mules" (762).

So "we came over the hill, and there our chimneys were,
standing up in the sunlight, and the cabin behind them and
Louvinia bending over a washtub and the clothes on the line,
flapping bright and peaceful," and they are home (762).
"Stop the wagon," Granny says; and when they are out, "We
lied. Kneel down." "Then we all three knelt by the road
while she prayed" (762).

QUESTIONS (page 871 of *Modern Short Stories*)

1. What is Granny Millard's plan for the recovery of the
silver, the mules, and the Negroes?

2. Why does she send the boys to Jefferson to borrow
Mrs. Compson's hat and parasol? Why does she write the note
to Mrs. Compson in pokeberry juice?

3. Why does Ringo think it foolish not to drive the
horses to Jefferson? Why will Granny not allow it?

4. What are Bayard and Ringo most interested in about
the ruined plantation house at Sartoris? What interests
them most about Hawkshurst?

5. Why are the Negroes walking in great masses toward
the river? What is Granny's attitude toward these Negroes?
What is Aunt Louisa's? What is Drusilla's?

6. What is Drusilla's attitude toward life in general?
What has made her take it?

7. What happens when they get to the river in the wagon?
How does Granny meet the disaster?

8. What is Colonel Dick's attitude toward Granny and her
request?

9. What is Colonel Dick's attitude toward Bayard and
Ringo?

10. What causes the mistake that leads the union troops to give Granny so many chests of silver, mules, and Negroes?

11. Why does Granny keep them? What does she think of herself for doing so?

12. How does Ringo use the order signed by the union general? Why?

13. Why does Faulkner emphasize the peacefulness of home when they finally get there and follow immediately with Granny making them get down and pray?

ROBERT PENN WARREN

WHEN THE LIGHT GETS GREEN

WHEN THE LIGHT GETS GREEN is a story about the necessarily uncomprehending and hopeless fight that love and
pride put up against change and time. But it never speaks
of this subject directly. The speaker in the story—though
he is presumably now an adult who understands his boyhood
relations with his grandfather—wants to tell us about those
relations as they were when they existed, not what he has
thought about them since, as an adult. He therefore shows
us, through the understanding of the boy he had been at the
time, without comment from his present self, what we need to
know about Mr. Barden and his grandson. That boy had been
old enough to comprehend what he felt about his grandfather's life but too young to understand what it meant for
his grandfather or for him, or what it implied for the
future when he would be as old as his grandfather.

There are great dramatic advantages in such a narrator.
He makes it possible for the story to be told as if it were
random recollections, and that allows the author to leave
out all the insignificant facts that would have to be in-
cluded in an orderly biography and—as long as he stays
within the limits of a boy's understanding—to arrange the
facts he does include in the order that emphasizes their
meaning. He could not have the boy consciously arrange the
facts in such an order; the boy did not understand their
meaning. But as long as the boy had some boyish reason for
grouping them as he did, the author can achieve his different end. Consider, for example, the final paragraph on
page 766. The reason the boy thought of these things in the
order he did is obvious and plausible. Grandfather cared
about tobacco; he had cared about horses and even had cups
to show for his success with them (only one of them, to be
sure, real silver). But now he hadn't any decent horses:
Uncle Kirby thought horses foolishness and grandfather said,
yes, they were. So then he had only tobacco to care about.
He had once been a tobacco-buyer but had failed and was
thought by his daughters to be visionary and impractical.
When the storm came up he was nervous as a cat, worrying
about the tobacco.

It is easy to see the reasons—at least the conscious
reasons—the boy's mind moved from one to another of these
thoughts, and its doing so helps to bring him alive for us
as a boy. It is not so easy to see why Mr. Warren wants to
fix our attention on these details in this order, but when
we do see that, it comes to us, not as something Mr. Warren

has told us <u>about</u> life, but as something we have seen <u>in</u>
life, in the <u>felt</u> experience of a convincing boy.

This method of narration has the further advantage of
allowing Mr. Warren to mix things the boy saw that reveal
something about Mr. Barden with the things he noticed that
reveal his own nature, and to mix them in such a way as to
make us see how much the boy responded—without understanding it—to what Mr. Barden was, and how much more relevant Mr. Barden's old age was for the young boy than he
could imagine. For example, as the two of them went across
the lot and along the branch, the boy noticed that this "was
where I used to play before I got big enough to go to the
river with the niggers to swim" (764-765). That was an expression of his pride in now being grown up enough to swim
in the river with the big boys. But he was now grown up
enough to see that the passage of time that made this
triumph possible would continue inexorably, carrying him on,
willy-nilly, to an inconceivable time when he might, like
Uncle Kirby, die in a war and leave his wife to work in a
store, or, like Mr. Barden, not die in a war and survive
into a useless and humiliating old age when no one understood how he felt about the places where he had played as a
child or about the things he had loved in the innocent pride
of his young manhood.

Mr. Barden's grandson—though in his own way and time—
loved some of the things his grandfather had loved and,
without understanding why his grandfather was what he was,
admired him. He too loved the familiar natural world, "the
limestone bunched out of the ground," "with cedar trees and
blue grass" (764), "the sassafras bushes and blackberry
bushes," the sight of the house as he looked back at it from
the rise (765). He hardly realized that he was loving these
things, and never thought that his grandfather must have
been renewing similar feelings as the two of them went across
the lot together in the spring morning or as his grandfather
rode along the edge of the field, sitting up pretty straight
in the saddle for an old man and holding the tobacco stick
he could not use on Uncle Kirby's field firm and straight up
like something carried in a parade (765).

The grandson cannot be blamed for not having understood
all this. His failure is in the nature of things, inevitable;
no one can love the things his parents and grandparents have
loved, because no one has had the experience that created
their love. It is impossible for the young to know the old
as they really are. All Mr. Barden's grandson could do was
love him in an uncomprehending and inexpressive way, not
understanding why he felt a puzzled uneasiness when he looked
back from his work in the tobacco field and "the lane would
be empty and nothing on top of the rise, with the cloudy,
blue-grey sky low behind it" (766). He was equally incapable
of wondering why he went to his grandfather's room so that
"he and I went down to breakfast" together every morning
(764), why "grandfather went off with me" to the fields when
the tobacco was set (764) or he with his grandfather to the

cedar tree to listen to Gibbon read or Byron recited or the
battles of the Civil War described. All he consciously knew
was his small boy's anxiety to discover whether grandfather
had ever killed any Yankees (768).

Most of the time he was conscious of his grandfather
only as the cliché the mind of the young requires grand-
fathers to be, as an old man who "had a long white beard and
sat under the cedar tree" (763). "Almost every afternoon
right after dinner, he went to sleep in his chair . . . his
head propped back on the tree trunk. . . . Usually I remember
him that way, asleep" (768). But unlike his aunt and uncle,
he was still young enough sometimes to see the real Mr.
Barden with his clipped grey beard and good profile that
made him look "like General Robert E. Lee, without any white
horse to ride" (763)—or "any horses that were any real
good" (766). His grandfather had been a soldier, one of
Forrest's men and, later, the captain of his own cavalry
company. But he had never been made a colonel or even a
major by that species of post-war promotion that was a
measure, not of a man's soldiership, but of his civilian
prestige; on the contrary, he had been slowly demoted
socially for failure in the post-war world until he was now
plain Mr. Barden, as he had been slowly turned by time into
an old man with shrivelled hips and legs and scrawny neck.
Without understanding the helpless humiliation of honorless-
ness and old age and physical decay, the boy still "felt a
tight feeling in my stomach," seeing all this, "like when
you walk behind a woman and see the high heel of her shoe is
worn and twisted and jerks her ankle every time she takes a
step" (763-764).

Mr. Barden had the added humiliation of living on the
charity of his daughter and her husband, kind, even considerate people in their way, but too taken up with their own
lives to have an inkling of his, and with the frustration of
not being able to do anything, not even supervise the setting
of the tobacco that was not his but Uncle Kirby's. In his
wisdom Uncle Kirby had decided that the horses Mr. Barden
had loved were foolishness, and when fire destroyed Mr.
Barden's tobacco sheds and ruined him, his daughters had decided, in their wisdom, that "Papa's just visionary, he
tried to be a tobacco-buyer, but he's too visionary and not
practical" (766). They were sure they were right because
Mr. Barden was an inveterate reader—of Macaulay and Gibbon
and *Napoleon and His Marshals*—and an unaffected reciter of
the *Rubáiyát* and *Childe Harold*. He never read anything new,
just went on living with the literature of his time, as he
went on living with its values and devotions.

Thus, gradually, through the haze of the necessarily
uncomprehending judgments of later generations, there
emerges for us a sadly old but genuine and unselfconscious
representative of the pre-Civil-War world. Little by little
we begin to understand through him that world's adaptation
of the impractical "visionary" virtues—the love of horses,
heroism, poetry, growing things—to a simple rural

environment that gave its activities an almost comically
provincial air. There it is with its country fairs and imitation silver cups instead of tourneys and priceless prizes,
its illiterate ex-slave-dealers like Forrest instead of
Napoleons, its sights like the dead in the cold river bottom
after Donaldson instead of grand visions of the carnage
after "the Janizaries took Constantinople amid great
slaughter" (767), its social life of cob pipes and country
phrases ("Don't it stink" [764]) instead of the courts of the
mighty and regency graces. One wonders for a fleeting
moment whether medieval jousts and Flodden Field and the
Isles of Greece where burning Sappho loved and sung were not,
despite the stylized splendor given them by Scott and
Macaulay and Byron, really like this too—whether perhaps Mr.
Barden had not known in his life the true relation between
reality and the vision in men's minds that makes it beautiful
and endurable.

Not that Mr. Barden would ever have had such thoughts,
or his grandson either. There was nothing spectacular about
Mr. Barden, nothing either grandiose or subtle; there never
had been. He had won his plated cups with the innocent delight of a man who loved horses, not silver cups, had admired
Forrest for being a great general without caring or even
noticing that Forrest was not Beauregard or even a gentleman,
had cared for growing tobacco but not for trading in it.
Without making anything of his silver cup one way or the
other, he kept it on his dresser, and kept string and old
minnie balls and pins in it (766).

He had tried without selfconsciousness to adapt his
talents to the practical, money-conscious world of his
children by becoming a tobacco-buyer; but he conducted the
business in the only way he could, with the good cavalry
captain's necessary daring—too little insurance and too
much faith in the generosity of his competitors—that was
sure to make him unsuccessful in Uncle Kirby's world. When
Uncle Kirby pronounced horses foolishness—meaning unprofit-
able—"he reckoned horses were foolishness, all right" (766).
After all, he had only loved them—as he had loved the idea
of the Confederacy, enough to have been willing to follow
Forrest's radical policy "and clean out the country ahead of
the Yankees, like the Russians beat Napoleon" (767). The
Uncle Kirbys of the Confederacy would have thought that
foolishness too, and no doubt Mr. Barden would have agreed
that, yes, it was foolishness, all right.

Until he had his stroke, Mr. Barden met the humiliations
of old age with an habitual dignity and the splendid easiness
of manners of his generation's code. When Uncle Kirby,
meaning to be thoughtful, reminded Mr. Barden each morning
whose breakfast he was eating, he always answered, "I'll be
down in a minute, thank you, sir" (764). When his daughter
—fighting her own battles with Uncle Kirby and innocently
unconscious of her effect on her father—complained about
his cob pipe, he kept on smoking it but gallantly conceded
his daughter her right to a ladylike disgust; "But he always

brought it down just the same and said to her, 'Don't it
stink'" (764). He accepted without any sense of injury or
any protest the cost of having been visionary in a sense his
daughter's generation could not understand, never questioning
the superiority of his own values but never obtruding those
values on those around him. Only, he could not stop caring
about tobacco; "he had to go down to the tobacco field to
watch them sucker or plow or worm, and sometimes he pulled a
few suckers himself" (766), though it was not his tobacco.
"'God-a-Mighty,' he always said [when it hailed], 'bigger'n
minnie balls,' even when it wasn't so big" (768). It killed
him, that caring. Not that he was lucky enough to die
literally when he had his stroke; literally he died four
years later in the flu epidemic. But his grandson was
right when, hearing the news, "I thought about four years
back, and it didn't matter much" (770).

It was when the light got green for Mr. Barden and he
was struck down that his pride failed him and he admitted to
himself and his grandson that it was time to die because
nobody loved him. That was not completely true. His grandson loved him, in the only way he could. When they got his
grandfather to bed after his stroke, the grandson's impulse
was to pick up the broken glass and pitcher and wipe up the
floor with a rag, as if, shocked as he was, he felt for a
moment as if the damage to his grandfather could be made to
disappear along with its accidental consequences. Then he
went straight up to see his grandfather. Both these gestures were the uncalculated acts of love. But his grandfather looked to him like the undisturbed image that slept
afternoons in the chair under the cedar tree. The grandson's mind wandered from his actual, living grandfather, and
he almost jumped out of his skin when that grandfather—out
of his now desperate need to be loved for what he truly was
—spoke to him. But the love Mr. Barden in his desperation
was asking for was a love no grandson can give. The boy
tried, but he could only lie. Out in the yard afterwards,
noticing with the irrelevant acuteness of shock the fool
chickens and the dry spot on one side of the gatepost, obscurely aware that it was as important for him as for his
grandfather, that he should succeed, he tried and failed
again to give his grandfather the love everyone needs and
nobody can have.

Perhaps the most important thing to notice about this
story is that, though its meaning is lucid enough, it contains a great deal of contingent matter, a great deal that
is there because "it happened," because it is part of the
actuality, whether it fits neatly with the meaning the author
finds in the events or not. For Mr. Warren, the final truth
is what happens. Men can lose themselves in unthinking action or in abstract thought. But reality is in the "being
done," where thought is brought to the test of action and
action subject to the judgment of thought, and both are
modified by the mess of contingency, happenings that action
ought neither to cause nor to involve, events unplanned and
unforeseeable: accidents.

That the "being done," not the theory about the done or the neat plan for the "to-be-done," is Mr. Warren's truth is evident from the fact that, twenty years after he wrote this story, he returned to the actuality that is its substance, the "old man and small grandson" "under the cedar tree" in a poem called "Court-Martial." In this poem the grandson is trying to "untie / The knot of history" by thinking in terms of separate and neatly defined past and future; "And the done and the to-be-done / In that timelessness were one./ Beyond the poor being done." Then, for an instant, his grandfather's talk makes him see a violent occasion in his grandfather's past as actual, as being done, and he suddenly thinks, "The world is real. It is there." Both the point of this poem and the fact that it exists at all, the same situation seen with a very different meaning from the one Mr. Warren was concerned with in the story he wrote about it twenty years before, show that for Mr. Warren, the world is real, the only place where action and thought are inextricable and neither can falsify the ultimate and—because of the confusion of its contingency—always puzzling truth. A similar conception of the truth lies behind the second poem Mr. Warren wrote about this boy and his grandfather, the poem called "A Confederate Veteran Tries to Explain the Event."

QUESTIONS (page 872 of *Modern Short Stories*)

1. Why does Mr. Warren select a narrator who is remembering an experience from his boyhood? Why does Mr. Warren limit what the narrator tells us to what he had understood at the time, when he was a boy? (Be sure to keep this narrator in mind when you come to Andrew Lytle's *Mister McGregor*, which has a similar narrator but uses him differently.)

2. How much do we understand from the boy's account of his grandfather that the boy himself did not understand?

3. How does the narrator make us see these things without saying anything that the boy himself did not understand?

4. How does the boy see his grandfather most of the time? What does his grandfather look like in fact?

5. What kind of a man had Mr. Barden been when he was young? What things did he love? How did he love them? How good had he been at doing the things he loved?

6. What does our understanding of Mr. Barden as a young man tell us about the ante-bellum and Civil War South?

7. What kind of life has Mr. Barden lived since the war? Why?

8.   What kind of people are Mr. and Mrs. Kirby?

9.   How had Mr. Barden dealt with the difficulties of living with Mr. and Mrs. Kirby? How does his way of doing so fit with his character?

10.   Why does Mr. Barden say to his son, after his stroke, that it is time for him to die?

11.   How does Mr. Barden's outburst affect his grandson? How does his death?

12.   Why does Mr. Warren include the information that Mr. Kirby was killed in the war and that Mrs. Kirby works in a store?

EUDORA WELTY
A WORN PATH

A WORN PATH is an exquisitely controlled story of unconscious heroism. Old Phoenix's name suggests the way her
spirit almost miraculously renews her worn old body each
time she must return again to the doctor's office for the
medicine to sooth her little grandson's throat, that has
been badly burned by lye. She has her own standards of
right conduct and of dignity, and she is proud of them.
When she cannot resist the temptation to fool the hunter into going off in pursuit of the black dog so that she can
pick up the nickle he has dropped, she does not deceive herself: "God watching me the whole time," she says to herself.
"I come to stealing" (775). She has come to begging, too,
saying stiffly, when the receptionist offers her "a few
pennies," "Five pennies is a nickle" (778). But she neither
steals nor begs for herself. Without clearly remembering
that it is Christmas time, she says, "This is what come to
me to do. I going to the store and buy my child a little
windmill they sells, made out of paper. He going to find it
hard to believe there such a thing in the world." Then, so
she will not forget what it is after she buys it, she reminds herself to "march myself back where he is waiting,
holding it straight up in this hand."

Her dignity is equally firm. When her memory fails her
momentarily, as it so often does, at the doctor's office,
"then Phoenix was like an old woman begging a dignified for-
giveness for waking up frightened in the night" (777), and
it is with equal dignity that she asks the "nice lady" to
tie up her shoes (776). Self-pity is inconceivable to her;
the physical handicaps of age that make her trip to the
doctor's office an odyssey for her are to her only part of
the job, and she has done it so many times that her feet, as
it were, know the way and can follow by themselves the path
they have worn.

Miss Welty takes us into old Phoenix's mind with great
delicacy. She begins with an objective description. We are
told Phoenix is very old, that she wears a long dress and
"an equally long apron of bleached sugar sacks," that she is
"all neat and tidy" except that her shoes are unlaced (771)
—because, as we learn later, she "can't lace 'em with a
cane" (776) any more than she can get up by herself when she
has fallen (774). Presently, "in the voice of argument old
people keep to use with themselves" (771), Phoenix starts
talking, and we move a step closer to her perception of
things and Miss Welty begins to tell us, though still in her
own terms, what Phoenix is thinking: "she could not let her

-194-

dress be torn [by the barbed-wire fence] now, so late in the
day, and she could not pay for having her arm or her leg
sawed off if she got caught fast where she was" (772).
Then, almost imperceptible, Miss Welty slides into telling
us things just as Phoenix knows them: "Big dead trees, like
black men with one arm, were standing in the purple stalks
of the withered cotton field. There sat a buzzard"; and
Phoenix says defiantly, "Who you watching?" For the rest of
the story Miss Welty moves between these points of view, as
the occasion requires, with unobtrusive skill, and we are
gradually made to feel how desperately long this journey
really is for Old Phoenix, and how formidable both its
physical and its spiritual dangers seem to her.

She is sharply aware of the dangers of getting knocked
over by some wild animal and being unable to get up again
and of being just plain exhausted. "Keep the big wild hogs
out of my path. . . . I got a long way," she says (771);
and, when she comes to the hill, "Seem like there is chains
about my feet, time I get this far. Something always take a
hold on this hill—pleads I should stay." When she is
caught in a thorny bush on her way down the other side of
the hill ("Old eyes thought you was a pretty little <u>green</u>
bush") and, trembling with exhaustion, finally frees herself,
her only thought is for the delay: "'Sun so high!' she
cried, leaning back and looking, while the thick tears went
over her eyes. 'The time getting all gone here.'" Then
comes her severest physical trial, crossing the stream by
the log (her walk is very unsteady; she moves "a little from
side to side in her steps"). When she makes it she is
pleased; "I wasn't as old as I thought," she says (772), but
she has to sit down and rest. She does not dare close her
eyes for fear of falling asleep, but even awake she dreams
that a little boy brings her a piece of cake, and comes to
herself only when she reaches for it and finds nothing.

Next she has to crawl under a barbed-wire fence into a
cotton field, and from that she moves into a corn field,
where she sees a "tall, black, and skinny" ghost. When she
realizes it is only a scarecrow, she is highly amused at
herself: "I ought to shut up for good. My senses is gone.
I too old. I the oldest people I ever know." And then,
with gay defiance, "Dance, old scarecrow, while I dancing
with you." And dance she does; "she kicked her foot over
the furrow, and with mouth drawn down shook her head once or
twice in a little strutting way" (773). At the far end of
the corn field, she at last comes to a road, or at least a
wagon track, and begins to pass cabins, "all like old women
under a spell sitting there. 'I walking in their sleep,'"
she says (773). Then, past the danger of being knocked over
by wild hogs, she is unexpectedly rushed and knocked into
the ditch by a dog. She lies there helpless but undaunted
until a white man comes along and asks her what she is doing
lying in the ditch, and she raises her hand to be lifted up
saying that she is "lying on my back like a June-bug waiting
to be turned over."

When the white man, with friendly but characteristically mistaken self-confidence, says of the incredibly long trip she is taking to town, "I know you colored people! Wouldn't miss going to town to see Santa Claus," Phoenix does not correct him; all she knows is that "I bound to go to town, mister. The time come around" (774). Finally she reaches the doctor's office, knowing she is there by "the document that had been stamped with the gold seal and framed in the gold frame which matched the dream that was hung up in her head" (776). She has her momentary complete lapse of memory; then, when memory returns, she says, really talking to herself to remind herself of what is the whole motive of her life because even that—so old is she—sometimes slips her mind: "My little grandson, he sit up there in the house all wrapped up, waiting by himself. We is the only two left in the world. He suffer and it don't seem to put him back at all. He got a sweet look. He going to last. He wear a little patch quilt and peep out, holding his mouth open [because of his burned throat] like a little bird. I remembers so plain now. I not going to forget him again, no, the whole enduring time. I could tell him from all the others in creation." After what she has done for that little grandson, we feel that her words—"whole enduring time," "from all the others in creation"—are hardly hyperbole at all.

QUESTIONS (pages 872-873 of *Modern Short Stories*)

1. Why is Phoenix taking this long trip to town?

2. Trace the various obstacles old Phoenix comes up against between the valley where we first pick her up and the wagon track, and describe how she deals with each.

3. What does old Phoenix do when she is knocked down by the dog?

4. How does she describe her situation to the white man who helps her up?

5. How does she feel about stealing the nickel he drops?

6. How does she explain where she is going to him?

7. How does Phoenix know she is in the doctor's office?

8. What happens when old Phoenix is first spoken to by the receptionist and the nurse?

9. How do we know how much old Phoenix loves her grandson?

10. What does old Phoenix plan to do with the money she has got during the day? Why?

ERNEST J. GAINES
THE SKY IS GRAY

THE SKY IS GRAY has certain important characteristics in
common with the selection from Ralph Ellison's *Invisible Man*,
called *Battle Royal*, in Part One of this book; both stories
take their heroes through an elaborate series of events that
offer an almost formal demonstration of the black man's situation in a predominantly white society. But in its basic story,
the journey, and in the heroic character of its most significant figure, Mama, *The Sky Is Gray* has much more important
resemblances to Eudora Welty's account of old Phoenix's heroic
journey in *A Worn Path*.

In narrative technique Mr. Gaines's story differs from
Mr. Ellison's only in its greater emphasis on its eight-year-
old narrator's consciousness and in its fuller realization of
the other characters in the story. The very fact that the
narrator is too young to understand fully the implications of
what the other characters do and say means that we must often
infer from his literal reports of them what they are. He
cannot tell us directly what they stand for or what their conduct implies about the social conditions it reflects; he can
only show us. This requirement of representation imposed on
the story by the innocence of its narrator is very valuable
because the story is, like Mr. Ellison's, systematically
symbolic—almost allegorical—and could easily become abstract
and unmoving. It is the intervention between us and the
story's moral implications of the small narrator's vivid and
literal consciousness that prevents this, his habit of telling
himself what is happening as if his life were a story he is
trying to understand—"G'n be coming in a few minutes. Coming
'round that bend down there full speed. And I'm g'n get out
my hankercher and I'm go'n wave it down, and us go'n get on it
and go" (779). This way of presenting the story is beautifully suited to its double purpose—to make us know the story
as human experience, as pain and suffering, determination and
courage, and at the same time to make clear to us that this
odyssey is, in every detail, a particular instance of a general situation, so that by the time we finish it we feel that
it constitutes a fable of the impoverished black in American
society.

We eventually learn from *The Sky Is Gray* nearly everything a third-person story would tell us about this particular
family, though the information comes to us very indirectly:
the little boy knows it too well to have to tell it to himself
systematically. Nevertheless we learn that the father has

been drafted and that the mother is barely able to keep them
all alive by working in the fields; she cannot afford to miss
a moment. Even the eight-year-old narrator works in the
fields whenever he can. We even catch a glimpse of the complex social customs of the black community in which these
people live: Monsieur Etienne Bayonne is comically irritated
by James's habit of praying Baptist instead of Catholic; how
can anyone expect Baptist prayers to cure a toothache? We
know that this family, despite its desperate struggle, somehow manages much of the time to live in a richly human way.
When the narrator is dying of the cold and longing to be
"home 'round the fire," he thinks of Ty, who "can make
ever'body laugh mocking Monsieur Bayonne" (799). Ty is
"always trying to make some kind o' joke" (798), a classical
example of the grimly comic grumbling with which so many
blacks confront the pains of life ("'Got to get up,' he say.
'I ain't having no teef pulled. What I got to be getting up
for" [783]). On the bus James is almost immediately involved
in a miniature war of the sexes with a little girl across the
aisle; and, struggling against the cold of Bayonne, he thinks
of *Annabel Lee* and his schoolteacher—"I'm sure Miss Walker
go'n make me recite it when I get there. That woman don't
never forget nothing" (802).

     But all the time we are aware of the general implica-
tions of these events, especially after James and his Mama
reach the dentist's office. We listen to the solid, common-
sense woman who is impatient of mere ideology but has a sharp
awareness of the injustice of life—"I often wonder why the
lord let a little child like that suffer"—and of the special
injustice of life for the poor—"And it looks like it's the
poor who do most of the suffering" (789). We listen to the
pious old man who James thinks of as a preacher. "'Best not
even to try. He works in mysterious ways. Wonders to per-
form'" (789). We hear him attacked by the bitter young man
who James thinks of as a teacher; this young man has the
whole rebel package (religion is just the white man's device
for keeping black people down; words are rubbish; action is
everything). Nonetheless, he constructs a witty verbal
parable out of "the wind is pink," "the grass is black," "we
are citizens of the United States" (793-794). He knows too,
sadly, that "the ones who come after" will have to believe
something "that they can lean on," and that he, believing
nothing, has nothing: "For me, the wind is pink; the grass
is black" (795). James feels instinctively that "when I grow
up I want to be jest like him. I want clothes like that and
I want to keep a book with me, too" (793). The preacher and
the teacher—the first with a Tennysonian trust in "the
heart," the second committed to what he calls "cold logic"—
seem neither quite to meet the reality of the life of James
and Mama, much as the first appeals to the elderly and the
second to the young. "Monsieur Bayonne say it wasn't fair
for 'em to take Daddy and give Mama nothing and give us
nothing. Auntie say, Shhh, Etienne. Don't let 'em yer you
talk like that. . . . Yes, you right, Monsieur Bayonne say.
Best don't say it in front of 'em now. Bit one day they go'n
find out' (799).

   James and his mother are treated kindly by the tough
people who run the Negro café, but Mama is attacked there by
a pimp and has to stop him with her knife.   They are treated
kindly by the old white lady who feeds them with the special
tact of an older generation which Mama also knows how to deal
with ("'Your kindness will never be forgotten,' she say.
'James,' she say to me. Us go out . . ." [806]). But at the
heart of all this action is the way she herself faces life
and the way she is determined to teach James to. Mama is not
resigned like the old preacher; she is in a steady rage at
life. But she is not in any sort of ideological rage, like
the young teacher; her rage is an immediate response to the
practical facts of their life, and she worries and cares
every minute:

      She thinking if they got 'nough wood—if she left
      'nough there to keep 'em warm till us get back.
      She thinking if it go'n rain and if any of 'em go'n
      have to go out in the rain. She thinking 'bout the
      hog—if he go'n get out, and if Ty and Val be able
      to get him back in. She always worry like that
      when she leave the house (779).

   She is bringing James up to take the same responsibility;
"I'm the oldest and she say I'm the man." She is grimly determined to do what she must to make sure he is a man. She
hates to kill the pitifully small birds James and Ty catch,
but she knows it must be done if they are to eat, and knows
that James too must learn to do it.   "'Octavia,' Auntie say;
'explain to him. Explain to him. Jest don't beat him. Explain to him.' But she hit me and hit me and hit me" (785).
James understands; he remembers this lesson because he sees
"a bunch of pull-doos" on the river and immediately begins to
wonder if you can eat them (783-784).

   Mama is indomitable; she knows that what sustains men
and makes them wholly human is pride; she will not yield herself in the smallest thing, nor will she allow James to. She
pays for the heat in the Negro café by buying something; she
refuses to accept food from the white woman until the woman
has found work for James to do (he knows she is following him
"jest's quiet's a mouse" for fear he will look inside the
garbage cans he is carrying and see that they are empty); she
will not let the old lady give her more than the exact two
bits worth of salt meat: they have a comic battle over it
which Mama wins.

   In his childlike way James understands all this almost
perfectly. "I look at my mama and I know what she thinking.
I been with mama so much, jest me and her, I know what she
thinking all the time." He tries to hide from her how much
his tooth hurts "'cause I knowed it didn't have no money, and
it jest was go'n make her mad again" (780). He often feels a
small-boy longing to show and be shown love, but his mother
will not have that.

> I love my mama and I want to put my arm 'round her
> and tell her. But I'm not s'posed to do that.
> She say that's weakness and that's cry-baby stuff
> and she don't want no cry-baby 'round her. She
> don't want you to be scared neither. . . . I make
> 'tend I ain't 'cause I'm the oldest, and I got to
> set a good example for the rest (780).

He hates to see his mother "wearing that black coat and that
black hat and she looking sad" (779). As soon as he can
make some money picking cotton, he's going to get his mama a
new coat. "And I ain't go'n get a black one neither. I
think I'm go'n get her a red one" (792). When the sleet begins to fall, "I want to stand close 'side her, but she
don't like that. She say that's cry-baby stuff. She say you
got to stand for yourself, by yourself" (797).

James is her oldest child, even if he is only eight; she
depends on him. "S'pose she had to go away like Daddy went
away? Then who was go'n look after us? They had to be somebody left to carry on" (785). All her sternness is to train
him for his responsibilities.

> "You got yourself a little man there," the lady
> say.
> Mama don't say nothing to the lady, but she must
> 'a' grin a little bit, 'cause I seen the lady
> grinning back (792).

But above all, her sternness is an expression of her love for
him, of her fierce determination to inculcate in him the
pride, the sense of his own dignity, the independence that
she lives by.

> The sleet's coming down heavy, heavy now, and I
> turn up my collar to keep my neck warm. My mama
> tell me turn it right back down.
> "You not a bum," she say. "You a man" (806).

QUESTIONS (page 873 of *Modern Short Stories*)

1.   Describe the situation in *The Sky Is Gray*.   Where is the father?   How does the mother support the children?

2.   What is the cause of the byplay between James and the little girl on the bus?

3.   What attitudes toward the lot of the poor are represented by (a) the lady who is quite sure the grass is green; (b) the boy who is pretty sure the grass is black and the wind pink; (c) the big fat man in the black suit who feels sorry for the boy?

4.   Which one of these people most attracts James?

5.   How would you compare James's mother's attitude to the attitudes of the three speakers in the dentist's office?

6.   Why does James's mother insist on his killing the little birds he catches even though she knows he can't bear to do so?

7.   How does James's mother deal with (a) the café, where they go to get warm; (b) the white woman who offers them food; (c) the old lady who tries to sell them too much meat for a quarter?

8.   What kind of coat does James dream of buying his mother?   Why?

9.   Why must James resist the temptation to put his arms around his mother and tell her he loves her?

10.   Why must James not turn up his coat collar, even to keep the sleet out?

11.   Why is James's mother so anxious to teach him to act in the way she approves of?

ANDREW LYTLE

MISTER MCGREGOR

MISTER McGREGOR has, perhaps, a certain advantage over
many stories in its slightly exotic subject matter; there is
a special fascination in the day-by-day relations between
master and slave—especially when those relations involve
the most intimate and violent human feelings—for those of
us who know they once actually existed but can now hardly
conceive them. These people existed, as Mr. Lytle's
narrator says, "in a way that folks don't understand no
more" (808). But there is a danger in such subject matter,
too, for in the hands of an unskillful writer it can easily
become the mere wooden melodrama of stock historical fiction.

Mr. Lytle keeps *Mister McGregor* from becoming so largely
by his use of the narrator. This narrator is used in a way
that has been largely developed since Henry James began it.
The narrator is an old man remembering and commenting on
something that happened a long time ago. But he was, as a
small boy, present when it happened. Thus he can give us
his recollection of the small boy's direct experience of the
occasion, with all the immediacy and the minute awareness of
physical fact that are the unique possessions of the young,
and can, at the same time, give us the full benefit of the
mature man's long brooding over the meaning of the episode
he observed as a boy with such vividness of perception but
such limited insight.

Mr. Lytle takes the most skillful advantage of both
these possibilities. The small boy—"there I was, a little
shaver of eight, standen by the window a-blowen my breath on
it so's I could draw my name . . ." (807)—has a boy's
natural way of seeing things as physical actions. His capacity to generalize or to draw conclusions from these actions
is limited, with the result that he sees the action unblurred
by ideas about it. As his father walks across the room
toward Rhears, he is aware of "the even distance each boot-
heel made" (808); as his father and Rhears fight, he sees
every muscle move: "I looked at pa's breeches. They fit him
tight; and the meat rolled up, snapped, then quivered under
the cloth. His butt give in at the sides and squeezed away
its sitten-down softness" (812). "Slow as candy pullen he
broke the nigger's holt on the front muscles of his thighs.
But that nigger's grip never give. No sir. What give was
two drippen hunks of leg meat" (813). He counts the drops of
blood that fall to the floor as his mother and father grip
the gun and his mother's "left little finger, plunged like a
hornet's needle when the skin drew tight over pa's knuckles"
(809).

These quotations show another boyish characteristic
that Mr. Lytle is making careful use of. The boy naturally
made his descriptive comparisons out of the material his
experience has provided him, which was necessarily limited
but, as a consequence, minutely observed; these comparisons
thus build up for us a vivid image of the physical appurte-
nances and social customs of the world the action took place
in. When they all freeze at Rhear's knock on the door, for
instance, "I remember thinken how much we favored one of
them waxwork figures Sis Lou had learnt to make at Doctor
Price's Female Academy" (807). He did not "see" and therefore could not say that his mother shivered with tension as
she challenged his father; what he did see was that "a light
sorghum color slipped up and down [her hair] as if it were
playen on grease" (809). He does not tell us the watching
Negroes turned gray with terror as they watched the fight;
he says they looked "like they had fell in the ash-hopper"
(814), and his way of making us understand how fast the
blood spouted from Rhears's back when Mr. McGregor's knife
went in is to say "it fell back from the knife like dirt
from a turnen plow" (815).

Mr. Lytle takes equally skillful advantage of the fact
that the narrator is an old man who has thought long and
hard about this episode by the time he comes to tell it. He
uses this characteristic of his narrator to justify the
narrator's skill as a story-teller ("one of them no-count
gifts like good conversation that don't do you no good no
more" [807]) and the subtlety of his explanation of motive
and meaning in the events. "For a long time," the narrator
confesses, "I never could make out . . . why ma done what
she done. . . . It's bothered me a heap in my time, more'n
it's had any right to" (809). Mr. Lytle also uses the
thoughtful maturity of the narrator to suggest to us, indirectly, the tragic character of this episode; no doubt Mr.
McGregor triumphed, over both Rhears and ma; the story has
what appears at first glance a satisfactory ending by which
readers—possibly Northern readers particularly—may conceivably be fooled. But what the narrator knows very well
is that it shows the necessarily tragic character of human
experience, a character that only becomes more inevitable as
people become finer.

He understands and respects Rhears. Rhears was proud
and dignified. "He was proud [and pure-blooded], black like
the satin in the widow-women's shirt-waists . . ." He
"warn't no common field hand . . . [and he] didn't mean to
run away from his home like any blue-gum nigger. He jest
come a-marchen straight to the house to settle with pa . . ."
(808). If Rhears was spoiled too, we can hardly blame him
for that under the circumstances. Nor do we, any more than
the narrator, blame him for not being able to think through
the implications of his situation to the end: how many
people can? "Niggers," as the narrator puts it, in the terms
of the perhaps fallacious racial generalizations that are
habitual in his culture, "can think straight up to a certain
point, and beyond that the steadiest of'm let their senses

fly like buckshot, high to scatter" (810). The narrator
understands why, and clearly feels Rhears's attitude is, for
all its limitations, understandable and human. Rhears's
"feelens was bad hurt" (808), but not by the mere physical
fact that his wife had been whipped. It was fixed in his
mind that "Folks just didn't whup their house servants," and
he had been brooding all night on the blow to his social
vanity and his pride of spirit of Della's whipping, fretting
and sulking over it and thinking about "what was be'en said
in the quarters and how glad the field hands was she'd beén
whupped" (808)

The position Rhears gets himself into might, of course,
have been avoided if he had had some rare, ideal power of
understanding the situation completely—or if he had been an
ordinary, inferior, cowardly man, such as the narrator pro-
fesses himself to be, unwilling to fight proudly for the
woman he loves. (The narrator wryly offers the demand for
heroism imposed by marriage as his reason for remaining
single; "That's how come I never married," he says. "I'm
peaceful by nature"; then he admits there is one thing he
loves enough to fight for, his whisky [811]). As it is,
Rhears comes through to us as an admirable if humanly—and
colorlessly—imperfect man, and therefore a pitiful rather
than a villainous one.

All this the narrator can see and can make us see because he has, as an adult, been thinking about that experience of his childhood for a long time. Even more important,
he has also come to understand the more significant meaning
of the episode, its effect on the relation between his
mother and father. These two were even prouder, more
fiercely independent and unbending than Rhears, and up to
the moment that Rhears challenged his father, the battle
between them had been a stand-off. It is settled by Mr.
McGregor's fight with Rhears. But what the narrator's long
brooding about that conflict and its outcome has shown him
is that, just to the extent that these two were fiercer and
prouder than Rhears in their independence of spirit, so the
outcome of their battle was—though a necessary and workable
personal relationship—nonetheless even sadder than Rhears's
death, in the sense of being a solution that required something quite wonderful in Mrs. McGregor to be given up. No
doubt she was, as the narrator says all women are, "proud to
think she'd picked such a game one" as Mr. McGregor (811).
But when she surrendered at the end, she was no longer that
beautiful and fiercely independent wild creature, the lover
of "horses that wanted to run away all the time" (808), who
"would have taken the breeches away from any ordinary man"
(809), and stood watching the fight between Mr. McGregor and
Rhears "stiff as a poker, her head thrown up and her eyes as
wide as a hawk's" (811). The only alternative to her surrender would have been for Mr. McGregor to surrender to her
and, as it were, be "put . . . down amongst the chillun and
[given] . . . a whuppen when he forgits his manners or
sasses back" (810). Nonetheless, something beautiful and
proud dies when ma "walked over and handed [Mr. McGregor]

the gun" and volunteered to sell Della (815).

That surrender is necessary, inevitable, and perhaps
even some sort of fulfillment for Mrs. McGregor; it is nonetheless sad, and it is his awareness of its sadness that
makes the narrator always come back in his thoughts to this
episode when he "gits melancholy and thinks about how he
come not to be president and sich-like concerns" (809), or
how he is doomed, like all men, by his own nature to do what
he knows very well is senseless—in his case, drink "up my
kidneys" (810); "jest enough to settle the dust in my belly.
I'm about to choke to death with the drought. . . . Aah
. . . that's sweet to the taste" (810).

It is thus that the narrator's double understanding of
the episode—the young boy's and the old man's—gives the
story its richness, allows Mr. Lytle to show us the sheer
physical manifestation of tension when Rhears knocks on the
door and says, "in a respectful-arrogant sort of way with a
basket-knife in his hand" (808), ". . . I want to speak to
Mister McGregor" (808) and at the same time make clear to us
the full meaning of the moment. "My heart flopped down in
my belly and commenced to flutter around in my breakfast,"
the narrator says; "then popped up to my ears and drawed all
the blood out'n my nose except a little sack that got left
in the point to swell and tingle." ". . . I knowed it was
the knock of death" (807). It is this that allows him to
show us the precise, economical movements of Mr. McGregor at
the sound of that word "Mister" and to make us understand
that they are the controlled movements of a man who has
guessed instantly that he is in deadly peril and must act
both quickly and efficiently. "He didn't waste no time, but
he didn't hurry none either. He just got up, took off his
specs, and laid them as careful on the secretary, just like
he meant to set'm in one special place and no other place
would do. He reached for the gun and turned" (808). It is
this, too, that allows him to make us understand that the
fight between his father and Rhears is really a part of the
struggle between Mr. and Mrs. McGregor. "Rhears was
a-meanen to teach pa his manners" (810). "For you might
almost say pa had whupped ma by proxy. And here was Rhears,
agen by proxy, to make him answer for it . . . a nigger and
a slave, his mistress's gallant, a-callen her husband and
his master to account for her" (812). The real fight, then,
is between husband and wife, and it is no less deadly because
both would rather die than derogate in the least from the
dignity of politeness. When Mr. McGregor could not get the
gun from his wife "without acting ungentlemanly [he] gave
her a curious look and a low bow; then turned it loose" (809).

"The construction the kin put on it" was that "it was
a question of authority" over the slaves, and as far as that
goes, it was. Without such authority Mr. McGregor "might as
well have sold all his niggers for any work he could a got
out'n them" (810). But more than Mr. McGregor's authority
over his slaves was at stake, as the narrator has slowly come

to realize. His mastery of Mrs. McGregor was at stake, too.
Mrs. McGregor was going to make sure he established his
mastery over her "gallant" in equal combat before she would
admit that he was her master. She had already defied him in
the argument over Della; and Mr. McGregor had recognized the
challenge for what it was and had accepted it. "Mister
McGregor," she had said evenly, "you're not going to punish
that girl. She's mine"; and Mr. McGregor had replied "in a
hard, polite way," like a duelist addressing a deadly
opponent, "And so are you mine, my dear" (811). Neither
yields an inch, even when the crisis is reached and Mr.
McGregor is close to death. He makes no appeal for Mrs.
McGregor to shoot Rhears, and she makes no voluntary move to
do so: "Have you ever seen a long dead limb stretched
between sky and droppen sun? Well, that's how still ma held
onto that gun of pa's" (814). But when Mr. McGregor kills
Rhears and Rhears says as he is dying, "Marster [not now
"Mister McGregor"], if you hadn't got me, I'd a got you,"
Mrs. McGregor "walked over and handed [Mr. McGregor] the
gun" (815).

QUESTIONS (pages 873-874 of *Modern Short Stories*)

   1. What do we know about the narrator of this story?

   2. How is his telling of the story affected by the fact
that he is a mature man remembering an experience he had had
when he was eight? (Be sure to remind students of the
narrator of Robert Penn Warren's *When the Light Gets Green*,
and ask them to compare Mr. Warren's use of his narrator
with Mr. Lytle's use of his.)

   3. What were Rhears's motives in coming to the house
with a knife and asking for Mister McGregor?

   4. What kind of woman is Mrs. McGregor? Why does she
like spirited horses? Why is she so good at running the
place when Mr. McGregor is away?

   5. Why is Rhears's request to speak to Mr. McGregor so
shocking?

   6. How does Mr. McGregor react to Rhears's request?

   7. Why does Mrs. McGregor force Mr. McGregor to give up
the gun? Why does Mr. McGregor agree to do so?

   8. What can we deduce from the fact that, even when
Rhears is practically killing Mr. McGregor, Mrs. McGregor
never makes a move to shoot him?

   9. Why, when the fight is over, does Mrs. McGregor walk
across the room and hand Mr. McGregor the gun and volunteer
to sell Della?

PETER TAYLOR

What You Hear from 'Em?

The interest of Mr. Taylor's story depends on the subtlety with which Aunt Munsie is conceived. She is anything but a simple person, though because of her spirited unconventionality—which is in fact an evidence of her real quality—we may at first think of her as just another quaint old Southern Negro woman, slightly touched but harmless and therefore tolerantly indulged by the community. This impression ought quickly enough to be brought into question by the evidence of her ironic shrewdness and impatience in dealing with those who do not understand her. Her trick of repeating her favorite question two or three times when she gets what is to her an irrelevant answer "from some fool white woman, or man" is a formidably scornful one: if they are fools enough also to believe her so deaf "she couldn't hear it thunder," they deserve no better. She "knew what [the mill hands and such] thought of her—how they laughed at her and felt sorry for her and despised her all at once. But, like the has-been quality, they didn't matter, never had, never would" (822).

For Munsie has a subtle conception of quality, even subtler than Miss Lucille Satterfield has, though Miss Lucille is quality too. Miss Lucille is rightly impressed with the way the expatriates—"Mine and yours," as she has sense enough to say (823)—are prospering in Memphis and Nashville, but she does not understand that being rich somewhere else is not the point. She tells Munsie that Munsie ought to go see Mr. Thad in Memphis, as she goes to see "hers." But Munsie will have none of that. At first she tells herself that is because in Memphis and Nashville they did not "own any land, or none in Cameron County" that they saw after themselves (824). Then she remembers she had mocked old Doctor Tolliver when he had taken this line. "No, it wasn't really to own land that Thad and Will ought to come back to Thornton. It was more that if they were going to be rich, they ought to come home, where their money counted for something" (825).

There is truth in this; the mill manager from Chicago who has made so much money in Thornton will never be really rich as Munsie has known it, rich in the sense that the old, vigorous quality of Thornton had been. When Crecie, not getting the point at all because she has been filled with a sentimental view of what quality is by "the has-been quality" who have brought her up while Aunt Munsie was busy bringing up real quality like Mr. Thad and Mr. Will, said "Quality's better than land or better than money in the bank here,"

Aunt Munsie sneered at her, "It never were" (825).

Munsie knew very well that what makes quality is not
living on the distinction of one's ancestors; what makes
quality is the vigor to be quality in the present, to get on
and to keep up with the times. Aunt Munsie knew that "there
were things under the sun worse than going off and getting
rich in Nashville and Memphis and even in Washington, D.C."
(821). She scorned the people that did not have the gumption
for that, as her Mr. Thad and Mr. Will have. Such people
were has-been quality; but if it had to be in Memphis and
Nashville, well, she would put up with that—temporarily.
For what she cannot face is the possibility that keeping up
with the times means moving permanently from Thornton and
never reestablishing the old Tolliver family existence that
she lives for. Munsie knows that you must keep up with the
times if you are to be real quality because Doctor Tolliver
himself had been one of the first people in town "to widen
his porches and remove the gingerbread from his house," and
just a few weeks before he died, he had taken down the iron
fence around his yard and replaced it with a hedge (818).
She could see too that in the "houses in Thornton the heirs
had never left" and that were kept unchanged were the
biggest fools in town (821). No, you had to put up with
the boys' absence temporarily, knowing they would soon move
back to Thornton permanently.

Munsie puts up with this temporary absence proudly. It
is not easy for her. She is old and deaf and half blind.
But she must keep going until Mr. Thad and Mr. Will are able
to come back to Thornton in the style she wants for them and
believes is the object of their exile in Memphis and
Nashville. She moves spryly about the town with her slop
wagon, spiritedly defying "strangers in town or trifling
high-school boys" who do not know any better than to blow
horns at her (819). She takes the same attitude toward has-
been quality like Ralph Hadley, who lives with his mother and
has nothing in life to do but drive to the drug store in his
mother's coupé for his mother's prescription (824). People
who really know who Munsie is lean out of their cars and say,
"Aunt Munsie, can you make a little room?" and she always
hears them and moves over promptly, waving and grinning as
they pass her (820). She is firmly convinced that "no one
would dare run into her or her wagon" (820).

She has taken her position in the community with the
directness and the simplicity of her whole nature. There is
a childlike simplicity about Munsie's feelings; they are as
vivid and pure as they were the first time she had known
them, and, like a child, she is incapable of thinking that
any incongruity of mere outward show has anything to do with
them. Wearing her white dust cap and her apron, she drags
her old slop wagon about the streets of Thornton with unques-
tioning dignity and proud assurance. Everything is as fresh
for her as if it were brand new and she turns "her head from
side to side, as though looking at the old houses and trees
for the first time" (819). She is as direct as a child too,

"calling out at the top of her lungs, when she approached
the house of one of the elect" of whom she still asked her
question about Mr. Thad and Mr. Will, and greeting her
friends with cries of "Hai-ee, now! Whee! Look-a-here!"
(820).

There is nothing shiftless about her, as there unfor-
tunately is about her daughter Crecie, who has been brought
up by the wrong kind of white people. Munsie knows that her
job is to work hard and keep her independence by collecting
her slops and raising her pigs and chickens, just as she
had, "without being able to book-read or even to make
numbers," raised "the whole pack of tow-headed Tollivers
just as the Mizziz would have wanted it done" when Doctor
Tolliver asked her to (825). She does these things with
pride because they are her jobs in the family, of which she
has become a member by virtue of her love and devotion, a
devotion so intense and so proud that she is a very stern
task-master of the young—"hard about people and things in
the world" as Crecie puts it (825); all the Tolliver
children except Mr. Thad and Mr. Will had quarrelled with
her by the time they were grown, just as they had all
quarrelled with old Doctor Tolliver (826)—and for much the
same reasons.

Just as her proud devotion accepts no compromises and
knows no tact in dealing with the rest of the Tolliver
children, so it does not in dealing with Mr. Thad and Mr.
Will, whom she loves best. When they come to see her, she
is happy welcoming them home ("Mama," says Crecie, "some of
your chillun's out front" [822]), her eyes blinded by tears
and her arms flung around them—around their waists, for she
is "hardly four feet tall" (819)—taking them about her
house as if it were theirs, just as she will go about theirs
"'a mile north of town' or 'on the old River Road'" (817)
when they get around to building it. She does not hear the
tone of voice in which Mr. Thad and Mr. Will tell her they
are going to build these houses, the same tone in which their
wives say politely "how good Aunt Munsie's own house" is
looking (817).

But these visits are not important and she never pretends for a moment that they are. What is important is that
Mr. Thad and Mr. Will are coming permanently back to
Thornton where they can be properly rich and the family can
once more be united, as Munsie expects to hear daily that
they have decided to do—"What you hear from 'em?" Do they
say they are on their way back?

In the purity of her love and the pride of her heart
Munsie will never admit that times have changed in any
fundamental way. Of course Mr. Thad and Mr. Will would
never live in the old house like has-been quality. It was
just as well the old house had burned down. Not that Aunt
Munsie does not secretly regret that even it had to go, just
as, in their way, Mr. Thad and Mr. Will do, so that when
they come to see her their hands rest "a moment on [the]

familiar wrought-iron frame" of the old gate from Doctor
Tolliver's house that Munsie has so carefully preserved
along with the banister from its porch (818).   Still, she
knows from the very fact that Doctor Tolliver himself had
discarded these things that "someone . . . with a special
eye for style and for keeping up with the times" (819) refused to cling to such old things and to rot away along with
them, and she does not want Mr. Thad and Mr. Will to.   What
she imagines for them is that they will become rich, return
to Thornton, and build new houses in some smart part of contemporary Thornton where they will recreate the old family
life in a properly up-to-date way.

     She does not admit to herself that this is not going to
happen until she discovers that Mr. Thad and Mr. Will, instead of coming back to Thornton where they can take care of
her like family in her old age, as she had taken care if
them like family in her childhood, have instead conspired
with the law to take her pigs away from her and get her off
the streets, now that she is too old to be safe there any
more.   Then she has to admit to herself that "They ain't
comin' back.   They ain't never comin' back.   They ain't
never had no notion of comin' back. . . . Aunt Munsie, she's
just their Aunt Munsie here in Thornton.   I got sense enough
to see that"—and she always has had (829-830).

     What she had not admitted until now is that for Mr.
Thad and Mr. Will Aunt Munsie, like the other remnants of
the old Tolliver home—its gingerbread, its porch banister,
its iron fence—must, however regretfully, be discarded.
Once she does admit that, her conviction that she is still a
living part of the Tolliver family, duty-bound to assert
with spirited pride the family position in Thornton, is
gone.   She becomes the human equivalent of gingerbread and
wrought-iron fences, the stock old Negro woman, separated by
a deliberately cultivated and impenetrable inequality from
all white folk—including Mr. Thad and Mr. Will and their
families.   She ties "a bandanna about her head . . . [and
talks] old-nigger foolishness" (830).   "Her spirit softened
and she became not very reliable about facts"—because she
could no longer endure to face them squarely.   "And the
children never set foot in her back yard again."

QUESTIONS (page 874 of *Modern Short Stories*)

1. Why does she disagree with Crecie about Crecie's idea that quality, not money, is what counts?

2. What is Munsie's attitude toward mill hands? Toward "has-been quality"?

3. Why will she not go to Memphis or Nashville to see Mr. Thad or Mr. Will?

4. Why is Munsie so insistent on continuing to move about the streets of Thornton with her slop wagon? Why is she so sure she will come to no harm in spite of the traffic?

5. Why does Munsie act one way when high-school boys blow their horns at her and when someone she knows says, "Aunt Munsie, can you make a little room"?

6. What is Munsie's attitude when Mr. Thad and Mr. Will come to Thornton for brief visits?

7. What finally persuades Munsie that Mr. Thad and Mr. Will are never going to return to Thornton? How does it do so?

8. What change occurs in Aunt Munsie when she does admit this? Why does that change occur?

THE TECHNIQUE OF THE SHORT STORY

The arrangement of the stories in *Modern Short Stories* has been determined by the conceptions of reality that govern them. Some teachers may prefer to teach the short story in other ways. They may, for example, want to pick out the stories that have a particular subject matter or a particular concern with social doctrines and problems, such as Mary McCarthy's concern with anti-Semitism, Richard Wright's with discrimination against black people, or Dan Jacobson's with apartheid in South Africa. It is easy enough to identify this subject matter and to pick out the stories that illustrate it, and there are a good many stories in *Modern Short Stories* that do. A good many teachers will like to begin teaching fiction by studying the techniques of the short story before going on to discuss individual stories as wholes; they will want to make some preliminary definitions of plot, characterization, point of view, and symbolism. It is not so easy to select the stories that are most useful for these purposes.

Most stories depend primarily, of course, on plot or characterization, the two basic resources of all fiction; but few depend exclusively on any one narrative device. Most use several others in a supplementary but significant way. Even so strictly constructed a story as Edith Wharton's *Roman Fever*, for example, though essentially a story dependent on plot, has considerable subtlety of characterization. We may feel, with some justice, that the characterizations of Mrs. Slade and Mrs. Ansley serve the plot of *Roman Fever* too well, that as characters these ladies have been reduced to neatly complementary types so that the plot may balance them against one another without leaving any loose ends of characterization unused by the plot. Nevertheless we have to recognize that each lady is a remarkably convincing character. Each has the marks of the developed character; that is, each frequently says things that surprise us and yet that turn out, on second thought, to be exactly what she would think. Moreover, each has a past history that, though often startling, also turns out to fit her character quite strikingly. *Roman Fever* certainly depends primarily on its plot to convey its meaning: the ingenuity with which Mrs. Wharton maneuvers the discussion to make Mrs. Ansley's "I have Barbara" the final dramatic speech is enough to show that. But *Roman Fever* is also a story in which the characterization is full enough and subtle enough to require some attention.

In many stories the effects of devices other than plot and characterization require similar attention. Scott Fitzgerald's *Babylon Revisited* depends primarily on the contrasts among its three main characters—Charlie Wales,

Lorraine Quarrles, and Marian Peters—to convey its meaning.
All three people are convincingly characterized in some detail. At the same time each one of them carries a burden of
general, almost abstract meaning; each represents an idea
about the best way to live that is easily reduced to a set
of moral propositions. At one point Fitzgerald even has
Charlie Wales, the most important of them, openly state his
idea when he says, "He believed in character; he wanted to
jump back a whole generation and trust in character as the
eternally valuable element." We cannot quite describe these
people as symbolic, if for no other reason than that their
characters always dominate our impression of them and are
clearly the sources of their ideas of how to live: they are
too well developed as characters to be thought of simply as
symbols. On the other hand, each of them clearly acts
according to a "philosophy of life" in too obvious a way to
allow us to think of him simply as a character.

In addition, *Babylon Revisited* has a carefully organized plot that comes to a logical climax in a quite painfully dramatic scene when Lorraine and Dunc arrive unexect-
edly at the Peters' house. We cannot therefore ignore the
effect of plot in *Babylon Revisited*. The story clearly depends on its plot in a secondary way, but the plot is not
insignificant. At the same time the story frequently
ignores its plot in order to introduce scenes like Charlie
Wales's taxi ride through Paris, scenes that do nothing to
advance the plot, which is concerned with Charlie's efforts
to regain legal control over his daughter. This taxi ride
is described in order to give us a sense of the atmosphere
of Paris, of the real Paris that Charlie had never seen before but which, in his new mood of sobriety and responsibility, he is now acutely sensitive to. This creation of the
atmosphere of Paris in order to emphasize Charlie's new state
of mind is also a minor element in the story, but it is
beautifully done and makes a significant contribution to the
story's meaning.

Fitzgerald communicates this atmosphere—the feel of
the Ritz Bar at cocktail time, of the Place de la Concorde
and the Opéra at twilight, of Montmartre after dark—through
the consciousness of Charlie Wales. *Babylon Revisited* is
told in the third person, but not in the traditional third-
person voice, the voice of some one so undefined that the
story comes to us as from a great distance, as if told by a
remote omniscient creature like a god on Mount Olympus.
Instead *Babylon Revisited* uses what Henry James called "the
central intelligence." This means that, though the story is
told in the third person and the author can draw back from
the main character at any time and tell us things that character cannot know or does not understand, what the narrator
actually tells us is, on the whole, limited to what the main
character does know and understand. By and large, what we
know and the interpretation we put upon it as the story pro-
gresses is what the main character does. This procedure
gives the story a great deal of the suspense and the dramatic
immediacy of a fully developed first-person narration like

Frank O'Connor's *My Oedipus Complex* or Andrew Lytle's *Mister McGregor*. At the same time it allows the narrator more latitude than first-person narration does, so that he can explain directly things the main character does not clearly understand.

Fitzgerald makes his own special use of a central intelligence by identifying the narrator's thoughts and feelings most closely with Charlie Wales's when Charlie is most deeply moved. The narrator is almost indistinguishable from Charlie Wales—even using as his own words and phrases those that Charlie is speaking to himself in his own mind—in those moments when Charlie is feeling most deeply the rightness of his way of life, the waste and deprivation of living as Lorraine and Marion do. Fitzgerald's main use for the central intelligence is to give emotional force to his statement of the superiority of Charlie's way of life and of the justice of his claim that he would make the best home for Honoria.

Though *Babylon Revisited* depends, then, primarily on characterization, it nonetheless makes important use of symbolic effects, of plot development, of atmosphere, and of point of view. No doubt we will begin a discussion of the story with students with the characters and the contrasts among them, simply because it is the most prominent and obvious way the story expresses its meaning. But we will have to go on from that to discuss the ways the story uses other technical means to reinforce and enrich its meaning. Something like this combination of technical means will appear in most stories. Nevertheless, most of them, will, like *Babylon Revisited*, depend primarily on one technical device and will therefore be most interesting as illustrations of that device. For teachers who would like to begin their discussion of short stories with a preliminary discussion of technique and for those who are exclusively interested in technique, here is a table of the contents of *Modern Short Stories* in which the stories have been arranged according to the technical device each of them most interestingly illustrates.

I have limited the number of technical devices in this table to the major ones, to avoid the complication and confusion of listing a story under several heads. The uses of minor devices such as atmosphere are often very interesting, as is evident in such stories as *Heart of Darkness*, *The Jolly Corner*, *Araby*, and *Entropy*; in all these stories an atmosphere is created, a mood in the reader, by a persistent use of poetic effects. But to try to make lists of stories that illustrate these minor as well as the major techniques of fiction would clearly be more confusing than helpful. Within each of the lists in this table of contents, the stories are arranged according to the obviousness with which they illustrate the technical device in question.

Table of Contents for the Illustration of Technical Devices

I. Stories that Illustrate the Uses of Plot

    1. The Tightly Knit Plot

        Edith Wharton, *Roman Fever*
        Bernard Malamud, *Take Pity*
        William Faulkner, *Raid*

    2. The Loosely Knit Plot

        Saul Bellow, *Looking for Mr. Green*
        Dan Jacobson, *Beggar My Neighbour*
        William Faulkner, *The Fire and the Hearth*
        William Faulkner, *Delta Autumn*

    3. The Plot of Interior Action

        James Thurber, *A Couple of Hamburgers*
        Diane Oliver, *Neighbors*
        James Agee, *The Waiting*
        D. H. Lawrence, *The Shadow in the Rose Garden*
        D. H. Lawrence, *The White Stocking*

II. Stories that Illustrate the Uses of Characterization

    1. The Mature Character Described

        Shirley Jackson, *The Flower Garden*
        Sherwood Anderson, *The Egg*
        Eudora Welty, *A Worn Path*
        Peter Taylor, *What You Hear from 'Em?*
        Vladimir Nabokov, *Pnin*

    2. The Mature Character Dramatically Revealed

        F. Scott Fitzgerald, *Babylon Revisited*
        Philip Roth, *Defender of the Faith*
        Mary McCarthy, *Artists in Uniform*
        Henry James, *The Lesson of the Master*
        D. H. Lawrence, *Odor of Chrysanthemums*
        J. F. Powers, *A Losing Game*

    3. The Immature Character and
       the Crisis of Maturity

        John Updike, *A Sense of Shelter*
        James Joyce, *Araby*
        Joyce Carol Oates, *Out of Place*
        Katherine Mansfield, *Her First Ball*

III. Stories that Illustrate the Uses of Symbols

    1. The Uses of Symbolic Objects

        Katherine Anne Porter, *The Grave*
        Henry James, *The Jolly Corner*
        Thomas Pynchon, *Entropy*

    2. The Uses of Symbolic Events

        Joseph Conrad, *Heart of Darkness*
        Ralph Ellison, *Battle Royal*
        Flannery O'Connor, *The Artificial Nigger*
        Ernest Hemingway, *The Gambler, The Nun,*
                                    and The Radio

IV. Stories that Illustrate the Uses of Point of View

    1. The First-Person Point of View

        Frank O'Connor, *My Oedipus Complex*
        James Alan McPherson, *Gold Coast*
        Virginia Woolf, *The Mark on the Wall*
        Robert Penn Warren, *When the Light Gets Green*
        Andrew Lytle, *Mister McGregor*

    2. The Central Intelligence

        Henry James, *The Tone of Time*